Choestoe Book II

Living Where the Rabbits Dance

J. R. Collins

W & B Publishers
USA

Living Where the Rabbits Dance © 2017. All rights reserved by J. R. Collins.

No part of this book may be reproduced or transmitted in any form or by any means, graphic, electronic, or mechanical, including photocopying, recording, taping, or by any informational storage retrieval system without prior permission in writing from the publisher.

W & B Publishers

For information:
W & B Publishers
9001 Ridge Hill Street
Kernersville, NC 27284

www.a-argusbooks.com

ISBN: 9781635540727

This is a work of *fiction*. All of the characters, organizations and events portrayed in this novel are either products of the author's imagination or used fictitiously.

Book Cover designed by Capsaician

Printed in the United States of America

Living Where the Rabbits Dance

Prologue

Trouble was stirrin' in the mountains of the Southern Appalachia. The wise ones of the Cherokee was havin' visions of strangers trailin' through their mountain home lookin' for the sacred yellow rock the ancestors left for all Cherokee. A wanted treasure for the invader, layin' hidden in the caves and in the water. Dreams of blue soldiers killin' Cherokee who dared to fight, simply because they refused to be driven from their homes like animals. The trails was showin' signs of searchers movin' through. The creeks started givin' up color. Wouldn't be long 'til word got out there was gold in them hills.

The Indians saw what was happenin'. Got to worryin' over it. Many started hidin' all the gold they had or could find. Murder happened on occasion, settler and Indian, as the search for the yellow rock brought evil to the mountains. The comin' caused much trouble for the Cherokee. Many fled south and west. Others stayed and fought for their homes, only to be forced at gun point to leave the mountains they'd lived in all their natural days; their ownin's, land and property, took.

Greed is a terrible sin. America's people, and the ones who spoke for 'em, got greedy. They'd moved on from the Will of God with no thought to take care from Him, the Great Creator. Their loss 'a sight from what was right made blue soldiers do things they did not believe in.

The U.S. Government became a hated enemy of the folks livin' in the mountains and was plumb awful to the Indians as time went on, because of broken treaties, personal attacks, takin' of properties, death and destruction, just to name a few. These were the gifts our young nation afforded the natives of the Southern Appalachian Mountains. The

Cherokee would cry…

Preface

My name is Jebediah Collins. Folks call me Jeb. Some 'a y'all might remember me from before. We spoke a while back on my growin' up years in a most wonderful place to grow up in, the Choestoe Valley. Said by folks as Cho-Ē-sto-Ē. How, by my own choice, I near-lived with the Cherokee Indians for many years. How my best friend, my Blood Brother, Wolf, was a full-blood Cherokee Indian from the Choestoe clan. His folks was Dancing Bear and A-Ga-Li-Ha. My dad and Dancing Bear also shared the blood bond. They was closer than brothers.

For those of us just meetin', I hope you enjoy my story. Here now, listen close. I'll fire my pipe and commence to tellin' you about a time most folks don't really understand, nor know little about. It was a time when life could be no better, a time when folks lived by their word. Died by it, too. I've draw'd air over ninety years on Mother Earth. Seen many things. Learned many things. Made many memories. Almost all my loved ones are waitin' on me to cross the Great River, and I look forward to bein' with 'em soon. But first, I want folks to hear my tale. It's important we don't forget. I see folks forgettin' . . . the Cherokee will never forget.

Chapter One

Two Skinny Ol' Mules and a Marryin'

I was born in 1815 to Thompson and Celia Collins, whose folks come from the Mother Land, Ireland. I had a brother, Cain, and a sister named Anne. Cain weren't scared 'a nothin' I ever know'd of. He'd proved that over and over; tough like a boar hog. Anne was special. Had a gift for healin' she'd learned from an old Cherokee medicine woman, Owl the Wise One. We all called her Old Mother.

I was raised in a most beautiful place. A valley so wonderful that many stories told around the Cherokee smoke fires claimed the Great Creator Himself would come visit on occasion. I believed that. The settlers called it Choestoe. The Cherokee said it as Cho-Ē-Sto-Ē. The name means "Land of the Dancing Rabbits". There was lots 'a Cherokee in the mountains when I grow'd up. Wish they was still there.

I'm an adopted Cherokee, too. My Native family lived on the east side 'a Slaughter Mountain, close to the gap. My father was Dancing Bear. My mother went by her Indian name, A-Ga-Li-Ha, which means Sunshine in the English. Their son, Wolf, was my Blood Brother and my best friend from since I can remember. All are across the Great River waitin' on me to come. I reckon I'll get around to it 'fore long.

My ancestors settled a good-sized piece 'a land what laid at the base 'a Ben Knob Mountain. That was hard for folks to say so everybody just said it as Ben's Knob. My granddad passed the land on to our family after he'd got feeble and had to move to the flat ground around the bottoms of the river Notla. He worked a sawmill there, hired on by a cantankerous, old Irish gentleman.

They'd both come to the southern mountains as boys. Spoke true Irish speak I could hardly make out. Couldn't understand a word lessin' they was meanin' to speak the English.

Me and Wolf was hardly ever apart once we'd got old enough to go stay in the woods by ourselves. We happened into all kinds a doin's durin' our time together. We never did no real wrong, though. Always put our faith in the Great Spirit. Trusted Him to guide and protect us. Never stole or lied or killed no person what didn't deserve killin'. We hunted, scouted, fought, and went on walks lastin' days, even attacked enemy soldiers when life or family depended on it. We was always respectful of our elders, women folk, and kids. Made sure the old ones never went hungry. For safety, we kept up with what was happenin' all around the valley; didn't wanna miss nothin'. Oh, and I worked a lot. Dad owned a mule tradin' business, which meant tendin' to mule needs constant. We had to farm all we ate, or we'd not eat. Our place was heated with firewood. A good-sized cabin with big fireplaces required many loads 'a wood to keep it warm. Cain, Dad, and me spent a lot 'a time cuttin' and splittin' firewood 'fore Cain got hitched to Wolf's sister, Rose, and moved on. My momma liked bein' warm. Dad made sure she had plenty 'a wood to keep her that way. He loved my momma. *I* loved my momma.

Me and Wolf savored our lives of freedom in the mountains, knowin' it could end any time. Our folks let us walk our own trail long as we followed the rules. We had many adventures, with Wolf the cause 'a most of 'em - him and his curious nature. He was brave with much courage. He led us many places.

Let me tell you about a time recent concernin' one certain hunt that come to teach us a lot about the depth of our souls. What I'm fixin' to tell you changed my life forever. I praise Jesus for seein' me through it all alive. Really, I do.

It was late winter, gettin' close to early spring, a while 'fore some trouble we had with the government and gold miners fired off. Wolf and I'd turned twelve recent. I was just healed complete from bein' jumped by a full grow'd bobcat a couple years earlier. I was hurt bad! That thing tore me up good. Healin' was a long time comin', but I'd healed whole by this hunt. Praise God! My sister, Anne, who was learnin' the healin' way from the old Cherokee medicine woman who tended to me, Owl the Wise One, stayed with me constant; seen to my healin'. Anne called her Old Mother out 'a respect. Momma never left me the whole time I was down, neither.

I'd finally worked my way back to trailin' the mountains with Wolf. We'd grow'd enough to hunt together, takin' game without nobody havin' to go with us. Our folks had taught us the way. The only thing they worried over was us leavin' Choestoe. They'd tell us, "stay together when travelin', or huntin', or on a walk. Stay clear 'a strangers and U.S. Government folk." We did what we was told... most 'a the time.

Wolf and me was camped on a big ridge east of Levelland Mountain hog huntin'. We was lookin' to get us another that mornin' to meet the two we had hangin'. Winter could go long in the mountains. Meat was important for survival when it did. Our folks know'd we was huntin' the big ridges. Know'd when we'd be back. They'd be worried over us, but not much. The woods had become our home; comfortable. We'd got good at stayin' safe. Bringin' back meat.

We'd crossed a fresh hog trail just 'fore good daylight the third mornin' of our hunt. Stayed on it 'til we slipped up on 'em rootin' around in their chosen feedin' ground. We was watchin' the lead boar as he wandered off from the rest of his bunch. He looked big easin' through a small stand 'a white oaks tryin' to fill his big ol' gut with some late season rotted acorns. One of us was gonna put an arrow through that critter. Then it, and the others hangin' in camp was gonna feed our clan for the next few moons. My mouth was waterin' just thinkin' on it. Baked, boiled, smoked, or fried, Momma cooked hog perfect. I was ready to taste it. Wouldn't be long now 'til we was back home in her cook room.

The pig was only twenty paces out makin' its way toward Wolf. The frozen leaves and sticks of the forest floor crunchin' as it walked. The cold air, such a dark gray in that time 'a darkness just before dawn, makes it hard to tell just what's what.

The big boar moved slowly. Rootin' for the slightest scent of a grub, or left-over acorn, or chestnut waitin' on him there in the rotting mast. He was payin' no mind to the danger he'd walked in to. Trustin' what gentle morning breeze was movin' to carry the warnin' he would need to stay safe … that warnin' had just been carried.

The pig stopped its searchin' real quick, jerkin' its head up from the ground with a hard grunt. A sudden shift in what gentle breeze was stirrin' filled his snout with my scent, makin' him turn toward where I was squatted. His huge, curled tusk now showin' white in the morning darkness. I know'd he weren't seein' me good 'cause it was still dusky dark. Hogs don't have the best eyes in the woods no how. I couldn't move, though, or he'd see where I was. That would not do. He was turned dead at me as he chomped the last mouthful 'a whatever rotten stuff he'd scoured, the foamy slobber drippin' off his bottom jaw and chin.

He raised his nose to the breeze. Scented. Then blow'd out a big ol' snort sendin' nose makin's flyin' out like bats leavin' a dark cave. Hateful mad at the nasty now locked in his snout, he followed the scent in my direction while liftin' his ugly ol' head even more. He was tryin' to find exactly where the foul smell was comin' from. That quarterin' move opened up a killin' shot for Wolf. I know'd my friend would not miss, bein' so close to what he was aimin' to kill.

It was a sight to see when that arrow shaft pushed a big, sharp, black flint point out from behind the boar's left shoulder. Plumb covered in dark blood, drippin', its turkey feather fletching stickin' out behind the right shoulder. Perfect killin' shot. Didn't even spook him. The boar stood for a second 'fore the pain hit, then let out a holler to beat all. A pig's squeal is ear piercin' if you're close by. I was. My ears rang so I could barely recognize the thud of its feet hittin' the ground as it charged right at me, blood blowin' from its snout every time its front feet landed.

I was in a bad way as it commenced its charge. If I moved too soon, the pig would move with me; open me up where he could rip my leg with them sharp tusks from behind. My only defense was knowin' what all mountain folk know'd: a pig can't cut left or right quick when chargin'. I was gonna have to wait 'til he was near on me to move. That was gonna be dangerous for me in what little light there was.

One thing was sure, I weren't gonna have to wait long to jump 'cause he was comin' full on. I let it charge to within' a couple paces 'fore I made my move. Throwin' myself hard to the left side of his charge, hittin' the ground with a thump. The pig stopped spot on. Dead still. Right where I'd been squatted. He turned slowly to his left, movin' closer to where I lay tryin' to find me, his head held high. The blood comin' from its snout now coverin' my foot-skin boots like a soft rain on dry garden leaves. Without no sign, he blow'd out hard. I watched as the sides of his rib cage kept movin' in and out with each desperate struggle for air. It made Wolf's arrow do a kinda killin' dance as it stuck out both sides of the hog's front quarter. Wolf could not 'a put that arrow through no better. Took out both lungs while slicin' through the top of it's heart. The thing was just a tough ol' mountain pig what was fightin' death with all it had.

I dared not move. One rip from those tusks could jerk a main blood line open. That would put us in a bad way bein' we was a couple miles from the nearest help. I tried to stay hid. I could not figure how that hog could 'a stopped so quick, but he did. Standin' near on me. He was a *big hog*, too.

A slight wobble to the right, then back left, his spirit was startin' to slip. His family from across the river would see him soon. He was fadin'. I know'd the danger was passin' as it's eyes went dark. He stumbled again. Left, then right. A last lunge 'a mad fell him right at my feet snout first. He never made another sound, 'cept for a dyin' grunt as the last draw'd air left his lungs.

The Cherokee believed his spirit would now cross over; that we would see him again on the other side when our days was finished. The Christian ones believed Jesus when He said He'd make all things new. Naturally, me and this hog would meet again, but Wolf is the one who set its spirit free. He would be the one to run it when we crossed the river.

That pig got harvested, gave up its meat, and it's spirit was now in paradise. That's how the Wolf believed it. I know human folk who trail with Jesus will spend forever with Him in Heaven, but animals was different in my way 'a thinkin'. Who could argue? I would just look forward to the hope that we'd get to hunt the big boar again.

We had our meat. Wolf had another story to tell around the Cherokee fires that spring. Course, he had a good laugh at the pig nearly gettin' me every time he told it. I didn't cotton to it. I don't see the funny when a wounded hog is tryin' to kill a body. Cherokee warriors did. Not one I ever know'd feared death.

Indians had their own way 'a lookin' at things. You just had to respect that. No figurin' 'em sometimes. They was family to me. I was with Wolf most 'a the time, that is if I weren't needed on the farm. It never gave out, neither. We'd be at my home at the base 'a Ben's Knob Mountain, with him and his family on Slaughter Mountain, or on a trail somewhere in the mountains. We was all tight.

They was a lot 'a Cherokee in the mountains when I was bein' raised. I lived as much like one 'a their kind as I did a farmer or mule trader like my dad and granddad. They was true mountain men, both of 'em, born and raised.

Dad made his gold coin tradin' mules with folks. They'd come from all over to buy his stock. You'd hear it told in stories that Granddad even sent some across the great water back to the Mother Land. I didn't know if I took to all that or not. Still, folks told it gospel.

Dad tended over forty head, includin' his jacks and the draft horse mares he bred 'em to. Each year he'd raise to sell at least a dozen good mules. Them jacks was mammoth jacks from the stock 'a General George Washington's own rake. Folks claim he was the first mule breeder in America. That made me proud. They say his stock was brought across the great water, too, in boats. Can you believe that? It was always hard for me to figure all that; mules crossin' the great water on boats. I reasoned I'd have to see that 'fore I'd tell it. To me, that was like a body walkin' on the moon. Just weren't never gonna happen.

The jacks Dad used was big, and when they mixed with them draft mares 'a Dad's, you had a solid-bred mule you could count on in the mountains. Dad give me my own as he did my brother, Cain, and his wife, Rose. My mule's name was Peter. We went all over together. He could ride, plow, pull, and log. He was *real* smart, just as savvy as our main lead mule, Big Jim. Me and Jim had a history. I was on his back when that bobcat attacked us. Got him good, too. Took Jim nearly a year to heal. He was a *great* mule. He was black where Peter was gray with black. Both was huge animals. They liked runnin' together, too, like Wolf and me.

Wolf didn't have no mule of his own 'til later on. He'd been ridin' a certain young mule 'a Dad's. Him and it was bondin'. My dad was watchin'.

***

Yeah, Cain and Rose got hitched. Become one. Tied

the knot. Moved in together. Jumped the broom. Made their covenant with God. It weren't long after the trouble from the Yonah clan was done with, that terrible winter of all the killin'.

Dancing Bear and A-Ga-Li-Ha throw'd a big comin' together at our place for their doin's. It was a sight. They was brought together at sunrise. Standin' on a small rise facin' east about a half mile up the trail above our farm in late spring. It was *real* special. Most everybody in the valley come. The Cherokee brought their families. I'd not seen so many females in one place ever, young and old. Never know'd Choestoe had so many women.

I saw the widow England from up on Wolf Creek makin' camp near our barn. My insides got tight as I remembered the blue-eyed, chestnut-haired girl I'd seen when me and Dad first trailed to Slaughter Mountain. I got a knot in my throat that tasted like salt. The center of my bein' was jumpin'. *What in the world?* I thought.

The women all cried at the vow takin', them knowin' what all the young couple had gone through to get to that day. Once they was done marryin', my brother was made a full warrior of the Choestoe clan. He and Rose lived mostly like Cherokee anyway, 'cept Cain helped Dad farm. He loved bein' Cherokee. He loved Dad, too. Farmin' was how he was raised. Sides', the food was needed. He had two families dependin' on him to provide. He'd swore it to Rose.

Their marriage ceremony was a story in itself with many more stories to come from it. Dad bein' who he was, Cain bein' who he was, and Rose bein' who she was, you could figure the comin' together of Cain and dear, sweet Rose was gonna be a time to remember. Every settler in the mountains know'd what Cain had gone through. They'd all be there. His name was smoked over 'round many fires.

Rose was the daughter of Dancing Bear. Every young Cherokee buck I ever met wanted her for his wife. They'd all be there. Good or bad, she chose a white settler. But, as they all had learned, not just any white settler. She chose Cain, a most respected warrior. They was to be wed. The marriage would demand honor. Many didn't cotton to it but respect it they would. Cain didn't care. He'd already put his life before hers more than once. He know'd Holy Spirit protected them. She know'd he'd always be there for her. His devotion made her love him beyond any feelings she could put to words. Divine. Right. From deep down inside. And when you met them together, you could feel it was right. They made the time you spent in their presence seem proper.

The word was sent out from Slaughter Mountain by runner about Rose marryin' Cain. Folks come to our place in bunches several days 'fore the preacher was supposed to be there. The Cherokee would light a sacred fire that required seven full days to burn. Seven full days 'a grow'd folks havin' fun, settlers and Indians mixin', a special time. The smoke from the fire would cleanse the ground, along with the folks, both family and visitor. Prayers was offered up, makin' everything havin' to do with what was goin' on acceptable to Holy Spirit. They was so many folks come they ended up coverin' most all our pasture. The families from each clan was allowed the cleared spots along the edge of our woods, which was close to the creek. They got those out 'a respect. But, Cherokee families was all over. Most camped deeper in the woods. They took folks joinin' as one *real* serious, same as settlers.

Both sets 'a people brought their music. Dancin', some lastin' all night, was a big part 'a marryin' for Indians and settlers. They came to celebrate and enjoy time from the hard work 'a providin'. They passed the jug, smoked, gambled, passed the jug, slept, hunted, ate, passed the jug, and danced ... oh, the Cherokee was amazing when they danced! They just had themselves a big ol' time, with Dad right in the middle as usual. It was such a goin' on!

Me and Wolf didn't see Cain for three days after his kind arrived. His friends was wild. All trainin' to be warriors. Cain was way ahead of 'em on that for sure. Rose was everywhere. I spent a lot 'a time with her. Loved her as much as any did, 'cept maybe Cain.

Dancing Bear had come with his whole family clan. He'd brought George Black Oak, the biggest Cherokee Indian to have ever lived, I was sure. My true friend. They lit the ceremonial fire, which had to burn constant for seven days. That's why guests was there. Nobody wanted to miss out on such a happenin'.

Me and Wolf had been wrestlin'. We'd whupped most all the boys our age, then began movin' on up on the older ones. They stopped us. My nose was bleedin' and I'm almost sure Wolf had a shoulder out for a bit. One 'a the warriors watchin' us wrestle seen what happened. Grabbed Wolf under the arm without askin', then lifted up with a quick pull settin' the joint back right. I heard it pop. Wolf went to his knees in pain. His face turned white, but he never made a sound.

We weren't lookin' too good when all the women folk got to stirrin' around us that evenin'. We'd been wrestlin' all afternoon. Covered head to foot in Mother Earth's finest dirt. Blood and bruises on our faces and arms. We was *plumb ugly*. It *would* just have to be the time when the little chestnut-haired girl showed herself. I couldn't believe it. I looked like a pig. But she was, oh, such a sight. She made my legs weak. My vision go foggy. I hadn't seen her for a *long* time. I'd thought about the time at her place a little, more lately than normal for some reason. She had on the most perfect dress I could've ever imagined, homespun sure.

She come from a small pond 'a females millin' about like young doe trailin' by the base of a huge mountain white oak in heavy fog, floatin' as it were. Her chestnut-colored hair, tied back with a single-beaded hawk feather laced just behind her right ear, was callin' to me like a warm fire. She laughed. I died. She walked straight to me. I looked for a hole to crawl into. I didn't know the feelin', but it had to be what bein' shot with an arrow felt like — burnin', no air, hot, sweaty. I wished she'd walk away. No! Don't! Stay! I couldn't think straight. Wolf was hidin' his laughin'. I had to look a sight.

She stopped dead in front of me. Stared me straight in the eye, and spoke the first words I ever remember hearin' her say, "My name is Elizabeth, Jeb Collins, and *you will* dance with me tomorrow night," then she turned and left. The pull on my heart took my breath as her scent filled my lungs. I had to stink. She acted like it weren't nothin'. I didn't see her again 'til the day 'a the doin's. Without knowin' it, I'd planned a trail for her in my heart.

***

God could not 'a given Cain and Rose a better morning for their vow takin'. They weren't married all Cherokee, nor was they married all Christian. They had some 'a both to show respect to all folks attendin'.

The holy man for the Nation had come for the Cherokee part. He blessed the intended and their families with the smoke from the sacred fire. Now that the ceremony was commencin', he blessed the visiting folks who'd come, too. He turned his attention to Cain who was holdin' part of a fresh venison ham rolled up in a deer skin, a sign to show he'd forever provide for his wife and their offspring. She returned the favor by placin' a small pouch 'a dried corn in the holy man's palm. It proved she'd always be there to take care of the family. He then took the victuals, prayed over 'em, and sanctified the couple.

The path the families walked to the top 'a the rise for the Christian part of the ceremony was lined with women folk — Indians on the bride's side, settlers on Cain's side. The Cherokee girls weren't wearin' nothin' above their middles but flowers wove together. Their hair was full 'a fresh dogwood and azalea blooms. They wore full beads all over. Some wore gold bands around their brown-skinned upper arms, while others wore gold around their necks hangin' from braided leather cords. It was a most beautiful sight.

The settler women was lined up wearin' their best

homespun. The chestnut-haired girl was one of 'em, standin' with her friends along the side of the wedding path. My throat went dry when I seen her. I had to walk right by her, bein' that I was part 'a the direct family. I was in my finest homespun. My hair was combed, and I was havin' to wear boots. I didn't like boots. They hurt. You couldn't feel the ground through the sole. I was clean this time when I saw her. I liked what she was wearin', a mix 'a homespun and Indian. The same dress I'd seen her in the day before, but she'd added beads all through her beautiful hair, hangin' 'round her neck and wrapped around her wrist. She was like honey to a bear for me. I had to get closer; smell her scent one more time.

  I stopped. I didn't think. I just did it. Right in front of her, I stopped. I couldn't help it. I had no control. No doubt in my mind, she was a witch throwin' a spell on me, but I liked it. I turned, walked over to her real close like, and looked down into her eyes. She weren't laughin' then. I never said nothin'. I just kinda stared. She stared back with those piercin' blue eyes. I smiled. She smiled. We both smiled. I near fainted as Wolf dragged me away 'cause I'd forgot to breathe durin' all the starin'. It took me a minute to realize what'd happened. I looked back. Gone. Nowhere in sight. She made me feel funny. I couldn't figure if I liked it or not. It did somethin' to me I was gonna have to study on, smoke over.

  The preacher took charge once the Cherokee Holy Man had covered the shoulders of the two with a white blanket. He said some stuff I didn't understand 'cause my mind was twisted from seein' Elizabeth, then he quoted scripture for the Christian part 'a their marryin'. Women was cryin'. Men was standin' around fidgetin', wishin' they was somewhere else, anywhere else. It was gettin' hot. Old Man Sun was wakin' to bless Cain and Rose for their eternal bond. A bond held by oaths. A gold circle made for both by my dad for commitment.

  "Rose," Cain near-whispered as he turned to look

into her eyes for the vow sayin' part. "My life is yours. I wish I could tell you all will be fine. I cannot. I have seen suffering as have you. But I can tell you sure, I will stand with you in everything we face. I will provide for our family. In times of happiness, we will smile. When you are sad, we will hold each other close. When you are mad, you can hit me and feel better. I will love you until I can breathe no more. My strength will be yours if you find yourself scared, lonely, or threatened. Call for me. Know I will be there. Trust me, I will never let you down. I am now ... and forever ... your husband."

Rose held tears when she answered him back, "Cain, I am your wife. There is no other for me. My heart has surrendered the fullness of its ability to love you. I devote myself to you. I will care for you. I will carry our children. You will be their Father. I will be their Mother. I will be there for you, our family, 'til my eyes close on this world. If I go to Glory Land before you, I will wait. If you go before me, you must wait. I will be at your side for the good and the bad. We will be one."

With that said, every Cherokee in the place shouted loud as they could then took off down the hill to commence dancin' around the sacred fire, singin' and chantin' holy songs all the while. Girls danced with boys. Boys danced with girls. In the Cherokee tradition, the celebration lasted all night. Music played. Jugs was passed. Rose and Cain disappeared. I danced with Elizabeth. Most everybody there stayed up near two days feastin' and dancin'. When the morning light come on the third sun from the union, not a Cherokee could be found.

The families got together after the wedding and built Cain and Rose a small cabin on some land Dancing Bear owned not far from the base of Slaughter Mountain. Their new home place was a bit lower down in the valley, not far from Wolf Creek, the biggest creek in Choestoe. Me and Wolf would stay there when we was out on a hunt or a walk; for sure on cold nights. It was warm and cozy with a main room in the front what had a huge fireplace for warmin', a loft for beds, and a sleepin' room in the back for Cain and Rose. That had a fireplace, too. Dad and Momma give 'em a cook stove for a wedding gift. It was in Rose's cook room. She learned how to use it after a time.

Me and Wolf loved it there. They liked for us to stay. We'd help Cain get in firewood most all year, so they'd be plenty for 'em durin' the cold time, then they'd be enough for us when we come to visit.

***

As life in the mountains went, it weren't required that folks make it known they was comin' to visit. Nobody thought no different of it. It was always expected that some poor soul may wander in needin' food or shelter or warmth or healin'. Folks in the mountains was always ready for most anything. Even cooked extra when makin' meals. We had somebody in for a meal at our place at least once a week, almost always Indian. Many would come, eat, and leave, never sayin' a word. Then again, some would stay to smoke with Dad or Cain, then sleep the night or leave out in the dark. I learned most 'a the ones who didn't speak was the ones who hadn't learned English words. But then without knowin' who'd done it, you'd find a fresh pile 'a venison on the back porch wrapped up in a skin or a gift like new foot skins or beaded necklaces and bracelets or a pipe or knife. That was some Indians' way 'a sayin' thanks without callin' notice to himself.

I loved the Cherokee for how they was. I once caught a very small, old Cherokee elder leavin' Dad a flint knife blade wrapped in an old piece 'a rabbit hide. He'd most likely made that blade, or he'd not be lettin' go of it. I remembered him, all right. He'd come early one morning to have breakfast with us. He'd eat a lot, too, to be so small. Never said a word when he'd cleaned his plate, neither. Just got up from the table, nodded a little toward Momma, then left.

***

Everybody know'd Cain. He got lots 'a visitors, mostly Indian. I met a bait 'a warriors when we stayed there through the years. Heard many stories. I really liked stayin' with Cain and Rose. A boy could be all the Indian he wanted to be at their place, didn't bother Momma one bit. She liked us livin' mostly like settler folk.

Me and Cain got to be more Cherokee as time went on; *really* got that way after learnin' how government folks could be. Gold miners and Federal men – all of 'em was liars as far as the Cherokee in me was concerned. I didn't hardly trust none of 'em. I trusted the miners more than any government folk, though, and that weren't much. But you could smell the evil in them government men. They smelled like where rats'd been livin' in the corn crib. I reckon some 'a them "polick-tisians", as Dad called 'em, was good the way he saw it. I trailed away from 'em when they come for visits. Regrettably, as time went on, they come a lot.

Wolf and me met our first government man early in the fall 'fore Killin' Time commenced. He was ridin' an old horse and had all kinds 'a truck with him. Carried it strapped on a couple 'a wore out lookin' mules with a "US" brand burnt on their rumps. Me and Wolf figured the U.S. Government must not have much coin if that was the best they could do for their man. Two skinny ol' things like he was near-pullin'. Them two put together wouldn't 'a made one 'a Jim or Peter.

I didn't like him much. I got to know him some as he traveled in and out 'a Choestoe near two years. It got too dangerous for him to be near the Cherokee after a while, some settler folk, too. He was what folks called an "A-gent." He never looked no different than a regular body to me. Bein' government meant he was an outsider, an enemy to the Cherokee. Outsiders had to be watched 'cause they weren't trusted. That man never know'd it, but he was near killed by some concerned Cherokee when he first come to the valley. They watched him constant. Could feel the federal government in him. Me and Wolf know'd him showin' up meant trouble for all.

The way 'a the Cherokee would change. Of this, I was sure. Freedom, the Spirit Bear, had told me in my dream after I got hurt that the Cherokee was facin' changes. And 'cause of all the government's greed, lies, and evil, Choestoe would change, too. It weren't right for a bunch to take a man's home just cause they was better armed than the weaker party. In this case, that was the Cherokee. Most of 'em was forced to give up everything they'd worked for, so the government could give it to some other folks what was gonna move in. They ought 'a left 'em alone, let 'em be. The mountains would 'a been a sight better if the Cherokee still lived in 'em.

***

It was on toward mid-day when me and Wolf near slid down the east side 'a the ridge toward our camp. The hog we was draggin' was heavy in meat. It weren't no struggle, though. The ground was steep and the mast wet from the morning thaw. That helped with the draggin'. It was cold, bein' late winter like it was. Still, the days would warm some with spring close, so we had to watch for flies blowin' our hangin' meat. We'd already had to scrape a place or two with our knives.

Old Man Sun liked to hide early that time 'a season, makin' for short days. We decided to hang the fresh kill with the other two and stay over one more night instead 'a travelin' in the dark. Break camp at daylight, load the mules with our meat and campin' truck, then be on our way back home. That would give us the most travelin' light for our trip to Ben's Knob. It was a good plan. We was both comfortable with it. But, as we'd learn time and again, even the best thought out trails can take some curious turns. Our visitors durin' the night would prove that.

At least the fire was warm, the coffee hot, our tobacco dry, and we had fresh meat, weren't havin' to chew jerked. We was plannin' on havin' us a restful night after huntin' hard for several days, at least most of it was.

J. R. Collins

Chapter Two

Samson and Toad

The fire was down a right smart as me and Wolf settled back a'gin a big ol' log we'd camped by and got comfortable. The coals circlin' the dyin' flames turnin' from orange to gray. Takin' out our tobacco pouches, we packed our pipe bowls with some 'a the best air-dried, homegrown burley tobacco in the mountains, then used a dried splinter to fetch a flame. The taste from the sweet smoke after a good supper was a gift from Heaven for true mountain folk. We'd eat enough roasted hog to fill two more and my full belly was makin' me near lazy. Our hunt had beat us up good. We was both tired; wore down. But the meat hangin' made the effort respectable. Dad would salt cure at least four 'a the hams, most of the tenderloin, and near all the bacon, then smoke the rest for sausage or stew meat. A body never eat a better breakfast than when Momma fried some sausage, ham and eggs, baked a skillet full 'a cathead-sized buttermilk biscuits, then finished the meat grease by makin' a sausage gravy what had meat chunks laid all through.

They was only one way to eat a mess like that proper. First, you'd lay a thick slab of the skillet-fried, salt-cured ham on a long plate. Slice one 'a the skillet baked cathead biscuits in half across the middle, then lay it inside-up flat across the top of the ham. The two halves touchin' side-by-side. Cover both sides with a fried egg for each, yokes hot and runny. Lay on a generous coverin' of meaty sausage gravy then add a chunk 'a honey comb dropped square on top filled with rich, dark, sourwood honey to melt over the whole pile. This plate full 'a the best tastin' breakfast a body could stand was what local folks called the "Choestoe Blessing." It was hard for me to eat a whole plate full. Dad, Dancing Bear, Cain, and our Cherokee friend, Black Oak, could eat the whole put-together. Sometimes two. You'd not believe it 'til you saw 'em actual. I watched Black Oak eat near three one morning when he come easin' up on our back porch just after daylight. He was back from scoutin' new huntin' grounds. Been days without solid food from gettin' turned around in a strange land. Only had water with a bit 'a jerked meat to fill his big ol' gut for over three days.

Hog meat was cured for breakfast; some jerked near-dry for takin' on the trail. We'd use the whole of it when we killed one, 'cept for most 'a the bones or such as that. I liked the best cuts for eatin', favorin' the ham, tenderloin, shoulders, and bacon best. I never held a taste for what I'd seen some folks eat like boiled or smoked ears, skillet-fried boar balls, snout meat pies, mush made from bone marrow mixed with fresh blood and flour then skillet-fried, eggs scrambled in brains seasoned with hot dried pepper laid over cathead biscuits with a heavy puttin' on 'a red eye gravy, guts baked into cornbread called chitlins, and pickled feet. *Whoever eat them first I wonder?* Lot's 'a folks liked 'em for some reason. Now, the sun-dried hide scraped clean 'a stiff hog hair then skillet-fried in bacon drippin's, I liked that. We'd cut it up in pieces, tote it with our jerky. The older ones liked them nasty kinda fixin's mostly. I know'd a few common folks who favored 'em as well, but I never brought myself up to eat that kinda food makin's. I really weren't never that hungry, praise God!

The night was dark as dark gets. They weren't no moon showin' none. We couldn't see much, 'cept by what light was shed by our little fire. Peter was tied close, actin' edgy, kinda restless. I didn't think nothin' of it. I know'd he was ready for home. I should 'a thought more on it.

I never cared for mean Indians, still don't. The mountains had their share. Fortunately, there was only a few. Dancing Bear taught Wolf and me to always watch for 'em when we was out on a trail. They could come on a body at any time. You'd not know it, neither, 'til they was on you. The one who'd just walked into our camp was mean. You could tell by lookin' at him. His friends was mean, too. They was what mountain folk called rogue Indians. You'd cross trails with 'em if you didn't watch.

We was tired. We'd grow'd lazy from the long, hard hunt mixed with a big supper 'a fresh-kilt, skillet-fried hog meat. We weren't watchin', now here we was eye-to-eye. They smelled bad, too. Dirty.

Most times foul Indians like the ones payin' us a visit set out for what they could find or take, but I could feel they was somethin' different 'bout what they was interested in. All had a look to 'em like they was on the hunt for somethin' they meant to find. I remember thinkin', *"They must be good 'bout slippin' around 'cause we never know'd they was in the world 'til they come in on us."* Peter tried to warn us. He was comin' on to be a really good mule to have around.

I weren't scared none, Wolf, neither. I looked to where he'd stood once the visit commenced. He done had his knife draw'd, right hand low, blade up. My senses come to me when I realized I was standin' beside him. My right hand laid across the hard bone handle of the knife Black Oak give me on my first ever camp with Dad. I had no memory of ever movin'. Wolf said later what we done was spiritual, Cherokee learned.

The lead Indian, the ugliest one 'a the bunch, moved in closer, squattin' across from us in front of our fire, palms up, facin' forward. He looked over at us and started talkin', "I am Blood Moon. I am a warrior of the Cherokee from over to the west. Many call our clan 'The Lost.' I mean you no harm as we are in search of an evil one -- a woman who can kill with the knife. She took the life of my brother. Have you seen such on your hunt? Tell me true as I will know your words young ones."

The Lost, they was a bad bunch. We know'd it, too. Believed they was attached to mother earth by spiritual roots like you find under a tree. The stories told how many Choestoe folk throughout the early years had fallen to their thirst for blood. I thanked God those days was in the past. They'd let folks be for many years; lived across the main ridges to the west while mostly keepin' to themselves. Folks didn't speak on 'em much anymore, 'cept in a few stories I'd heard around smoke fires. They'd never crossed the main ridges into Choestoe that me or Wolf ever know'd of, but here they was. I'd heard of 'em, but never met one. Wished I weren't meetin' one then.

What few stories we'd heard told around the fires spoke of how the old ones of The Lost would eat their enemy if the spirit provoked 'em. The thought made my gut sick as I looked across the fire at the ones who'd come in on us. That kinda eatin' just weren't right. I saw no sign of it, but lookin' at 'em, I did not doubt it could be so. Made me wonder what folk meat would taste like. My mouth turned sour. I near wretched at the thought 'a meat like that cookin' over a fire. Folk meat grease poppin' in the coals as it dripped.

They was plain nasty, not clean like the Cherokee I run with. Their home spun shirts was dirty, blood stained. Their leggin's and foot skins was covered in what looked like bear grease or dried lard. They had story marks on their faces, which told us they was battle tested. I still weren't scared. I couldn't figure why not. I should 'a been.

Everything they had on was near wore out. Nothin' fancy at all. Had no beads wove into their stringy hair; none hangin' from their necks or skins. They carried few weapons. Most likely had some back in the woods out 'a sight since they was lookin' to talk on what we know'd. Only one of 'em had a bow. They all had pouches. A knife sheathed to a leather belt. A couple had two. The youngest 'a the bunch wore his hair braided. Couldn't figure that.

Wolf was first to speak 'tween me and him, "Why would you come to this ridge to look for your brother's killer? Has she trailed this way? Did you think we would know of her?"

It weren't real nice the way he'd said it. I think Wolf was feelin' a little nasty his own self since the strangers just kinda walked in on us without welcome. We'd been camped where we was for a few days. Hadn't seen hide nor sign of a single soul. Now here walked in four stinkin', dirty Indians with brother warriors likely watchin' off in the dark. We was ill 'cause they'd messed up our smoke. Wolf seemed mad.

That little push from Wolf got 'em to start actin' like they was gettin' on the edge 'a mad. I was concerned, watchin' close. Wolf's words had kinda made the whole come together a little uncomfortable. He didn't seem to care.

"We have not seen another living soul in many days," Wolf kept on. "We have been on a hunt for the grunting one. You see the Great Spirit has blessed us with some late winter meat. You are welcome to take some as you go."

Blood Moon suddenly wore a more hateful look as Wolf stood his ground. He'd just invited them to leave.

"What might your name be young one?" asked Blood Moon.

"I am Wolf," he replied as he put his knife away, layin' his right forearm across the top of his chest. "Son of Dancing Bear, council member for all Cherokee."

"I have heard of your father. Among my people, he is an honored man. I wish to go visit with him if my time here will see it. It is a good fire to meet his son ... and his white skinned friend," he said as he turned to look at me with a strange kinda want on his face.

I felt like he was sizin' me up, maybe thinkin' on what kinda seasonin' he'd cover my hams with while I roasted hog-tied over his fire. I pulled my hand from the handle of my knife, then squatted down close to the bed 'a hot coals. I laid on a couple 'a small sticks to make more light. I wanted to be able to see these visitors better if things turned against us all of a sudden.

Wolf still didn't act like he was gonna be real gracious, even though this stranger said he know'd Dancing Bear. Truth was, Wolf had never heard his father say one word about this hateful-lookin' Indian. Could be Blood Moon was tellin' the truth, could be he weren't. Wolf was gonna be careful 'til he know'd one from the other. I figured him for the truth. He didn't sound fetchin' to me.

I turned my head, lookin' over at him with wonder about the woman they was chasin'. I spoke as I got more comfortable, takin' a draw from my pipe, "I am sorry for your loss. I will ask the Great Creator to give your brother peace across the river. But, where do you figure this killer is ya'll are lookin' for? We've hunted this ridge and the two east of here for several days. We've seen no sign of any human. Did she move close by? Did we not see her?"

"She did move close by. She was in your camp just today when Old Man Sun was resting up high. She took only meat from your kill then went on. She is mountain-born, purebred Cherokee. I will cut out her heart when I find her, roast it over my fire. Then leave the rest of her to fill the bellies of the wild ones. My brother's spirit cries to me from the other side each night she lives. I cannot sleep."

He did look tired. No doubt, he meant what he said. There was no question in my mind he intended to do just what he figured right. I reckon most folks would 'a been doin' no different when family was concerned. I only know'd one soul in my family I'd not take an arrow for: a cousin on Dad's side. He was so aggravatin' you could hardly stand to be near him. He'd set out to make you mad on purpose. He didn't like folks, neither.

His name was Toad, or at least that's what me and Cain called him. Dad's sister, Aunt Sophie, married a Cherokee man who never cared for us much. He'd not come to visit. We never went to their place. Aunt Sophie would come stay with us some. She and Momma was close. When she'd come, she loved spendin' time with my sister, Anne. She'd teach Aunt Sophie about the plants. Share the healin' Owl the Wise One had taught her. Toad always come when she visited.

He was short for his age. Had a big face. Wide like a frog. Kept a strange look on it all the time. Nasty in his doin's. Mean if he wanted to be. You couldn't trust him no more than you could a rattle-maker or a copper-backed snake. He didn't like folks. Very few cared to be around him. He thought he was the sweetest corn in the field, but true to callin', all folks like that get found out. It weren't gonna be no different for him.

He acted like he weren't scared 'a nothin', yet had a secret he thought no one know'd. Aunt Sophie had told us without his knowin'. She wanted us to keep an eye on him on account of it. It worried her a right smart. Made her fear for him. What she told us was, he was really scared 'a critters, bears mostly.

He was the kinda person that'd say hateful things to weaker folk. Make fun 'a things they said or did or how they looked. He figured himself better than they was and had no respect for nothin', includin' himself.

Cain got riled up at him one time. Had to settle with him on account. Toad saw a part 'a Cain that day what didn't show itself around family much.

Aunt Sophie had come to visit. I weren't but six year old at the time. Toad was some behind Cain in age. Me and Cain always liked seein' her. Gettin' to spend time with her when she'd come to visit. Neither one of us liked that snake son 'a hers, though.

One 'a Cain's favorite knives went missin' after one of their visits. Dad had give it to him, makin' it even more special. We know'd Toad had it. Anne seen him handlin' it 'fore they left for home. Cain decided he was gonna get it back from him the very next time they come for a visit. Him travelin' would mean he was prob'ly carryin' it.

Dad took us all down to the river to wash a bunch 'a mule shoes him and Cain had made that winter. He liked to rub 'em with the river sand from off the bottom of a deep hole to make 'em worn some. That rubbin' made 'em easier on the mules feet once they got nailed on. I learned later in life that new mule shoes was kinda like store-bought clothes – stiff and uncomfortable, 'til you wore 'em a season or two. They'd made a poke 'a nails, too. We was gonna wash them along with the shoes 'fore we was done.

Soon as we got there, Dad told us to go about fetchin' some dry wood to build a fire with. Then strike flint to steel to get it burnin' good while he finished goin' about collectin' the things we'd need to do the mule-shoe rubbin' chore. Proper sand was very important. We needed a place to warm ourselves, too. It was sure enough cold that day.

Cain, me, and Toad 'a followin', took off into the woods to get the makin's for a fire. We'd only been gone a few minutes when Cain turned, givin' me one 'a them little grins he'll give you 'fore he gets up to mischief. Toad was on a trail to be had. He didn't have a notion for it, neither.

I wanted Cain to get his knife back, but Toad was spiteful, so he might not. We'd soon see 'cause Cain had just turned complete around, walked right by me after we'd made it into the woods good, and went straight toward our back trail, stoppin' dead in front of ol' Toad. Cain did not look as mad as I know'd he was.

Toad nearly run into Cain as he stopped and looked up askin', "What are you doin', Cain? Why did you stop?"

"Bear," was all Cain said as he leaned in close starin' down into Toad's dark eyes.

"What? Bears?" Toad said, real nervous-like, lookin' around. "We should go from here. Look in another place for fire makin's. Huh, Cain? Don't you think? I think we should."

"We can't," said Cain, cool as winter's breath, showin' no fear.

"What? We can't? Why not? All we got to do is walk to some other place. We can get wood *there*. Now, I mean, let's go," Toad replied as he started to walk off.

"Go ahead. Suit yourself. You know more than most folks I reckon," scolded Cain. "Take your trail. Just be on the sly 'cause this bear is mean. I know the track. We call him Samson. He is strong. Been known to kill. We must be very careful.

"Kill?" asked Toad, turnin' back toward Cain, near shakin' he was so scared.

"Yep. Kill, Toad," replied Cain in a calm, hushed voice. Lookin' around like he was tryin' to spot ol' Samson for real. "He likes folk blood, the fresher the better. Likes to crush their skulls. Lick the brains right out. There are stories told around the smoke fires about this bear, 'bout the youngsters he's killed and eat. However, we must not be scared. If you show fear, he can smell it. That's how he knows an easy meal is about. Then he'll come fetchin', tryin' to eat what he smelled. Stay calm, Toad. I do not want to die today. I sure don't want to be eaten by no killer bear when my time comes!"

"Eat us! What…? Cain, what do we do? We can't just let him eat us. We got to do somethin'. Tell me what to do. I'll do anything. Tell me now!" he near hollered he was so scared.

Cain worked him up so he was near wettin' his skins. I was just waitin' on him to let it go Cain had him shook so. I figured it for soon. No way he was gonna come out from this with dry britches. His fear 'a bears was worse than some town-raised girl. Samson, Cain had told him. I nearly laughed 'a loud thinkin' on it.

"Okay, here is what we're gonna do," Cain whispered real quiet-like while lookin' around, puttin on an act like he was watchin' for ol' Samson to come bustin' through the brush at any minute. "Toad, you're gonna stay right here. Remember, don't show scared or that bear will smell you and have you for supper. Me and Jeb are gonna move out to see if we can find where he went. Right where we are is the safest place around right now, so don't move 'til we come back for you. You hear, Toad?"

Toad whispered, "Yeah. Stay here. Don't leave. Try to not be scared. I got it. Is that it? Just stay here? Wait?"

"Yep. Just stay here. Don't move unless you have to. If you hear bear gruntin', then pull your knife and hold it like this," Cain said as he pulled another of his knives showin' Toad how to hold it. "You got a knife with you, don't you, Toad?"

"Yeah, I got a knife. Sure, I do. It's in my pouch."

"Well, take it out. Let me see you hold it where you can fight a hungry-folk-eatin' bear."

"No. I don't want to take it out unless I have to. I might need to haul off runnin'. I'm scared I might trip and fall and poke myself. I'll only pull it if that bear comes 'round."

"*No!*" Cain whisper yelled as he grabbed him by the shoulders to let ol' Toad know he was dead serious. "Has no one ever told you not to run from bears? They are lightning fast and'll tear your head clean off if they have to chase you. Havin' to run down their meat makes 'em mad. Steady yourself right here. We will go and find this bear. Talk with him." With that, we both turned and left, not givin' Toad a chance to follow.

I walked behind Cain as we took a small deer trail out from where Toad was standin', shakin' like a scared young'un headed for the woodshed. I know'd Cain's plan. He didn't need to tell me. We was gonna scare that knife right out 'a his pouch. Cain *would* have it back. He needed it to cool his vengeance. I figured it was gonna be painful to watch.

It weren't long 'til we'd made a big circle out around ol' Toad; come right back to where we'd been not a half hour before. He was still standin' there, lookin', but no knife... yet. It was comin', though. I know'd it.

I wish folks could 'a seen Cain the way he done. He got down on all fours, just like an old bear. Had his head down gruntin', gettin' his mind in the bear spirit. He turned his head to look up at me, near whisperin', "Watch ol' Toad yonder, Jeb. Tell me what he does when I get to carryin' on. If he pulls out my knife, let me know. We'll go in on him. Take it away. Watch close now."

Cain lowered his head some, breathed in deep, raised up on his back legs 'til his hands was off the ground 'bout knee high, then with a smooth jerk, he slammed his hands and front half back down to the ground, landin' square on both his palms while lettin' out the nastiest soundin' grunt you'd ever hear. It sure enough sounded like a big ol' mean bear done wallered in close. I looked up to study Toad. It near made me laugh out he was carryin' on so, spinnin' around like one 'a my toy tops Dad made for us to play with, bouncin' from behind one tree to the next, searchin'. His eyes was wide, like when the moon is full. He was shakin' hard. His arms was straight out from his front, both hands squeezin' tight to the hickory handle of Cain's knife. I seen right off it was Cain's. It was the one Dad give him for Christmas a few years prior. It was Cain's for sure. This was gonna be ugly.

I kept my eye on Toad while tellin' Cain what was goin' on, "It worked, Cain. You've near scared him to death. He's got your knife held tight in both hands. He's spinnin' 'round like a dog chasin' its tail. I ain't never seen such. What a sister he is."

That's what Cain was waitin' to hear. He jumped up from the ground. Commenced to runnin' from the woods toward Toad with a loud growl and a snarl, soundin' just like a big ol' mad bear. Cain made it seem so real, Toad allowed it was Samson comin' hard to get him. He wet his pants right there — I promise you he did — but that never stopped Cain. He run right up to his face. Grabbed Toad's wrist with his left hand while givin' it a hard twist. I heard a sickenin' meat tearin' noise as Cain snatched back his knife with his right hand, then let go 'a Toad's wrist while switchin' the handle back to his left hand, bringin' his right arm up hard to backhand Toad plumb flat to the ground. He squatted down over him, puttin' a knee square in his chest while layin' the sharp point of his knife in close to Toad's eye. With a simple flip of his wrist, Cain sliced the left side 'a Toad's face nose to ear, makin' him let out a scream. The blood flowed from just below his eye while followin' the slice down the side of his head 'fore drippin' off his ear to the ground. Cain wanted folks to know when they saw the scar that Toad weren't no good.

"You better never let me hear 'a you stealin' from folks again," Cain hollered in his face. "We are family. That kinda behavior goes against our reputation as a family. I won't have it, hear?"

Toad started to cry. I worried what Cain might do next. Nothin'.

Cain got up to leave still holdin' his knife, the tip covered in blood, Toad's blood. He wiped it on the leg 'a Toad's skins to clean it. We simply left him there cryin' and bleedin'. Dad never asked us nothin' about why Toad weren't with us when we come back with more fire makin's.

Toad wandered home a little while later. The blood had been cleaned from his face. The scar fresh, swollen, and red. As far as we know'd, he never said a word to nobody 'bout what Cain had done. At least we was never scolded for it. He just went on like nothin' happened. I don't think he ever really cared he got found out over stealin' Cain's knife.

A year later, he got caught takin' from his neighbors. My uncle got so full of him he sent him off from home on his own. He was too sorry to fend for himself. Got caught stealin' valuables from different home places. We heard he near got himself tarred over that. Then he robbed a family; murdered their man in cold blood. Claimed he was fightin' for his life when he was the one doin' the stealin'. They sent him off to prison that time. They should 'a hung his sorry carcass then for murder plain and simple. He left that man's family there without a provider. A woman with five young 'un's. He just weren't no good.

They kept him in prison to the ripe old age of eighty-nine. He lived his life behind those walls for over seventy years. Finally, dyin' of old age. They burned him when he died. He weren't worth the trouble it took to bury a body.

Luckily, that widow woman married a proper man a few months after the killin'. He raised them kids like they was his own. All good folks far as I ever know'd. Shame they lost their natural man to the likes 'a Toad. No sir, forgive me God, I don't believe I would 'a taken an arrow for that sorry varmint, ever.

Chapter Three

We Know'd to Help Folks 'Cause It's Right

The ground was hard where she found herself wakin'. Cold. The limbs of the huge oaks overhead hung like dark spirits watchin' her sufferin', waitin'. The wore-out old homespun covered what it could of her body, but weren't keepin' the sting of cold time off her person. She shivered constant. The pain was near too much. She had no food. No sleepin' truck. She was powerful hungry. What little raw hog meat she'd stole earlier in the day weren't enough to fill a week old empty belly. Her life-savin' run from The Lost had been exhaustin'. She was thirsty; dry. The hole in her side was threatenin', leakin' out what she needed. She'd left a faint blood trail all along her escape. Even more so since leavin' the top 'a the ridge headin' into the valley. The cool waters she'd found there were a comfort, but she couldn't seem to drink enough to kill the burnin' thirst sufferin' inside her.

Her weak mind remembered havin' family what lived in the valley. She was hopin' to find some of 'em. Beg for help if she had to. Weren't her fault she was there. She'd been captured in a raid. Made slave to the women folk of The Lost for more than a year. She hated their very souls; a way down deep inside kinda hate. Who could blame her? They'd treated her just like a dog. Kept her tied no different. Same food. Same water. Same sleepin' place. She'd been stole from her clan when the men folk of The Lost made a slave run south 'a Choestoe near two years back. The heathens killed her husband and parents and took her one-year-old son, then sold him to a tribe to the north two moons after their capture.

It was common among Indians to have slaves. Most time they was tribal enemies what was captured. Sometimes they was bought. She hoped one day she'd see her son again. Prayed to the Great Spirit that she would. Hoped she would. Feared she would not. She missed her husband.

She'd turned different after bein' a slave for so long, stronger. Most likely they kept her close 'cause 'a that strength. She was right for child carryin' but was never raised higher than an outdoor slave for a reason only The Lost could know. May 'a been she was too orn'ry; needed tamin' down some 'fore becomin' part 'a the men folks doin's. Then again, could 'a been she weren't there long enough; women hadn't had time to break her spirit. Indians do things in their own understandin'. There are things they do you can't figure. You just settle on it bein' their way 'a thinkin'. Go on from there. Whatever the reason, she was off limits to the men folk 'til she weren't a woman's slave no more. The chief weren't allowed to get at her 'til the women give her to him, which kept her safe, without child. She was pretty. There was no fat layin' on her at all. Her muscles was hard from all the long hours of slave work they'd put her to; cut through her skin when she moved like the muscles on a mule's shoulders when it was pullin' hard.

She could smell the blood so strong it left a taste in her mouth; know'd it was hers. It was layin' thick where it'd run down her side from under what was left of her wore-out homespun top. The flow stained her leggin's, if you could even call 'em that, down near to the top 'a her knee. She felt the fear rise up again as she remembered runnin' for her life. How the arrow sounded slicin' the air as it flew toward her back. She'd turned away from the cuttin' sound only quick enough for the deadly flint point to miss hittin' vitals. It simply punched a hole down low in her right side from behind. Its path headed away from her center, stoppin' just shy 'a breakin' through the front part of her right-side. It would 'a been best for her had the arrow hit hard enough to poke all the way through. Way it was, it left a sharp-edged stone in the hole, slicin' meat and muscle with every step she'd took since leavin' the valley of The Lost. She'd broke the poplar shaft in a fall after she was hit. A short piece was pokin' out from the hole, keepin' the blood goin'. It hurt like nothin' she'd ever experienced, 'cept child birthin'. Her thoughts turned to her son.

She was fortunate in a simple way. The Indian what shot her used a bird huntin' arrow instead 'a one made for killin' deer or bear. Those was made from hickory. Wouldn't 'a broke durin' her fall. Instead, it would 'a ripped that point right through her body as she ran, tearin' up her insides. The death spirit would 'a been on her already had that 'a happened. Painful as it was, she was mighty fortunate.

She was weak, too weak. She'd come to sense, as she woke, this might be as far as she was gonna go. If so, it would be a relief when the brother finally found her. Plunged his knife deep into her chest, takin' out her heart. A calm come on her knowin' the evil one she'd killed would never hurt nobody again.

She thought to fight the notion of death while sittin' up some from the cold ground, facin' the morning light. In her wakin', she felt the crampin' knot of hunger and the burnin' thirst of blood loss as much as the pain from the hollered out wound in her side. She felt the need to stay where she was, to rest for a spell, even though she know'd warriors was followin'. Her strength near gone, 'bout bled out, she allowed again this might be her last morning on Mother Earth as she laid back flat on the hard ground. She stared up at Old Man Sun's early morning light as it breached the tree tops above her and started to sing her death song. It weren't much more than a whisper, but sing it she did. It give comfort knowin' she'd be seein' her husband soon in the land across the Great River. The thought made her smile what little smile she could do. Her world grow'd dark as she finished the final words of her prayer song. She wondered what death had waitin' for her. All she could do was done. She was goin' to see Jesus.

***

Them Indians believed us when we told 'em we'd not seen hide nor hair of the woman they was trailin'. They know'd we ain't when they come in on us at camp. Wolf allowed they was after some easy meat while lookin' to find out what we know'd. I was just glad they'd gone and left us be. They was four of 'em what come in on us. I figured they was more hidin' in the dark. They'd found us by trackin' the woman. How she found us left me wonderin'. Most likely luck. Could 'a been guided. Holy Spirit has His reasons, too. What little fight me and Wolf could 'a put up would 'a been nothin' compared to their fightin' ways had they been sour. Dad, Cain, Dancing Bear, or Black Oak would 'a had no problem with 'em, but me and Wolf would 'a, if they'd been lookin' for trouble. It was the revenge on their minds what kept us safe. That's a hard trail to leave 'til it grows cold. Still, we would have to pay mind on our way home. Watch for 'em to settle back in their thievin', killin' ways and maybe come on us. We was over a day's travel from Ben's Knob and the trail back would now need to be guarded. This bunch could turn on a body like a mad dog over nothin' more than a change 'a heart. I would learn they could get plumb mean in their doin's if their thinkin' got troubled.

The trail home weren't really no trail at all since we was followin' the tops of the smaller ridges what laid down in the valley, or at least we did as much as possible. Slippin' through the giant chestnut and oak tryin' to find the best trail possible so's not to be seen, watchin' constant. Peter and the pack mule was loaded heavy with hog meat and all our campin' truck. The weather was easy with Old Man Sun shinin' high overhead. Hardly no breeze. It was some warmer durin' the day. We both had our lamb's wool homespun on under our winter skins with the hair turned in.

We was comfortable. It was cold outside 'a mid-day, though, as winter held strong late.

We stayed to the shorter ridge tops for as long as we could 'fore havin' to drop down for water. They weren't none where we was trailin'. Our water skins was near empty. The mules was startin' to get white around their lips, which meant they'd be needin' a heavy drink 'fore too long.

We turned east, trailin' down a long ridge toward the valley floor. We'd only carried enough water for a couple days huntin' and had stretched our store by stayin' an extra day. We just had to keep after them hogs, though. The weather was perfect, the time was good, and we know'd where they was usin'. We stayed 'cause our folks needed the meat. Neighbors, too. We was just proud for the water to start the day. Now that dark would be comin' on, the day was drawin' long. We needed to be findin' us a drink. It weren't no chore to find water. You just had to get down off the ridges. Trail lower where spring heads was more common. That's where we was headin'.

It was a fair-sized branch that satisfied our need a good ways from the main tops, but still a piece from the Keowee Path; the main trail through the valley. We'd use it to make home next morning. It was good light. We had in mind to drop the loads from off the mules' backs, take off their lead ropes, leave 'em free in their halters to roam while we commenced to settin' up camp. They'd fetch a drink, smell around some, then find a place to do their natural business. When they figured it was time to eat, they'd wander on over to get their feed sacks strapped to their heads. We'd need to fix a good place to tie 'em off while they took their oats. As I've had to say many times, it would 'a been a proper plan, too, 'cept for things ain't always proper when Wolf and the ways of his life are figured in; no different that evenin', neither.

Me and Wolf was movin' to untie the campin' truck when we both saw it, a streak 'a wet black movin' across a small top just above us, kinda off to the south, back toward the way we'd come and a long way from where we'd camped for our hunt. Nothin' was said between us. We both know'd what it was. The only question was - why was she there? It was Spirit, a full-grow'd black mountain cat, or "painter cat" as the old-time mountain folks called 'em. They figured 'em for panthers. She'd takin' on as Wolf's guardian, his kinda totem mate. We found her mother dead at the Rock Ridge a few seasons back durin' Killin' Time. Now, she was payin' us a visit. Wolf didn't see her as much of late as he did durin' the time after we first found her. She followed him home when Killin' Time ended that year. He'd still see her time and again. I'd see her, too, if I was with him when she show'd herself. Sometimes she'd come in close, but never close enough to touch if a body was fool enough to wanna touch a full-grow'd mountain cat. Wolf did, bein' Cherokee. Not me. She made the back 'a my neck cold when she come anywhere near close up.

We'd not seen her on this trip 'til she'd made herself known that afternoon. She'd follow us on some huntin' trips, some she didn't. There weren't no figurin' it 'cause she was full-grow'd now, had to pay mind to her natural callin'. Most likely be matin' come spring. Like as not, we'd never see her again once she got with her own bunch. I know Wolf hoped we would. I guess I did, too. She was the deadliest killer in the mountains outside 'a folks or maybe bears. That held weight with me. Wolf never cared. Me and him didn't always see square on things. Havin' a full grow'd panther for a friend was one of 'em.

She was actin' strange by showin' herself full, then turnin' to run away, then comin' back, almost like she was wantin' us to go with her. Wolf noticed her goin' on and studied it.

"I believe she is asking us to come, follow her, Jeb. Let's go up. See what it is she is wanting. The packs can wait," he said without much thought.

"No, Wolf. I'm tired from walkin' all day. I don't want to. Let's make camp. She will come to us. My two legs feel lazy. I don't want to climb back up to where she has chosen to play on her four legs. She can come down here if she wants. I ain't goin' up there. I want some coffee. I want to eat, then smoke and rest. Now, c'mon. Let's get to it," I grumbled as I turned to head back to the mules.

"Yes, Jeb," he replied as he took off up toward where she was standin'. "That sounds like a good plan. I will lead."

What? Where was he goin'? I don't know what he heard me say, but it weren't what I said. Somehow, what I said made him think I was ready to see to it 'cause he took off straight away, makin' a beeline for her trail. What was I gonna do? He weren't gonna listen. They weren't no stoppin' him. Dark would be comin' on in a while. It only made sense we get to settin' up camp while still light enough to see. No, foolish me. Why would I think reasonable? Nope, we was goin' back up a trail we'd just come off to try and follow a full-grow'd mountain cat. I put the leads back on the mules, tied 'em still packed to a young dogwood, but it weren't what I wanted. Her goin' on had Wolf so concerned he'd not even heard the words I'd said proper. I silently prayed a little prayer, then started up the ridge followin' Wolf... like normal.

When I got to the place where we'd first saw Spirit, Wolf was there, but she was gone - nowhere in sight. I looked over at him, standin' there still as a stone with his eyes closed, his face raised to Old Man Sun. He had his arms out to the side near hip level, palms turned up. His nose was raised to the air like he was tryin' to scent that cat or somethin', which worried on me 'cause I hadn't learned whatever it was he was doin'. I was curious.

"What is it you are scentin' my friend? Do Painter Cats have a scent strong enough to smell? Or are there other things you are searchin' for in the air above?"

He never opened his eyes or lowered his head as he answered, "It is very hard to learn what it is that I am doing. My family is teaching me. I have learned well. Listen close. You must be able to sense from what you smell, that which you will see before you ever actually hear it, to know where it might be going some time before it ever gets there. I cannot explain it any better. That is all I can say about what it is I am doing. Cherokee learn this as we grow. I am without words to make you feel it. One day you might be able to do as I am. Until then, you will need to understand the ways of Mother Earth better. I will guide you as much as one can, but this is a spiritual gift you will need to own for yourself. I can never share the blessing. You must walk with it many moons. Learn as you grow. Only then will you be able to understand what you do not know about the unseen - the things Cherokee know."

    I just stared at him. *What in the whole put together had he just said?* That had to be the biggest mess 'a Indian mumblin' I'd ever heard. Yet, it kinda made sense later on when I thought it through. He was sayin' you wouldn't know what it was you was gettin' ready to see if you couldn't figure out what it was 'fore you ever sensed it, so you could then figure where it might be goin' once you was sure of what it was you was gonna see before you saw it. I understood that clear as spring water. It was just learnin' how to do all of it that would take the effort. I would smoke on it later. Try to figure it proper.

    Wolf lowered his chin then opened his eyes while turnin' his head in my direction, sayin', "We will find her back to the west of this place. She has moved toward the base of the ridge toward Old Man Sun from where we camped on our hunt. Come, we must hurry. She is nearing the place while we stand here talking like sisters."

    You don't ask no questions when a Cherokee as spiritual as Wolf and his bunch tell you real knowin' like what to do in times like we was in. Us not knowin' which way Spirit had gone so we could follow was a problem for Wolf, but he sorted it out in his own way. Got us goin' on the right trail. It must run in the family. Owl, his grandmother, had the gift. I was just glad he was my friend.

We took off for her trail soon as he finished sayin' where she'd gone. He was sure she was headed there. He did not have one doubt. Me? Now I weren't so sure about all this. I had to follow if I wanted to know the truth, so I kept up. It weren't long 'til we seen her, 'cept she'd never made it to the base 'a the ridge.

She was standin' in what looked like an old trail, most likely used back durin' the war times. It was grow'd up with small saplings and ivy. She stood lookin' right at us not thirty 'a Dad's paces away. She was swishin' that long, beautiful tail 'a hers. She liked doin' that. I hadn't seen her this close in some time. She'd grow'd considerable. Her magnificent tail was now very long. You could tell she was proud of it. She raised up some on her back feet, then turned off the trail to the south out 'a sight. Wolf and me nearly ran to where she'd been standin' so as to not lose her again. She was gone, nowhere in sight.

"She is like a spirit, this one. I have named her well," Wolf said as his eyes searched the woods for her black, wet shine. "She is leading us, Jebediah. We must find her to see what is drawing her near. I believe this to be true."

I weren't gonna doubt nothin' he said. If he believed it, then I would as well. She seemed to be headin' toward somethin', that's what he believed. I'd figure it to be the truth, too, if we saw her again. Sightin' her that many times on the same trail would mean Wolf might be right. Wild critters didn't like bein' seen, and even though she know'd us, she was still a wild mountain cat. A full-on, adult. If, or when, we ever saw her out in the mountains, it was only for a short time, then she'd go. Seein' her for another time as we made our way up the mountain followin', could mean she had a place in mind for us to go. Turns out she did. Wolf's thoughts show'd true. How could I ever 'a doubted?

We saw her again after a bit. Wolf had found her trail after a short look; led us to where she was. We'd gone a ways back south when we finally seen her. She was sittin' this time. Her tail had grown quiet, she had her head up, her ears turned straight at us, her nose twitchin' while scentin' us drawin' closer. She was not movin' away, which surprised me and Wolf. We must be where Wolf believed she wanted us to be, 'cause she let us get close enough to see the greenish-yellow of her eyes. The black shine of her nose looked like creek water sparklin' late in the evenin' of a clear day as she kept tryin' to taste our scent.

She'd let us slip in close. Close a plenty for me. After all, this was a wild mountain cat. She'd lost the innocent look of her youth I remembered from the last time I'd seen her close. She'd replaced it with the eyes of a hunter. Keen and narrow, with thick whiskers to help catch the slightest warm-blooded scent. Her feet was huge, the claws visible, makin' her a sight. Death on four legs with a taste for blood no critter in the mountains could match. She was plumb scary lookin'. I would go no closer.

Of course, Wolf didn't see it the same. He kept on slippin' toward her 'til he got to within' a few paces of where she was sittin'.

Why did she not run off again? I realized, as I watched, even now that she was older, her and Wolf still know'd each other.

In my life, I don't think I ever really understood that bond, even though I saw it on many occasions in our growin'-up time. She stayed close to Wolf for many years. Then one day, she never returned. Wolf told me 'fore he died later on that he saw her in a vision late in life, not long 'fore he crossed over. She was sittin', waitin' for him on the other side. She was beside Jesus, and He was rubbin' her on top of the head, right between the ears. They both were smilin'.

She didn't care if Wolf got close but would not let him get too close. She stood on all fours as he moved to within a few feet 'a where she was sittin', then walked off slowly to the north. The sight we saw when she eased out 'a the way made the air go right from my lungs.

Spirit know'd exactly what she was doin' when she led us to this spot. It was a faint deer trail leadin' through a stand 'a yellow locust. Tall and dark they was, with a hard bark, kinda like the chestnut, but not as big. The inside 'a them trees was pure yellow; long in the grain, not hard to split. Folks made posts and rails out of 'em 'cause they took a long time to rot in the outside weather.

    The way Spirit had been sittin' you couldn't see the trail, or the woman's body layin' a ways on down. We was sure it was the woman Blood Moon had been lookin' for. Me and Wolf could tell. It was the slave clothes she was wearin' what led us to figure it. Spiteful owners always made 'em wear the worst thing they had so folks would know they was property. Kept most of 'em from runnin' off. She looked dead, but I figured if she'd made it this far, there was a good chance she could still be alive. We ran to her at once gettin' close to her face to feel for her air. We found life was still there, but only by a little. We both know'd it would run short if we didn't get her to a warm place. Her life had near leaked out from a wound we found down low on her right side.

    Wolf stood. Began to look around real worried like. He even walked a circle around where she was 'fore lookin' back to me. The look on his face givin' voice to the wonder I had in my mind, too. We was both thinkin' the same thing. This woman was trouble for us. If she was here, and she was, Blood Moon with his warriors would not be far behind. Revenge keepin' the fire burnin' in their hearts; a need for killin' fillin' their very souls.

    After lookin' to her, Wolf spoke his mind, "If we take this woman to either of our homes, she will die before we get there. She has gone as far as she can on her own. Death is near. The trail is long to both our places. If we stay here, the warriors from the The Lost will find us. Kill us all. We must move. Take her with us if we mean to save her. There is only one place close where I know we will be safe. By good fortune it is near since we dropped off the ridge tops where we did. It is a climb from here, but we can make it before Old Man Sun returns to his home at dark. We must take her to Panther Cave. It is our best hope if we care to save this woman. The hole in her side will not kill her. The blood she has lost and the poison that is running inside her will. We need to get her warm, so the blood will come back. Once we get her settled, you will go get Anne. Bring her to Panther Cave. There she can work her healing. This is the only way I see we can save her, if saving her is what we choose. Speak if you think this is right, or if you know a better way, Jeb."

I had nothin' to say. He'd thought this through. I agreed with everything he was thinkin'. It'd come to mind takin' her on would be dangerous. Wolf and me could end up as an enemy of Blood Moon, his family, and the whole rest of his clan. That was a bother to me, for sure. We talked about it later. Strangely, both of us had the thought to leave her where we'd first seen her — not take on all the trouble tendin' to her would bring — just turn and go on our way. But, that just weren't the way mountain folk saw what was now laid out on our plates. Cherokee, neither. She needed help. We know'd to help folks 'cause it was right. If she was guilty 'a killin', it'd be show'd true under oath. But until she was found to be guilty, we was obliged to help her. That's what we'd both settled on in our hearts 'fore Wolf ever spoke. It was the proper thing to do for as long as we could. 'Sides, I believed Holy Spirit had guided our trail to the hurt woman.

My first real trip to Panther Cave was gonna be interesting. Dangerous, but interesting. At least we had plenty 'a meat.

Chapter Four

My First Time in Panther Cave

She was alive when we got her slid back down to the mules. It weren't by much, but she was alive. Bloody, dirty, her thin clothes barely hangin' on her, and she smelled. Reminded me of an old hog waller used fresh. She was drawin' breath, only barely. She was near froze, bein' it was the dead side 'a winter and her only wearin' one layer 'a homespun. Them laid full 'a holes providin' little to no comfort against the cold mountain air. Her foot skin boots was in fair shape. I figured she'd stole those 'cause they weren't wore out like the rest she was wearin'. She must not 'a had time to get somethin' warm to cover herself in. I fetched one of our quilts from the pack mule and we wrapped her head to toe tight as we could. The wound hole in her side would have to wait for any tendin'. She grunted in pain as I lifted her by the shoulders, Wolf lifted her by the legs. We laid her across Peter's back longways, head to tail, comfortable-like across the top of our campin' truck. She fit just fine.

We took for the cave once loaded. Our water sacks filled. It was gonna take most 'a what light Old Man Sun allowed us to reach high on Blood Mountain. That's where Panther Cave was. I got to watchin' while makin' that climb, knowin' killers was trailin' her. It made a body think on things a little different.

Movin' through the mountains as light's fadin' or growin' is near spiritual. Makes for a different world when travelin' the woods at dusk or dawn. Things ain't as they are. They're what your eyes see, makin' for a real soulful time if you don't pay mind.

As the light grows dim, you get your back up for danger. Your heart beats so hard it thumps inside your chest. Your strainin' to hear so hard your ears move. You can feel 'em when they do that, like haints pullin' the tops of your ears up on both sides of your head.

All you see comes to life. Saplings move as silent hunters stalkin' game for meat. Rotting logs look like deer or hogs tryin' to slip by so's not to become a hunter's meat. It's a gift from God how critters can see in the dark the way they do. Old stumps seem to move like black bear. Dark trees are giant warrior spirits makin' their way through the mountains, just watchin'. Half-light gets a body lookin' close for trouble. Half-light in the mountains of Appalachia makes things different. You'd have to trail it to feel what I'm sayin'. But trust me, it gets spooky trailin' in the near dark. For sure, when folks are followin'.

We made it through, though. Never seen no other Indians. We felt hurried, skittish. That made me nervous. I know'd movin' in the woods that way raised the hair on back of Old Man Trouble; made him lay for you. Try to make you get careless. Hurryin' on a trail brought danger in close. Thankfully, the Great Spirit watched over us. Knowin' He was near give a body courage.

It was my first-ever real sight of Panther Cave. It was a beautiful place. The view back north let you know just how big the valley was. I could feel right off why the Indians called bein' there spiritual.

The front weren't much. Nothin' more than a slit in a sheer rock face, opened up a little higher than what my dad was tall. You had to be movin' in from the west or you'd not see it. If you trailed in from the east, you'd walk right by never knowin' the cave was there. The openin' looked like God Almighty hisself sunk his pole axe in the bottom of the rock face. Sharp side first. It weren't no trouble to walk through 'cause it was wider than two grow'd men standin' side-by-side. It laid in what seemed like a forever-high rock cliff grow'd full 'a ivy, dogwoods, grapevines, and ferns - lots 'a ferns all over. Made you look straight up to try and see the top. Lookin' around on the ground give me shivers up my back. Felt like it could rain boulders down at any time from way up high above. They was spirits near, too. You could feel 'em. Made the cold even colder. I liked bein' there.

    The opening to the cave was guarded by big boulders you kinda had to walk through. You could tell they'd fell straight down from somewhere above 'cause they was sunk in like they'd plugged right where they was layin'. That got me to thinkin' 'bout how they come to be there. I'd 'a liked to 'a been near to see 'em fallin', then hittin' the ground. Watchin' off at a distance, of course. Not Wolf. He'd 'a wanted to be in close for that. Feel the spirits of them rocks go into Mother Earth as they made their beds. His thinkin' got off from mine on occasion, bein' full-on Cherokee like he was. Put me into all kinds 'a doin's as we was growin' up, too. I liked it all, though, good and bad!

    Wolf led us to the front of the cave, then pulled the mules up short while turnin' toward me real serious like. I got nervous when I saw them looks he'd get. I felt better after rememberin' this place was like home to him. He was born here.

    "We must build a fire. Find the black smoke pine and cut some torch knot limbs. Get them burning for light. The bear likes to make camp in the high-up caves during the cold time. Sometimes they will bed here in Panther Cave when the Great Spirit leads them to Blood Mountain. We will need to share this winter home if one is sleeping here. Take care to not wake it while we tend to the hurt one. If the Spirit is with us, they are sleeping some other place for this cold time."

    Wolf's thinkin' near froze my blood sometimes. Sharin' winter sleepin' quarters with bears? Stand by as boulders rained down from above? Trackin' down hurt panthers? The Cherokee way took some doin' to get comfortable with. I don't think I ever come full circle with it in all my days of runnin' with 'em. Wolf called their way spiritual. I called it dangerous. Either way, it made for some excitin' times throughout my life. I'd trade it for nothin', 'cept salvation as paid for by Jesus' sufferin'. That's how big it come to me.

The woman was comfortable stretched across Peter's back. She actually 'rous'd up a little when we started gettin' her down; no more than to open her eyes some and moan. We eased her down slow. Laid her 'a top a separate folded quilt while keepin' the one she was wrapped in around her. Wolf put a rolled sleepin' skin under her head for a pillow. She looked comfortable as could be but was in bad need of food and drink, shelter, and cleanin'. We had to get her warm soon, cleaned up. She stunk somethin' awful from all the dried blood on her person. The rot in the hole. We needed to get her in the cave next to a big fire.

God, don't let there be any bears in there, I prayed silently.

"Jeb, you should go find more water before the dark comes on us. What we carry will not last long after we wash her. I will fetch what is needed for the fire. Search the black smoke pine for torches. If a bear has settled here, I hope he will share his lodge with us without a fight."

"Share with us, Wolf?" I finally asked. "They'd never stand for it. She's smellin' strong from her wound. All the dried blood. The scent will go with us. Draw whatever bear might be in there like a cat hearin' rat scratchin'."

"My friend, you must remember you have never seen the inside of this cave. We will have the torches lit soon. You will understand my words."

He weren't exactly right on that as I remembered. I had seen the inside when the Spirit Bear, Freedom, visited me in a dream. It was the night after Old Man Bobcat tore Jim and me up but good. He'd led me inside, showed me the secret room, and the rock coverin' the front of it. I heard his words again. He told me it would save Wolf and his family when the time comes. I wondered then if Wolf know'd of the secret room. I reasoned he didn't or they'd been no call for Freedom to 'a come to me. I thought to show Wolf 'fore we got out from there for good on this trip. It might be time.

I'd not made mention of my dream to Wolf or his family, yet. I'd tried, but I couldn't. Somethin' about it was troublin', like when you feel haints movin' about or catch one blowin' out a candle. I was takin' my time tellin' it, hopin' the vision was wrong. This would be a good time to make it known, seein' how they was more strangers than normal bein' seen in the mountains. I prayed for the time to be right; for Holy Spirit to show me when that time was proper out 'a respect for that knowledge. What was comin', meant killin'. I would pack me a pipe of weaver later. Smoke it over. Pray. Then wait for the right sittin'.

The dream I'd had would be took real serious by Wolf's clan when repeated by Dancing Bear at the story fires. It would be truth to the Cherokee brought to mind by me. The one they know'd as "Spirit Filled One." I'd be in for it then. Elders would start comin' 'round our place once they heard, lookin' me over for truth. They'd rub their leathery old hands over the top 'a my head, under my chin, down my arms, and pinch my fingers from tip-to-palm. That always hurt. I never did figure why they did that. A couple would get real close to my face. Look deep into my eyes. Wolf allowed they was hopin' to see the spirit what guided my tellin'. I'd smell the woods on 'em. They'd run the tips of their fore fingers over my teeth makin' sure I weren't no real bear. That near made me sick. I don't think they ever found no spirit talkers, but it never stopped 'em from pesterin' me all them years. Indian ways didn't set well with me at every doin'. Purely aggravatin' sometimes. I didn't care to be touched by folks. I never said nothin' to 'em. I didn't figure to show no disrespect to a folk that deserved respect when it was to be show'd.

The makin's Wolf found was dry. It weren't no time 'til we had us a roarin' little fire jumpin' and poppin' and puttin' out precious heat. We piled on 'bout a third 'a the wood he'd got. Propped two pine limb torches I'd found over the new flame to get 'em caught up. The knots on the end of the limbs would burn for a good while, bright too. Their flames would light up the cave plenty good enough to see once we went in.

I had a lot 'a questions about what we was doin', but I know'd to wait and ask at a better time. Livin' with Indians like I did, a body learned sometimes it's best to stay quiet, watch, and learn. It was time to go in. The pine torches was burnin' hot.

Wolf grabbed the torches. Raised 'em up high while keepin' 'em out in front of his person. Small licks of lit pine tar was fallin' off, splatterin' the ground. You didn't want them gettin' on your skin. Burned like hell's fire if it did. I could hear the roar from the flames. Smell the rich pine tar burnin', lightin' up our little camp, the hurt woman, the mules, and all our truck. Dark had rolled in by the time we'd got the torches goin'. It was cold. I don't think the hurt one felt it.

"I will take the light and go in. Look to see if the cave has visitors," Wolf told me. "You stay with the woman. Keep this fire up. We will need the hot coals to start a fire inside. I will hurry back with word."

He turned and left without sayin' nothin' else. The light from the torches hidin' from sight as he breached the openin' to the cave.

I went over to sit by the injured lady, watchin' and listenin' as I waited. The flames from the outside fire kept her face lit so I could see if she moved any parts. My hearin' turned to what was out stirrin' on such a cold night. I could just hear a wolf singin' 'way off down in the valley, somewhere on Wolf Creek. It was a lonely song 'cause they weren't many left in the mountains. Folks had killed lots of 'em. Many had moved on, followin' their need to find a place with less folks and a heap more food critters. Deer weren't near as plentiful, neither.

I figured it would be but a short while 'til their songs was gone from Choestoe for good. That made me sad in a strange kinda way. I know'd them devils was most dangerous. I'd seen what they'd leave, but the mountains wouldn't be the same without 'em.

I laid on a couple big sticks to the fire. They'd last a while, then do for back sticks when startin' the fire inside. I'm sure whatever bear was in there would favor a good warm glow... right after it ate us.

I weren't troubled by the fire keepin'. I sat and looked close at the woman, saw her pain. Her face show'd it in the fire light as the big sticks caught. She was a handsome woman, not pretty like Momma or Wolf's folks, but she was easy on the eyes all the same.

I started uncoverin' her. I wanted to find out just how bad it all was. I could see her clear when I pulled the quilt back. I looked back at her face. She was lookin' at me with slightly opened eyes — lips dried, cracked, and bleedin' — no real thought showin'. I laid the top quilt to both sides leavin' her lower half covered. It was clear she'd lost a lot 'a blood. That loss was gonna need seein' to. Anne always said, "It takes time, nourishment, and broth for a body to make more blood." I figured this woman would be in Panther Cave for a while.

***

Dad was up late worryin'. He know'd the weather was right for huntin'. It was straight thinkin' we might stay another day if we'd found hogs. But only one day, no more. His rules was simple. Tell him where you'll be, for sure what day and time you'd be back. You'd get one day's time after that day to get home. If not, he'd come to find you. Because 'a that rule, Dad would know when somethin' weren't right. He know'd we'd be home if possible then since our extra day had come and gone. It was dark. We was now late. A dangerous time to be out for tired young folk. He know'd it.

His pipe was burnin' clean. He was pacin' back-and-forth on the back porch of our log home with a fresh full bowl 'a weaver tobacco. Studyin' on the conversation he and Momma was gonna have when he went back inside to the warmth of a hot fire. It was cold. He only had on his homespun shirt and britches, and lamb's wool socks. Momma would fuss at him for that - wearin' homespun socks bare out on the nailed-down wood porch boards full 'a splinters and nail heads that was liable to snap the wool and tear it enough to need mendin'. Just like it tore my knee meat when Dad poured me out on 'em at my birthin'.

His blood was warm from bein' inside. He'd just come out for a smoke to see if maybe we was walkin' in since dark had just settled. His mind told him we should be back. We would 'a, too, had Spirit not shown us the woman. He looked up to the heavens. Breathed a short prayer on the burnt tobacco smoke. The stars was shinin' bright, it bein' a dark night with no moon. He silently hoped we weren't havin' to travel since Old Man Moon was sleepin'. He hated tellin' Momma 'bout things that caused her worry. Us bein' uncommon late would truly do that.

He went back inside to where she was rockin' by the fire reading. She liked to read. Dad would always bring her a book or two from the market when we went south to Gaines Town every fall to trade mules. He never brought her back no Bible, though. He allowed, "All 'a them said the same thing on the inside." He figured, "One was all we needed." Believe you me, ours was big enough to service everybody in the family, guests too, when they come.

"Celia," Dad said, as much to the fire as to Momma, takin' a seat on the hearth in front 'a where she was rockin'. "We must talk, Celia. Jeb and Wolf should 'a been home by now."

She looked at him over her book, "Yes, I could see your thoughts were afar. The boys should be home, I know. What is it we should do, Thompie? What is it I can do?"

"Black Oak trailed 'em east. Said he'd look in on 'em secret-like while they got camped. I'm sure he found 'em. That's why I'm worried. Them not bein' back would mean they's somethin' keepin' 'em from makin' trail. I feel I should leave in the morning if they don't come in overnight, go to where they camped on the ridge near the Levelland, find their sign, and trail 'em. They should be home havin' supper with us tonight. I gotta feelin' they need help. Somethin' ain't right."

Momma laid her book down on the rocker as she stood, moved to sit in Dad's lap, then laid her arms around his neck, lookin' him in the eye. She loved my dad. "We must put their care in the hands of our Savior. He will watch over them come what may. All things pass through the Throne of God, Thompie. But if Holy Spirit is telling you to go and see, then I will make ready a traveling pouch for you. Will you be going by to get Cain? Take him with?"

"No. No need, and don't be worryin' so, Celia," Dad answered as he reached around her with his arms pullin' her up close. The fire was makin' her eyes sparkle like two lone candlelight — soft, warm, welcoming on such a cold night. A slight smile appear'd at the edge of her lips, even though she had worry, too. "Cain's place is out 'a the way. I'll have no trouble findin' the boys. There will be a reason why if they are still not back by morning. Black Oak is most likely with 'em. My trail could end up bein' no more than a long walk for me. That'd be fine, though. I need to get out; been on the farm all winter. A good long walk will do me some good. I believe, when I do catch up to 'em, I'll find 'em with health. Maybe wettin' a sore-footed mule that's slowin' 'em up; somethin' such as that anyhow. One of 'em might 'a twisted an ankle makin' 'em take longer to get back than normal. They's no way 'a knowin'. I believe it will be somethin' simple, yet serious enough to keep 'em from home. I'm sure they're fine. Still, I feel I should go. They may need an extra set 'a hands."

"I fear the weather could get bad soon, Thompie," Momma said in a most serious tone while layin' the left side of her head against the side of his face, snugglin'. "It's been cold this winter. We've had no bad storms or snows, so we're due a good comin' down. I feel it could be soon."

"Aye, you're right, Celia," Dad said as he squeezed her tight, closin' his eyes. "I'll pack an extra layer 'a homespun for me and the boys."

He was ponderin' how it was gonna feel to be missin' her over the next few days. Holdin' her, thinkin', tryin' to hold as tight as he could without hurtin' her. He draw'd back, then brought her face to his with a soft touch from his hand. Scentin' her beauty, while movin' to kiss her for a while. Passion rose in his soul, wanting. A longing to stay with her warmth — not to take the cold trail his duty as a father called for — wishin' to wake up to her under heavy, layered quilts and nothin' else but her soft skin for comfort. But, it weren't gonna happen. He was to find his son. Leave his woman ... then he remembered ... he still had the night. His soul smiled.

***

George Black Oak was huge, but he could move through the woods as quiet and unseen as most any Cherokee. You'd find no truer warrior. His rewards across the Great River would be many. He deserved 'em all for the good he'd done folks all over the valley, settler and Indian. Everybody liked him. We all loved him. Many owed him much.

He was squatted on his haunches behind a young white pine. His arms laid over his knees, eyes fixed on the six little men of The Lost boilin' their supper. Fresh kilt turkey. He did not like these men bein' in the valley. He'd been watchin' 'em for a couple days. Crossed their trail on his way to find where we was makin' camp. Them bein' in the valley was causin' him concern. Still, he did not follow their trail when he first found it. Dad asked him to look out for us, that was his first callin'. He went on and found our trail. Followed it to our camp to make sure all was proper. Careful to make no noise or leave any sign we'd find, he then went back to watch the troublesome little warriors.

His movin' that day scared a bunch 'a hogs back up the ridge toward where we was lookin' for sign, which gave Wolf a broadside shot on a big sow as she trotted by within' thirty paces. Our first kill of the hunt.

Most times Black Oak would not 'a scared them hogs. See, he was havin' to travel with the breeze, against his instincts. It couldn't be helped. Black Oak had a direction to go. It just so happen'd, the breeze was goin' that way, too, which give them hogs a snout full 'a him from a ways off. Spookin' 'em back up the ridge toward us. We didn't know he was there. You hardly ever know what spooks a critter. We just took advantage of 'em bein' on the move, not knowin' we was anywhere near. That kinda huntin' makes for an easy kill... most every time.

He had no trouble locatin' the evil pack after checkin' our camp. Hadn't been watchin' 'em long. He'd never seen any warriors from The Lost up close. All Cherokee in Choestoe had heard of 'em, but nothin' since he was very young. Then he remembered the stories told by the old ones about their killin' ways. He was gonna make sure they did no harm while they was near.

It seemed they'd been on a track 'til now, kinda like one of our Redbones chasin' a ring tail on a dark night. Settin' up camp meant they'd found their purpose or lost the trail. Either way, they was holed up in a shallow holler east of the Levelland, less than a half mile from the ridge where we'd made camp. This concerned Black Oak. They was close, as woods travel went. He was well aware of how an evil bunch like this could turn, especially for gain. He figured to not let 'em out 'a his sight 'til they left the valley. He weren't gonna worry over us for the while. It was these unwanted that held his mind. He left us to our own trail, feelin' comfortable we'd collect our meat, then head for

Ben's Knob when Old Man Sun woke next morning. He was sure we would after he watched the warriors visit us in camp the night before. He would 'a been right, too, but he did not know about the woman Spirit had found. Nor did he know we was headed to Panther Cave. Nor did he know Wolf was goin' into the cave alone to make sure there weren't no sleepin' bears layin' around.

***

It weren't no real big bear, but it was a big enough bear to cause worry. It was layin' up high on a ledge, several feet off the floor of the cave. Both legs on its right side hangin' off, it had perched just a few feet shy of the high stone ceilin'. Made me wonder how it got up that high.

Wolf jammed the two pine knot lanterns into rock cracks. They was burnin' bright together, lit up the whole cave. I'd never been inside Panther Cave before. I'd heard Wolf talk about it, but never been. So, when I come through the crack openin' and looked up, it was like lookin' into a whole new world. Huge! A big opening like a room! Smelled different than the woods, though, kinda old like. Cold. If it hadn't been for the bear, it would 'a took my breath plumb away. Knowin' that thing was sleepin' nearby made me uneasy.

It was quiet on the inside, other than a small trickle from water fallin' somewhere off on the dark edges. The bear was snorin'. That's how Wolf know'd it was there; heard it 'fore he ever seen it. I thanked the Great Spirit they was only the one... that we know'd of.

You could see most all the inside, as the cave was just a big hole in the rockface off the side 'a Blood Mountain, leadin' to nowhere. It didn't take me long to find the rock from my vision with Freedom. I felt a shiver run down the center of my back rememberin' it. I thought to take Wolf later, to look for the opening to the hidden room after our chore was done with the woman.

We had to be real careful not to start her to bleedin' again as we carried her in. Wolf laid another blanket down on the ground in a spot where somebody else had slept not too long before. It was near a fire pit circled by several rocks each about the size of a one-pie pumpkin. I figured we'd be usin' it for our fire. The wounded one would 'a no doubt died where she was if Spirit hadn't shown her to us. Either by the cold mountain air or by the hands of those mean little warriors of The Lost. They'd 'a found her no problem come daylight. I wished they would go away. She did not look like a killer. Strange that she was saved by a mountain cat. I wondered at how she would take to that thought once we told her, if we got to tell her.

"Jeb," said Wolf kinda soft-like as he looked down at her. "We need the lit wood from outside to get a fire started in here, but we must be careful of what might have followed us here. We will ease out to the fire, bring in as much wood as we can, and gather some hot coals to start our fire inside. We must get her warm, so her blood will start moving. If not, she will walk across the Great River this very night. We will boil some venison jerky. Help her to drink the broth. These things we can do may keep her with the living until Anne can get here to work her healing gift."

It was curious to me that we was gonna leave her in the cave with the bear, so I asked, "Should one of us stay with her? Mind our sleepin' friend up there? He might wake while we are out to the fire. Decide he don't like what he's smellin'?"

"No, I think if we are quiet, he will stay in the sleeping world he is sharing with his ancestors. I believe he will be of no trouble to us if we move like the cat. The smoke from our fire will trail out the back of the cave into the mountain. This will keep the sleeping one from scenting us. I have stayed in this cave many times. I was born beside the fire pit we will share with this injured one. It is like home here to me. Our worry now is if we have been followed."

There it was then. We was gonna share a cave with a sleepin' bear and a hurt woman covered in dried blood. Just the slightest scent from that blood could bring that bear back from his dream world. And on top of all that, we know'd she was bein' trailed for blood. I was troubled, my Cherokee friend was not. He was none the worse for it. To him, it was spiritual. I wondered if the rest 'a the folks comin' to the cave was gonna feel like he did. I was glad to be leavin' to go fetch Anne soon. Sharin' a cave with a bear could get bad real quick if things went wrong. I hoped Wolf know'd what he was doin'. Then I righted myself, rememberin' who he was. He was Wolf of the Choestoe Cherokee clan, a grandson of Water Runs Deep — one 'a George Washington's favored scouts — son of Dancing Bear, my best friend, and one of the bravest folk I ever trailed with. It would be best for that bear if it never woke. Thinkin' that, I was comfortable. It was time to build a fire. Do what we could for the hurt woman.

Chapter Five

A Trail for Purpose

It weren't long 'til our fire in the cave was goin' good. Wolf figured it right, the smoke draw'd out the back, keepin' the cave from fillin'. That would help about botherin' the bear up high in its restin' place. So far, he'd been most affordin'. Hadn't woke nor moved none, which would change in a hurry if he come awake enough to get his nose full 'a folk scent and blood. I was hopin' things would stay the way they was. I had all the worry a body cared to stand with what we had workin' at the time. Didn't need no bear trouble to add seasonin'.

The woman was knockin' on death's door, her breathin' barely there. She hadn't made a sound nor moved a bit since we'd laid her out by the fire. A study of her chest would make you figure she was dead, and at one point we both thought she was, but her heat was up. There was no doubt she had the fever. Her skin was hot to the touch.

The meat around her wound was sourin'. We both know'd she'd be courtin' blood rot soon if she weren't already. I was sure I saw a maggot or two fall out as I eased her up on her side, proppin' her there with a quilt. I slit her shirt with my knife. We needed a better look at her wound. The site near made me wretch. The smell from the infection was sure, but it was the hole that near got me.

Oh, it was bad. That little bit 'a arrow shaft left pokin' out had jerked at her while she was runnin' and fallin'. The hole had been tore open a right smart; waller'd out full circle. Small chunks 'a meat fat and muscle was hangin' loose around the edges. Looked like a bunch 'a raw liver mush 'fore Momma dropped it in a fryin' skillet, 'bout the same color, too.

God help her, I prayed. I know'd what the flint point could do. I'd seen vitals, like the heart and lungs, from critters that'd run some after bein' stuck with a sharp flint arrowhead. It weren't pretty. It would be a mess inside her where the point had settled; sliced up bad for sure. The damage you could see would take moons to heal. No doubt, there'd be a lot 'a pain for a time to come. The wound, bein' so open, though, would help yield its maker and graciously save havin' to poke the point on through her front. That alone would help her a sight durin' the healin' time. Still, gettin' it out without doin' more hurt depended on the kinda point she was shot with. We was sure it hadn't sliced no vitals or we'd be home asleep. Hopefully, all the important stuff was still sittin' as it should. Meat and muscle only cut and fetch. Bad off as she was, God had to be lookin' after her. That thought give me comfort.

"We must heat some water, clean this wound best we can, then remove the arrow point, Jeb," Wolf said as he leaned in for a closer look. "We must do this quickly." He put water on to boil then moved away. Squattin' down next to the fire, he put his arms over his knees. Lookin' at me with concern, Wolf said, "Her blood is turning. It will not be long until Holy Spirit takes her across the river. Anne must come soon, tend to her. When we finish this cleaning and remove the arrow, you will go find Anne. Bring her here with medicines for healing. We can save this woman if we get Anne to her soon." His eyes moved to look at her, then said, "I believe she is strong. Her spirit is fighting, but she is losing."

It was never really spoke over, but Wolf was in charge when we went out on trail. That was just a given. He was at home in the woods. Kept a way about him when he studied on things that was near unbelievable, spiritual for sure. But then, that was the way with most all Cherokee I ever met. It always seemed to me they was more to their bein' than others, like their souls grow'd more cinched to the spirit world than non-blood folk.

Me and Dad talked about it on occasion. He understood my thinkin'. They just weren't no puttin' words to it, really, but it made you mindful. How'd they know the things they know'd? How could they tell what was gonna happen 'fore it ever did? And Old Mother, how'd she know to come see to folks when bad things got to 'em? It'd make a body shake their head to study on some 'a their goin' on's. It gnaw'd at me that those things weren't part 'a my put together. I wanted to learn.

I studied on how different the Cherokee was over common folk for years after I'd left Choestoe, me included, and it finally come to me one day. I put together everything I'd learned livin' with 'em over my time. Mixed in all the things I'd heard 'em say, watched 'em do, or learned from their story dances. It was their world, made by the Great Creator same as them. They felt a soulful connection to their home, Mother Earth. The way it made sense to them was: God, the Great Creator, loved the earth, made it beautiful. The earth was their Mother, a living being. So, since He made the first human folk from the makin's of the earth, then breathed in life, all Indian folk come from that. To them, everything had life. It was different in their hearts than in non-bloods. They believed they was a real part of the earth, made from it. It was almost like the Spirit of the Living Earth could get in 'em. Make 'em be a part 'a the woods. They accepted it as the way.

Many I met durin' my time believed the spirits could change 'em into things that belonged in the woods — trees or critters or even runnin' water. I never doubted they could do just that. But me, nor Wolf, nor any of our folks ever changed into anything that we know'd about. We never thought on it as somethin' our clan did, but there was strange happenin's with other folks that made a body wonder. Some

Indians would go missin' from time to time with no sign to tell their tale. Then just when you'd think they was gone for good, there they'd be. Show up for supper one night with the family that was missin' 'em, just walk out from the woods one mornin' at daylight, or just appear at the fire durin' a smoke. We know'd Indians that'd been down that trail. They was spooky like haints after they come back. I ain't sayin' that's where they was, but none of 'em ever remembered where they'd gone, only the comin' back. The stories told at the fires spoke of it. The older Indians believed it true. Fine by me was all I allowed. I know'd Jesus went down a death trail and whooped it; come back to life for the rest of us. So why couldn't their spirits change if God's hand was in it? Made sense when you thought of it like that. Anything is possible with the Great Creator.

As I looked him in the eye face on, I asked Wolf, "Do you really think she can make it through this? It'll be the evenin' of the next sun earliest 'fore I can get back with Anne, if I can find her. I fear it'll be too much time for the body of this one to fight without proper lookin' after."

Wolf thought for a second, then answered, "She is strong, this one. She will wait for Anne to come. I will see to it."

The cleanin' chore was due. Me and Wolf obliged its callin'. He'd already got the kettle settled on the fire for the water to boil so we knelt one on either side of her to start removin' the quilt she was wrapped in. Her clothes was *filthy*. They had to come off. You could see them threads was crawlin' full 'a bugs. Poor thing. To be treated this way by folks, then stripped naked in front 'a strangers. But, we was all she had. We weren't gonna worry over it, and she weren't, neither. The dried blood showed where the wound was poutin'. She had scars from beatings and bein' tied, but no brand that we could find. No wonder she'd run off. I reasoned if it took killin' to get her free 'a the meanness she was livin' under, then killin' needed to be done. I studied over it while we was washin' her body clean. That's what I figured happened after seein' her close up, stripped down.

She was a beautiful woman. Bruised up, scarred, and near starved, but still beautiful. I really hoped we could help her make it. God would decide. It was our job to do all we could. Pray for the best. That's exactly what Wolf had in mind 'fore we got started removin' the wound maker.

"We must pray for help to free the stone, then clean her wound." Wolf said as he raised his hands and his head to pray. I bowed mine. "Guide our hands, our thoughts, Great One. Make your way our way. See to this poor woman who has suffered much. You are the giver and the taker. Now we ask that You decide how it must be," then he lowered his head, slid his knife free plungin' the blade into the boilin' water, then takin' it out, he moved in for the deed. It was time to stir the shadow of death what was hangin' over her body. The wound maker was fixin' to be out. We'd know her fate soon.

I remember thinkin', *It would 'a been a good thing if she'd 'a found time to sing her death song 'fore we got to her.*

"Jeb, put the butt of each palm on either side of the wound. Push down and away to both the east and the west. Pull the hole open only a little. Hold solid as I try to slip the point out by pulling on the shaft. I will move slowly so you can watch her face to see if we make pain. Are you ready?"

I thought I was ready. When I did as Wolf wanted, opened the hole some, the smell hit us both right in the face makin' me turn away quick. I didn't know if I'd ever smelled live death before. It was a different smell than dead rot. It was sweet, like soured milk or old churned butter that's got too hot. It was a gut turnin' smell. Wolf never flinched. He just kept at it. Hardly made a sound as he commenced to slippin' the arrow from the hole. A small meat cut with the tip of his short knife about half way through the pulling out, freed the point. A gentle tug, a slight turn of the shaft, and the blood-covered point jumped from its hidin' place in one quick, smooth motion. I was just recoverin' from the stink. Not expectin' what I was lookin' at when Wolf held it up . . . maggots! It was covered in maggots! There was many showin' in the hole after he slipped the arrow from her side.

Her face never changed.

He moved my hands away puttin' his palms on either side of the wound; his right palm more in front, the left below the wound. Holdin' flat to her back, he mashed in and down real gentle like.

I watched. I shouldn't have. I could not believe, and was not ready for, what I saw next. It is difficult to describe what laid inside her wound. I don't ever wanna see it again. A mush-like stew of maggots, blood, infection, and folk meat rolled out the front of the hole, slidin' over the back of Wolf's left hand as he gently kept pushin' with his right. The rot eased down across her bare back to the quilt we'd wrapped her up in like somethin' with a mind of its own. Reminded me of when Momma poured out the left-over breakfast gravy in the dog's trough after it'd cooled. The light from the fire made the mess show thick, alive.

I removed myself as calmly as I could from the cave to empty what little food and water there was in my gut. That wound cleanin' was more than I could tolerate. At least the arrow was out. I was glad Wolf did the takin' 'cause I couldn't 'a done it once that pile 'a grubs come sloppin' out. I could 'a gone my whole life without seein' what he done. *God help her*, was all I could muster between wretches. It was all the prayer I could do.

Wolf was washin' out the hole with boilin' water when I got back to the fire. He'd washed her face and wet down her hair; 'bout cleaned her good as she was gonna get without her helpin' or doin' it herself. I know'd that weren't gonna happen for some time, if ever ag'in.

Her hair was long. He'd most likely cut it all off after I'd left to get Anne 'cause it was 'fested. When you got close, it looked like her scalp was movin' with all the bugs crawlin' on it. Fleas and lice mostly. No tellin' how long she'd been tormented with them things. Right then her life was more concernin'. Cleanin' the wound had been most important. Wolf had done a fine job, but it would not heal her. Only Anne with her knowledge of medicines and healin' would stand a chance with that.

It'd took a while, but the chore was done. We smoothed out the quilts. Laid her flat down on the cave floor, a sleepin' skin rolled up under her head. We used the same quilts we'd first wrapped her up in 'cause she still had the crawlies. Didn't wanna soil no more truck. Wolf took another small skin and made a roll from it to lay on the ground below the hole, raisin' her up some from the cave floor. That held her back up so the wound could get air. He'd cleaned out all the infection he could with the boilin' water, but it would be back. They was way too much rot in that wound for it not to. Her blood would spoil complete 'fore long. She was fightin' death, a powerful spirit.

Wolf sat back by the fire and laid on a good-size log. It was dry, so the flames jumped on it, got it growin'. The warmth felt good. I, too, sat back. Studied what we'd just finished. I'd been keepin' an ear and one eye out for our sleepin' friend above us on the ledge. The snorin' was near funny if you got to thinkin' on it.

"My friend," said Wolf, "we have done for her all we can. I will boil some jerky. See if I can wake her to drink in a while. If you feel you can, I think you should make time, head for home. This woman needs the talents of our sister, Anne. I pray she is there. Owl the Wise One will not come to us. She has grown too old to hear the calling. Without Anne, this hurt one will never make it to the top of this healing mountain she is climbing. I believe you should take the mules, all the provisions, and hurry. Watch as you go. The little ones may be following."

The pack mule was still loaded with all the meat and camping truck we'd packed on it the morning before. He'd had to stand all night with his load. I know'd he was ready to move.

It didn't take long to cinch Peter's packs back up and to separate what provisions Wolf would need. I made to leave as Wolf finished tyin' off the last of the load.

"I am worried for you, Jeb," Wolf said as we locked forearms to say goodbye. "The Cherokee's path can be dangerous when one is traveling alone. Folks are about. I would tell you to watch, but I know you are able to think with your own mind. We have not traveled alone like you will be alone this day. We are young for such as this. Be very careful. My father would tell me to stay calm as I traveled, take care to listen to all around me. Watch everything you can see. Keep your eyes focused, your mind clear, smell where you are as you go. Find the wind, scent the things that don't belong. Do what he has told me. You might catch evil before it can make trouble for you. May Holy Spirit guide you and keep you safe. I will pray for you until you return."

"I'm scared, Wolf," I replied, grippin' his arm even tighter. "I do not want to take this trail alone. It's not proper for us to be doin' this without grow'd folks guidin' us. But I know if I don't make the effort, she will die for sure. The Holy Book reads we must love one another; that to offer one's life for the life of another is right up there at the top 'a what God looks for in the heart of a body. It's near Christ-like knowin' what He did for folks on that old rugged cross. That is why I believe I can do this. That is why we both can be brave. He will watch over us come whatever. I say, let it come on. But, my friend, it's not me who's gonna sleep this night with a bear overhead. That is a worry. It concerns me greatly. You watch yourself as well while you keep the hurt one with us. I think I would like to get to know her if she makes it. My spirit feels she is a lot like us. Goodbye for now, my friend."

With those words hangin' in the air, me, Peter, and the pack mule headed out for the Keowee Path, the main trail what connected all the Cherokee towns throughout the mountains. It was the way folks traveled in and out from Choestoe. Unfortunately for me, it was the most used way.

Folks traveled on it goin' south to market in Gaines Town or trailin' north into the valley. I know'd takin' it could be more dangerous than the back trails 'cause lately the Cherokee Guard was findin' sign from visitors - gold lookers and government men mostly. I was more likely to meet strangers on the path, true, but it was the fastest way home. For me, there really weren't no other choice. Gettin' Anne back as soon as I could was most important.

It was my first time ever to trail by myself for purpose. My hope was I could make it home 'fore dark, then get help back to Panther Cave 'fore dark of the next sun. The woman's life was dependin' on me makin' it home, then fetchin' Anne back. She needed for me to stay safe, not get hurt, took, or kilt'. I was gonna do all I could to not let her down.

My first trail alone. I was dead tired from no sleep. My belly was plumb empty, which made me weak. Somehow, I had to make it. I was leadin' a good mule. I'd use him to help me watch, but I also had a pack mule with fresh, bloody meat layin' over its back, which proved to me God has a sense 'a humor. I prayed as I went that He'd send His angels to trail with me. That settled me some as I led the mules off the steep side 'a the Blood Mountain. Back down into the valley. I could not wait to get home. I wanted to hug my momma. That always made things right.

Chapter Six

A Reckoning in Chestnut Holler

Me and Peter was on our first ever trail by our lonesome. I was nervous. More nervous than a long-tailed cat on a porch full 'a rockin' chairs at a family come together. I hadn't got to know the young pack mule yet, so I weren't gonna depend on him for no danger signs. Peter had a trail sense about him he'd picked up from our lead mule, Jim. I couldn't help worryin' over a hundred concerns or more. I was dependin' on Peter to help keep us safe. Dad wouldn't let me tote no gun when Wolf and me went huntin', lest he was with us. All the weapon I had was the knife Black Oak give me, and my bow. It weren't real strong, not near as strong as Wolf's. He'd grow'd up shootin' with his brothers. He was bow strong. He could even bend his dad's heavy locust bow. Mine would put a point in most critters or folks but would not break bone. My only real protection was to not be seen while keepin' a sharp eye out for trouble. Hide if I come up on danger, or folks. It was a good plan. Give me comfort, for what it was worth.

  Old Man Sun was just wakin' when I left Wolf at Panther Cave. It was still cold. My air was showin' when I breathed out, which could give me away if I weren't careful. The trail off the mountain dropped off steep for a ways 'fore levelin' out, then cuttin' through a long flat holler full 'a huge chestnut trees. I stopped the mules on the high side 'a the steep 'fore headin' into the flat. Stood for a minute studyin' all I could see. I moved back. Stood beside Peter.

Listened to his breathin'. I watched close for several minutes, listened, scented. Nothin'. I felt safe, so we kept on. Me leadin' Peter with the young pack mule tied behind. Dried hog blood stainin' its haunches and underbelly.

I was hungry, growin' weaker. We'd not made breakfast to save time, and 'sides, hunger weren't pangin' me at daylight no how. I was still gettin' over my spell 'a gut wretch from what come out 'a that woman's wound.

Wolf figured it best to leave what little jerky we had for her. She'd need broth to drink for strength and blood makin'; that is, if she woke enough to take any. It was all the jerky we had, so there weren't none left for me to take on the trail home. We had mule oats, but no food for folks, save for the fresh hog meat, and there weren't no time for stoppin' to cook that. I'd left Wolf a thick slice. He'd stick it over the fire to cook. He'd have to be careful makin' food 'cause the sweet smell 'a meat cookin' or jerky boilin' might wake the bear. But, he really had no say in it 'cause the injured one needed the broth. I was trailin' toward food, so I could handle the hunger pangs, seein' how it was just for the day. I'd be home to some 'a Momma's cookin' 'fore dark. That notion give me strength, but I was still weak. What food I'd eat recent was lyin' on the ground outside the front of Panther Cave. I'd got nothin' out 'a them eats as far as the day went. I was hungry for sure. I could feel it in my legs; wobbly kinda, heavy. Shaky, like when you get really scared. Not that I'd ever been really scared, 'cept for a couple times.

The holler was long, wide in places, not so wide in others. It was full 'a huge chestnut trees, only chestnut trees, not a small tree of any other kind growin' in that whole holler. Never saw anything like it anywhere else I ever went in the mountains. They was growin' so it looked like they'd been planted as a garden by God Himself. It was like another world where things was all big. Folks like me, was small. The huge trees made you feel like what an ant must feel when he's runnin' around tryin' to store up food bits in the outside world.

I stopped again on the edge of the holler 'fore goin' in to look and listen one more time, but sensed nothin'. I checked with Peter. He seemed to allow all was good, so we moved on down the trail. Walkin' through that stand 'a trees made one know just how powerful the Great Creator is. A growth like that was nothin' short of a wonder, near a miracle the way I saw it, bein' they was only tall, straight, dark chestnut trees. You could smell the sweet in 'em. Kinda like Momma's berry jam when she boiled it for makin's.

I was edgy in my travelin'; feelin' most uncomfortable 'cause they weren't no other folks with me. Peter could sense it. I'd catch myself jerkin' my head one way then another, lookin' all around, not really seein' nothin', worryin' more than trailin'. Worst of all, I weren't makin' no time easin' along all careful and such. That was bad. The whole purpose to my travelin' was to get home quick as could be. I weren't doin' it. It was makin' me mad, like a cat caught out in the rain, just thinkin' on it. I was different in my movin'. Bein' alone on the trail was makin' me too skittish. I was pushed past my comfort. I couldn't get settled. Weren't feelin' the spirit of the woods like on a normal trail with Wolf. My spirit felt wrong, lost.

I'd trailed partway through that stand 'a huge, giant trees when I come to a realizin' 'bout how I was travelin'. My deep down bein' got stirred with concern 'causin' me to hold up. Take time to figure on what I was doin' actin' like a scared young 'un, not mindful like grow'd folks. Dad would 'a expected better. The understandin' started in my center workin' its way out, then commencd to givin' me strength and courage. In my thinkin', I got to kickin' fear out the door. I come to see how the way I was studyin' everything was foolish. Not feelin' my surroundings was makin' it all unsettling. Guardin' against goin' on was gonna get me to makin' mistakes. Bein' careless could mean I'd miss seein' the very danger I was lookin' so hard to see. I needed to settle down. Feel the spirit of the woods, the cool mountain breeze passin' on my face, the ground beneath my feet, and the calmin' warmth of Old Man Sun as he rose higher in the eastern sky. As Wolf called it, "the voice of my spirit."

Yes, I was on the trail. Yes, I was alone. Yes, somebody might get me. What could I do about it, but fight if a fight come? If a body was on me in these woods, they'd be no way 'a gettin' away from 'em no how. Where in creation would I go? They weren't no hidin' places to keep us safe, 'cept all the big trees, and they was easy enough for folks to pass around. No real protection there. I come to realize I was bein' worried by my fears, not by where I was, or by what was really happenin'. That was hinderin' my walk. Slowin' me down, and me slowin' down would make the hurt woman suffer longer. How selfish I was bein'! I felt like I'd put myself in control of my wellbein', takin' God's work on myself. It was makin' me trail too careful. My mind was different than when Wolf and me was out on trail. I studied on it. Come to see I really weren't in no more danger alone than if Wolf was with me, hardly so. What was I thinkin'?

I'd got so tight in my body I couldn't feel myself movin' from all the caution. I was missin' my comfort of bein' in the woods. Missin' the adventure of bein' out on the trail. That made me mad. I always felt at home in the woods. I loved bein' on walks, takin' trails. I was a hunter. I mostly lived in the woods. Someone else was usually around to make me feel safe, though. Now it was just Peter and me. He was dependin' on me, so was the pack mule. I reckon the worry of bein' lead on the trail was weighin' on me. I recognized the fact I was actin' different. My senses had got numb. My eyes was foggy. Puttin' us in more danger than was there. I weren't movin' like normal, that was foolishness, and it made me mad. Burned me deep inside. My soul come alive through that fire of anger. Holy Spifit come on me like water fallin' from the sky. Caused me to walk on through the fear about what was happenin'. Changed the way I felt things. Made me put in mind to be more settled. Act on it. A need to pray come over me. Smoke it all over while doin' some thinkin', then have a little talk with Jesus 'fore I trailed on.

    I found a nice place to sit under one 'a them big nut trees, fetched my steel and flint from my possibles bag, then leaned back against the trunk. I wiggled my rear side-to-side to make a comfortable spot to settle, leavin' my legs laid straight out from the tree flat to the ground. It felt good. On a little rise, not far off the trail, no higher than I was tall, I got my fixin's out. Near had the bowl 'a my pipe packed when a coldness come over me. Made the hair on the back 'a my neck rise up. I froze. *What in the world?* Here I was, kickin' fear out the door, gettin' calmed with my thoughts 'a courage, when the hair starts risin'. I guess me bein' comfortable let my natural senses perk up. I noticed the feel of the woods again. Gatherin' my steady, I looked all around slowly, carefully, all proper-like. Peter weren't riled. All seemed right.

    I spent a minute listenin', watchin', just to answer what must 'a been the cold from an awakening. A reckoning as the old timers would say. They weren't nothin' near. I got comfortable the woods around us was empty, just me and the mules. I bunched a little pile 'a dry leaves up close between my legs then struck flint to steel. A couple hot sparks, a little fannin' with my hat, and small flames got to jumpin'. I finished packin' my pipe, lit a small stick, then put fire to tobacco. The dried burley tasted good after I'd been so nervous. The flavor was refreshing. I drank in the smoke like hot cider at Christmas time. I'd done made my peace with the Woods Spirit, makin' me calm as water behind a beaver dam. I figured I needn't bother the Savior with my concerns for the time, but I did. Didn't need to since He know'd 'fore I ever bowed my head anyhow. He'd done give me the peace 'fore I ever even asked Him. Made my faith a might stronger whenever He did that.

    My prayer was true, from the heart, "Thank you, Holy Spirit, for guardin' me. Thank you for your blood that saves me from hell. My soul washed white by your pain. I sure appreciate what you did for me today. I will not fear with you near. I will be strong in you, holdin' my fear for thought. Listenin' for you when you speak. Guide me in thy will. I trust my life to your hands on every trail I will take in this life. Praise be to you, Jesus."

The prayer was a comfort as I finished my bowl. I made for the Keowee Path without fear. My Jesus walkin' alongside me. I felt Him. I come to realize that day I should not fear when trailin' alone. Even if death found me, He would be with me always. Just like He promised in the Bible. I would never forget that.

The trail out to the path was short from where I'd stopped for a smoke. I felt a fondness for this special holler in my life now. I'd figure chestnut trees different from then on, too. They was spiritual as far as I was concerned. Bein' in them trees when I come to my confidence was what I thought of every time I saw one from then on. Them big nut trees took on a whole new thought in my mind. They'd become real special to me that day. I will never forget them... or my reckoning with the Great Spirit in the chestnut holler.

***

Wolf had sat by the fire watchin' for life from the woman, or death, for about as long as he could sit by a fire watchin' life or death come to a body. He'd not be surprised by either, as he moved to see if the small place on her neck was still showin' blood movin', it was. He'd gently tried to wake her to take food and water a few times. Nothin' from the woman, she was out. Wolf know'd she had to have some broth 'fore long, or Blood Mountain was gonna be her burial place.

No sign 'a life was in her, 'cept for the little lift on the side of her neck. The heartbeat so weak you couldn't feel the blood pass if you mashed fingers to her neck. You had to look close at the place just below her ear to make sure her heart was workin' at all. I'd seen Momma use a mirror under Dad's nose lookin' for air movin' when he was hurt in that

Yonah trouble 'cause he'd got so faint. If his breath made the glass foggy, she'd know he was still breathin'. The hurt one weren't breathin' hard enough to see with the raw eye. A mirror would be the only way to know if she was still alive. We'd not thought to pack no lookin' glass. We didn't use 'em. Of course, we weren't plannin' on tryin' to save no folks, neither, when we packed our possibles and truck for our hunt. It was unfortunate, but it was lookin' to Wolf like we weren't gonna be savin' no folks no how.

    Wolf didn't believe she was gonna make it. He told me so later around the fire at our place. He started thinkin' on the proper death song for this strange woman who laid near dead in a land that was not hers. Where was she from? How did it come to be that somebody shot her? Where was her true family? He wanted to find out all these things. He wanted her to live, to talk to him. He thought if it could help, he would try and talk to her, convince her to stay. He wanted to ask her his questions. Made sense to him, bein' Cherokee. He moved over beside her head. Squatted close on his heels. Leaned down to her ear.

    "Young woman," he began, "I am Wolf, of the Choestoe clan. You are in the Choestoe Valley. Choestoe means 'the land where rabbits dance'. They do dance. I have seen it. They rise up on their back feet toward each other, and they dance. You will see it, too, one day. I know a place where they dance every morning when the season is right. You and I will go there. You will see. But, to be able to travel to this beautiful place, you must stay alive. I cannot trail across the Great River to visit, then take you to see the rabbits make their dance. You have to be in my world, here, where we are now. I will have a mule you can ride. I will lead you, take care of you, and protect you like a warrior.

    "I do not have this mule yet, but the Great Spirit has shown him to me. My friend, Jeb Collins' father will make him mine. At least, that is my wish. He is a good mule. Big, like the one my friend has already. Jeb's mule goes by the name of Peter. Him and the mule I aim to have are friends.

Mine already has a name that only I know. Would you like to hear what I am going to call him? Woman? Do you hear me? Would you like to know his name? Can you hear me? I am talking to you. You should answer. You are being disrespectful. I am telling you what you will miss if you leave us here and go.

"I know you are resting. That is good. But listen close now for there is something you should know. I don't want to worry you or make you concerned for your life any more than you are, but you should know we are sharing our sleeping shelter with a near full-grown bear. He is black. Sleeping above you on the ledge. He does not look to be at full growth yet. Still, he is big enough to tear your head from your shoulders. With a slap of his claws, he could kill you, drag you outside, and eat you for his breakfast. Do you hear me, woman? You're gonna get eaten by a bear if you don't wake up. He is sleeping right over our heads. Open your eyes if you hear me about this bear. I do not want him to eat you. I do not like bears much. They are different from the other critters I live with. You can't speak to them. They do not listen. If he wakes, we must kill him. I will need your help. Can you help me? Listen, can you hear me talkin' with you? I just wanted you to know we are in much danger. It would be good if you could wake and drink some broth, then we could leave this place. Leave the bear to his dreams. Yes, that would be very good. I hope you decide to do this. Now, I will make the fire bigger. Heat the broth again. This time I pray you will wake. I have promised you a time with the rabbits. I want you to see them dance. It will be spiritual."

Wolf rose from beside her head, moved to the fire, and put the boilin' kettle half full 'a broth back near the heat to warm. He sat back on his haunches again, stared into the hot coals. The small blue and yellow flames rippin' at the darkness from the half-burnt sticks hangin' on as the day aged. Somehow, he knew, he had to get her to drink some broth. If she didn't, her body was gonna shut down full. That would be the end of her visit to Choestoe. They weren't no way to feed her if she stayed out like she was. He figured he should start thinkin' again on a good death song for her. It might just be the last time he would need to think on it. He laid back in his quilts and sleepin' skins. His mind was studyin' on a song. In no time, his eyes got too heavy to hold open. Sleep took him over. He'd not slept since the morning before, same as me. He needed it. It was good he was gettin' some rest.

***

The Keowee Path weren't much better than the trails we traveled on in the mountains, just a little wider in most places. Cleared 'a trees good enough but didn't lay very solid. Stayed muddy long after it'd quit rainin' in the spring. It was froze on my trail. Travel was good.

I was handlin' my trailin' better since I'd got myself back to thinkin' my normal way 'a woods doin'. Least it seemed like things was goin' smoother. I could tell Peter weren't near as nervous as when we was comin' off Blood Mountain into the chestnut tree holler. He was good now.

What about that? Ain't that somethin'? He could tell I was more at ease, which put him in a less-worrisome mind, too. *Good.*

We made decent time travelin' the Path, then takin' the side trail to our home. Bein' winter, the leaves was all off. I come to a place just before dark where I could see a window light on the backside of our house. It was like an angel shinin' in the night. I cried, but only Peter and the Good Lord know'd it. I ain't never been so glad to see a place in all my put-together. I wanted to shout, but I was cold and thirsty and hungry and tired, and I wanted my momma. I was still just a boy. The trail had no more slow downs once I'd made my mind not to let fear make me weak. We never saw a soul. Thinkin' back on it, you might not that time 'a year. I reasoned if I trailed on enough, and me and Wolf would, I'd prob'ly meet some kind-hearted and not so kind-hearted folks. It just didn't happen on my first trip. I was lucky. Sometimes good fortune itself keeps you safe.

Peter and the pack mule stayed strong for me all the way back. Totin' their loads without complaint. It was a hard trip for 'em. Two full days without much rest. Three full hogs was a heavy load for a young mule. Peter was loaded heavy, too. Dad was gonna be proud 'a the meat we'd took, but his back was gonna be up 'cause he'd be concerned over what'd kept us. I know'd he weren't gonna be none too happy about us not bein' back at our called time. He'd made his rules clear. And we know'd 'em clear. He only gives us a day after the day we are to return. If we ain't back, he... the thought stopped me dead still on the trail... he'd come to fetch us.

Oh, good gracious! Dad's on his way to where we'd made camp near Levelland Mountain, and the little ones are there searchin' for the murderin' woman! He was gonna have to watch his trail, or they'd find him. Once I thought on Dad out lookin' for us, it give me worry just for a minute. Then I reasoned it better. Dad was all healed. He was one 'a the best in the woods when it come to slippin' along without bein' seen. Second to only a few in readin' sign. He'd done it a lot. Learned his talent from a battle-hardened Cherokee warrior, Dancing Bear, who was the best. My worry settled thinkin' on that.

My trail calm was workin' as I thought this new circle through. I was no longer worried over my dad. He would take care of himself - meanin' the evil little warriors had best leave him be. Wolf, however, I weren't so founded on. He could not fight the warriors the way Dad could. Stayin' hid was his only weapon, really. He might get one if they come in the cave on him. They'd proved how sneaky they could be when they walked in on us at camp, showin' no fear. I prayed it didn't come to that for Wolf and the injured woman as I led the mules through the back gate of our barnyard. I was cold, hungry, and exhausted.

I was home. I'd not worry over nothin' for now. Momma would make it all right when she got word of it. She always did.

I took the mules to the barn. Dropped their loads in a pile just inside the door. Then turned 'em to pasture. I'd hang the meat, put up our truck, and scrape the mules' feet later. Those things could wait. I needed a plate 'a Momma's cookin'. I walked up the back-porch steps, and when I saw the back door to our home, I felt complete. I reached for the latchstring, give it a pull, then stepped inside. Soon I'd eat, get warm, and sleep. I just hoped for the injured woman's sake that Anne was there.

Chapter Seven

The Lost Slave

Wolf woke to find the fire near out. He moved over to the sleepin' woman and realized quick the talkin' had done no good. She was gone. His questions would never be answered. The young woman would never see the rabbits dance. Wolf was sad. The sign on her neck could be seen no longer, and unknown to him, it had been unseeable for a bit. She was turnin' cold. The blue was comin' in her fingernails. Her mouth had fell open. Wolf leaned her up to look at the wound. It was turnin' white with gray around the edges. The leakin' was no longer runnin'. The rot in her blood had turned to death. Her trail across the river had begun. She'd be with her folks soon, whoever they was. She'd fought hard. It seemed she never really had a chance even with all we'd done for her. It's hard to shake Indian warriors when they've swore a path to kill you. You will die if they ain't kilt first. Their trail of revenge had ended while Wolf slept. The arrow had finally done its chore.

A quick look at the sleepin' bear gave Wolf no concern. He commenced rollin' her body up in the quilt she died in to bind it for burial. Gettin' her ready while prayin' to Jesus the whole time to let her stay a while longer. He moved her closer to the fire, so he could see to do the bindin' chore better. As he worked her body straight squarin' it up from her feet to her top, he couldn't help but notice how handsome her face was, even in death. He felt a sadness come to his spirit for her passin', so he halted what he was doin' for a minute. Sittin' back on his heels, arms on his knees, starin' at her, he reached from where he was squatted and pulled each of her arms up across her chest. Leavin' her right palm flat on top of the back of her left hand. After seein' to it they laid across her middle, he sat back to give her a once-over. She still looked like she was in pain the same as when she died, 'cept her mouth had closed.

"I am going to miss getting to know you, woman," Wolf said to her spirit. "I hope your coming journey is comforting. I will see you again one day. But for now, I must complete your time here on Mother Earth. I will bind you proper. Place you in the ground somewhere sacred; fitting for a woman like you. It is the way to hide you from the evil one before your ancestors learn of your fate. Cross over to take you with them. I will not like this chore, but I will do it. You are a fighter. A warrior. I respect the way you chose to challenge death. There is honor in your passing." With much honor, Wolf sang her spirit a song of life.

As soon as he was done singin', he slid the quilt with her in it back some away from the fire. It was gettin' too hot for him after movin' it closer earlier. Takin' hold of the quilt on both sides of her body, he pulled it up tight across and underneath her person. Startin' at her feet, pinchin' them together so the toes was near touchin', he used the strength in his left arm to hold the two quilt corners together. Then, he used his right arm to wrap it around tight up to her waist. The upper part of her body still exposed. The right palm still layin' flat to the left-hand center of her middle.

Needin' straps to do the bindin', he went to his possibles pouch to fetch 'em. They weren't none. We'd used 'em all tyin' our extra late winter meat to the pack mule. He would need to find something that would work. The quilts had to be bound or the swellin' of her body would break the wrap. Critters would find her if that happened. Dig her up for food source. Bein' cold would slow it, but she still needed to be bound.

He had to study on things. Think for a bit. *What would work?* He allowed they weren't no real hurry, so he moved over to the fire for a smoke. Fetched his tobacco pouch and pipe from his possibles bag 'fore gettin' comfortable in his place by the fire. With hands skilled in the act, he packed a short bowl in his favorite white oak pipe. Made flame from a wood splinter then sucked it through the dried burley. Raisin' his chin while closin' his eyes, he savored the taste. A kinda pullin' wave with his right hand moved the smoke over his head; prayin' all the while 'til dozin' off again for a minute. Durin' his wakin', he felt more than saw that things didn't seem the way they should be across the fire. Different than from before his smoke.

He sat lookin' at the woman, searchin', feelin', knowin', but not figurin' what it was. It was different for sure. They was somethin' out 'a place from when he'd wrapped the woman just a little time before. Lookin', knowin', seein' but not seein', he looked closer. The quilt, her head, her hands... her hands, they weren't the same. He'd laid the right palm on the back of the left hand; left 'em that way. Now the right was layin' flat to her belly. *What? How'd it move? Is she alive? No, she couldn't be!* It must 'a slid off when he was layin' her lower half back flat on the cave floor. He just hadn't noticed it 'til now. Lightin' one 'a the pine knot torches, he eased over for a closer look. There was a flicker of hope in Wolf as he moved to her side. Jesus might be seein' fit to let her stay a while longer.

He settled up close to her. No doubt, the right hand was in a different place than he'd left it. *But why? How? It had to be her.* He moved the torch close to her neck. Got real close down to see if the tiny bump was showin' any blood travel at all, it weren't. He checked the flat of each wrist just above the base of her palms. There was no feelin' of her heart beatin'. This woman was dead. There was no doubt about it. She show'd no signs of life in any knowin' of the word. She was dead. Gone. No life. Finished. Done with it all. Wolf looked mighty hard to try and find life sign of any kind. It just weren't there. He cried. Nobody but one ever know'd of it.

Wolf whispered to her, "I am sorry young woman. I thought maybe the Great Spirit had sent you back to us. I am praying very hard. I know He is listening. However, I believe it might be that He wants you home. I wish you to stay, to live here with us in Choestoe. Poor fortune for you I am not the one who will decide that fate. It is in His hands. I know your body cannot hear me. I believe your spirit can. Be safe in the crossing. May your ancestors come swiftly."

After the short-lived, small hope, Wolf was still at a loss as to what he was gonna use to bind her death roll. He smoked it over again. Studied the problem whole. He finally come to a simple conclusion, considerin' he'd spotted a stand 'a hickory trees just off to the east where he'd got wood. He'd use young hickory bark. All mountain folk know'd you could tie a young hickory's bark into knots. It would hold stout. Not break or tear, hard to cut. He just had to go and harvest as few strips. It was easy enough to do. You just needed a young hickory to skin so the bark would be soft enough to twist. The only problem was, he had to leave the safety of the cave to do it. Was the little warriors outside? What would he find when he went to harvest the strips? Could he wait for morning? No, her body would need bindin' sooner rather than later. It would be too much for Wolf by himself once she commenced to swellin' up. He had to go. He was all there was to go. He moved back beside the woman, explained it to her.

"I am going out for a little bit of time. I will be back soon. We will finish this binding when I return." So sayin', he took the torch and left.

He didn't worry over them little warriors gettin' the woman 'cause she was already dead. They couldn't kill her again if they found her, but they would be vengeful to him for helpin'. Knowin' that made Wolf get real careful as he started out for the strips. Stoppin' just inside the opening of the cave, he stuck the torch handle in a crack about shoulder height from the ground back a little ways from the front. Nobody on the outside could see the light, nor his shadow movin' out quick. He knelt low easin' on in silent like a mountain cat prowlin'. Listenin', watchin', scentin', stayin' squatted for several minutes lettin' he eyes get to where he could see a little. Watchin', listenin', waitin' to go on 'til he was sure no noise or movement was there that could be taken for danger. Saw no shadow move for cover. Felt no bad spirits. When he was certain it was safe, he went back inside the cave and fetched the torch, then went back out movin' east to the hickory stand.

***

Dad was doin' the warrior's trot to make time when he found our camp. He followed the trail off the big ridge to where sign show'd Spirit had come to us. She'd left no sign he could read, but we had. It told him what we'd done and the way we'd gone after we'd done it. He started trailin' us.

The sign told him something had made us backtrack up the mountain, then return, carryin' whatever it was that prob'ly made us do the backtrackin'. Something heavy. What made him unsure of our trail was we'd not turned toward home or made camp since dark was near. But instead, headed off to the south. He really had to study hard, look close to see where our trails all crossed. We'd come down from the big ridges, then back up, and then back down again. It was most confusing for him, but he figured it all out in a short while. He was wise to woods travel.

He'd also found the smaller tracks of the little people around our fire pit at the huntin' camp near Levelland Mountain. Figured their comin' and goin'. He know'd right off who they was. Remembered their small tracks from bein' with his dad when they hunted some of 'em for stealin' one 'a Granddad's mules a time back. Dad said they never caught 'em. *No. Not right. I know'd better. That weren't the way of it.* Never settled straight with me them just walkin' away without their mule. I know'd my granddad better'n that. They weren't no way he was gonna let some rogue Indian thief take his property and not settle with 'em. I figured they'd— no, I know'd they'd made it right. Took the mule back. Dad just weren't gonna tell it, which was fine. I know'd what I felt was true. My grandad was tough, but fair.

Dad spoke to no folks in particular as he moved on our trail south. He prayed to Holy Spirit, "They've gone from this place, Holy One. Headed south when it is west they should be movin'. It is cold. The dark will be on them. Their back trail has slowed their travel. Somethin' has caused this. What is that, Great Spirit? I wonder for my son and his friend, Wolf. Send your angels to surround them, your blood to cover them. Protect them from the evil walkin' our valley. What fate has come their way to make them seek the shelter of Panther Cave? I will listen' for Your thoughts."

***

It'd took Wolf a while to cut the hickory bark strips. He'd found three perfect sized trees growin' right next to each other, all havin' the right age bark for tyin'. The strips was near as long as Wolf was tall. Had to be for them to reach around her body whole with enough left for the tie knot. Hickory bark was strong in its makin'. Folks would use it for all sorts 'a different chores. A thin strip could make a great basket tie or hold poles together or hang deer and hog. Many laced the seats of chairs with it. The stuff is natural strong.

Wolf was havin' to walk back to the cave mostly from memory. The pine torch had burnt plumb out and he couldn't see the ground. It'd taken him a while to work the bark free. He needed a good bit to bind the quilts proper. The long ties would tighten snug around the woman's dead body as they dried.

As he entered the cave, headin' for the fire, he could see the flames had died down. Small licks was fightin' for life around the edges. He used them to catch it back up once he bunched the coals and laid on some dry wood. It weren't no time 'til the flames made the darkness begin to back away. He looked toward the woman but could barely see her, even close as he was.

There are times, Wolf and me would learn again and again, darkness is preferred to what the light makes known. That sometimes the unknown is better than the known, or, many times, safer. This was absolutely one 'a those times. It would take all Wolf's warrior trainin' to remain calm and do things proper. His world was fixin' to change as he settled back in his sittin' spot while fetchin' his tobacco pouch. He wanted to drop some dried burley into the building flames. Pray to see if evil was near him. He should 'a saved that pinch 'a tobacco for a later time.

Wolf squatted on his heels across the fire from the woman once he'd got the little bit 'a tobacco he'd use to speak with the fire. He dropped it, prayed, and watched. Nothin'. The small burst of flame from the dried bits 'a burley said nothin'. He stayed squatted there to think. Watchin' as the fire got bigger. He felt the heat warm his cold face, his feet, and his hands. He felt comfort, sadness.

His raised his eyes, lockin' on to the body lyin' across from him. Looked at the quilt roll he'd started. His gaze moved up from her feet to the split where her upper body was still showin'... *Huh?* It weren't right. The arm was moved again. A cold chill started runnin' down the back 'a Wolf's neck as he followed the roll to the top where it opened. No, it can't be. The lady's head was now turned toward the fire. Her eyes open . . . she was starin' at him. It weren't no death stare, neither. The light from the fire was shinin' from the wet in her eyes. Wolf fell back on his rump from the shock.

No! This could not be. She was dead for sure. He couldn't be seein' it right. He closed his eyes tight, then opened 'em back up quick lookin' right back at her. Yep, the eyes was open. She was lookin' at him through the fire. She was movin' . . . no, bein' moved. He took another hard look. Somethin' was on her . . . no, it couldn't be ... a huge black paw? . . . Claws? A black paw... layin' across her middle. *What spirit was this that had come to her? No, what?*

Wolf felt he had to be seein' a vision. This could not be real - a dream, maybe. He had to be asleep. He took another close look. It was there. A black paw... with long, dirty claws... holdin' her to the earth. He looked harder. A deeper gaze over where the paw lay into the darkness. A pair of eyes starin' back. Red eyes. A face trimmed in firelight. A shiny nose tilted up tryin' to scent. *No!* A bear... sittin' on its haunches... near the woman. *Alive! She looked alive! How? Was it this bear? A spirit bear?* He froze. His woods mind come to him. He did not move or even blink. The bear was starin' right at him.

Wolf know'd bein' up close in a cave to a huge black bear with no weapon could mean he'd pay with his blood if the bear sensed him an enemy. Wolf needed to think, to control himself. The bear seemed fine with stayin' right where they was, for now. This had to be handled without fear. It could mean death for him and the woman, the second one for her.

***

"Jeb," Momma said as I opened the back door of our home, near fallin' into the cookin' room from exhaustion. She hurried over to hug me. I'd made it home just in time for supper. The scent from the food Momma was cookin' made my belly growl. My mouth tighten up.

Momma stepped back, looked me over good sayin', "Praise the Lord you're home! Where have you been, Jebediah? You look worn, hungry. Come, sit at the table. I will get you something to eat. A mug of cool buttermilk. Is your father with you? Wolf? Black Oak?"

"No, ma'am," I said as I took a seat at the eatin' table. My mouth waterin' like the spring run-off from the smell 'a her cookin'. "I'm all by myself. Just me and the mules. I left Wolf in Panther Cave on Blood Mountain. He's with a woman who's hurt bad - near death. We run up on her trailin' home. Could be she's already dead by now. That's how come I'm late gettin' back from huntin'. Wolf stayed with her. I come for Anne and her medicines. Is she here?"

"Yes, she is here. Up in the loft sewing a new pair of foot skins for your dad's birthday this spring while he is out on trail looking for you," Momma said as she laid out my food on the table. "You eat your supper. I will go up and get Anne. No need you telling this twice. Now eat, slowly. You might want to drink some buttermilk first to settle your insides."

I felt sorry for Wolf. I was sittin' in my warm home lookin' at smoked venison, fried potatoes, and boiled cabbage seasoned with sun-dried peppers and onions. A small pone 'a cornbread lay close on the table, thin, golden brown, just the way I liked it, still steamin' in the skillet. Fresh butter and Cain's honey sat with it. This was sure to be comparable with nothin' no better than what folks eat in the Glory Land. I mean, Momma's cookin' was *good*. None better no place I'd ever been. Near painful good if you was starved like I felt.

Anne come down from the loft with Momma. Thank God Almighty she was there! I was lookin' at her. She'd come down to see me. Hear my tale. She walked over to the table to stand beside me while wrappin' her arms around my head pullin' me tight against her chest. She said somethin' to me, but I couldn't hear it. Her arms was coverin' my left ear. My right buried against her bosom. I could feel the vibration of her voice on the side of my face but couldn't make out one word she uttered. I weren't troubled over it though. I liked her huggin'. She smelled clean, like Momma always did. Made me know I was home. I loved my family.

"Okay, Jeb?" I heard her say as she let go huggin' my head. "Don't that sound like a good way? Now tell me what's goin' on. Tell it straight so I can figure what to take back with us in the morning."

I hadn't heard most a' what she'd said. That last part told me it was time to tell her and Momma what was happenin', so I commenced. Between bites of meat, taters, cabbage, cornbread, and slurps of buttermilk, I began tellin' 'em all I know'd, for the most part. Her and Momma sat across from me as I told 'em mine and Wolf's tale, leavin' nothin' out 'cept the part about Spirit leadin' us to the woman. As I told it, we just happened on the hurt one's trail. I was really tired. Near wore plumb out, so my mind weren't workin' proper. Still, I told it square enough they understood. Momma was real concerned about us runnin' into the warriors of The Lost. She remembered the stories about 'em from days gone by. They had few questions when I'd finished tellin' it all. Fortunately for me, I made 'em understand how things was.

I got done eatin', stood from my place at the table, then went and hugged Momma and Anne real big sayin' goodnight. I could go no more. The rest would have to wait 'til morning.

***

She was alive! By the Great Spirit, she was alive. Bein' guarded by what Wolf figured to be a spirit bear watchin' over her like food.

Wolf was in a fix, with very few protections, as he tried to stay perfectly still. The bear was gonna lead this dance. Weren't much Wolf could do about it. He started figurin' on how to fight the bear if things turned, prayin' in the slilent he'd not need to. No doubt he'd lose 'cause he was lookin' at full-grow'd adult male bear not over four paces away. An old bear what lived back in the mountains. Weren't never close to folks. Seasoned with years 'a bear doin's. Prob'ly a smart bear, too. Wolf figured if he left him be, then the bear would leave him be.

A quick look at the woman's face told Wolf he weren't dreamin'. It was no vision. The woman was lookin' at him, scared, half out, but her eyes was open. That was more life showin' from her than Wolf had seen since we'd found her. He was thankful for that.

He looked back at the bear. It was movin' some. Stood on his hindquarters enough to raise up on all fours. While Wolf watched, he put his snout down behind the woman flippin' her over with just the slight raisin' of his head. Without call, the bear let out a soft grunt makin' Wolf go dead still. The bear went to lickin' the woman's back. Cleanin' the wound with it's mouth, tongue, and lips. Sloberin' foam over it like washin' soap. Bitin' at it like a dog nibbles an itch from a flea on its leg. He reached up with a front paw. Rolled her up on her side then back and forth while mashin' down on her some. Her eyes still open. Her face showin' pain, yet she made no sound. She was bein' doctored by an old black bear straight out 'a the backwoods of the Appalachian Mountains. They weren't no doubt in Wolf why that bear was there.

Songs and stories would come from that night's bear visit. Wolf watched close everything that happened so he'd remember. The bear never minded Wolf none while workin' its cleanin' chore. When it finished tendin' to the woman, he shocked Wolf by lookin' right at where he was sittin' close to the fire, grunted, raised its head to scent, then turned and eased on out from the cave into the night.

Wolf said later it was spiritual. I believe it was 'cause it was a whole different critter than the one sharin' the cave. That bear was still sleepin' hard on the ledge. Could 'a been Brother Bear, but we'd never know. Wolf didn't see its chest.

Chapter Eight

The "What-for" of the Matter

There was no doubt where we was headed. It was just the what-for of the matter that he couldn't cipher. Dad walked our trail 'til he was certain where we was goin', then cut across the big holler at a trot under the steep to Panther Cave.

He was standin' out front as daylight got to showin' over the top edge of the big ridges to the east. The sign he found markin' up the ground outside the cave was like words on paper to him. He know'd by all of it what'd took place to a notion but couldn't be for sure. He checked the charge in his gun, then walked into the cave. He'd been there before with Dancing Bear. Yet, none but me know'd of the secret room inside.

Wolf had used the rest of the wood we'd gathered to build up the fire. He needed to warm the woman now that she was alive again. He heated the broth, then soaked a small clean rag of homespun he'd took from his possibles pouch offerin' it over her mouth to drink. She was able to open enough to let some of the meat juice drip in, but weren't near strong enough to suck juice from the rag. The cave was lit good, allowin' him to see her struggle as she drank what little she could. He recognized a strength for life in her as she swallowed the salty broth. Wolf was humbled.

The sight Dad saw through the flames as he entered the cave give him answers about why we was out past our time to be home. Two folks, one flat to the ground, a woman, the other sittin' over her. Wolf he know'd. The woman concerned him. Was this why the warriors of The Lost was in the valley? Dad allowed the only reason they'd be in the Choestoe Valley was they had business. Turns out them little heathens weren't allowed to be in the valley by order from the Cherokee; banished 'cause 'a their killin' and thievin' ways durin' the old days. Wolf and me learned that from Dad around a smoke fire one night. Made sense then, them slippin' around like they was. They never bothered us after our spell with the hurt woman, but they did trouble the England folks one winter later on. Elizabeth got fetched up in that business.

"Wolf," Dad said softly.

"Thompie Collins! I am so glad to see you, Uncle," Wolf said as he rose to meet Dad with a hug. "Jeb is not here. He is gone to fetch help for this woman here. Come see. She has found her life again. It is growing."

"What is this, Wolf?" Dad asked as he moved over beside the fire. "How is it you've come to be here, to have this woman? Who is she? Is this why The Lost warriors are here? Lookin' for this one? Is she the reason they are in the valley?"

Wolf replied, "Yes, she is, I know that to be true. Four warriors visited us two nights ago. They followed her trail to our camp. Surprised us. Said she had visited while we were out on a hunt. That she took meat to eat. They were very quiet slipping into our camp looking for her. Claimed she killed an honored man of their people with a knife. They trailed her into the valley a few suns ago. I believe one of them tried to kill this woman as she ran from her life as a slave. What she wore spoke to us that she was owned. We pulled this from her wound." Wolf reached for the arrow point to show Dad.

"I know that stone," Dad said as he took the point, studyin' it close. "It's a trade stone from the north. A kind of stone those warriors would have. They trade north 'cause nobody here will trade with 'em. I'm sure one of their kind has done this. They are very angry with her. We must watch. Make sure they don't pay us a surprise visit, too. They will most likely find our trails. Could be on us soon. Of that, I have little doubt. They will know by readin' the trail sign she's been helped. That y'all are the reason they could not find her. This will make them very angry with you and Jeb. We may need to fight these unwanted visitors. We must be ready if it comes to that."

Dad stepped outside the cave into the early morning light to see what was what, to think. He studied the woods all around. Saw where he figured the little ones might show, if they show'd. He know'd these warriors was good trackers, skilled. They'd trailed their slave for miles just on what little sign she'd left behind in the frozen woods. He know'd they could find Panther Cave, too, if they sorted out the trail sign proper. It was powerful confusin', even for him. He was sure they could find the cave, even though the crossed trails where we found the woman was confusin' to read. Only time would tell.

The story of her fate, told in the sign left behind, would keep their blood up for revenge. The trail she now shared with me and Wolf could mean death to all what lay tied to it. They could be out there, trailin', lookin', knowin' the way. Dad really needed Black Oak to come, but there was little chance in that now, since our huntin' camp was broke. It was possible he could be followin' the unwanted visitors, but one couldn't know for sure. No, he know'd he'd be facin' 'em alone, a musket and two pistols backin' him up. He said a short prayer for Holy Spirit to protect him, Wolf, and the woman, too.

The more he studied it, the more he settled with the notion it might be best for everybody if they did find her. After all, she was still their slave. As a council elder, Dancing Bear would have no choice but to rule against the slave if the little folks did find her. Prove she did murder. It would mean justice for The Lost, since some Indians owned slaves. It was a tolerated infection in lands outside the valley.

They weren't a owned body ever in Choestoe that I'd know'd about 'til after the U.S. Government come in. Give all the Cherokee land away. Same in the Yonah Valley, but other clans owned 'em. Trade was still held in those places. The Lost bein' one bunch what still stole folks for slaves or sale. They raided and took from their enemies when threatened, slaves included. Folks in the mountains didn't like it, but that's just the way it was with some Indians. Later on, some whites, too.

***

Daylight was crackin' when Anne walked out from the light shinin' out the back door of our log home. Her soft, worn, doe skin pouch of doctorin' possibles slung over her shoulder, layin' in the small of her back while bein' held in place by her right arm. It looked like a part of her person, natural. Herbs, wraps, salves, mixed powders, and clean rags of homespun had a home in that pouch, so did the spirit beads woven into the hangin' strap, flap, and along the edges. It was one thing she never went any place without. That, and her special knife Old Mother had passed on to her. She kept it strapped tight to her belt just above her left hip, handle forward for easy grabbin'. It was sharp enough to split a hair. I'd watched that blade slice flesh and it hardly felt, at first. For wound cleanin' and nerve calmin', a full jug 'a Dad's hard cider dangled from the bottom of her right arm gripped tight by her strong right hand.

She'd come far in her learnin'. Old Mother was teachin' her the medicine woman trade, so she was bein' taught proper. Owl mostly stayed home now that age had caught up to her. It got to where Anne would have to go visit her to get on with the learnin'. Stayin' for days at a time. She'd trail to secret places Owl would tell her about way out in the mountains to gather a type 'a root or a certain tree bark or sometimes even special dirt. Wolf and me went with her on many trips. She taught us about healin' when we was out with her. We remembered how to get to them places so we could go back and tend to the plants or collect provisions.

Anne wrote down all the mixes for herbs she'd use for this or that. We'd read her words to learn so we'd know what herbs to look for. It weren't hard to find Old Mother's hidden gardens. The old woman's thought was clear as she told Anne to the rock or tree or trail it took to find what she wanted Anne to find. Then they'd mix those things and make medicines great for healin' folks. We all know'd Anne had the gift. She was special; called to it by the Great Spirit, so Owl claimed. That was good for all 'cause healin' folks was needed in the mountains.

"You got all you think you're gonna need, Anne?" I asked as she stepped up, takin' her seat next to me on the harvest wagon. We'd both done hugged Momma goodbye. Wiped our tears. It was always hard to leave her.

"I do, Jeb. There won't be much we can do at the cave other than clean out the infection again, like y'all did, try and get some medicine tea in her. If that much can be done, then she will have a chance. What is her name, so I can start prayin' for her as we travel?"

"We don't know her name, Anne. She ain't been awake enough to say since we found her. She looked dead to me when I left Panther Cave yesterday morning. I feel this whole trail may be like chasin' a shadow. My gut tells me she's across the river, runnin' with her folks what done gone ahead of her, which may be for the better anyhow. We know she's a slave. Wolf spotted that right off. We believe she's the one what run off from The Lost. Them little warriors is bent on findin' her. That's why I packed these."

I reached down under our wagon seat turnin' up a top quilt to uncover two 'a Dad's .36 caliber flintlock handguns. They was both loaded with custom shot, primed with dry powder, propped up, handles forward, ready to cock and fire. I had 'em layin' real gentle-like in the fold of the quilt so they'd be handy if they was needed. That give me extra comfort from the worry of makin' trail back to Panther Cave. I know'd the evil little warriors was out searchin'. If they was savvy warriors, they'd be trailin' toward Panther Cave by now. We'd not run into 'em. That would put 'em in for Dad and Wolf, though, if they'd figured the sign correctly. I said a prayer for Dad, Wolf, and the woman. Momma had asked about Black Oak when I first got home, maybe he was near. I'd seen no sign of him durin' our hunt or my time on the trail home. I give his whereabouts little thought. Knowin' him, he could be anyplace, or no place. Choestoe was a big valley. He had no common home. The whole valley was his to travel. The thought come to me he might 'a found the visiting warriors' trail and was spendin' time watchin' them. Who would know? Like as not, he was back over toward Slaughter Mountain with Dancing Bear.

I'd not shot no folks before, only hog and deer. My thought with the short guns was to make sure Anne stayed safe - me too, of course. I figured I could pull the trigger on danger if I had to. I didn't feel I couldn't. I would know one day. I was sure of that. I just hoped it would be when I was older.

Anne took hold 'a my right forearm with her left hand as we took our seats, looked me dead in the eye, and said, "You're growin' more like Dad every day, Jebediah. I feel better knowin' those guns are within arm's reach. I know how to fire 'em. Dad showed me a while back. I can hit where I'm aimin' as long as its close. Now, give me them reins." She turned back square to the front, give Jim a little pop sayin', "I ain't drove ol' Jim in a long time. I sure have missed him."

With a wave back at Momma, we took for the trail to Panther Cave. Anne know'd she had a chore to get at. She was ready. Healin' was excitin' to her like a good hunt was to me and Wolf. We was in for a time. Of that, I was sure.

Jim jumped to Anne's voice commencin' to pull the harvest wagon. Peter trailed on a lead tied to the back. Sittin' next to Anne, I rode watch. Momma had laid a fresh roll 'a quilts and homespun in the back as we was leavin'. It laid up against the front side 'a the wagon rail d'rectly behind where we sat. She'd tied and bound it all in homespun strips. I'd told Momma and Anne about the woman's need for cover and the nasties she was crawlin' in. I saw Anne pack a powder that would rid a body 'a them bugs. It worked, too. I'd seen it sure. Cain got bugs on a huntin' trip once by allowin' one 'a Dad's old hog dogs to lay up ag'in him on a cold night. He never let that happen again. It was terrible what folks had to go through when they got fetched up in them crawlies. The healin' Cain got was truth to that. I tell you, we ain't never let him live it down.

Anne made him go out to the back porch in the cold and strip down plumb naked. Bare as a new born baby. That was bad enough, but then she commenced to dustin' him with this stinky yellow dust all over his whole put together. It clung to every part 'a his person. Coverin' him complete top to bottom with not a spot missed. He looked like a yellow haint come to scare all what walked Mother Earth. Cain allowed the powder burned some. He didn't care, though, when he seen what it could do. That yellow dust killed straight away every one 'a them varmints it landed on. Makin' the rest jump plumb off his body gettin' away. It was the devil's time when she got to powderin' some poor soul. You had to watch bein' too close to the dusted one when she got the healin' goin'. I'm speakin' truth when I tell you them critters would settle on your person if you was in range 'a their leavin' jump. That powder had a strong healin' spirit. Shed a body 'a them crawlies real quick-like. I prayed silent, not out loud, I'd never have to go through one 'a them dustin's as I stood by watchin' Cain's sufferin'. I prayed silent cause I didn't want the evil one to hear my mind, torment me with them critters, no sir. It took Cain three moons to get clear 'a all that yellow powder. He never got near them dogs ag'in. He got in fights over folks laughin' at him. Callin' him "yellow boy while covered in that powder. He could take a kiddin' on such as bein' a different color and all, but you'd better watch if you ever called him "yeller". He didn't take to bein' called that at all. They weren't nothin' in all the world he was scared of. I'd seen his courage many times.

Silent, quiet prayers, not spoken aloud, that's what I believed. The way I seen it, you had to watch how you prayed about certain things. I'd learned from the old timers you had to pray in the silent for stuff like: torments, needs, wants, weather, stock, and for sure, folks. A body needs to be careful. Accordin' to them, the devil listens in on your talkin' with God if it's said aloud. And if you speak it out, he'll pester you with what you pray for 'cause he's learned what you want if he hears it. It's like if you prayed out loud to God for courage, Satan will hear and send somethin' that'd require a body to use his courage. All mountain folk know'd the great deceiver was always on the prowl, listenin' close. Granddad believed every livin' soul had a demon spirit watchin' and hearin' everthing they say, seein' everything they did. Same as an angel from the Great Creator who'd look after you. He allowed them demons let ol' Lucifer know what was goin' on. See, the way the Bible tells it, the devil ain't all in everything like God is. God makes our lives complete. He is part of our bein'. The evil one ain't by nature all knowin'. He has to be told, thanks be to Jesus! So, I pray in the silent just in case. Listen in the silent, too. I figure that's best.

"That woman is gonna need you bad if she is still with us," I said to Anne as she drove the wagon. "Me and Wolf got the arrow point out, but the hole is real nasty with maggots and infection. The way her side is tore apart from the inside, she must 'a been runnin' for days. That arrow slipped right out when Wolf give it the slightest pull - like it was stuck in some 'a Dad's fresh-mixed hog sausage. The worst of the takin' out made him have to slip the point of his small knife back in the wound some to slice a little meat. The bottom edges of the arrow point was stuck deep inside. She never felt it, 'cause even the slicin' didn't wake her. She is bad off. Don't feel hurt if she can't make it once you get her settled. I prayed for healin' power to come on her. That's where I left it."

    She thought for a minute, then said her mind, "Each body is different, Jeb, some are strong and can come back from near death. Some are weak and die like they should. Then, some stay when all signs tell you they should go, leave when the signs say stay. We will give her every chance that I know to live. Do all we can for her. Life or death is in the mighty hands of the Creator, Holy God, Jehovah. Old Mother has shown me all healin' comes from the Great Spirit. He is the source for healin' — Him, and only Him — and I believe that. The Cherokee say I am called to heal; no other trail would be accepted for my life. I feel their words are true."

    She weren't speakin' from no book, nor was she sayin' anything she'd just thought or come to mind on. She was speakin' what her soul felt. She had a talent provokin' her to be the earthly hands for Holy Spirit's healin' work. That would scare the devil plumb out 'a me and most anybody else called to work that close with Holy Spirit. She never minded it none; just went on like it was meant. Momma said she was watched over by special angels what led her trail. I wanted to know more about that. I took a mind to watch her close as she worked healin' on the hurt one. See if I saw any 'a them spiritual happenin's. Somehow, I know'd just by her bein' there I would. It was strange, and I'd heard other folks carry on about it, but you could feel Anne when she was close. Like a haint lookin' over your shoulder, or a slight warm breeze in the woods on a cold dark night. Old Mother called it "The Gift." I wondered while we was ridin', *Would she follow the way? Know when to go doctor folks like Old Mother?* It would be interesting to see her bloom in them kinda doin's. I was glad she was my sister. I loved her very much.

    I could tell the day was gonna be clear, but cold. Old Man Sun was lightin' up the valley as we made our way out to the Keowee Path. Anne and me had our cold weather truck on. The warm foxhide head skins we wore run down the side of our faces, then slipped around behind our necks 'fore wrappin' back across the front. We was sittin' close together to keep warm, too, sharin' one 'a Momma's thick quilts wrapped complete around us both. You could still feel the sting of cold air passin' by as ol' Jim pulled with a haste he was feelin' we needed.

We was makin' good time. Jim was trailin' smooth as fresh, cool buttermilk bein' poured into a wooden mug. Peter was followin' without no fuss. The Keowee Path was froze solid makin' for easy, but bumpy, travel. The birds had commenced to makin' songs to start their day. I'd already seen some game. It was a good morning for 'em to be out movin'. A couple 'a whitetail deer spooked and run off, wavin' their white tails at us as we topped a small hill where the path cut through a stand of white oaks. Some ways on we saw turkey hens scratchin' out old leaves lookin' for grubs and such. They weren't far off the path to our left. On up we saw a squirrel hoppin'. It crossed in front 'a Jim. He saw it. I watched as the squirrel was busy - movin' from a log to the base of a tree, to an old stump, to the place where turkeys had been scratchin', findin' nothin'. Seemed he couldn't find the acorns he'd hid before the cold time set in. He knows he hid a bunch somewhere not long after Mother Tree had let them go, but exactly where was turnin' out to be hard for him to remember, near frustratin'. He was older. He'd have to find 'em, though, or he'd starve.

Seein' them critters was special. Those are things you expect to see in the woods; look for as you travel when you're out on trail. It's special when you do see 'em.

It's the things you see that don't belong that catch you up -- bring on worry. The squatty warrior standin' in the middle of the path as we turned the long curve around Sharp Rock Point was just one 'a those things. I'd hoped to never see that face again. Anne whoa'd Jim up. Stopped him short from where the dirty little Indian stood. I didn't get too concerned at first, then the rest 'a his bunch come out from hidin' all along where we sat. They was on both sides of us, and in back. That concerned me 'cause all of a sudden we was surrounded by six warriors of The Lost . . . and this time they wore paint.

***

Wolf felt the skin on the side of the hurt one's neck. It was cool, slick, like sliced bacon ready to fry. He was leanin' in close watchin' her lips. Her breath was still faint. Her eyes opened but barely. She was no longer dead.

How? He wondered on all that had happened. *Where had that bear come from? Why was it there? What made it come? How in the whole put-together could that just have happened? Do healing angels take on the form of critters? Did Old Woman change into Spirit Bear, then come save the injured one? Was it just a vision?* No, he was certain it was no vision nor dream, neither. He would have to smoke on all this when we got the woman home. He would speak to the old ones concerning what happened. They would have knowledge of such things. Like as not, they'd seen it before. He would just have to wait. Figured he would tell only me 'til he spoke with them about it. This was a wise choice.

Chapter Nine

A Need for Killin'

He wore red paint. Three turkey feathers hung from the right side of his now mostly shaved head. He'd left a single strip 'a hair down the middle startin' at his forehead, stoppin' somewhere in the back. Made him look much more evil than the last time I'd seen him. It was Blood Moon, the same warrior who'd walked into our camp a few nights back lookin' for the hurt woman. Wearin' paint throw'd me 'cause they weren't no need for it; this time he had weapons. A long knife slung to his left side, sheathed from his waist by a braided leather belt. He held a short war club in his right hand, stained from what looked like years of old blood. His worn-out homespun had been replaced with a full-on set 'a battle skins. They was painted on, too. He had mad on his face, near ready to kill from what I figured was the recent comin' on of a burnin' need for revenge. Justice had escaped him. It was clear his bunch had become desperate. That made 'em dangerous, unpredictable. Fear was makin' a trail up my back, raisin' the hair on my neck. I stayed calm. Tried to not let him see my fear as we stared hard at each other.

We was far from where the woman lay. Weren't no way they'd made trail to Panther Cave, then back to the valley in the time it'd took me to trail home to fetch Anne. That meant they'd not found what they was searchin' for. I know'd then that's why they was riled, wearin' paint. I wondered why they'd not followed our trail to Blood

Mountain? Somewhere on the mountain is where I'd figured 'em to be when me and Anne left from home 'fore daylight. It was possible, since they seemed kinda stupid compared to most Indians I'd met, for them to 'a not found the cave. I was sure they'd 'a been close to it 'cause of the trail we'd left . . . then it come to me. Hit me like a punch in the gut. They'd messed up in their sign readin'. Got confused over who'd gone where. Followed the wrong trail by readin' the sign to say we'd packed their slave out on our mules.

    I had to study on that for a minute, even though I was starin' down a full-grow'd, battle-scarred, adult Cherokee warrior wearin' color. No doubt they'd found where Spirit show'd us the woman. Made a circle out wide from there lookin' for sign. Prob'ly crossed up on my trail headed home, never circlin' back to find the trail we'd made to the cave. That was somethin' Dancing Bear would 'a never done. He was the best in the mountains at trail sign readin'. My sign I'd left goin' home show'd both mules was packin' heavy — naturally figurin' we must be carryin' the one they was searchin' for — they followed my sign. In their mind, one of us ridin' to hold her from fallin' off, leavin' one set 'a tracks leadin' the mules, which told me they figured her to be at the end 'a that trail... the trail I'd left the day before... my trail home to Momma.

    My blood went cold, then fired red hot 'fore I know'd what I was thinkin' good. They'd followed that trail to my home. They'd gone there figurin' the hurt one to be hidin' with us. Didn't find her. She weren't there. That's why they was down this low. That's why they was mad. This could get bad. I could feel killin' was gettin' close. I wondered where my dad was. I needed him somethin' terrible. My silent prayer was short. *God help us!*

    He was dirty. I could smell him. The paint made his face look fierce. I could feel the scare in my back even stronger. I felt near sick, weak. Jim could tell things weren't right. His mane hair was stickin' straight up, quiverin' with mad. He was blowin' snorts while bouncin' his head up and down tryin' to get the Indians' stink out from his nose. That caught the little warrior's attention. He reached out takin' Jim's lead with his left hand, while starin' even harder at me -- if that were possible.

He weren't happy. I weren't, neither. Fact 'a the matter, I was mad; scared mad. My back was up knowin' they followed my sign to our place. I figured they'd got there not long after dark, watched 'til we left at daylight. But what then? I worried for Momma.

The anger I felt when I realized these varmints had been near my momma turned quick to hate. 'Fore I know'd what I was doin', I was standin' up in the wagon starin' hard at the little warrior in the road. I didn't remember movin' to get it, but somehow Dad's short gun was solid in my right hand pointed dead center of Blood Moon's chest, and him but a few paces away. Death was starin' him square in the face from the barrel of Dad's gun, but he never flinched, never even quivered. His eyes held locked into mine with the trail calm of a true warrior, evil or not. I had to respect his courage.

I felt a jump. The move near made me fall off the wagon as Anne reached for the second of Dad's short guns. Turnin' it on the Indian to her right, she cocked it square in his face with her thumb. She show'd him by movin' so quick she know'd what she was doin'. At that range, he'd better watch his topknot. He did, must 'a been smarter than he looked 'cause he stopped dead in his tracks right where she halted him. Anne had caught the seneaky little Indian mid-stride makin' a move toward the wagon while we was all lookin' the other way. Spottin' him tryin' to slip up without us seein' him was real woods savvy of Anne. I'd never seen that side 'a my sister before. Made me proud. Later on, her bravery was talked about in stories around the smokin' fires where talk was made.

I was growin' tired 'a these rotten eggs. I was wishin' Dad and Cain was with us so we could settle up and be done with the parasites. As I stared him hard, I could see by what his eyes was speakin' he know'd I know'd. Now he was wonderin' what I was gonna do.

I was so mad, I near screamed at the ugly little man, "You are not welcome at my home! Why did you go there? The woman is not there. You know this. That is why you followed us here. She is gone from you. You should go home. Her family has her now. They will see to it that you leave her be. They have many warriors who will fight for her. You must know, if you go there lookin', you will die."

The way he took what I said, and the look he give me after, said he weren't real happy with my words. He replied calmly, even though I know'd he wanted to tear my heart out for speakin' so disrespectful, "I do not believe she is with family, young brave one. Yes, we visited your place. We did not trouble the mother after you left before Old Man Sun's first light. We want the hurt one. We searched the house, all around outside. You are right, we found no sign from her. Of that, you are speaking truth. But, she is not of this land. I know she comes from south of this valley of dancing rabbits. No, there has been no time for her to be found. She has no blood here. You are not speaking truth, boy," he near-growled as he dropped his forehead some like he was gonna come on at me. His face was locked in pure hate. He let go 'a Jim's lead from his grip.

I'd crossed the line with Blood Moon. The meanin' of his words was clear to me. Anymore hard talk toward him would mean the fight would come sooner rather than later. It did not matter that he was grow'd and I weren't. He was Indian. I'd insulted him in front of his warrior guard. He would stand for no more. If I had not pulled the short gun, I believe he would 'a been on me 'fore the insultin' words had ever reached his ears good. The gun was keepin' him from charging, even though it was just a boy holdin' it. Warriors respected the smoke pole for the death it held when it spoke. The way they saw it, their leader had no choice but respect it. They believed there was no lack of courage from any warrior's soul with such an evil spirit as the gun holdin' you true. He'd lost no respect from them. Yet, he was still on fire at me. I'd just made an enemy for life, however long that life may be. No matter to none how our unfortunate comin' together went, we would be lifelong enemies.

I never said a word. I know'd better. If I said anything more even hintin' at bein' disrespectful, he'd charge like a mad bear; leavin' me nothin' to do but pull the trigger on the short gun. Try and put a .36 caliber lead ball through his chest in hopes that would stop him. I did not care to do that. I felt I could but hoped I wouldn't have to. I was mostly sure my soul would let me 'cause the fear I felt was cold. I'd never killed folks before. I was froze stiff. Out 'a fear, mad, and hate, I kept lookin' him square in the eye; could sense this was not gonna end well. I figured I'd better get ready to defend myself. So, usin' both my hands and thumbs, I cocked the gun quick 'fore ol' Blood Moon know'd I'd even done it. The sound was like a scream in the night shoutin' danger. Time seemed to stop. The woods went plumb quiet. My world got to feelin' really small, but still, too big.

It can't be good for a body to be lookin' down the barrel of a powder primed flintlock short gun, and it cocked. Knowin' they's no way to get out from the lead ball headin' your way if it fired. No sir, that sound got his attention. Let him know I'd look after myself if pressed. I was near shakin' with fear. What had I done?

"I aim to kill you young one," said Blood Moon. "I know your name, Jebediah. I know your family now, too. I have seen the mother. I know of the father. He troubles me very little. We will find what we search for. Nothing can keep us from our path. The woman must come back with us across the big ridges to the west. Once there, our women will cut her, so she can never run again. Remove her tongue to end her talk. Her words will have no place in this life. I know you are going to where she lays. The spirit one has her medicine pouch. You have made a threat against the brave warriors of the west. We do not need you, boy. I have decided it is time for you to die. Now, make the evil one smoke, or I will take it from you, then send you to be with the ancestors. Which will it be, brave, foolish child?" He paused for just a second 'fore startin' at me like a cat.

I never saw any movement, but somehow, he sent an unseen word to the others. They all started movin' toward us at once. I looked around at Peter. He was gettin' nervous as one 'a the warriors was comin' up from behind. I could tell Jim was ready to fight by how tight his neck muscles had got. His ears commenced to turnin' front to back, strainin' to follow the danger. He was mule mad. His eyes show'd it when he turned his head back to see about me. I loved that mule.

This was not goin' good at all. To protect me and Anne, I reasoned I was gonna have to shoot the mean, little man comin' at me. He weren't givin' me no choice. My gut told me it was him or me, no matter what the rest of 'em did. I steadied the barrel. Closed my eyes tight. Started pullin' on the trigger waitin' for the gun to explode against my arms, then kill. It seemed to take forever. The trigger pull was firm. I weren't ready. I wondered if Anne was, now that there was a need for killin'. I kept pullin' the trigger, thinkin' it should go off. The thuds I heard shortly after closin' my eyes was not the boom I was expectin' when flint hit steel. Then I realized of a sudden, I never pulled the trigger.

The next sound I heard was from the gun Anne was holdin'. She did pull the trigger. I figured for sure at least one Indian was dead. I opened my eyes to see Blood Moon layin' to my left flat out on the ground along with the warrior closest to his right. Blood was leakin' from their ears, nose and mouths. The others was still alive, backin' up ever so slowly from the biggest Indian the mountains had ever seen, George Black Oak. He was usin' his favored war club. The rest 'a them varmints was fixin' to have a really bad day if they stuck around. Black Oak was known all over the mountains, and among The Lost, too.

Two of the warriors broke, run off like scared chickens. The third weren't as lucky as his mates. Black Oak took him to his knees with the front edge of his war club as he turned to try and leave with the others. The warrior was kinda sittin' on his rump with his head tilted back to the sky. His hands held together in front of his face. White bone stickin' out from the top of his thigh. I could understand enough of their language to know the warrior was pleadin' for his life in Cherokee. It was a sight I would never forget. Black Oak laid him out cold.

The one Anne shot at made three what run off. I don't think she give him nothin' more than a deaf ear. We couldn't find no blood like he'd been hit. Even Black Oak looked but found nothin'. I allowed he could just go on. That was one lucky Indian 'cause all three of his friends had busted heads, thanks to Black Oak, brought on from their desire to kill us. We left 'em layin' stone cold dead where they fell.

Black Oak got Jim by the lead. Started walkin' on down the Path like nothin' was wrong. Leavin' the dead where they'd fell, their blood soakin' the ground around 'em. We simply left the curve at Sharp Rock, makin' our way on down the Keowee Path to Panther Cave. Not a single word spoke between us — Black Oak leadin' Jim, Peter followin', me and Anne now sittin' with the pistols back in their place. We got to feelin' the cold after a ways, so we wrapped Momma's heavy quilt back tight around us. Somehow, I could smell her sweet scent in the quilt. My senses had never been so sharp. I reasoned that's the way it was when killin' had to happen. I liked it.

None of us said anything for a good while. Me and Anne weren't used to all this type 'a goin' on; where Black Oak, Dad, Cain, and Dancing Bear was. We weren't warriors. We'd never seen real killin'. Anne had seen folks die from different ailments or hurts, but never seen killin' in full person. It just didn't seem like what happened was real. Them warriors was alive just some time before, now they was dead. I felt like I had a part in their death. Like I'd help land the killin' blows with Black Oak. The thought grabbed me in the gut. Talk wouldn't come for me even if I'd 'a tried. My gut was sick.

I felt for Black Oak. He'd made the killin' blows but weren't showin' no feelin's over what he'd done. I know he felt different inside. It had to be hard for him, judgin' from the way I felt inside, even though their aim was to kill me. Seein' death, and causin' death, was two different things. The gut sick I felt was just from seein' life taken. I couldn't imagine what his guts was feelin' like from takin' life. He had to be handlin' it in some way I couldn't understand. Still, you'd not know it by lookin' at him. He was a true Cherokee warrior.

I studied on what happened as we rode 'til way past where we split from the Keowee Path, takin' the side trail to Panther Cave. I settled on the fact it was just a life-changin' reminder to all of us how close death really was when you called the mountains home. More so, if you went around threatenin' folks and scarin' young 'uns. The Cherokee, for sure, had a real concern over that type 'a behavior. They'd not stand for it, which was now upfront obvious to me.

I couldn't wait to talk with Wolf and Cain about all of it. I would feel better after I did. Of that, I was sure. I didn't figure they'd find much concern from the killin'. Death like that was a part of the Cherokee life. They was raised to it. Common to the Indians who fought for all they had.

***

I was not the one Dad was expectin' to see walk out from the woods just as Old Man Sun was settin' for the night, so he didn't shoot me. It was still good light. Dad know'd right off who I was. Anne and Peter was followin'. We'd left Black Oak with Jim and the wagon at the bottom of the steep. They weren't no trails Jim could pull the wagon on anywhere near Panther Cave. We'd tied him off a ways from the side trail out 'a sight, then Black Oak slipped away into the woods to watch from a hidin' place. Me and Anne left leadin' Peter headin' for the cave. It was most important to get her there quick as we could. We'd still not spoke of the killin'.

Dad was hid off to the east away from the front of the cave openin'. I never seen him, even though I was watchin' close as I walked. When he seen me come from the woods leadin' Peter, he hollered. I near died 'a fright. I weren't healed up from seein' folks get kilt yet. Got me more nervous than common. My heart was already beatin' hard from the climb, and I weren't expectin' to see Dad. He must 'a know'd about the visitors from the west to be outside the cave sittin' watch. Maybe it was a sign the woman still walked on our side of the river. He broke from the place he was hidin' and come our way as me and Anne started toward him.

"Dad," I near hollered back as I left Anne and Peter and took off runnin' toward him. I was so glad to see him I near cried as I ran and jumped up to give him the tightest hug around his big ol' neck I could muster, my feet swingin' free from the ground. It made my soul complete bein' in his arms. I squeezed hard as I could. It felt so good holdin' on the way I was. It didn't hurt him. He was strong like the bear, and tough.

"I'm sorry we weren't home at the proper time," I said as I pulled back some, starin' him in the eye. "I figure you've been in Panther Cave, seen the hurt woman. I trailed home by my lonesome, Dad, with Peter and the pack mule to get Anne. Ain't you proud? Now we are here for Anne to mend the hurt one if there is still a need. I hope the woman is alive. When I left to fetch Anne, she looked ready to go on home to Jesus. I was tellin' Anne on the trail here I thought she would be gone when I got back. Is she alive? How is Wolf? Is he okay? How 'bout you? How are you, Dad?" I moved in for another squeeze around his neck, then kept on, "I am so glad you are here. We've brought the harvest wagon to take her home in. Black Oak is back down in the holler with Jim, waitin' to hear from us. He said to tell you the valley has visitors. Some are travelin'."

"I am well, Jeb," Dad answered as he unwrapped my arms from his neck. Set me back down on the ground. He give Anne a quick hug, then commenced to leadin' her to the cave door.

Then, Dad said, "The woman is alive. I think Anne will have good fortune with her. She has some strength, but I have yet to hear her talk. I came to the cave early this morning. I was waitin' outside for any unwanted folks to show. I am glad it is you that came, not the mean ones. Black Oak needs to come here. Help us guard this woman until she can grow strong enough to leave. Her healin' enough to travel could take a few days. The warriors of The Lost will find us here in time. They are sure to find your trails same as me. We must be ready."

Anne and I stopped cold in our tracks. Looked at each other kinda strange like. What Dad said *weren't* funny, but for some reason, we started laughin'. I mean belly laughin'— gut bustin', tear makin', muscle crampin', fallin' to our knees laughin'. We couldn't help it. It felt like we was laughin' at the dead, which could bring trouble for Anne, but they weren't no stoppin' it. We laughed for a good while. We'd get a hold on it for a bit, then a quick look up at Dad would get us goin' again. He just sat down to wait. This went on 'til our bodies just plain run out 'a laugh. After we settled, we looked each other in the eye. That started us to huggin', and cryin' hard.

The look on Dad's face was pure question mixed with a little mad. We weren't actin' right for woods livin'. It was reckless. But what he didn't know was, we'd near been killed. Seen killin' close up. Threatened with death, then saved from death. The hurt built up after it all happened had to get out. The feelin's we was sufferin' from proved too hard to hold in. Our little fit was the worry of it all bustin' out. Them warriors was bent on killin' at least me. Then seein' 'em dead from bein' alive right in front of us confused our spirits. It felt to me like I'd held a sickness in as long as I could, and it had to come out. Obviously, Anne felt the same. We'd held it in all we could. It was time we let it out. I felt normal again, once the fear, anger, and hate got clean of me. We settled down.

Anne got control enough to explain to him why we was carryin' on the way we was 'cause he looked real confused. "You don't gotta worry over them Indians no more, Dad. That is why we carried on like we did. Don't ask us to tell you the what for of all of it. Just sit with Black Oak when you get time. Maybe he will tell you. It is only something he should speak of. Trust us when we tell you, the warriors who are visiting from The Lost will no longer be a problem on this trail. In fact, those visitors won't be a bother to anyone, if the truth is told. But as I said, Black Oak will be the one to tell this story. Out of respect to him, it is not for us to tell. Now let's go in to see the one who has caused all this trouble. If she lives, maybe we can help her."

She explained it clear enough. Dad know'd Black Oak had done somethin' serious. Seein' the look on his face, I believed Dad know'd what. To him it was simple, the little warriors was a threat… now they weren't. Could only mean one thing if Black Oak was there. He'd told Dad in his message the visitors was "travelin" or "some was travelin," which had meanin' to Dad after Anne's words. It wouldn't 'a been no surprise to him what George did. Black Oak was a Cherokee warrior. Cherokee took care of their own. We was part of Black Oak's own. To Dad, it was just that simple.

Chapter Ten

Momma Takes a Trail

Momma didn't like the thought 'a bein' alone after she'd found trespassin' sign the morning me and Anne left for Panther Cave. She had no notion as to when Dad would be back for sure. Maybe a few days; several days; weren't no tellin'. No tellin' how long it'd be 'fore we all got home, neither. She weren't scared to be by herself on occasion, but knowin' folks was about made her more nervous than common.

She reasoned it'd be a good time for her to go visit Rose and Cain. She'd not seen 'em in a while. Felt the need to make sure all was fine in their new home. She got excited at the thought 'a goin' for a visit. Been a time since she'd got out in the woods on her own to enjoy the Great Creation. Got her blood up thinkin' on all of it. She loved the freedom of trailin' alone. She was comfortable doin' it.

She'd seen the trespassin' sign just after daylight on her way to the barn for feedin'. There was tracks in the yard, circlin' 'round the barn and near the wood shed. She could tell they'd been in the house, too, searchin'.

Findin' all that got her worried at first, then she got mad. Started wishin' she'd got a look at the rude visitors what trespassed on her home. It would 'a been good to know who they was, where they'd come from, and why their tracks was so small.

Momma didn't typically mind folks comin' around, but she'd not tolerate rude behavior. Them slippin' around like they did, not lettin' her know they was there, was considered rude behavior. It spooked her. Got her back up. 'Sides, they'd got mud and dirt on her fresh-swept floors from dirty foot skin leavin's. One of 'em track'd in chicken droppin's from the back 'a the house. They was spots of it stuck to Momma's cook room floor. You could see where he'd walked through the back door, 'round the Lazy Susan eatin' table, and back out. She figured that Indian to be stupid. What warrior would step in a pile while he was watchin' where he was steppin', slippin' around all quiet like?

Ooh! She was mad. A little scared on top of it. She cleaned up their mess. Changed into her winter skins. Laced up her Cherokee-made, beaver skin, knee-high foot skins with beaver tail soles. Ready to go, she raked down the fire, closed the damper on her cook stove, and packed a pouch with all her possibles, allowin' space for a thing or two she'd made for her new daughter-in-law, whom she adored. She left word on the message stone what laid on the hearh tellin' Dad where she'd gone and for him to come to Cain's when he got home. She planned to stay there 'til he come for her. Fetchin' her rifle, powder and ball, a couple quilts, her best tobacco pouch and favorite pipe, she closed the house and headed for the barn. Once there, she throw'd enough heavy meat-bone scraps out to last the dogs a few days, put out extra hay and meal for the stock, then saddled Dad's best ridin' stallion, Brutus. Man, that horse was strong. Smart, too. It was all Dad could do to ride him. Momma never had a problem, though. He minded her much better than Dad. It kinda seemed like that horse had a fondness for Momma.

Tyin' off the poke across the horse's rump, she slid her rifle into it's leather home to the right side 'a the saddle. Her left foot found the leather-backed stirrup to mount. With the smoothness of a hawk jumpin' from a tree limb, she swung her right leg across the horses back, settlin' her bottom in the saddle's seat. Her right foot landing solid in the base of the right-side stirrup. Easin' Brutus out from the barn toward the woods, she give him some rein. With a big nod of his head, and a hard shake that had Momma standin' in the stirrups to stay mounted, he calmed and trotted off toward the trail that would take Momma for a visit. Cain and Rose would be surprised. It weren't but a half day's ride if you was a good rider, Momma was.

She had plenty 'a time to get there. Her desire was to make it 'fore dark. Supper would soon follow since it got dark early. It was still first of the morning, so she had no intention of hurryin'. She figured to stay a few days and wait for Dad. It would be good for her. She'd been needin' time away from the farm. Some fresh trail air was just the thing to revive her spirit. Folks spent a lot of time indoors durin' the cold time. They got stale. The thought of bein' out was refreshin' to her soul. It was a good time since spring weren't due for a few more moons. They weren't much in the way 'a chores to take care of. 'Sides, everybody was gone.

It was cold. She didn't care. Her clothes was first-rate, Cherokee-made skins. She'd be takin' her time, enjoyin' the trail. The thought of seein' her family got her excited. Cain and Rose's place was deep in the woods. Not a problem for Momma. Her growin' up in the mountains with my granddad made her trail savvy, and we all know'd she could shoot.

The weather was near perfect for the ride. And as Old Man Sun got to shinin', Momma could tell Dad's horse was lettin' her know he needed to cut loose some, achin' to get on down the trail, feelin' the call so to speak. She'd kinda been havin' to hold him back ever since they'd got out in the woods good. She know'd it'd been a while since him and Dad was out for a good run. He was feelin' the pull of the trail. Momma know'd what he wanted; know'd horses well enough to understand his needs. She was skittish to turn him loose since she hadn't rode for a while, but know'd she had little choice in the matter if she wanted to ride. The only other option was to get off and walk him. That was not her plan for this trip. She got excited in her middle knowin' what was fixin' to happen. Brutus was makin' it clear, at some point he would go. He was gonna run out. That was a given. Better for her to pick the time.

She could not hold him much longer. The muscles in her arms got to screamin' the farther they rode. She got shaky, her legs began to quiver, and there was cramps in various places from her feet on up. It was time. The trail was opening up — the trees farther apart. The ground now smooth and flat. She know'd the trail. Weren't really a better place to let him go than right where she was. He'd calm down once he got the need from his run out, so she decided to give in to him. She got her body ready. Bending from the waist in a solid ridin' position, she caught a strong hold on the reins givin' Brutus some slack to move his head. Set her legs back a little for better balance, then tighten'd up her knees in a kinda pinch to help hold steady. She leaned in close to his neck whisperin', "Okay boy. I'm with you." Committin' herself to him, her heart began to pound. She could feel his, too, in the sides of her knees. He was ready. Both know'd what was comin'. She was dizzy with excitement.

He felt her relax. The reins loosen a bit to free his head for runnin'. Know'd she'd just give him permission to take her for a ride.

So, it commenced. He got to lettin' his legs out slowly, reachin' fast not long after she'd settled in. It was dangerous, her ridin' like she was. Trees was flyn' by like the wind. Horses could run, but they could fall, too, and a tree could come on her real quick if she didn't ride tight. Holdin' the side of her face flat against his neck, the reins held short but firm in her hands, she could smell him. Hear his breathin'. Felt his mane blowin' against her neck and shoulders, in her face. The trail, bein' more open where they was, allowed Brutus to stay clear of all the trees. They weren't much danger to Momma, 'cept for the chance of fallin' off a full-grow'd stallion runnin' wide open through the woods. Death was close, him movin' like he was, but she trusted him; know'd he would make sure the ride was safe as possible for her. He did, fast but smooth. She was as close to heaven as a body could get on earth. She loved ridin' a good horse. Brutus matched 'em all.

He was down the trail like a rabbit bein' chased by a slick hound dog. It was all Momma could do to stay the saddle in a few places, but she did. It'd been a while since she'd rode like that. Made her wonder how long he would run the way he was. It would be a chore to stop him if he weren't ready. She reminded herself she was in no hurry, wantin' to take her time. She know'd no horse can run such distance through the woods at the pace he was travelin' for very long, so she let him keep on. He proved her right. Weren't long 'til he got to slowin' down, 'bout the time she figured him to. Knowin' he just needed to get the smell of a stale barn out from his nose. Loose the stiffness in his legs from not gettin' to run much. Momma had obliged him by stayin' the saddle. Keepin' him headin' straight. Her backside would pay the price for the ride, but to her, it would be worth it.

The excitement of bein' on the edge, like you are when a horse is runnin' right out, made her feel free like young love again. Made her remember the time when she and Dad courted. Ridin' Grandad's horses back-and-forth to each others' homes. Runnin' through the mountains without a care other than for the love you was feelin' for the one you was with. I loved my momma. She was the best. I praised God for her, and my dad, every day that I lived. They was good folks. Brought me up proper.

I hated to think about the day they would go home to be with Jesus. I'd catch myself thinkin' on that at times. I reckon a young 'un thinks on them things. Kinda selfish really, if you thought it through. Dad never seemed to study on it none; least he never talked about it. He was never worryin' over things he had no doin's with. He told me true many times. He turned all his worries over to Holy Spirit when he prayed at night. Then again when he read the Good Book in the mornings. That was it whenever it come to strugglin' with concerns. He said it was the way God wanted us to be. No need for worryin'.

"The Bible says you get one 'a them sin marks in the Life Book whenever you worry over things, not let God tend to it," Dad would explain to us. "He knows the worry 'fore you ever tell him. He just wants you to talk to Him about it, let Him know your troubles. I study things out, layin' my burdens at the foot 'a the cross. The worry spirit stays shed 'a me."

She'd rode near halfway to Cain's when the hunger hit her hard enough to make her need to stop and eat. Her dinner camp was by a little branch in an open sunny spot just under a small top west 'a Cain's place. She built a good size warmin' fire, took off Brutus' saddle and blanket, then tied him to a small saplin' just off the trail. Grabbin' a heavy quilt from her possibles, she hurried back to the fire to get warm. Once there, she commenced to rollin' it out on the ground in a sunny spot up close to the fire. She sat on the folded side while she ate a bite. The food made her realize she was more hungry than she'd felt.

Done with her eatin', she got kinda lazy feelin'. Removin' her foot skins, she laid 'em out flat close to the fire crossways on the quilt for a pillow. She planned to lay on the fireside half 'a the quilt and use the other half to lay across herself for cover. Wanted to take a nap to let her food settle.

She then took off the heavy outside layer of winter skins, strechin' 'em out flat from her footskin pillow to lay on. She was wearin' a single layer 'a homespun garments under her skins for the trip, but they weren't enough to turn the cold without her top skins. The fire, with half the quilt, was gonna have to help with that. Old Man Sun was smilin' down on her. She could feel his warmth as she crawled inside her quilted cocoon. It was a reminder just how cold it got in the mountains and how the winter skins she wore kept her warm, alive. She thanked God for all He'd blessed her with. She wrapped half of the thick, heavy quilt over her person as she laid down on her skins. Her backside howled as she rolled up tight in the quilt, already feelin' the rub 'a not ridin' in a while.

The heat from the fire, the popping of the coals, the warmth of the quilt and Old Man Sun, left-over biscuits and ham from breakfast, and the winter quiet of the woods where she lay made her plumb comfortable. Without her stoppin' it, she fell asleep. Life was good for her, good for her family. Before her eyes got too heavy and closed for sleep, she prayed it stayed that way.

It was some time past mid-day when she woke. Her fire was down, growin' cold. Old Man Sun was nearly finished with his hottest shinin' of the day. Wouldn't be long 'til he would head more west to start the evening.

The heat from Old Man Sun felt good on her body as she laid half the quilt back on the ground, exposin' her full body to his light. Oh, the heat felt good, so warm and comforting. She felt as though she could bathe in it; soak it up through her skin. Her spirit wanted to drink it up. She couldn't help herself. She wanted to feel the light on her body full-on. She stood, tryin' to get even closer to the heat, but could not feel it enough. She stripped off her top layer of homespun, lettin' her bare bosom show to the midday light much like the Cherokee. It felt hot, soothing. She held her arms out to the side to catch more heat. Old Man Sun was burnin' into her body, stingin' her breast. She needed more. With a quick slide of her arms down her legs, she dropped the bottoms of her homespun, then stepped out onto the quilt. She now stood full-on naked head-to-toe before God, and whatever else was in the woods. It didn't bother her none. It felt spiritual, natural, her naked body standin' before the heat of God's own creation. She soaked in it. Rubbing herself like water was runnin' down over her. She felt like bein' in our hot tub right after Dad filled it with hot water. The heat steamin' through her blood. It was too much. She was overcome. Fallin' flat to her skins, she laid out whole in her body's weakness. Her soul was full. Complete rest had found her.

She come whole after a bit. Slipped on her homespun undergarments and winter skins, then slowly commenced to lacin' up her foot skin boots. She had to do it slowly 'cause her fingers weren't workin' just right from the cold. She gathered together her truck and saddled up Brutus. The skies was growin' darker lookin' like they might shed some snow later. She hit the trail at a good walk. It was a couple more miles to Cain's. She'd slept a bit longer than she'd intended, but there was light enough 'fore dark to arrive by supper, even though the days was short durin' cold time.

It was hard to see in places 'cause 'a clouds that was blockin' the light. She know'd the trail, though, makin' it fine. The woods was thick, oak and chestnut mostly. The dogwood, maple, and hickory found a place to root there, too, but they weren't many of them. Dancing Bear had give Rose and Cain the choice of any of his land to homestead as a wedding gift. They'd chose a near-perfect spot for their homeplace, left by a Cherokee man and his wife who had to move on. A flat clearin' with an orchard already growin' in among the giant trees. They was room for a stock barn and corral, a good-sized garden, and corn field. And, it had good water, Wolf Creek branch, which was important if you wanted to grow enough vegetables to store year 'round, have food for folks and stock. The peach and apple trees was important, too, for makin' dried fruit, jams, and brandy. Of course, hard cider was for medicinal needs and celebrations.

Dad, Dancing Bear, Black Oak, and some others had helped Cain and Rose set up their new home. They'd all worked many hours buildin' them a smokehouse, wood shed, spring house, corn crib, chicken coop, ground cellar, and a fresh water still for turnin' apples and peaches into hard cider. The earth around the place was rich. Food grow'd good if planted when the signs was right, which was also very important if you wanted to eat year 'round. The land had been cleared by the Cherokee family and farmed for many seasons. When they got too old to keep a place, they'd give it all back to Dancing Bear. Moved on to live with younger family. The branch was close to the east, providin' fresh water.

Like Dad's, from his pond to his tub back at our place, Cain run a bamboo trough from a little ways up the branch to a water barrel some thirty paces off from their back porch. It ran constant, keepin' a barrel full with a spout about half way down from the top, runnin' steady for drinkin'. Real good for fillin' jugs and buckets. The water from the spout filled a short trough that carried it on to a cistern that lay in the ground some three feet deep just inside the corral. It was lined complete with smooth flat rocks carried from the branch. It held all the water the stock needed. From there, the overflow ran back to the branch. It was smart the way they'd done it. Mindin' the troughs was the only real concern. Leaves fallin' in, or hard rains and run off, messed 'em up at times.

Down at the end of the clearin', the branch come close to the edge of the woods. Dad and Cain built a hemlock washin' tub just like ours with an iron pot for heatin' water. It was just as nice for them to bathe in as the one Dad built for Momma. Seems like most of the Collins folk I ever met was smart; respectful too, mostly. Never met but a couple I'd not claim as kin.

Dad's horse was strong, he could ride all day at a good clip if needed. Momma was just walkin' him while she rode; watchin', lookin', kinda huntin', not payin' much mind. Her backside was sore. Dark was comin', but she was well within' range to make it to Cain's 'fore it come on good.

She'd eat and rested and was now enjoyin' God's creation from the back of a smooth ridin' horse. The woods was so nice with all the sounds you'd expect, includin' the near-constant breeze; gentle, slippin' through the trees. It was like a quiet voice whisperin' you a story as you traveled;

seemed like you could hear the words if you listened real hard. She loved it all: livin' in the woods, survivin' the way she and Dad and all of us did, and bein' a family together. They was good providers. She and Dad loved each other more than the whole put-together of the whole of it all. She loved her family, too. She was most thankful for the wonderful woman God had chosen for Cain. He seemed to be happy. The last she'd seen of 'em they was cozy in their new life.

It was a glimpse, just a glimpse, but it was a glimpse. It got her attention. Somethin' movin' through the woods caught her eye. She turned in the saddle, unsheathed her gun while easin' off the horse. An unseen slip of her hand into the oilskin shot pouch fetched her small antler powder horn carryin' five good loads. It took her skilled hands next to no time to prime the gun for live shootin'. Bein' skilled got her movin' on whatever it was she'd seen real quick-like. Her motion from her seat on the horse to the ground was fast. I know'd she could shoot. She shattered the bow out 'a the hand of 'The One Nobody Speaks Of' when he come to find Rose durin' all the trouble with the Yonah bunch. If it was a deer, she could take it to Cain. They would have fresh meat. If not, the gun would give her protection. But either way, she was goin' to see what it was. It looked dark in color.

She was cold. The excitement of the hunt, along with bein' chilled near to the bone, made her body quiver. She thought to hold real still when she draw'd a bead, if she draw'd a bead. Her stalk could work. She know'd she had a chance at a shot. Her feet was findin' quiet footin' as she slipped along on the thawed forest floor. Watchin'... listenin'... feelin'... easin' along several paces 'fore seein' it again. It moved in behind a huge chestnut, but never come out the other side. Turnin' the tree on her, hidin' as it slipped off, it put the tree directly between it and the thing it didn't know, which told her it was game meat. Deer, she figured. She moved on toward the huge tree to try and get close.

It was gone. She walked to where she'd last seen whatever it was. No sign. No stirred-up leaves. She couldn't figure it. Game meat would 'a left a mark if just in the slightest way. Here, there was nothin'. Dark. It was dark in color, but what kinda critter could move like that and leave no visible sign? Her senses was sharp from growin' up mountain folk, but the thing was gone. No sign 'a nothin'.

She moved back to the horse, took the powder from her gun, and sheathed it. Her left foot found stirrup again as her hands grabbed saddle horn; swingin' her right leg over the saddle 'til her tender backside found its seat. She was square on facin' forward, expectin' nothin' as she looked to the trail ahead while settling in the saddle. The dark thing was there. How had she missed it?

There is a look in the eyes of battle-tested Cherokee warriors once they've been scarred. The eyes starin' at her most assuredly held that look. Took her breath away just as her right foot settled into the leather stirrup. The sight made her heart near stop, her mouth go dry.

It was Indian, and not only Indian, but a Cherokee Warrior Indian. The thing she'd seen was human. It was standin' in the trail right in front of her with Brutus' reins in his right hand. His left arm raised to shoulder height. Palm open to her.

Where had he come from?

She never figured her sightin' for a man 'fore she settled in the saddle facin' him eye-to-eye. It was no Indian she'd ever met or seen before, but one she felt certain was no threat to her, even though he toted full battle truck with a couple warrior pouches. She sensed it right off after she gathered herself from her first shocking sight of him, and calmed down a little. It was his eyes what spoke to her. He had the eyes of Dancing Bear. It was not him, yet the eyes was his. Family, she reasoned, he must be family. He said nothing, simply turned with ease leadin' Brutus as they walked the trail on toward Cain's.

Who is he? It was botherin' her how he'd snuck up on her. The questions would have to wait as the solid-framed warrior released the reins, then broke into a trot, headin' east on the trail to Cain's. Brutus felt the pull. Momma give him rein to start his own trot. He was followin' the strange critter what was now leadin' his trail.

Her calm ride had turned into a story to be told around the fire about a meetin' from an unknown warrior who guided her trail. That was fine with her. She felt safe, more so than while she was travelin' alone. She'd be at Cain's soon. He and Rose would have answers for her questions. She hoped to talk to her new guardian. Expected to see him as Cain's log home come into sight. He was nowhere. The warrior had turned from the trail to Cain's.

Must 'a headed back up into the mountains. She caught another brief sight of him as he crossed a small top just south 'a Cain's place, trottin'. It always surprised her how well Indians moved through the woods. She wondered if he'd seen her by the fire after she'd woke from her nap?

***

She weren't dead, but she looked it. Her eyes was closed. Anne was on her knees to the woman's right, facin' the fire. Wolf was on his knees beside her head, next to the fire. Anne was lookin' to all the things Old Mother had taught her, tryin' to figure a way to save the woman. There was a milky-lookin' salve spread all over her side, in and around the wound. She couldn't figure what it was, nor what it meant. It weren't 'til Wolf explained what'd happened to us all that Anne understood.

"I believe it was the Spirit of the Holy One, Anne," Wolf told her. "It came as the bear. Left into the night without a word. Stayed only long enough to help. She woke while the Spirit was here. She was dead. I am sure. I was binding her for burial. She was cold. The wound had stopped leaking, yet, she woke for the bear. I believe what I saw happened. I also believe death still watches from a short distance."

Anne thought for a minute, then said, "No, Wolf, that's not how healin' in the body works. God can bring the dead to life, that is for sure. The Bible tells of great miracles done according to His will. But for this woman to have slept then woke, means only her blood is near dead. She has never lost the first life the Great Creator gave her. Old Mother has taught me, He will trespass into our lives very little. He expects us to learn. Do what we can with the talent He created us with. He is the Great Healer. I am nothing without His hand."

Anne woke everybody early the next morning after makin' sure the woman was still alive. She motioned for us all to go outside the cave; wanted to talk out 'a ear shot of the woman. I figured she had her plan to fight the woman's sickness as we gathered around outside the cave to listen. The top 'a Old Man Sun was just showin' over Horse Trough Mountain to the east. It was a beautiful morning to be in the mountains, but cold.

She began calmly, "Her blood is near turned. It's gonna be very difficult to save her here. I am sorry, but if we want to help her, we gotta get her back home into some hot, dry air. She has the lung sickness on top of all the other problems facin' her. Death is near, from the poison in her blood as well. She will die from either of those things if we don't get her home. It means we have to carry her down the mountain to the harvest wagon now, then somehow get her back to our place without all the moving killin' her. I gotta have my boiling kettle and dried herbs from home. I will brew up a tea she is gonna have to drink a lot of. We will need Black Oak to help carry her down. I will go tell him he is needed here, then I will stay with Jim and the wagon 'til ya'll come. Do not put her on Peter. Carry her in a quilt. Treat her gentle. Be careful not to drop her on the steep. We must do all we can to keep her still."

Anne was gone 'fore Dad ever said a word. She know'd he understood what to do. She left quick 'cause Black Oak needed to come as soon as he could to help get the woman down off the mountain, then loaded up so we could head for home. It sounded like time was fightin' hard against her.

Wolf and me went back in the cave and knelt down beside her to wait for Black Oak. Dad stayed on watch outside to be safe. Wolf began rubbin' her face with a wet piece of homespun, while we spoke for the first time in two days.

"She woke when Old Man Bear came to her, Jeb. I looked across the fire from where I was sitting. She had her eyes open as he nuzzled her. She was looking at me from back across the fire. I went to her. Spoke with her after the Spirit One went His way. I know her name. It is a name my mother will know. A name I know. She was stolen from the Yonah clan as a child. A raid from The Lost took her. She is of my mother's clan. That is why she came this way. They tell stories about her being taken away during a raid, of her father looking for many seasons trying to find her. My mother will be happy. The Yonah clan will be as well. Wind Is Strong, this woman, has finally returned to her home from a long journey. God is good. I pray he keeps her on this side of the river."

Wind Is Strong. It seemed a proper name for this creature of the woods who found herself in a strange land fightin' for her life among strange folk. She did not look strong right then, but common sense would tell, only a strong spirit could 'a come as far as she had with a wound like hers.

Wolf allowed she'd come home. I figured her home was across the low gap with the Yonah Valley clan. I still didn't trust that bunch. I know'd Dad and Cain had their feelin's, too, 'cause 'a some bad times there. This was different than those times. Wind Is Strong was not a part of all that. She was fightin' hard for her life and required help. We was helpin'.

We'd concern ourselves with who she was later. Everything would work itself out. None of it mattered anyway, if she died. I prayed she lived. Me and Wolf began to gather our truck and pack up our possibles. While makin' ready to leave, Wolf started talkin' to her as Old Man Sun climbed the eastern sky. She never said nothin' back. Wolf also thanked the bear sleepin' in the cave for his kindness in sharin'. I thought it foolish talk. That bear never know'd we was in the world. Lazy thing slept the whole time we was there. Wolf know'd it, too. He was just bein' polite. Showin' respect to its ancestors . . . to Brother Bear.

Chapter Eleven

Duty! Honor! Blood!

We left as soon as Black Oak made it to the cave. The cold mountain air felt like snow hittin' your face as the winter breeze snaked through the hollers, then up the sides of the big ridges surroundin' Choestoe valley. The ground was steep and rocky, which was hard on Dad and Black Oak as they near slid down the side 'a Blood Mountain totin' Wind Is Strong. She only had a simple layer of quilts keepin' the cold off. We was afraid to move her what it would take to dress her in winter skins. Anne allowed the cold was good. Slow'd the blood poision spreadin'. She still had the crawlies 'cause Anne weren't gonna fool with the dustin' 'til she got stronger; figured the powder might hinder her breathin' since her lungs was gettin' thick.

Wolf said our sleepin' bear friend never stirred durin' the whole put-together. Snored plumb through the whole of it all. Wolf said it was spiritual, but not near as spiritual as Old Man Bear comin' to heal the hurt one. Cleanin' her wound. Prayin' over her. That's what Wolf said it looked like. Kinda like a preacher prayin' over some poor sinner as he put his front paws up on her. Commenced to rollin' her like he did. He'd not told me the whole story yet, but he'd told me some. I wondered if it was my brother bear. We'd not know 'cause it never show'd Wolf its chest. He never saw whether or not it had the cross star.

Black Oak and Dad doubled one 'a Momma's big quilts in half. Then used it to carry Wind Is Strong down the steep to the wagon. She weren't heavy. They was handlin' her just fine once clear of the rocks. Me and Wolf was walkin'. Leadin' up front with Peter, while keepin' sharp eyes out for anything movin' up ahead. Dad and Black Oak had to watch their footin'.

The cold time was a dangerous time. Meat eaters was hungry. Leaf eatin' critters was hungry. Even Dad's stock was hungry. He'd put the stock on just a few oats, a little hay, and a touch 'a salt each day that he sprinkled over their oats. It was toward the end 'a winter. He had to watch out so we'd not run low on provisions. They weren't no tellin' how long the cold time would last. If spring was a long time comin', and no new grass got to growin' in the pastures, the stock would suffer. It would be a hard time if we ran out 'a food for them. They was folks that'd be hungry, too.

"I didn't have no troubles on the trail home for Anne, Wolf," I said as we finished the steep, stoppin' to wait for Dad and Dancing Bear in the flat next to the wagon. We climbed up on Peter's back.

Then, I told him, "I did have a come together in a big chestnut tree holler, though. It was plumb spiritual. Like haints was around me. I figure I got trail savvy now 'cause after I come to my realizin', I weren't scared no more. What say you, Wolf? You allow it was spiritual? Near Cherokee, reckon?"

Wolf was quiet for a spell, then he said, "My friend, you have said. We will smoke on this tonight. Ask the spirits if they see you as Cherokee or settler. It is my feeling you are on a trail that only time can make you see. You must wait for the answers. The woods are wise."

What? There it was then. More Indian mumble that didn't do no more than confuse a body. Wait for answers. The woods are wise. You'd 'a thought I'd asked him whether or not the world was gonna end. Sometimes you just did better to keep your thoughts to yourself. It was near frustratin' conversin' with a Cherokee. It felt spiritual to me. That's what I was gonna keep ahold to. He was my best and true friend, but there was times when I wanted to grab him up quick and shake the words from his mouth. I never did. I know'd better. We couldn't whup one another. It got real messy when we went to wrestlin'.

Anne had pulled the wagon to the flat where the main trail and the steep come together 'fore we got off the steep. Made a bed in the back with the extra quilts Momma sent. She was sittin' on the very back with her legs hangin' off from the knees when we got there, waitin', ready to get goin'. Dad and Black Oak had no trouble layin' Wind Is Strong on the soft bed, her feet pointin' forward toward Big Jim. Anne turned her back against the side of the wagon, then stretched her legs across the back so they could lay Wind's head in her lap. It wouldn't be real comfortable for Anne, but it would make the bouncin' of the wagon better for the hurt one.

She had survived the trip off Blood Mountain. She was alive, least for the time bein'. What little jerky broth Wolf was able to get in her had provided just enough strength to fight a little more. It would be better now with Anne tendin' to her. She might get well if she could tolerate the tea she was gonna have to drink for the next several moons. The blood poison was gonna hit her hard soon. Anne was prayin' Old Mother would come to help. She needed her wisdom for what Wind Is Strong was gonna have to suffer through. The healin' to come would be very painful for her. Of that, there was no doubt.

"I left the meat layin' in the door of the barn when I unstrapped the mules, Wolf. All our truck is there, too," I said as we pulled Peter in behind the harvest wagon, trailin' for home. "I hate I didn't tend to it proper. I was real hungry, near exhausted. All I could find strength to do was wash some, eat, and fall in bed while Momma packed our truck for the trail back. Anne and me left 'fore light yesterday morning to hurry back here. There was just no time to tend to it all. Cold as it is, unless somethin' hungry comes around, it all should be good. We can hang it today when we get back."

Wolf said, "It is good you made it back to Panther Cave with Anne, Jeb. You are right in thinking the meat will be fine because of the cold. There is plenty if we need to share with any of the woods. The cold time is hard on them as well. What's good is, the injured one is with the living. I believe Anne will make her stay. Her heart must be very strong; her spirit, too. We will sing songs about her around our fires." Wolf seemed more worried for the woman than our meat or truck.

He had a big heart. Felt for most everybody, but I know'd he could 'a pulled the trigger on them outlaw warriors. There was no question in my mind on that. Rightful killin' would not come hard to him. He would not 'a thought twice 'fore shootin' ol' Blood Moon. Him bein' Cherokee would 'a made that a fact.

I was ridin' front on Peter, Wolf behind. He'd learned he could stand on Peter's rump to see further down the trail than I could ridin'. He liked doin' that. Peter didn't seem to mind. He put his hands on my shoulders to stand when I turned my head a little. Told him to wait. I had somethin' I needed to tell him. He would know how we should feel about Black Oak doin' the killin'. He was gonna see it anyway. Their bodies was layin' by the side 'a the Path. I wondered if Black Oak had told Dad?

"What is it my friend. What have you to tell me?" asked Wolf as he settled back down on Peter's back.

I slowed Peter some, wantin' to fall back from the wagon a little. I needed to talk to my friend on the private, not be heard. Anne was watchin' us as she comforted Wind Is Strong. Probably wonderin' why we was slowin' up. I finally stopped Peter. Jumped down from his back to run into the woods like I was goin' for nature's call. I figured that would answer any questions she might have concernin' what we was doin'. Wolf followed me, once he know'd Anne couldn't see him anymore. He tied Peter to a young oak 'fore comin' on after me.

We moved off into the woods some as the wagon topped a little rise out 'a sight. Black Oak and Dad was guidin' Jim from the wagon seat, talkin'. Black Oak liked to talk to folks. They never looked back at us. Anne was rubbin' Wind's head last I saw. Looked like she was talkin' to her.

We sat so we could talk proper. I caught the strong, musty scent of the forest floor as we settled, crossed legged, facin' each other. It was a little sunny spot on the side of a little deer trail what caught the trunk of a huge white oak. He pulled his small knife. Commenced to shinin' the blade on his winter britches. He could see I was troubled. He waited for me to think a minute 'fore he said anything.

"What is so troubling to you, Jebediah? You look lost. Like you are in a place with no light," Wolf said kinda direct while lookin' me square in the eye. He reminded me of Cain the way he spoke when we made talk.

I was studyin' on what to say to him. It felt plumb sinful tryin' to find words about killin'. Just thinkin' on it made me feel guilty. Like I was a part of it. Caused it to happen. I should keep it to myself if I was to blame, but I couldn't. It was burnin' me up inside wonderin'. I had to have him explain it to me. Find peace with it all. Holy Spirit done heard from me quite a bit over what'd happened. Give me comfort. Yet, confusion was still rakin' at my soul. I weren't sure about the why of it all. Had I caused it? Was their blood on my hands? Would God judge me for it? I was strugglin' to understand proper feelings, bein' I was only a young'un. Wolf and me was close. I could tell him anything. He would hold my words. My trust for him was unbreakable, as his was for me. If I could not speak with him on this, then there was no other person I should tell. It was a habit I would tend to. I gathered myself for our talk. After thinkin' another minute, I was ready to speak.

"It was awful, Wolf. The sound of a head bein' busted by a war club, just awful. I can't get the hearin' of it out 'a my mind. Black Oak did not hold back." I dropped my eyes from his, my gut sick.

"What? What are you telling me, Jeb? Say it clear. You saw Black Oak kill? Where? Why was there a need for this killing?"

"Me and Anne was on the trail back to Panther Cave, ridin' the harvest wagon with Jim pullin', Peter tied on the back. Anne had the reins. When we turned the curve around Sharp Rock, Blood Moon was standin' dead center the trail. He was wearin' paint, Wolf, had all his weapons, full battle truck. Anne had to whoa Jim up 'cause the evil one never offered to move. Once we was stopped good, the rest 'a his bunch come out from hidin'. Moved in around us, worryin' me and Anne a sight. I'd stocked Dad's short guns under a top quilt beneath the wagon seat that morning. Did it 'fore we left just in case any evil was to show. Had 'em handy, ready to fire. I reached for one, Wolf. Pointed it at him. Felt I had to. Dared him to move. I'd settled on shootin' him if he did. That's when it got strange. A feelin' come over me. Made me feel like I was in another world lookin' down on what was happenin'. A place where you don't do what you want but what you have to. It was like somebody, or something else, is movin' for you. I was fixin' to be in a fight for my life. I know'd it. Weren't no doubt in my mind, killin' was comin'. It come as a hard cold feelin' down deep inside. I did not like the fear of it none, but I got my back up, got ready. I cocked the gun so they all could hear. Set myself to pull the trigger when needed. Even started the pullin' chore as he commenced to comin' at me, but the flint never dropped, Wolf."

"What are you saying, Jeb?" Wolf said kinda confused-like, worry creasin' the space between his eyes. "Did he go away? I do not understand. Why did you not drop the flint on that heathen? What happened that you did not send him across the river?"

"That's what I was tellin' you, Wolf. I closed my eyes as I commenced to pullin' the trigger. I didn't want to see the ball cause death. I feared it. That's when I heard death. The sound of wood hittin' skull. Stopped me pullin' back on the trigger all together. I never pulled hard enough for the gun to fire, but Anne did. She let go on the Indian she was watchin', makin' the woods explode in my ears. Once the boom died, I heard more thuds off to my left. When I opened my eyes, Black Oak was there. Didn't know where he'd come from, but he was there. He was backin' two other warriors away with his war club. Blood Moon was layin' out cold, along with one more of the little warriors. Blood was leakin' from their nose, ears, and eyes. Another was sittin' on his behind, his legs stickin' straight out, bone showin' just above the knee of his left leg. He was quiverin' all over. His hands held up in front of his face beggin' Black Oak in Cherokee for mercy. It did him no good. Black Oak swung his club with both hands flattenin' the left side of his head. His right eye shot out like a hot coal poppin' from the fire landin' near Peter makin' him jump.

"Once he'd run the other two off, he looked all over for blood sign from the Indian Anne was guardin' but found none. He figured her to have missed. We was both real out 'a sorts."

"Where did Black Oak come from? Why was he there, Jeb? Did you know he was near?"

"No, I don't know. I asked him when we got to Panther Cave, but he said very little, other than we would speak on it later. I know'd not to ask anything else, Wolf. We left them Indians there. We didn't touch 'em. We didn't bury 'em. We didn't drag 'em away from the trail."

"They will be buried," Wolf explained. "The ones who ran away will come back. They will tend to them, bury them close, take their possibles back to their families. Black Oak would know this. That is why he left them where they lay and did not touch them. It could fall that the families will come back looking for revenge when they find out about their loved ones being killed. If so, you will be to blame same as Black Oak. For us, that is bad. They will look to make things square if they come. It could be their clan did not like these men who died. But to be safe, we will keep watch after the time of mourning, not let them slip up on us. I do not want them to kill you. I will fight them. My family will fight them. The Cherokee in the valley will watch when the story of what Black Oak has done travels. I think you will be safe. Do not pay mind over it for now. They have not found you. They cannot kill you until they find you."

What in the world did he just say? Kill me. Did he just say kill me? I was sure he did. I was confused. Why would they want to kill me? I didn't swing the club that crushed their skulls and sent them away. I weren't near strong enough for that. I'd just turned twelve recent. I was strong for my age, but not near man enough to fight warriors. I'd grow'd some. Momma had fed us good. Dad worked me hard. My muscles showed when I was bare on top. I could lift a full bag 'a ground corn meal. Load it in a wagon. Tote oats to the trough to feed the mules and swing a heavy hammer and maul to split firewood. I was even good at splittin' out fence rails with a wedge, hammer, and axe, but I couldn't 'a done what Black Oak did to them warriors. Him killin' them rats saved my life. I was sure proud 'a that. I guess God figured it was better for us if it was Black Oak what done the killin'. He was good at it. I still didn't know how he come to be there. I thanked God for mine and Anne's life. I hoped I would know peace over it. Black Oak, too.

"I wish Black Oak had 'a killed all them snakes, Wolf. Cleaned out the whole pit. Not let none get away. I see the value in killin' for protectin' now," I said lookin' him in the eye real concerned-like usin' my new trail face. "I don't wanna walk around lookin' over my shoulder all the time wonderin' if killin' is near. Why would they want the trouble 'a comin' back over here to cause more killin'? Ain't three dead enough? Family or not, they ought 'a let it go. Comin' back lookin' for me ain't worth dyin' over. But if that's the way it's gonna go, I aim to protect me and mine."

That is how Dad and Cain would have it. I was learnin' to understand things. How folks lived with death always near. I'd seen firsthand how it must be with the way Black Oak protected Anne and me. Life can be taken very quickly in the mountains. I remember Cain sayin' that many times. From then on, I would stay my soul. Keep death on a string. If it come lookin', I'd oblige it.

"My friend, you are speaking as a true warrior," Wolf said as he put his left hand on my shoulder, wrappin' his right hand around the handle of his short knife. "Jebediah, we are older now. You must understand our responsibility to the peoples of this valley. Dancing Bear has taught me. As long as we run these mountains, take trails to hunt or go on walks, we must watch for our lives, our families' lives, and the lives of those we love who live here. It is the way. I am Cherokee, true blood Cherokee. My ancestors have been raised in these mountains. I am taught in Choestoe by my own clan. I was born from Mother Earth. We know that every step on our Mother's body can bring death, hurt, or joy. It is a fact all Cherokee warriors must face. Since you and I are coming of age, we must accept this as our fate as well. It is an honor for our people to call on us. We have a duty to God, The Three in One, Mother Earth, and our families. We must do our part as one body, so all the valley will be strong. You and me, Jeb, we are becoming warriors folks will depend on. Set your mind to that, settle with it. I have been taught this from my first knowing of things."

Well, sometimes, Wolf just had a way 'a sayin' things, kinda like Dad. When Wolf spoke at them times, you couldn't help but understand exactly what he was sayin'. It was as plain 'a English talk as I'd ever heard spoke, serious in its meanin'. I suddenly felt more grow'd up, like folks was gonna be lookin' to me one day to do what Dad, Dancing Bear, and Black Oak did every day of their lives. Each generation has its own chore to look after the one ahead of it, same as the one comin' on behind. This was more than I thought I was able to take on, but Wolf seemed settled with it. I figured I'd have to come square with the notion, too. Killin' and death now seemed a bigger part of my life than when I'd left home at daylight. Made me wish I'd stayed in the bed and not got out on such a trail as I'd ended up on. I could see growin' up was gonna be more difficult on a body than I ever figured it to be. *God help me*! was all the prayer I could muster. It'd have to do for now.

I didn't want to study on the 'how come' of what he'd said. The fact my world had just got a little less comfortable put worry on me. I didn't feel scared about dyin' with the next sunrise, but I did start lookin' at my surroundin's different. Was the trail gonna bring us trouble around the next curve? *Could be*. Might strangers be makin' themselves seen as we pass through the next holler? *There was a chance*. Is death waitin' on us up ahead across the next top? *That was possible for sure*. Is there an ambush in the next ivy thicket? *I hoped not*. But if it come, I was ready. I allowed my experience in the chestnut holler was now most important. Had it not been for that little bit 'a spiritual growin', my day really would 'a been troublesome.

My mind jumped to folks. *Was Dad, Black Oak and Anne okay? Momma? Why am I worryin' over them? If they couldn't take care of themselves, what am I gonna do?* I wondered about 'em anyway. It was proper thinkin' for me as a coming warrior. I felt taller.

Something. I'd have to do something, now. Wolf said clear his dad would expect us to do whatever it took to make things safe in the valley. We must help whatever way they needed help, any way we could help. Life opened my eyes through the words and thinkin' of my best friend. Wolf had just changed the way I looked at the world by makin' me understand the responsibilities I had to accept over life matters. It matched the revelation I'd had in the chestnut holler. Holy Spirit was talkin' loud at me. It was a big chore for a little ol' body like me. I felt the weight. It felt… right.

"You have come to a reckoning, my friend, Jeb Collins," Wolf said as he took my right arm in his left hand. We stood. "It is with honor I call you my brother. It is with great concern that we leave our time as young ones, start down this trail of true life. This trail will have us see many things: good and evil, right and wrong, beautiful and ugly. We will make this walk as brothers. Now, let us share our spirits. Be true to the Great Creator as the brothers we have become."

As he draw'd his knife, I kinda know'd what was fixin' to happen. I just didn't know the exact of what it involved. My body went stiff, like I was gettin' ready to wrestle. He leaned his head back. Raised the knife overhead. Commenced to speakin' a prayer foreign to me. It was in perfect Cherokee, which I know'd very few words of. I was learnin' their talk but was far from knowin' what any of it meant, really. Most 'a the ones I ever met spoke good English. Made common talk among settlers with it. Of course, they all spoke their native tongue. Prayed that way often. It was difficult for me to understand.

He got done with his prayin', dropped his eyes square with mine. Lookin' at me like I was supposed to be doin' somethin' Indian. I had no idea what it was so I leaned in close. Asked him kinda in a whisper, "Do I do somethin'? I don't know what I'm supposed to be doin' now, Wolf."

"Yes, my friend. You are to hold still."

'Fore I know'd it, he moved rattlehead quick with his short knife cuttin' a two-inch slash on the inside of my right forearm just in front of my elbow. His cut was deep.

It hurt. I looked down. It was startin' to leak plenty, runnin' down my arm, then drippin' off my elbow to the ground. He'd cut me deep, but I acted like it weren't hurtin'. I watched as he changed hands with his knife. Moved the blade tip to the same place on his right forearm as he'd cut me. Without slowin' at all, he sliced his arm same as mine. Just as deep. It started leakin' quick too, about the same time as the real hell-fire stingin' of my cut hit me. It burned like when Old Man Bobcat tore me up. Felt like the claws what ripped my person. My mind flooded with painful memories, makin' the stingin' in my arm much worse. But, I couldn't show it. I never let on it hurt a bit. Wolf never did, neither.

He moved toward me. Slipped his bleedin' forearm inside my bleedin' forearm. Crossin' the inside of our forearms up cut-to-cut, settlin' his slash over mine. He pulled us up tight 'til our faces was near touchin', our eyes starin' tight. I could feel his blood mixin' with mine. It was the strangest thing. A stingin' feelin', but different than the stingin' what come with the slicin'. This was real. His blood and mine comin' together, our hearts pumpin' the mix. I seen then that's why the cut had to be deep. Our bloods was bein' pumped into each other's veins. I felt dizzy - like I could sleep. I leaned my head back and stared at the sky while Wolf held us tight. I saw Brother Bear walkin' in the clouds as my eyes closed. I could feel my soul bondin' with Wolf's. I promise you, I could. This was more than just swappin' some surface blood, this was real mixin'. We would carry the other's blood 'til death. This was serious doin's. Spiritual. I prayed God would hold me worthy of this new bein' I was becomin' as I lowered my eyes to meet Wolf's again.

"Listen to me, Jebediah Collins, my brother in blood," he said while holdin' our arms tight together, our faces close. "We are now holding each other's lives. You have a part of my life. I have accepted a part of yours. We are blood brothers from this day forward. Our lives now depend on the way each of us thinks for the other. We will watch each other's families. Protect and provide for them with our very lives if something was to happen, one for the other. May God, the Great Creator of all things, smile upon our bond of truth and friendship. My life for you and yours. Your life for me and mine. This is a binding oath for those closer than birth brothers, only to be known by blood-agreed warriors, a duty to honor for life. If you agree to this sacred covenant, then say. If not, walk away. Life will remain as it was before. I will still keep my blood oath to you. Which way shall it be, my brother, Jebediah Collins, of the Thompson Collins clan?"

There was only one thing I could or wanted to say as I draw'd us even closer with a pull of my arm, "Wolf, I am your brother, blood to blood. We are family, know I am true. My life for you and yours. Your life for me and mine. God holds our words as bond from this day forward."

He simply nodded to agree. Our lives had changed. We'd grow'd some. Now, we had more serious responsibilities to pay mind to. It was a lot for us to take on at our age, but I would have to worry over that later. My arm hurt.

Chapter Twelve

Brandy for the Pain

Wolf took a couple homespun rags from his possibles pouch. Wrapped and tied our arms 'fore we crawled back up on Peter. The cuts was still bleedin' some when we caught back up to the wagon. Anne looked. I know she saw the blood soakin' in the rags. A couple small streaks of crimson runnin' out from under then down our arms. She never let on she'd seen. She probably thought we needed tendin' to, but know'd what it all meant and kept quiet. Dad and Black Oak seen our arms, too, when we stopped after awhile to check on Wind Is Strong; but, they never said a word, neither. They had their own marks same place as ours. I'd seen 'em on both all my life. Wondered how they'd got such identical marks. Know'd enough about the way things was not to ask. Now I know'd first hand how they come by 'em. They was blood brothers, bound just like me and Wolf. Cain had a scar on his right arm from when him and Fox Running became one for the other as blood brothers. Least I know'd what mine was gonna look like. One thing was sure, bein' fresh blood brothers stung a right smart. My arm hurt a sight.

    I'd become a blood brother to a purebred Cherokee. Wolf was my blood brother. We rode on toward home after seein' to Wind. The more I got to thinkin', the more I figured Wolf got the slick end of that butter knife by makin' his oath with me. The Lost weren't gonna be mad at him over the killin'. That told me a lot about who he was. He know'd them dead warriors' families might want vengeance. Now he was tied in with me. I guess he figured that's what brothers do. I sure was proud.

They was gone! Nothing -- not a body in sight. We'd come up on Sharp Rock and the dead warriors was gone. No sign to tell they'd ever been a killin' there recent. Anne and me looked as we passed through the curve at Sharp Rock, the wagon never stoppin'. No blood show'd at any of the places the dead warriors had been layin'. I was up on Peter. I could see all around where the fight took place. No sign 'a nothin'. The leaves on the forest floor weren't even stirred up no more. The world had moved on. I watched Black Oak. He rode through like nothin' had ever happened there. Him and Dad just kept talkin' 'til way on past the Sharp Rock.

Wolf was right about them comin' back to fetch their own. They tended to the bodies. Packed their possibles for family folk, then trailed back west to tell what happened. My fate would prob'ly be decided by them when the time come. I, on the other hand, had decided their fate. If their decision was to come huntin' me, then them or me one would find death. Now I was thinkin' like a warrior, so rightful killin' weren't gonna bother me. I reasoned that was how Dad, Dancing Bear, Black Oak, and Cain all felt, too. I got to figurin' I ought to train better with the long gun. It made me a bigger enemy. I liked huntin' with 'em, too; although I'd rather hunt with my bow. I could out shoot Cain anytime, Dad sometimes, but *never* Momma. None of us could out shoot her.

Wind Is Strong was still livin' when Black Oak eased the wagon up to the back of our home. Dad jumped down from the wagon seat and rushed up the back-porch steps. He intended to let Momma know we was back straight away. Help her get ready for layin' Wind out on the bed. Maybe steal a big hug and a kiss 'fore anybody come in.

It was confusin' when we seen him bein' pushed back out the door with his hands held up. In the light shinin' out appeared a little old Cherokee woman with long gray hair, wrinkled hands, boney fingers, old beads, and the bone handle of a knife strapped to her tiny waist, doin' the pushin'. We was all still kinda shocked as Anne screamed, "Old Mother!" *She know'd about Wind Is Strong. She'd come.*

She'd figured it somehow. Holy Spirit had come to her, sent her to our place. It mattered that she was there. Wind Is Strong would have a better chance at livin' 'cause Owl the Wise One had come. She had the know-how from many years of tendin' to folks. Doctorin' up the evils of sickness, fightin', and death. It was good for Anne that she'd come. We all know'd the blood sickness runnin' through Wind Is Strong was gonna get mean.

By the looks 'a things, she was already gettin' took by it. Old Mother went straight to her, got busy tellin' Anne what all they needed for the tea. Anne commenced brewin' it up. Hopefully their efforts was gonna heal Wind Is Strong's blood, Lord willin'.

Anne had told us all about what Wind was facin' on the trail back from Panther Cave. It didn't sound like she would for sure make it. She was still gonna have to fight. How much more spirit did she have to fight with? Her will to live was strong. With what little help we'd been able to give her, she'd gotten to a place where her fight might be rewarded. She was still climbin' uphill in her healin'. And for her, it was gonna be a long steep ridge.

***

Me and Wolf'd had our fill 'a healin' and savin' and what not. Set our minds to hit the woods after chores the next evening for a full night 'a coon huntin'. The dogs hadn't been run in a while. They was itchin' to get at somethin', hog or coon.

We left all the meat we'd took on our hunt layin' where it landed when I'd come for Anne two nights back. There just hadn't been time to put it away proper then. We was home with Wind, but still had no energy to hang it 'fore gettin' some sleep. We was both dead tired from all the goin' on's we'd been into the last couple days. Our truck could wait, too, but not Jim and Peter. They needed tendin' to. For some reason, George Black Oak was stayin' in the house. He'd not come out to fetch up Jim like he always did. I wondered why he hadn't come out? I figured he was helpin' with Wind and couldn't leave her. That left the mule puttin' up chore to us. We obliged it.

Wolf and me took to the barn with both mules; me leadin' Big Jim, Wolf leadin' Peter. We tied 'em up to the side wall on the inside of the barn, scraped their hooves clean, give 'em a good rub down with a burlap sack, and filled the meal trough with fresh oats. We left the barn gate open so they could go out to pasture after eatin'. You ought 'a seen the way they jumped from side-to-side, swingin' their big ol' heads, makin' mule sounds once they left the barn. They was happy to be back home with their bunch. Black Oak never show'd.

We washed outside with water from the rain barrel 'fore we come in. Then walked right through the house up to the loft strippin' off our skins down to our homespun as we went. We both wanted to get in the bed. Neither of us ate a bite. Our bodies was just too tired to eat. I come to realize, right before I fell deep asleep, I hadn't seen Momma.

Old Man Sun was full on by the time we woke the next morning. The day was already warm. Black Oak finally made it to the barn to put away the wagon, all the mule harnesses, and the quilts left in the back what made the bed for Wind. I minded not to ask him why he hadn't come out after we'd got home. I did ask where Dad was, though, but got no answer. His mind seemed a hundred miles away. What was wrong with him? He was actin' strange for some reason. I just couldn't figure it.

Me and Wolf grabbed some cat-head biscuits out 'a Momma's stove. Stuffed 'em full 'a left-over breakfast sausage and apple butter. We washed 'em down with some cool buttermilk we fetched from the pantry. Wolf really liked buttermilk. He'd drink a bait of it if you didn't watch. I wondered who'd cooked breakfast, but there was leftovers for the takin'. It didn't really taste like Momma's cookin'. Most likely Anne.

We got busy after we'd eat. Cleaned and hung our meat in the skinnin' shed, gettin' it ready for curin'. Stored away our possibles and all our campin' truck. That took us most of the afternoon to do proper, then we went to the cook room. Packed a flour sack with some side bacon, left-over cornbread, dried apples, and a small tin of honey. I still hadn't seen Momma. I figured her and Dad to be off by themselves 'cause they'd do that a right smart, 'cept for some reason, this time Brutus was gone.

Anne was sleepin', so we got Old Mother to tend to our fresh cuts. She was watchin' after Wind Is Strong. Her and Anne had been at it all night. Owl treated our arms with some 'a Anne's salve layin' on a fresh homespun wrap with some dried herbs underneath. Them things commenced to burnin' our arms somethin' fierce. We both took to moanin' 'til she give us the evil eye, so we quit. They was done bleedin'. I was proud 'a that.

We went back to the barn just 'fore dark to load Peter. Got our heavy winter quilts back out. Wrapped up our possibles and food in those strappin' all of it to Peter's back. Then we fetched our knives, short bows, small arrows, and, most important for a good coon hunt - Wolf's lead-headed arrows.

After all our packin', we was ready to hit the woods for a dark night 'a coon huntin'. Coons run better on dark nights when they ain't no moon. Peter was rested but seemed anxious to get back out in the woods when I haltered him up.

We'd been trapped tendin' to Wind for so long our minds had gone soft. We was figurin' to take Dad's best coon dog, Stripe, for a run down in the river bottoms where the coons was easier to find. We called him that 'cause he had a white blaze runnin' down the back of his big ol' head square down the center between his shoulders.

Ol' Stripe was crossed with an American Fox Hound, and somethin' nobody really know'd for sure. He was the offspring of a bitch pup Dancing Bear had give Dad years back to raise up for huntin'. That dog didn't mind too good. Liked to wander. Dad would have to go fetch her home when she'd take off, which weren't a good trait for a proper huntin' dog to have. Caused way too much trouble on hunts.

Not long after gettin' full-grow'd, she felt the call and run off for several days. Must 'a crossed trail with somethin' out in the woods while she was heatin'. Weren't back but for a while 'fore she had a small litter 'a mixed pups. Stripe was the last 'a three.

They was somethin' strange about that bunch 'a pups 'cause she got to killin' 'em not long after they'd weened; started eatin' meat. Dad got to studyin' on the why of what she was doin' and figured it out on the short. Took Stripe out from her 'til he'd grow'd enough to defend himself. He allowed she'd mated with a wolf. The notion come to mind after she took to killin' her pups. It was clear to him she got to scentin' danger in their smell. Made her natural instincts take over. That's why she was killin' 'em. To her, she was doin' away with a threat. I figured Dad was right about all that. It made sense when you studied on it -- the pups smelled like baby wolves to her.

Stripe grow'd up to be one tough dog. He was big and strong. Calm around most folks, especially the little ones, but him and his momma would fight as Stripe grow'd. She hurt him good a few times. He finally got big enough to make sure she never hurt him again. Dad buried her in the woods next to the lower cornfield.

Ol' Stripe had the sweetest soundin' voice. Made the prettiest music when he struck trail. You could hear it for miles when the mountains was dark and calm. It come from the deepest part of his huge chest, rollin' through the woods like a thick fog hangin' low. Climbin' up the hollers to the highest ridge tops, while dancin' in perfect harmony with the night. Me and Wolf heard it many times growin' up when

Dad and Cain was out huntin' with him. That was back in the day when all we could do was listen from the porch 'cause we was too young to run. Wishin' the whole time we was out with 'em. It'd send chills down your back. Make your gut tighten up 'cause Stripe hollered out kinda spooky like. He was a great dog. Could run all night, never spellin' for nothin'. I couldn't wait to get him in the woods.

Dancing Bear and his clan raised a lot 'a dogs. They was all good huntin' dogs. Some hunted bear, some deer, coon, and some squirrel or rabbits. The original breeders of all Dancing Bear's dogs had also been gifts to his father, Water Runs Deep, from the Great General himself, George Washington. Dancing Bear said Mr. Washington had many different breeds. The foxhound Dad got was in the blood line from one 'a the General's pure stock. The original hounds was gifted to Mr. Washington by the head folks from another land across the 'Big Water' while he was President of America. Kinda like with his mules, Mr. Washington liked mixin' breeds to come up with some great lines 'a huntin' dogs, or so it was told. I never seen any personal other than ol' Stripe or what Wolf and his bunch owned.

Dancing Bear was proud of his dogs. The ones Dad kept from later litters from the old bitch was good coon dogs. Stripe was one 'a the best, even by Dancing Bear's thinkin'. He'd learned him to trail once he was old enough to be trained. Ol' Stripe weren't taught to hunt fox, bear, 'possum, or nothin' else. He'd only hunt coon or deer. If you wanted him to circle deer, you'd let him smell an old deerskin what was simple dried in the sun to keep the scent. If you wanted him to tree a coon, you'd let him smell an old coon hide dried the same. That was the only way to get him to scent proper. He'd trail either one, you just had to let him know which you wanted. It was real handy him bein' able to do that. It was like havin' a gun with two barrels but both bein' different.

We'd been bound to duty for too long. Our hog hunt ended days before. We had a need to feel the freedom of the woods again, to get out by ourselves for a while — smoke, talk, be free like folks of our time was, enjoy the mountains, feel the spirit of the creeks, and hear the voices off the ridge tops.

Momma had left some fried ham in the pantry. The biscuits had been put there now, too. All was covered over in wax cloth and laid on a shelf near the door. She kept cheese, butter, and milk in there. Granddad had left the floor of the pantry in natural red clay when he built the house. It stayed cool most of the time. Durin' the winter, food wouldn't freeze solid, neither. In the warm of late spring and summer, she had to put her stores deep in the cellar to keep 'em from turnin'.

We sat down at the table in Momma's cook room, slipped out our small knives, halved two biscuits each, and laid 'em thick with a slice 'a ham and some cheese. We eat 'em for our early supper, washin' 'em down with a mug 'a cool buttermilk. Oh, that was good. The food we'd packed would be eat as a late supper near the middle of the night around a good smoke fire. I was bad to fall asleep at them times if Wolf didn't keep me from it. I figured him and me would both sleep good this night.

Dad had found Momma's note. He was already for Cain's to fetch her. He didn't mind us goin' without him bein' home 'cause ol' Stripe was gonna be with us. He was a good dog that hunted hard. Know'd to look after his hunter, too, and Dad trusted him to look after us. He was a smart dog. He'd find the coons when no other dog could.

Peter could tell we was leavin' for a trail. His tail was swishin' good when we went back out to the barn to fetch him. He'd do that when he got excited. Goin' out with us got him that way. Me and Wolf had hunted Stripe with Dad a few times before always takin' Peter. That mule learned to know when we tied Stripe to his lead we was goin' coon huntin'. Stripe liked Peter. He'd walk right along tethered to Peter's halter.

We slung our pouches over our shoulders, leashed Stripe to the halter, jumped up on Peter's back, and started down the trail toward the river Notla. I was facin' forward guidin' Peter. Wolf was facin' backward watchin' our trail. We was leanin' back to back, and in no hurry. Peter didn't seem to be in no hurry, neither. We just let him walk. It was mighty peaceful walkin' through the woods. I couldn't wait to get after a big ol' river bottom coon.

I could feel my back tighten at just the thought of the chase. My heart jumped hard just rememberin' how pretty Stripe's voice was when he got on a coon. Only good mountain pickin' on a cold winter's night, when you could hear up the valley for miles, sounded better travelin' through the woods.

I got Dad's coon scent skin out from its pouch. Let Stripe have at it for a while 'til he started chewin' on it. His way 'a makin' it clear he was ready for the run, and the kill. He liked the killin' part. I let him off the leather to take the trail. Last I seen him, he was trottin' on with his nose to the ground, his long ears wavin' side-to-side as they hung down by his face. His tail wavin' 'come on' to us. He looked spirited. Like the scent he was gettin' was promisin'. Made me have hope for a good night 'a huntin'. All we had to do after Stripe left us was get a good warmin' fire goin', then sit, listen, and wait for him to bark trail. It was near too much for me to think on. I was ready for a good run.

We was sittin' with our legs crossed close to the fire, waitin', listenin'. It weren't good solid dark yet. The coons was just startin' to wake. Stripe'd not catch a scent 'til after the dark settled good. That's when them lazy coons come waddlin' out for their nightly food hunt. It'd give us time for a smoke. Wolf packed his bowl with some dried weaver tobacco, then offered his poke to me. I filled my bowl. Dad wouldn't let me keep weaver smoke. Said it weren't proper for young 'uns. Most settlers felt that way 'bout all tobacco toward any young 'uns. The Indians didn't. They smoked what they wanted with most warriors startin' young. The

Indians believed the smoke spoke for 'em as it traveled up to heaven. Maybe it did. I never read anything in the Bible what said that, but if they saw it that way, it was good by me. What I read in the Good Book was my body was the temple of Jesus. I should take care of it accordingly. I allowed I was doin' a fair job 'a that. I did feel older now that I'd come to my reckonin'.

Dad said I was too young for squeezin's. He kept hard cider and brandy for him and Momma, but not for us. I weren't allowed to have it. The Cherokee didn't see it that way. The little ones was kept from hard cider and drink, but not older young'uns. Wolf slipped me some one time. He won't never let me forget he done that.

It was at the end 'a my healin' time from when Old Man Bobcat had tore me up real bad. Wolf had come to our place. Been there a few days visitin', helpin see to me. We was out late one evenin' rockin' on the porch, watchin' things out on the farm. My shoulder was still really sore. My head mostly healed. I'd been strugglin' with my wounds for several weeks. The pain from my shoulder seemed to come and go a right smart every day. That cat had worked my back parts over real good. Well, the hard pain decided to come pay a visit while we was porch sittin' that evening, causin' me terrible strife. Wolf got to thinkin' a jigger 'a brandy would help me 'cause he'd seen Old Mother use it for such. We'd both seen our dads take a drink to 'help with the pain,' they'd say, so Wolf figured it'd help me. He fetched me some from Dad's jug real slick-like, meanin' all the time to ease my hurtin'. It was just a small mug full we allowed Dad wouldn't miss. It took me four big gulps to get it all down. It was *terrible*, burned like hell's fire when it hit the back 'a my throat. The heat flowin' on down to my gut. I saw stars when I closed my eyes after finishin' that mug 'a hard juice. Wolf laughed at the face I made tryin' to get it down. My first thought was how anybody would want to drink somethin' such as that? But once it hit me, it did help with the pain. It also made me near crazy. Wolf wondered about me after a few minutes.

"Jeb, how do you feel?" he asked as he leaned up in his seat lookin' at me close. "Your face is red like the flames in a fire. You are sweating from the top your head. It is running down over your face. Our fathers never sweat like that when they kill pain with the brandy. Are you in pain? Has the brandy helped with minding your pain?"

I leaned toward him enough to put my hand over on his shoulder. Looked him square in the eye, probably gettin' a little too close for boys like us, and said back to him all sweet-like and mushy with a smile, "Agh, Wolf, you're worried over little ol' me, huh? Just... now ain't that somethin', huh? Sure is... nice... And I want you to know I really appre... appre... appre - ci - ate the concern... worry... for my concernin' me. You're such the greatest friend for... a body... that ever could find a friend. And you know I know what you care over... same as me... and ain't that just the way of all of it, Wolf? We all just need what seems natural... won't study it... and I planted much you see... (hiccup) You won't needn't to worry none more... 'bout me none... 'cuzz me... I'm be strong enough so's to whup ol' Cain here himself and... and... uh... Wolf... uh... you and me... you know... I... ain't plannin' to whup at him none... hear? See... 'cause Cain... well you know him... and you... know... he... ain't whupupable none, Wolf, and... Wait now, I ain't right with that... Wolf, you won't tell him I said them words... no... don't do it Wolf. You gotta promise me. Don't be tellin'... don't be tellin' him... Wolf, I gotta... I gotta go."

I never finished all my talk. Kinda turned in my seat, stood right up, headed for nature's call. Took no more than two steps when I walked right off the side porch in a spot that was 'bout the height Dad was tall to the ground. I hit face first, dead center where Momma's herb garden would be come spring. I thought the world had just ended. That maybe Jesus was back. I can't tell you how the fall felt other than I weren't expectin' it. I'd forgot where the steps was from all the brandy I'd drunk. I do know it hurt when it ended. It jarred me like a mule kicked me with both back feet square-on solid in my center. Wolf said later it looked like I walked face-on through a door right into Mother Earth. Somehow, I'd forgot about the porch, and was thinkin' I was walkin' off the back steps. I don't really remember it all too good. All Wolf ever said was I smelled funny.

I was a lot older when I next had any 'spirits.' That's what my grandmother called 'em. It was stupid for anybody near my age to mess with such fool-hearted stuff. I learned from the pain 'a fallin' flat on my face into Momma's herb garden from off the porch why hard drink was for big folks. The devil was for spirits far as I was concerned. It took me two days for my head to stop poundin', my gut to quit hurtin', my legs to stop shakin' Didn't seem like I could drink enough water to calm my thirst. In the end, I'd rather have had the shoulder pain. But, I understood my friend was just tryin' to help me feel better, and I did, for a short time.

That would not be the last time I would have my best friend help me. It would be one of the least dangerous, for sure. Wolf had a way 'a keepin' me on my toes.

It weren't but a little after dark. We'd sat but a while when the sweet sound of a lone huntin' dog broke the silence of a poppin' campfire and a quiet smoke. It was ol' Stripe. He'd struck. The night was fixin' to get interesting.

Chapter Thirteen

A Strange Visitor to the Spirit World

The coons was easier to hunt in the low lands by the river 'cause of all the walnut trees. You'd find walnut stands all over, up and down the river. In the fall, folks would collect the nuts, get the center out from the husk, and take the sweet nut center south to Gaines Town for trade. They'd do the same with the chestnuts. Sometimes, when all the folks had put their haul together, they'd be a couple wagons full 'a bagged nuts headin' south; near a half dozen men escortin' it to market. Their wives and young'uns would be a'trailin', too. It took a lot 'a hard work to harvest that many nuts. Required patience from those removin' the sweet part. You could always tell a walnut hunter when you met one. Their fingers was forever black. They got gold coin for their effort. That made it all worth it.

    The woods down on the river bottoms was mixed like what grow'd up on the ridges, only not as thick 'cept in places. You had to watch 'cause they was a few big white pines ever so often that coons could belly-up in. They was hard to get at once they got up in the limbs 'a them big trees. Fortunately for coon hunters, they weren't as many on the river as what grow'd farther up on the ridges. They was huge granddaddy white oaks along the river, too. Most 'a them had limbs down low, easy to climb if the coon treed there. They was a few chestnuts growin' here and there. If a coon took off up one 'a them, you'd better get to it 'fore it got too high up or he'd be gone. Walnut trees was still king on the river, though. They was good-sized stands all over.

They was an art to killin' coons. Your aim was to get it kilt, but not mess up the hide or poke holes in it with a sharp arrow point. I took no likin' to the meat, it weren't important to me, but, their hides was. The Cherokee liked the meat. My granddad liked it. We never ate it.

Sometimes there weren't no choice. We'd have to use a sharp flint arrow to get the coon out from his hidin' place. Stripe would not hardly leave a coon once it treed. Near impossible to break off a hunt. You just as well climb up to get it or cut the tree down and let him have at it as wait. He'd stay days if he had to, I'd seen him do it. He liked the meat. Hide meant nothin' to him. He'd tear it all up gettin' at the meat. If a coon hit the ground movin' after bein' shot and Stripe got to it first, it was all his. You'd not get it from him. That's why we leashed him or held him after he treed. Nobody I know'd would take a coon from ol' Stripe if it hit the ground where he could snag it. Nobody, not even Cain. He'd figure your hand was just part 'a what needed killin' if a body grabbed it while he was on it. There you'd be out in the woods with a chewed-up hand. He was strong, he'd not let you take it from him. He'd break other critters' necks in one bite then leave 'em be, but not coons. He'd tear 'em apart. Never really understood why other than that was the way Dancing Bear had trained him.

He hated coons, but he liked eatin' 'em. He'd eat 'em bones and all, 'cept for the fur. He'd spit that out. It was a hoot watchin' his big ol' head start tossin' about tryin' to get thick coon fur out from his mouth, off his tongue and from between his teeth. Near made him yack. Wolf and me would laugh 'til we cramped-up watchin' him rid his face 'a coon fur. His big ol' ears would be floppin' side-to-side, slappin' his head. Slobber flyin' through the air like bein' slung from a rope. It would torture him somethin' fierce. But to him, it was worth it.

You could make all kinds 'a things out 'a coon skins, and we did. Pouches and sheaths mostly. We also used it for softenin' rags, table placin's, and neck warmers for rockin' outside on the porch or in front of the fire. Momma liked them things. Cold time was much more comfortable if you had a good pair 'a foot skins, a hat or gloves with coon fur turned in. It was soft, once cured the Cherokee way. I preferred them to store-bought later on in life. Never did figure why city folk didn't have such as we all wore growin' up. It was their loss for sure. Beaver skin and coonskin cured with the fur turned in was plumb comfortable when the cold was after your person.

We'd use arrows special made by my dad. He come up with the how-to of doin' it. They had a thick, flattened lead head wrapped tight and pinned around the end of the arrow shaft where a flint point usually went. The trick was to hit the coon upside the head. Knock it out cold makin' it lose hold and fall to the ground. Then we'd break their necks by layin' the handle of our pole axe behind their ears and jerkin' up on the tail real hard. It sounds bad for 'em, but it weren't, really. Once they got hit by that lead arrow, they never know'd about the rest of it; they was out solid when hit proper.

There was cane breaks up and down around the river in various places. They was the last thing you wanted a coon to run in to. You had to watch when trailin' near them growths of a night. Stay out if at all possible. All sorts 'a critters would use them patches to hide in like mean ol' hogs tryin' to stay clear 'a the big cats and wolves. We kill'd a bunch 'a hogs in the breaks up Stink Creek durin' the daylight, not of a night. Coons seemed to know they'd be safe in there. They'd run for 'em wide open 'til Stripe'd reason where they was headed. Turned 'em 'fore they made it.

Wolf cut a couple pine knot torches on the way to the river bottoms, one for each of us. The pine torches was already there, growin'. They lit the woods up just right when you held 'em overhead. You just looked for the little ball what grow'd off the limb of a yellow pine with some length to it; they was easy to come by. Then, you slipped 'em in the fire to get lit. If it'd been wet from rain or snow, we'd a been forced to bring a lantern to keep the light dry. I'd rather not tote no lantern on a coon hunt. The only bad thing about usin' yellow pine was the sticky pine tar what got on your knife workin' 'em up for lightin'. Didn't bother me much, weren't too bad to clean off. I figured the light was worth it, if needed.

Unlike a lantern, you could lift 'em high over your head. That made it where you could look under the light. See way up in tall trees better'n you could with a lantern. With a lantern, you kinda had to look through the light. Hard to see things straight in front of you or overhead. You couldn't see the critter you was huntin' as good as another hunter off to the side. I really liked that about usin' a knot over carryin' in a lantern.

The light was higher up with the knot, makin' it easier to see the coon when the shot come open. The head shot was best. Hittin' 'em in the shoulder or neck could bring 'em down, but didn't kill 'em, so some would get away if Stripe was leashed. That rarely happened with Wolf. He was quick on the watch. It was hard to hit the head let me tell you. Most 'a my shots found neck and shoulder. Wolf hardly ever missed. He was Cherokee. They didn't understand why other folks missed.

Wolf had a blowgun, as did most Cherokee hunters, but didn't use it much. Used his bow mostly for meat huntin'. Didn't care to handle the poison you had to use on the darts, havin' poked himself once when learnin' to use it. Got real sick. Near died, as the story was told. I'd only seen him use it when we hunted skunks. The poison would keep 'em from lettin' off their stink as they went to sleep. He made us several darts with thistle fletchin' and a pouch each for the poison powder. You'd mix it with water, or most often spit, then lay it on the dart's point. Didn't take much.

The mix would put whatever critter you shot plumb out. The hunter would have it once it was stuck if he simply watched and waited. He may have to trail it a ways 'fore it give in, but it would go to sleep. I got my blowgun after I got some older. Used it a couple times after folks got after me. Learned to work it proper, poison and all. Just the right mix would lay a body out without killin' 'em. Dad never took to usin' one, but Cain and me did. They come in handy, too, many times.

I put a few 'a them gold lookers asleep after they invaded the mountains later on. It was fun to watch 'em after they'd been darted. Some fallin' out in the creeks face first while they was searchin' for gold with their little pans. We'd have to go turn 'em. Keep 'em from drownin'. One particular low life we didn't turn. Don't know if he made it or not. I hated them gold-lookin' folks' ways. I didn't hate their souls, 'cause Jesus died for us all, but they brought nothin' but trouble to the mountain folk; for sure, to the Cherokee. Dancing Bear made me my blowgun out 'a good, solid river cane; Cain made his own. He know'd Cherokee ways better than me.

I'll never forget one old feller Wolf shot with his blowgun near the headwaters 'a Wolf Creek. It was not long after the gold lookers got to comin' to the valley. He'd made camp there with his Indian woman, a near wore out mule, and an old cur dog. He was plumb mean to his woman. Slapped her bare handed about the face and head and beat her with his belt across the back and shoulders.

She was a right smart younger than he was, and sickly lookin'. She seemed feeble for a woman of her age. Her clothes was wore out. Had holes all in 'em. She went barefooted all the time. She wore no beads. Her hair was short. Kinda looked like it was cut with a knife. Didn't look like the old man provided good 'cause they ate cold tack and pemmican or jerky near every meal. The old mule was left to fend for what it could find in the woods.

It was mid-year when we run up on 'em camped on the lower part of the headwaters. We was out on a walk followin' the creek south from the river Notla when we found 'em.

The weather was warm. Hot durin' the day. The woman didn't need what little homespun she wore. He made her stay covered from what we'd seen. Most Cherokee women went without on top when it was hot. She did spend the hot part of the day, while he was gone gold lookin', just sittin' in the creek mostly naked, coolin'.

We'd watched 'em for a few days, mostly in the evenin's just 'fore dark. We was curious to see how they done things since they was different from us. She was Indian. A mix 'a Creek or maybe some Choctaw or Cherokee. She weren't real pretty; kept herself clean bathin' in the creek, though. We figured her for a slave 'cause he made her sleep out in the woods on a blanket with no cover while he spent his nights under a stretched canvas. He even let the old cur dog sleep in there with him, but not her. Weren't long 'til Wolf had enough a' his meanness toward her. Decided to teach that trash a lesson.

"My friend," Wolf said to me as we returned to our camp from watchin' 'em one night after dark rolled in. "I see this man has never been taught the respect he should have for others. It is time we obliged him. I will go to Old Mother tonight. Get what is needed to open his eyes. You stay here. Tend to our truck. I will be back soon."

Done talkin', he jumped on Peter's back, takin' off for the trail to Slaughter Mountain. I didn't see him again 'til he woke me just 'fore daylight. He had his blowgun strung across his back; a small copper snakeskin pouch tied to his belt from Old Mother. I had no idea what he was plannin', but he had a look 'a mischief in his eye, which told me the old man was gonna have an interestin' day. We ate a small bite 'a breakfast. Washed it down with warm coffee from the pot we left near the fire constant. Followed all that with a good smoke 'a dried burley 'fore dumpin' our pipe bowls, grabbin' our possibles, and movin' on up the creek to where the nasty man was camped. It was shortly after Old Man Sun's first light when we seen their fire.

The camp was in a flat place a little ways west 'a Wolf Creek, near a half mile up from our camp. The creek weren't real wide where they was, but there was a deep spot not too far away to the north where the woman would sit. We slipped up close as Old Man Sun was startin' to peak over the ridges to the east. The early morning breeze began gently rollin' up the valley. We had to circle around their camp comin' on 'em from the south to keep our scent down.

The camp was small. Didn't lay like it should; kinda lazy lookin'. You could see clear this fool didn't know what he was doin'. Weren't no mountain smart in him fer nothin', if they was, he'd 'a turned his sleepin' spot different. North to south would 'a give him a way to cool as the air flow made its trip up and down the valley each morning and evening. Up the valley as the day warmed, back down as the air cooled at night. He was too close to the runnin' water, too. Be easy for an enemy to slip in. Never would hear danger comin' if it eased in by the shallow flow of the creek. That kind 'a thinkin' was crucial if you wanted to be comfortable and stay alive when livin' in the woods. The Indian woman slept on the highest spot in camp, a ways back from the creek. She know'd what she was doin'. Best natural spot in camp to sleep. It's where Wolf and me would 'a settled if it was our camp.

The fire pit, bein' laid out wrong, was what troubled me most. For folks what stayed in the woods a right smart, smellin' of smoke weren't good. Smoke meant danger. Critters would trail away from smoke. What was best was a fire with a lot 'a coals, not much wood burnin' constant. The Cherokee learned fire buildin' from the ancestors. They believe fire is alive. Wolf always know'd right where to lay the fire pit. He'd talk to it once it got goin' good. Learned it from his folks.

Fire pits was important. That's where most everything happens when spendin' time in camp — cookin', heatin', keepin' things warm, sleepin' by at times, and for gettin' hot water quick if needed. The way you dug your pit and the way you built the fire was very important. Warm water waitin 'in a pot on the edge of a steady bed 'a coals don't take long to heat up. They could be a call for a hot cup 'a black coffee to partner a good smoke; or to sterilize a knife blade right quick if a body needed an arrowhead or lead ball took out 'a their person. The fire was a good place to turn a blade red hot, too, if a wound called for closin'. You always had to be as ready as you could be. Life and comfort in the mountains depended on how proper a body did things.

Believe it or not, them Indians know'd just how to find the perfect place for the fire pit when makin' camp. They had some way 'a readin' the ground. The flow of the air what moved. They could put you on the exact spot to keep the smoke driftin' steady in one main direction. Meant eatin' or not on the occasion you trailed your food stinkin' like somethin' that scares it. Deer and what not fear that smoke smell. I liked to eat fresh meat when camped. I paid mind where to best burn camp fires.

We'd slipped to within' twenty paces of the camp 'fore Wolf grabbed my arm, stoppin' me dead in my tracks. He pointed with a concerned look. It was the woman. I don't know how she know'd we was there, but she'd made us. She was standin' next to the fire lookin' straight at us with a little smile at the edge of her lips. Wolf stood. The woman looked over to where the old man was sleepin', snorin' like a fat hog in a waller, then turned from the camp makin' her way to us stoppin' a couple paces in front 'a Wolf. She weren't no taller than we was. I don't think Wolf figured what she'd just done into his plan.

"Woman," Wolf whispered, while lookin' her eye-to-eye. "I am Wolf, Son of Dancing Bear, Family of the Choestoe Clan. What is your name? How is it you have come to be with this heathen white man? Do you wish to leave here this day? The Great Spirit has brought us here to you. We will help you if you want to leave. Speak so we will know."

Wolf said the "white man" part kinda careless for me standin' right there. I noticed it, too. I never studied over it long. The white men trailin' in the mountains now weren't real friendly when travelin' in the Cherokee nation. Rest assured, the Indians know'd the trespassers was there. They considered them enemy invaders. Once a camp was found, the folks stayin' there was watched. They was guests in a foreign land, and never even know'd it. At any time, they could die. Many never knowin' how close death had really come. One act of disrespect was all it took. No tellin' how many folks just simply went missin' back in them days. The old man we'd been watchin' never done nothin' we saw what would require him to die.

I felt for the woman now that she was face on good. She was older than we'd thought, but much younger than the trash she was with. Her beauty was gone, if she ever had any. The scars on her body told a story if you know'd how to read 'em. We did.

No doubt she'd been owned. Her neck held brandin' marks. The left ear was gapped with the lower part hangin' loose. She had a long scar on her forehead, which told what type slave she was, or had been. There was a toe missin' from each foot, which meant she'd run off at least twice from whoever owned her at the time. There was shackle marks on her wrists. One eye was turned white lookin'; most likely didn't work right if it worked at all. Her nose had been broke what looked like several times. It laid crooked across her face. There was slits in her lips that'd grow'd back thick. But the worst of it all was when she opened her mouth wide. Wolf seen why she couldn't answer his questions. Her tongue was missin'. Most of her front teeth was gone, too. The tongue cuttin' looked to 'a been done recent. That near made me sick. She pointed to the old man who was still sleepin' after touchin' her mouth with her first finger. We know'd then he'd done it. That kinda doin' might call for a killin'. I hurt for this woman. We both did. Wolf would not be so kind now. Our funnin' had just turned to anger. Vengeance was due.

"Woman," Wolf said in Cherokee as he stepped forward puttin' his hand on her left shoulder. "Go and gather your possibles. Leave this place. Honor the Great Spirit. His Son's sacrifice for all people. We will see to it this man never hurts you again. You are free. Go south through the low gap. Make your way to the great rock. There you will find friends. My people. The people of A-Ga-Li-Ha, my mother. Let them know it is Wolf, and his friend, Jeb Collins of Choestoe, who own your freedom now. They will know to find you a place to be. A home where you can live in peace. Remember, the one true God, the Great Spirit, broke you free through us, His warriors. Go now. Do not come back to this place. Your life is now your own."

The look in her face was somethin' I will never forget. Freedom was unknown to her. Tears filled her eyes as she silently went and did as Wolf had said. The old cur dog must 'a heard her 'cause it left the old man sleepin', went with her as she packed and left camp. The old man was now alone.

Wolf got that look in his eye I saw many times in our lives. Things was to be made right. Vengeance for the woman would be had. The old man's life had just took a turn for the worse. How far the turn went depended on how deep Wolf's hatred of this man went. I reasoned it was gut deep. This could be bad. I didn't care. We moved closer. Squatted behind some ivy, hopin' to not be seen.

The man rose not long after the woman left -- relieved himself in the creek. That was not proper in the Cherokee world. Mine, neither. We'd studied the camp. Seen he had an old flint lock musket leaned ag'in a tree beside the creek, a pole axe for wood splittin' near the fire, and a jug 'a hard cider beside his tent. He turned after finishin' his morning business lookin' around kinda dumb-like while realizin' things was different, then went to the fire, squatted down close. He wore only his homespun under garments. They hung on him like the loose skin around a hound dog's neck. His beard was long, shabby. When he walked, you could hear his bones poppin'. He was skinny like his old mule. Hair cut short like the woman's. His fingers was long and dirty. Boots near wore out. He smelled *bad*. But what caught our eye most, was the gold nuggets what laid in a wooden bowl not far from where we was squatted watchin'. We was gonna take them nuggets. Of that, I had no doubt. The way Wolf figured it, them belonged to the Cherokee. We would return 'em to the ancestors.

At one point, the old man walked to the opposite side of the fire and set his coffee pot on the coals, then walked to where the woman had been sleepin'. Stood there lookin' around scratchin' himself, actin' like he'd been stole from. He looked real close for a minute, then walked up the valley out a sight. Searchin' for any sign of what might 'a happened to her. When he did that, Wolf ran to his coffee pot. Openin' the lid, he commenced to pourin' a brown powder in from the copperback snakeskin pouch. He shook it up real good 'fore runnin' back to where we'd been watchin' with a big grin on his face. I know'd of what it was he'd poured into that heathen's morning coffee: powder the Indians used when they visited the sweat lodge for visions. I smiled as I watched Wolf. Me and him had used powder durin' my first sweat. I know'd what it did. We stayed where we was to watch for him comin' back to camp.

"Let us see how the evil man trails once the dream powder takes him, Jeb. I believe he will see many evil things on the trip he will be taking soon. I soured his coffee with enough of Old Mother's mix for two Cherokee the size of Black Oak. His mind may never come back from the world of our ancestors. If that is their decision, then so be it. He is an evil man. He will soon walk in a world of his own making. I believe it will be as evil as the darkness that holds his spirit."

"I reckon you're right, my friend. Folks like him deserve no respect. He will learn his true self here d'rectly. This is gonna be somethin' to watch. Your choice of punishment may be more than a person can take. I would not want to be goin' where he is headed. He is evil. Evil will be waitin'. We will have some fun with this lazy outlaw as he gets his due. You are wise beyond your years, Wolf. I am glad you are my friend, not my enemy."

Weren't long 'til the old man come back. You could see he was still confused over things. He got dressed with what little clothes he had, then commenced to washin' down a cold biscuit with what was now old, hot coffee mixed with plenty 'a vision powder. He drank three cups while we watched, then fetched his gold nuggets droppin 'em in a leather pouch. He tied his little sack under little mane the mule had, thinkin' nobody would find it hid there. Then he grabbed his musket and gold-findin' truck, loaded up his mule, and headed out downstream — gun in his left hand, mule lead in his right. I guess the woman bein' gone meant very little to him. Weren't long 'til he couldn't care where she was at, Wolf'd made sure 'a that. We followed, watchin' real quiet-like. I will never forget what a sight I saw when the visions come on him. The spirit world was gonna have a strange visitor. I kinda felt sorry for him 'til I remembered what he'd done to the woman... and why he was camped where he was.

His mule was the first to get paid his attentions. I reckon he thought that stinkin' thing was some woman 'cause he bowed-up real fast while leadin' it beside the creek goin' north, turned his lovin' eyes toward it, then started talkin'. When he put his hands up both sides of its head, rubbin' its nose with the palm of his left hand, talkin' in its ear all sweet, me and Wolf moved in close so's we could hear. We hid behind another ivy bush where there was very little cover. He was driftin' so, not sure he could 'a seen us even if he'd looked right at us.

Sweetly, he said to the mule, "Now, listen here, ain't you the purtiest thing this side 'a the mountain tops, honey? I reckon me and you been together a long time. How's 'bout a little smooch for showin' how sweet you is, huh? Me and you's been through a lot."

We couldn't believe it. His mind was foolin' him somethin' fierce. He leaned right in, grabbed the mule by both ears, then kissed that stinky ol' thing right on the lips. Finished with his kissin', he give it the biggest hug 'round the neck you ever did see. Well, that ol' mule got done with all that after a minute. It weren't in for such lovin' stuff. While the old man hung on, it raised up on its back legs, then slung its whole front part to the east hard as it could. That move sent the dirty old man flyin' through the air. Looked like chickens tryin' to fly. Landed him square in the middle 'a Wolf Creek. The water weren't deep where he landed, neither. Had to 'a been painful 'cause they was rocks showin' under his person. He never minded no pain if it was. What he did next showed us both he was wallerin' deep in the spirit world. Seein' folks.

"Momma," he said while layin' flat on his back reachin' up to the sky, creek water runnin' down both his sides. "Momma? Where you been, Momma? Where's Pa, Momma? He squeezin' mash with Uncle Bert today? I'll go ahead 'n pick some more apples fer 'em. Tell Pa I'll be back 'fore long. We'll have us a big ol' time. Bye, Momma. You tell him now." All of a sudden he come up out 'a the creek like he was shot out from a gun. Run to the nearest ivy bush and began pickin' leaves like a mad man. Smellin' of 'em just like they was apples. He eat a few of 'em, too. That weren't gonna be good. My, but we was havin' a time watchin'. Next thing he did told us for sure the spirits was on him.

"What?" he yelled, and stopped his leaf pickin', commenced to starin' out in the woods past the creek. "What is it y'all want? Leave me be, hear? Y'all got no call to come on me like this. I told you'uns before they weren't nothin' to all that. Stay clear 'a me now, hear? I ain't seen none 'a y'all since your passin' on. Hey! Wait now! How is it I'm 'a seein' you'uns here? Get away from me now. Leave me be. Take your meanness and get. I'll shoot ever last one 'a you'uns if'n you don't get."

    After that bold talk, he run and fetched his gun from off the ground where he'd started courtin' his mule. Aimed from the shoulder, then fired out in the woods toward whatever it was he saw. Just so happened it was over his mule's head near killin' the poor beast. It jumped scared, took for the woods plumb crazy. He put the gun back to his shoulder, pulled the trigger another time, payin' no mind to the fact it weren't loaded. He just aimed hollerin', "BANG!" real loud ever time he pulled the trigger. It looked like he must 'a been fightin' a whole army the way he was carryin' on. Slung that gun side-to-side with purpose, yellin', "BANG!". It was a sight. Wolf and me laughed considerable. He took on with his nonsense for the longest time. Run from tree-to-tree. Hid like he was fightin' off folks. Done it near to dark 'fore he fell face first beside the creek, wore plumb out. Laid there for a spell. Finally, he got up real slow-like to look around. That's when Wolf added to his misery. Darted him in his backside. He never even noticed the sting. Took a little while, but the poison worked its chore. Made him sleepy. He laid down on a log after a bit, groaned some, then fell asleep.

    Wolf run over to him takin' out his long knife. Carefully he started cuttin' the nasty old homespun from his person, not stoppin' 'til the old feller was plumb naked. Once he got the old buzzard naked, he laid foot to him, and kicked him off the log to the ground. Wolf then went to a big oak tree nearby with a plentiful source 'a poison ivy attached. He fetched a long length, usin' one end to tie the sleepin' man's foot to the lowest limb of a nearby dogwood, then looped the rest of it over the man's bare body, makin' sure it laid on the places he'd feel it most. His face, neck, and between his legs for sure. Wolf crossed the sleepin' man's arms over his chest to hold the itchy vine where he wanted it to stay, then come back to where I was. Oh, that feller would suffer when he come to.

We found his mule. Relieved it of the gold. Wolf would give it to Dancing Bear when we got home to his place. The mule weren't worth much, he was too old. We unbound him from the man's possibles, then let him go free. We never saw it or the old man again. I always wondered if he ever figured out what happened to him that day. No matter really. We cared nothin' for him; his kind, neither.

The slave woman made it to Wolf's folks across the ridge to Yonah. We saw her at Big Camp the followin' year Told her what we'd done. She smiled as Wolf explained it all to her in Cherokee. It was good to see her happy. Life turned out for her, I felt touched about that.

Chapter Fourteen

Not Just Another Dark Night 'a Coon Huntin'

The trail sign followin' Stripe told us it weren't the biggest tom coon we'd ever chased. No matter, he was big enough to make it worth the effort. We left Peter to fend for himself once we heard Stripe bark trail the first time. Stripe was pushin' his coon straight toward a huge stand 'a walnut trees. It would 'a been good if the coon treed in one of them. But of course, it didn't. That'd make it too easy. Who'd want that?

Instead, it made a long sweepin' turn headin' straight back to the place where Stripe first crossed its trail. Lookin' for its safe place after Stripe struck its trail for the second time. It weren't like him to have to locate the same critter twice. I'd not seen him need to do that, ever. Never heard Dad or Cain tell it, neither. He was too good 'a dog. Critters rarely got the best 'a him, but the one he was on that night did. All dogs would lose coons from time-to-time. Might be where they found to hide, or the ground got too steep for folks to trail on, but you hardly ever heard of a dog strikin' trail twice to the same coon. Most times if a coon got away, it stayed away. It'd not come back for seconds. That 'un did. It was just plumb strange the way it was carryin' on. Left me wonderin'.

As luck would have it, its safe place happened to be one 'a the biggest white pines on the river. A monster standin' tall at the south end of the Souther farm with no other trees anywhere close to it - a coon hunter's worst draw.

It had limbs so thick you could hardly find a spot to see through. Takin' this coon was gonna be a chore.

The tree was a little ways from the river, back near the trail we'd come in on. Big white pines simply made coon killin' hard 'cause of all the limbs. The ones standin' out alone, like the one Stripe'd treed in, was the worst. It could be daylight for we'd ever see our coon, if then. But if that's what it took, then that's what it would take. Once a dog treed, you needed to do all you could to get the coon. When you had to break off the dog after it'd treed for whatever reason, you run a chance he'd not tree again for a while. We didn't want 'a give no chance to messin'-up Dad's best coon dog. I don't think he'd ever 'a forgive us if we had. Sides, it weren't in ol' Stripe to leave a coon.

Wolf handed me his torch. I now had two. I got to shinin' the tree while he commenced to makin' his bow ready to shoot. He wanted to be ready in case we got there soon enough after it'd treed to get a shot at it as it started its climb. We didn't, but it worked out good, anyhow.

I couldn't believe it when I first seen it. It weren't near as far up the tree as I'd figured it would be. It was showin' good as it carefully walked a kinda open limb from Wolf's left to his right. It was gonna cross over Stripe in the air, then jump tree. Hit the ground runnin'. This struck me and Wolf as strange behavior. What was it thinkin'? He'd done made it to his safe place; found cover up the one tree he felt would protect his hide. There was a good chance he'd make it in that tree if he did right, but he weren't. He should 'a been goin' up. Headin' for the top away from us. Didn't seem the way he was actin' was right.

I was holdin' both torches high when we saw him movin' the limb. I dropped both my arms shiftin' the light off his walk quick as we seen for sure where he was. Wolf got ready. On his nod, I brought the torch heads back together at full height, that give him the most light. Wolf never hesitated 'fore he draw'd and fired landin' a hard, flat lead point upside the coon's head near to the second our light shined him. The hit knocked it full off the limb it was walkin'. The body bounced off white pine limbs as gravity pulled it to the ground. Took what seemed a minute to get all the way down, catchin' on limbs as it fell. It weren't too far up when he shot it, really, that pine just had a lot 'a limbs.

Wolf run to it the second it hit the ground to keep Stripe from gettin' it. He put his left foot behind its head, took a solid hold on the back two legs with his right hand, then jerked its backend straight up hard. The bones in its neck give way, killin' it quick. The coon was dead, and the hide was whole. It was a nice hide, too. Had a good feel to it, soft. Probably end up bein' part of a neck wrap, or gloves maybe.

We had a nice skin, but somethin' just weren't right. The woods was feelin' all wrong; uncomfortable. Stripe was still hollerin' treed. Him barkin' treed after we'd killed the coon weren't natural. Stranger even, he never looked at the coon where it tumbled down through the tree limbs, landin' not ten paces away from him. That weren't natural, neither. His paws was up on the tree as far as they'd go, diggin' at the bark. His eyes was lookin' hard at what he was seein'. He was mad, critter killin' mad. Makin' like he wanted to claw that tree apart after whatever was up it. You should 'a seen how mad he was — growlin' hard from deep in his big ol' chest with a bark that'd scare the spirits away - fierce actin'. Usually, he'd not get so mad at a simple ol' coon. Fact was, he liked chasin' the nasty things. Gettin' one treed had never bothered him so much before.

I held the pine knots high as I could. They was half burned up by then, not near as bright as when we'd started the night's chase. They weren't no sight 'a nothin'. There was a wrong about us, though; a body could feel it. Like a storm was brewin' overhead when you was out in the open woods huntin'. They was a pull in the air. Made the hair on your neck stand up. The dark night sky was clear of clouds. You could see stars shinin' like candles from the east to the west, but I couldn't see nothin' up that tree. What was it? It was obvious ol' Stripe couldn't help makin' the fuss he was makin'. I was startin' to get riled. I moved to quiet Stripe. See if we could hear anything to help make sense 'a the way he was goin' on.

I never got close. Stripe sprang toward Wolf as a hair-curlin' howl come from the top of that tree freezin' me and Wolf at the same time. A crashin', limb breakin' sound commenced about halfway up the huge pine after that howl tellin' me something big and heavy was tryin' to leave out. It was plumb frightful standin' there listenin'. I held our lights up far as I could, but they weren't much light left. Wolf grabbed Stripe by his leather collar, held him firm on the opposite side of the tree from me. The crashin' noise kept comin' bustin' through the heavy green limbs just over my head. It jumped from the tree with a bellow, 'causin' the crashin', limb-breakin' noises to scream out from over our heads a second time. The rich scent of pine tar leakin' from the freshly broken limbs burned my nose. The thing landed to the side of the trail nearest me some twenty paces away. Same trail we'd used to reach the bottoms on. Whatever it was, it hit the ground a good ways from the tree with a heavy, ground-thumpin' thud I felt through my foot skins. It followed its landin' by rollin' forward, then took off into the dark headin' south toward the big ridges.

It was strange the way it rolled after it left the tree. Kinda like kids playin' in the yard. What I saw struck me deep whether I was clear on what it was or not. Made me stop watchin' and look close. Take notice of how it did. The way it moved. Weren't common for the way most critters moved. It was big and dark, and left very little sign on the soft ground. It smelled like a salt-cured ham what'd soured in the heat. I'd watched many different meat animals in my short time - predators, too. Learned how they did when feedin' or what not. Made it easier to hunt 'em when the time come to get out in the woods after 'em. It moved like no critter I'd ever seen 'cept maybe a bear. The strangest thing was, and I've never told many folks this, but after it rolled a couple times, it seemed to me — and this is why I don't tell what I thought I saw much — it looked to me like it hit its feet and run off near same as me or Wolf would 'a . . . on two legs. I don't believe it possible, but that's what my mind said my eyes saw. I can for sure tell you I've never heard another howl like that in my life, nor heard a critter break white pine limbs like it did. Don't ever wanna hear them sounds again, neither.

I'd seen bears do that for a few steps while standin' on two legs, but you know'd what it was, a bear. So, maybe that was it. Maybe it was a bear. It would remain a mystery. It'll most likely stay a mystery to me 'til I'm across the Great River with Jesus. I'll ask him when I see him. He'll tell me if it's important. So be it, if that's what the Great Spirit wants.

Wolf never saw it. He was on the wrong side of the tree tendin' to Stripe. He heard it, though, and reasoned it for a bear. I never told but one soul for my whole life about what I'd seen on that coon hunt 'til here a while back. Of course, that was Wolf. He was there. He'd seen the limbs layin' on the ground from where the thing had broke through as it was leavin' that big White Pine. He heard the bellow as it jumped.

We saw somethin' similar to what I might 'a seen on that strange night 'a coon huntin' years later when Wolf and me was on a walk. It was draw'd on a cave wall up in the mountains four days north 'a my home at Ben's Knob in Choestoe. On the walls inside, made of solid stone, they was a drawin' of some critter jumpin' from what I figured for a white pine tree. Give me thought when I first ever seen it. I told Wolf then what I'd seen on our hunt many years earlier. He believed me. The Indians trusted spiritual critters what lived in the woods; believed they was there to protect the graves of the ancestors. He reasoned it for one 'a them spirit critters. No concerns to him, really - he was Cherokee.

I went back to that cave recent, as an old man. I wanted to see the drawin' once more. It was gone. They weren't sign of it nowhere. I recognized the boulders around where the entrance was, but it was all gone. The cave was just… gone.

**

My granddad on my momma's side had a simple way 'a catchin' coons. His way kept the hide whole for market, or for keep. Wolf and me never favored it 'cause you had to check it twice every day, mornin' and evenin'. We was too busy for all that. 'Sides, we liked a good coon chase. The way Granddad worked it there weren't no chase 'cause you didn't use no dog.

The way he done it was, he'd take his hand auger out in the woods. Find a persimmon tree, a wild apple tree, or some other type food source the coons was eatin' at the time he was huntin'. Locate a log or stump on the trail comin' or goin' to their food source that weren't too rotten. Then, he'd cut a hole in the top 'bout three inches deep with the hand auger. He'd say a little prayer or somethin', then drop in this particular small, shiny, silver ball 'bout the size of a ripe sweet pea. He kept them silver balls just for catchin' coons. It was strange how he said it worked. I allowed he only ever caught the ignorant coons, 'til he learned me different one cold, dark night. Some 'a the ones he caught was really big. Lots 'a times he'd catch 'em in places where stories say coons outsmarted good, seasoned dogs. He allowed his traps worked better than any ol' dog. I agreed with him, after I'd seen him work it with my own eyes.

He was stayin' with us for a while after Grandmother died, late in the time of fallin' leaves that year. He woke me early one mornin', fetchin' me to go with him to check his coon traps.

"Aye, boy," he said softly in his heavy Irish accent as he rubbed my head 'til I woke. "Come with me, lad, an' we'll get off to the furest for the fetchin' 'a the ring tail. You'll be gettin' the ready on while me tends to the necessaries. Ya hearin' me, lad?"

I loved my granddad. I jumped at the chance to go anyplace with him. He was most enjoyable to be on trail with.

"Yes sir! I'll be ready 'fore you know it," I replied, sittin' up, tryin' to wake quick as I could. "I'll gather my possibles, come down soon as I can. You eat breakfast yet, Granddad?"

"Nay, lad. I'd be 'a waitin' fer yourself, see," he replied in such a heavy accent I near couldn't understand him.

He could talk the English better'n that. He was just bein' lazy with it. He'd talk all old country speak if Momma'd let him, but she'd not have us talkin' it in her house. We was Americans, folks of a new country, and we was gonna talk like it. She held us to it, too. Granddad weren't no exception. It was hard for him. He'd slip often, especially when the jug was bein' passed. Made him mad havin' to hold his natural tongue, but he loved his daughter greatly, so he did as she asked — best he could anyway.

He was sittin' at the table when I come down. Momma was at the cook stove. I know'd by the cookin' scent what we was fixin' to eat, The Choestoe Blessing. It could not 'a come at a better time, neither. I was powerful hungry that morning.

Granddad walked near everywhere he went. He had a good mule, but he walked mostly. He'd use it to come and go to our place 'cause he lived a ways down in the valley where the settlement was; worked for another Irish man what owned the mill there. He and Grandmother kept a small place close by the mill. He'd be alone there now. That thought made me sad.

He'd not ride flesh into the woods for such a trail as we was on. He'd take a mule for bigger game hunts like hog, bear or deer, allowin' he needed his mule to fetch out the meat. Most times he'd not ride then, neither; just hold the lead, and walk. He reasoned mules weren't natural to the woods. Weren't made for havin' folks on their back for travelin'. All due them was packin', loggin', workin' the farm, or wagon pullin'. But let him kill a big ol' boar hog or such, and he'd fetch that mule after the meat quick as any of us. He weren't stupid, of course. He just figured man was born to walk. Jesus walked. God walked in the first garden of 'a evenin' with Adam. He figured man should walk as much as he could. He know'd Jesus rode a jack into Jerusalem on His death trail. Figured that forgave any aid provided by his mule while workin' a hunt or travelin'. He know'd God understood it was nice for a man to ride on occasion, since He did.

We'd cleared several small tops followin' the trail to his huntin' ground a good piece from our farm. Old Man Sun was showin' light near straight on as we come upon his first set. We stopped. He never said a word. Squatted down on one knee, he simply turned toward me, lifted his arm, and pointed toward a big chestnut log layin' only a few paces from us. It was a coon. A *big* coon with his leg down in the log strugglin' to get free.

I jumped at the sight of it. Started tryin' to pull him toward the chestnut log while whisper hollerin', "Granddad, look! It's a coon! Let's get after it or it's gonna get away. Come on, let's get with it. How . . . we gonna . . . catch it? Wait . . . it ain't runnin' off," I said, as I stopped pullin'. "What's wrong with him, Granddad? He looks… he looks… stuck? Grandad? He looks hung. What in the whole put-together is troublin' him that he don't run off? What's got his leg held like that, huh? Why don't he just run off?"

It was the craziest lookin' thing you'd ever think 'a seein'. This coon was a good-sized feller, pullin' hard as he could stand, tryin' to get his left front paw out from bein' stuck. He couldn't get free. He was growlin', snappin', and a gnawin' at his foot. I swear to you, he wanted free so bad he was startin' to gnaw his leg off. It weren't gonna be happenin' for him. His trail on this side 'a the river was at an end. His hide was had.

"Aye, lad, you sure on y'ur sight fer that," he said as he rose to go toward the coon. "He's 'a caught 'un. Shy 'a the smarts would 'a kept him from it so bein'. Come, let me show ya."

He stood plumb straight without another word. Not tryin' to be quiet or hid or nothin', walked right up to that coon. Its struggle with the grip death had on it was pure mad. A small hickory club carried in the side pocket of Granddad's homespun britches relieved the coon of all its trouble. Meat and hide was all it was after Granddad got to it.

"Here to me with ya, lad," he ordered after he'd killed the coon with a hard blow to the back of its neck. That kinda killin' saved the whole hide. Spared the critter much pain. "I'll show ya the trick that'll bag ya the ringed-tailed one, boy. Use it for the harvest but beg yourself to be on the secret against all souls, 'ceptin' the few close fer to fam'ly. Ya hearin' me clear, young 'un? Understandin' me, are ya?"

"I understand you, Granddad. Thank you for showin' me so's I'll know," I said humbly.

He reached and rolled the coon's body off to one side with its leg still caught. It was a hole. A clean, round hole. No doubt bored by a hand auger. Had four small, home-forged nails, no bigger 'round than a seeded stalk 'a wheat and about three inches long, drove in the log on angle from back of the hole's edge some two inches. Since the nails was drove on an angle, laid back from the edge like they was, the points broke through the wall of the hole 'bout half way down into it. This caused the points to come together about an inch or more off the bottom of the hole, makin' the openin' a lot smaller down where the nail points come together. I could see the coon had reached his paw into the hole, then found its fist stuck on the nails as he'd tried to draw it out.

But why did it make a fist? I wondered. *What in the whole put together would make him wanna do a thing like that?*

I watched as Granddad started workin' the coon's leg free. It proved simple once I saw it.

"Look ye here, Jebediah," Granddad said as he eased the coon's foot clear. He pinched a small, pea-sized silver ball from its hold. "Tis the silver makes death to the catch. He'll not be lettin' go fer nuthin' once he's grabbed to it. Look fer ya to see, he'd not let go for life. Ratherin' be chewin' the very leg he'd caught'n the hole. The silver they'd hold 'til death comes on. They'll all require it. Now be mindin' ya, boy, not jus' any ol' silver piece will be workin' for the catch. Look ye here? Only these blessed pieces from the homeland work for the catchin'. Me pap give this 'un to me. I'd be passin' the faith to ye and yer pap when the time fer 'crossin' over has come upon me, aye? Boy? Aye? Ya hear'n me, are ye, lad?"

"Yes sir," I managed to squeak out from all what my mind was takin' in.

I got to thinkin' as we checked the rest of his traps, they was three in all but only the first one had a coon, even the Indians couldn't do what I was helpin' Granddad do to get a coonskin. If this was gonna pass on to Dad and me, it would be one way 'a huntin' Wolf did not know. He could learn from me, which made me feel more important, taller. I didn't know if Wolf would like this way 'a catchin' coons or not, but it saved the hide. He'd like that.

But, as fate had to have it, the learnin' never happened. A chase with the dogs turned out to be the best way for us to get coon hides. Granddad's way worked. I saw it work, but only he could ever do it. Dad and me never caught one single coon workin' them silver balls once they was left to us. It would be somethin' he nor I could ever figure. I remembered later on Granddad told me they was some words, a prayer maybe, had to be spoke over the hole 'fore you dropped in the silver. We never know'd them words. Maybe that was why the silver never worked for us.

Old Mother was took by the tale I told over Granddad's way 'a gettin' coon skins. She wanted to see the three small pieces of silver Granddad had left to us. Hold 'em in her hand, but that never happened. It was a clan thing for my Granddad. Only the home folks could partake. I reckon the tradition died with him, 'cause we never got none 'a the silver peas to work proper. It wouldn't 'a mattered no how. Within' several moons of Granddad's death, they went missin'. We looked everywhere we could think to look. We never saw the silver peas again. They just went away like a soul in the night. I never heard 'a nobody ever findin' 'em, neither, in all my years.

***

Our fire was near dead when me, Wolf, and Stripe returned from the hunt to our makeshift little campsite where we'd loosed Stripe 'fore dark. I kicked the burnt wood ends in tight on the near dead coals from around the edges. In just a minute, the fire was up; flames heatin' our coffee pot. A hot cup 'a coffee was gonna be good. It was time for a smoke, too. Study on all that'd happened.

We only got the one coon. Stripe never found no other scent after the first one he treed. Strange he didn't, it was a perfect night for coons to be out runnin'. I don't think I ever hunted with Stripe, other than that night, where he didn't run half a dozen or more 'fore we was ready to give up the chase. Somethin' just weren't right about things that night. Got ol' Stripe out 'a sorts, me too.

Chapter Fifteen

Red Hawk

The Cherokee warrior watched as Momma made it to the front door of Cain and Rose's place. Saw the door opened to let her in. She was safe. He would sit close by watchin' the house 'til well after dark. Wanted to make sure she stayed safe. The wife of Thompson Collins demanded respect.

Family to the Choestoe Cherokee, it was good he crossed her path on the way to the big ridges in the south. He followed her, stayed with her while she slept, and made sure she weren't bothered with trouble while she made her way to visit family. He know'd where she was goin'. Depended on her to tell Cain he was near. His nephew never saw him when he come from the house searchin' shortly after they welcomed her inside the warm. They would talk later. Bein' cautious was a habit for a tested warrior of the Cherokee Guard.

He was concerned, ponderin' what he must do. There was folks about. The woods had become dangerous recent — trespassers lookin' for gold. Rogue Indians lookin' for easy pickin's. Government folk what made the Indian folk restless — and he despised 'em all. Now, he'd crossed trails with the mother of the one who survived the blue birth. She was trailin' by herself. He figured she weren't aware of the new dangers facin' folks in the valley. Him comin' up on her was the will of the Great Spirit. A call to duty. He felt the need to mind that duty. She must be protected. She was special in the eyes of the true warriors of Choestoe, near sacred. Her travelin' alone angered him. A Cherokee princess of her importance would not be left without at least two warriors of some experience watchin' over her. Even so, he respected her bravery; her ability to take to the woods without fear. She had courage to face a trail by herself. He respected that, felt honored to be chosen to watch over her, if just for a little while.

He'd met her once before at the home of his brother, Dancing Bear, elder and council for the nation. It was nice bein' near her. You could feel her presence. Her spirit was very strong. The warriors all believed the Great One smiled on her. She was the mother of Jebediah Collins, the 'Spirit Filled One'. He felt it his call to keep watch to her trail, to make sure she stayed safe 'til she got where she was goin'.

Red Hawk saw it as the Great Spirit needed someone to know she was in the valley. A body He could trust. There was few better ready for the chore. He was Red Hawk, a senior warrior of the Cherokee Guard. Brother to Dancing Bear. Proven in battle to be one of the deadliest warriors in the mountains. He'd been givin' no quarter for watchin' over the nation. The will of God must be obeyed, even to death… whoever's that could be.

Red Hawk was a full on Cherokee warrior who lived life with no regrets. He had no wife, no children, no family, other than Dancing Bear and his clan, and no home to call his own. Mostly stayed to the woods for his way 'a livin'. Not carin' to be near folks, lest it was a gatherin' of some sort. His heart had been cut from the inside out many years before; his young wife was taken from him in ambush. He was just comin' into manhood to serve as a warrior when they hit. He spent years tryin' to find her. The takin' of his wife changed him forever - near tore his soul clean out from his person. And because of that, his blood would always run cold with hate for his enemy. Know'd 'em on sight, even by name. He partnered that hate with a vengeance for any enemy what went against the Cherokee. Hate and revenge can drive a man into his own world. Make him do things he'd not do if all was square.

He kept himself hid from folks. He was rarely seen. So, when Momma told Cain about seein' him on the trail to their house, she found out how important he was. Cain lit out straight away to try and speak with him, see what was about. No surprise he weren't there. Cain know'd Red Hawk would not be found if it weren't time to be found, but he wanted to give him a chance if that time was then.

He searched all around outside. Never found any sign to prove Momma really seen him. He wondered if it was just a vision. But after thinkin' on how she told it, he know'd Momma had seen him. It was Red Hawk, for sure, which told Cain they could be somethin' stirrin'. Knowin' danger might be close made him glad his new uncle was in the valley; felt much safer for Rose and Momma. He allowed Dad would be there soon. That thought give him even more comfort. His place would need more protection than some real soon. His home family would be growin'.

Momma told about crossin' paths with what she called "a somewhat familiar Indian." He reminded her of Dancing Bear. She asked Rose all the things she was curious about. Rose did her best to try and explain once she'd listened to all Momma had to say. It was difficult. Her uncle was a mysterious man. The family didn't worry over him much. They know'd what kind 'a person he was. How he lived. Figurin' him was near impossible for non-warrior folk.

"Mother Celia. I know you have many questions. It is natural to be curious. Let me explain to you about the man you met. You will know my uncle better when you hear. Then I will answer all of your questions," Rose assured Momma, as they sat the rockers by the hearth, rockin'.

Momma had her pipe goin', enjoyin' a nice bowl full 'a weaver tobacco. Restin', after cleanin' up from a fine supper of rock-hard biscuits, skillet burnt yellow squash, near-raw sweet potatoes, which weren't all bad or Momma would be starved, and bark hard corn fritters. Momma was still tryin' to get the foul taste out 'a her mouth from whatever sweet cake it was Rose had made. Rose know'd how to store food proper. She was just havin' a hard time learnin' to cook it on her indoor stove, a gift from Momma. Rose could lay a fine meal with open-fire cookin', but the store-bought stove was confusin' to her.

Poor Cain, Momma thought, *at least they was tasty roasted meat.*

Cain had a good hand with roastin' meat in the smokehouse. She smiled rememberin' what Dad went through with her learnin' to cook.

"The man you saw is my uncle, Red Hawk," Rose began, "Dancing Bear's older brother. He is a stranger to me as an uncle. Few really know him. The stories told about him say he is out there always. Yet sadly, he lives to himself. Understand, he is of the Guard. Many of those Cherokee remain alone. They go unseen most all the time, a calling to be honored among the most respected of all warriors. They keep us protected. Spend a lot of their time speaking with the Great Spirit. Red Hawk is one of many. I've seen him but a few times in my life but haven't seen him in many moons. You met him once at Dancing Bear's. His being here is curious. There will be a reason, a meaning to his visit. He is not ready to talk, or he would make himself known. His intent is only to let us know he is near. It will be interesting to know how he came to be with you. Cain will go tomorrow with the hope of speaking to him. We will know his duty then, if it is his time for us to know."

Momma know'd about the Cherokee Guard and how they kept watch, especially durin' the cold time. All livin' in the valley know'd about the Guard; trusted 'em with their very lives at times. Nobody really ever talked about 'em. Few stories was ever heard at the story fires. Many of their doin's weren't to be spoke of, ever. They kept the valley safe. The warriors what trailed with the guard was seasoned, respected. Their judgement had to be sound. They was to know what trouble looked like 'fore it ever reared its ugly head. Threats was dealt with like-for-same. Everybody know'd what that meant. It just weren't somethin' folks wanted to spell over.

We all know'd it had to be the way it was. It was the Cherokee way. Had been like that for as long as anybody livin' could remember. The mountains was Indian land 'fore our kin ever settled there. It weren't near as safe for common livin' without the watchful eyes of the Guard. Choestoe settlers favored their common lives. They know'd who held a big part of that privilege for 'em. Respect was showed. The Cherokee Guard helped keep life livable in Choestoe. Folks appreciated it, even though they heard very little of it. Red Hawk was the first known warrior of the Guard Momma had ever met. She'd lived in the mountains for many years, too. It was important to the Indians that the Guard stay as secret as they could. Momma respected that.

***

Black Oak trailed the little warriors 'til they crossed the big ridges west into Coosa. He wanted to see 'em clear of the valley 'fore trailin' south back to our place to help Anne tend to the hurt woman. He learned healin' when he worked with Anne; had an interest in her ways. Amazed at how she had the gift. He could see healin' come natural for her. So, he watched her close, learned all he could, listened all he could. He figured knowin' more healin' might help at some time, the way he lived and all, Indian livin'. The hurt demon stayed close by in the mountains when you lived the way Black Oak did. Pain, death, or pure joy could be with the next risin' of Old Man Sun. Love, if a man didn't watch.

She was resting by herself in the great room, rockin' in front of a good-sized fire, starin' at the yellow and orange flames as they danced their jigs. Her legs up on the hearth; feet bare, warmin'. Around her shoulders was one 'a Momma's heavy quilts pulled tight. Only her head was showin' from the top of her shoulders up. A short bit of hair had managed to grow back from where Anne shaved her head clean. The crawlies had to go.

He could smell her as soon as he breached the front door. Her sweet scent slapped him in the face — clean smellin', like spring flowers after a rain. She had more strength than the last time he'd seen her. He expected nothin' less with Owl and Anne tendin' to her. She had a pull he felt comin' from her soul. He could sense it. Yet, he tried to not understand it.

His neck was tight; hard to turn. Figured it for a bad spirit. No, not so. Me and Wolf know'd it was from lookin' back from the front seat of the harvest wagon so many times while bringin' Wind Is Strong to our place. We seen him at it while we trailed behind - called him on it later. He said he didn't do nothin' of the kind. He was just worried over how she was, how the ride was treatin' her. Concerned for her life. Yep, he looked it, too.

He never spoke to her. They'd never had the chance while she was awake. Their eyes met as he closed the door. She smiled weakly as Black Oak nodded back kinda nervous like. He'd been on the trail for a few days. Hunger had a hold on him. He felt nasty and tired. Probably smelled bad for needin' a wash. His hair was dirty, but he didn't wanna be disrespectful, so he went and sat the hearth, close enough to speak to her. His words were hard for him to speak. She made him feel strange, different than he felt with most folk. He couldn't keep himself from lookin' at her. Her eyes was beautiful. They looked tired, weak, but at least they was open with life.

"You are feeling better, Wind Is Strong. That is good," Black Oak spoke as he turned to look at her. "My prayer for you is being answered. I did not know if you would be with us today when Thompie and I carried you from Panther Cave several suns ago. I am George Black Oak, Cherokee from the valley where the rabbits are said to dance, Cho-Ē -sto-Ē. I bid you welcome. I will be here for a while. I go where I am needed. I will do what you need. I am here for you." He bowed his head some.

She didn't know it, but that weren't the Black Oak we all know'd talkin' to her. He'd turned from fierce warrior into mush. She had a way about her he was fond of. We started to notice he was actin' like he was took.

Her voice was weak, even so, it sounded like honey drippin' from its comb to him — sweet, smooth, full, soft but firm. If he didn't watch it, they'd be a sting hidin' behind her kind smile.

"Thank you, Black Oak," she replied, rollin' her head over to her left some so's she could see him better. "I am thankful… to all."

The need to talk was too much. Used up her little bit 'a strength. She closed her eyes as her head laid back straight in the rocker, her smile fadin'.

"You rest. I will be here." Black Oak slid over to her from his spot on the hearth, near movin' her rocker with his leg he'd moved in so close. He folded his big arms over the tops of his knees, said a quiet prayer. His head leaned forward, slightly tilted so he could keep watch. He felt for her pain.

"Water… Black Oak. I need… a drink. If you would…" she said as a long brown arm eased out from under the quilt, then laid across the rocker arm like a snake settlin'. A portion of her left side then exposed. The fire made her skin look alive as her hand come to rest on his elbow. She never opened her eyes.

"Yes, Wind Is Strong. I will bring water."

He gently moved her arm back to rest in her lap, then covered her upper left side back over with the fold of the quilt. He near ran to the cook room. Nobody was there. He looked all over but found no drinkin' water. A trip to the well provided a half-bucket of some nice, cold spring water. He took it to her.

"I have brought you some cool, fresh water from the well. The cold will make you strong -- drink. Make the thirst go away, Wind Is Strong."

He dipped a small drinkin' gourd, which Anne had purposefully left on the hearth for Wind, into the bucket, draw'd out a good, cool drink. He held it steady for her lower lip with his fingers, give it a slight tip to help her drink. She responded. Her head straightened what it could to accept the offering. She drank. He watched as her lips worked to take in water. How her throat struggled to swallow the life-givin' liquid only Mother Earth could provide. The cool of the water killed her burnin' thirst. She thanked him again with a soft smile as she finished her waterin'. He liked her smile. No words was said to the notion, but feelin's was bein' birthed. He was enjoyin' the time with her. He hoped she felt the same way, if she could feel anything through the pain.

***

Dad was tired when he got to Cain's late in the night of the evening we'd got home with Wind. He'd struck out to fetch Momma soon as we'd got back. Momma put him to bed after he'd washed and eat. He was still sleepin' when supper was served the followin' evening. Momma fed him as he finally woke early the followin' morning. Makin' his first trip outside in over a day, he never know'd he was so tired. Thinkin' on it, he'd not slept in near three days. His trail had been a sleepless one. Cain understood the need for rest, as did Momma and Rose. They all left him be 'til he come awake good on his own.

Cain went out lookin' for Red Hawk again, knowin' if he was ready to talk, he'd be outside waitin'. He didn't bother to go look out in the woods. He wouldn't 'a found him no how. He just weren't showin' himself.

Momma wanted to stay a while with Dad, visit with Rose and Cain. They talked about it after he woke. She just weren't in no hurry to get back. She wanted to spend time with her new daughter. Anne was home with Wind Is Strong. Jeb and Wolf was there. Black Oak would be goin' there. She weren't needed. Winters went slow in Choestoe. They all know'd where her and Dad was. It was decided in her mind, which meant it was decided in Dad's mind, too.

    Momma always got her way in matters of what they did together. And if somethin' weren't pressin' him, he'd make time for what she wanted, no questions. He looked forward to pleasin' her. Spendin' time with Momma was his thought of what Heaven would be like. She made his life pleasurable, complete, and he was gettin' to be with her at Cain's for a few days. She know'd there weren't nothin' on him, bein' winter and all. Livin' close up for a spell would make the cold time much more tolerable for the both of 'em.

***

    The camp was small. They was keepin' the fire down so Indians wouldn't find 'em. Little did they know they'd been watched by the Cherokee since the morning they crossed the Duncan Ridge three days before. They didn't even know where they was.

    Red Hawk had cut their trail 'fore he run into Momma. Followed it south. Deeper into the heart of the valley. They'd stayed on the ridge tops 'til they come to the low gap, then followed the trail north to the headwaters of the west fork of Wolf Creek. They was on foot with a near wore-out, old jack totin' their truck. Somebody got 'em good tradin' 'em that ol' thing.

    You could tell by lookin' at 'em they was poorly clothed to be wanderin' the mountains durin' cold time. All three was wearin' single layer homespun wool suits and undergarments, slick bottom leather boots with no fur and flimsy little city-bought hats what didn't even cover their ears. They was cold, shiverin' cold. The blankets they was wrapped in weren't near heavy enough. Worn plumb through in a few places. At least they was smart enough to camp down out 'a the wind. That would help.

Red Hawk draw'd his hatchet, then threaded the handle through his belt next to his long knife, lowerin' it to the hilt. Leavin' his sleepin' truck in a small pile behind a good-sized ivy bush, he stood to take a final look at their camp, then walked straight on up to their fire. He wanted to speak with them. Warn them of the danger they faced from the bad weather he could feel comin'. They never moved. Their only weapon, an old smooth bore musket leaned by a tree several paces away.

Fools. These folks are fools. I should kill them for being stupid. Put 'em out of their misery, he thought as he walked to their fire.

There was three men: two grow'd, one near half grow'd. The older two had thick hair on their faces grow'd down to their middle. The third had very little hair on his face. He was sufferin' bad, too. So cold he couldn't even raise his head good when Red Hawk come in on 'em. Folks what kept themselves the way these did was a most disgustin' sight to a Cherokee – dirty and filthy. The way they kept their hair was wrong. He thought again to kill 'em just for that. Near did after the breeze shifted, puttin' him downwind 'a their foul odor.

Fools!

Red Hawk figured he near scared the life out of 'em. He hid a grin at the looks they gave him as he walked in. No way they'd ever seen a seasoned Cherokee warrior wearin' battle truck. From what they'd most likely been told, you'd not live through it if you did meet one.

The two men jumped up like scared rats when they seen him. Slingin' their quilt from off their backs while movin' toward the old gun. The boy could not move more'n raisin' his head some. Red Hawk thought he might be plumb froze. Figured the other two for cold crazy.

"You leave us be wild man," the taller of the two said. "We've heard what the likes 'a you do. Eat us if we let you. Well, you'll not eat me!"

In one motion, the stranger reached for the long gun, then swung it around toward Red Hawk while pullin' back the hammer. The long knife split his heart 'fore he could ever lift the heavy gun to hip level at Red Hawk. The warrior would not be shot by the likes 'a him. What kinda death story would that be. He pulled his hatchet while turnin' on the dead man's friend. The bearded one simply went back to sit by the fire, wrapped himself whole with his quilt. The younger man had already snatched the dead man's quilt for himself. They was both shakin' without stoppin'.

Red Hawk was big for an Indian, tall like Dancing Bear. Their father was tall. His mix of winter skins and homespun clothing was somethin' the strangers needed badly. His knee-high beaver skin boots with the hair turned in kept his feet warm where their feet was froze. His feet dry where their feet was most likely wet, 'fore they froze. They wore the white man's boots. Nothin' much at all to keep the cold out or turn water. Red Hawk was warm standin' there lookin' at the two sad sacks. He felt for the boy as he raised his hatchet. Spoke to the pitiful sight before him.

"You are fools to come here as you have. You would be wise to go home. The cold time is long this season. This young one looks cold struck. He needs to be warm. Your blankets are no good. Your fire is little help. The cold wind is coming. The white cold could fall this night. If it does, you will die, the boy first. Why would you come here in such a foolish way?"

Neither of 'em spoke. Red Hawk went to the dead man. Fetched the bloody knife from his chest; rubbed it off on the sleeve of the dead one's wool coat. He'd throw'd it from several paces hittin' him square. It always amazed me watchin' Indians throw knives and hatchets. I could do it decent. Hit things some. They could stick you in the spot they wanted in a second. Cain was good at it. Dad was real good at it. Wolf was good at it, too. I saw him throw his knife plenty. He could pin squirrels to the sides 'a trees, if they was low enough down. He know'd how. There was a trick to it. If you caught 'em just right, they would stop for a brief second just as they hit the tree they was aimin' to climb. Right then, when they made that slight pause just after jumpin' up on the side of a tree, was when you let it fly. I'd seen Wolf kill a bait of 'em that way.

"My trail is away from here. I must go. I hope you do well, young one." The boy looked up at him much as he could. Red Hawk saw death.

Without hesitation, he moved on to the duty he was sworn to 'fore trailin' up on the small camp. The duty he was workin' on when he crossed trails with the wife of Thompie Collins - to protect the valley from a sure threat. Strangers what looked like enemy soldiers. A good-sized bunch with more than a wore out jack and a few diggin' tools. Them in this camp was a mix of U.S. Government men, led by Indian scouts and settlers -- gold searchers workin' for the Federal men. They had two cooks with their own covered wagons for food cookin'. By the way they built their fires, and the look of their one camp — several horses, two teams 'a mules, and hogs for meat — show'd they was planning on camping there a while.

Total to all was twenty, plus three rogue Cherokee scouts hired to show the intruders through the sacred home of the Cherokee. They would never see their clan again for becomin' traitors to their people. Red Hawk had already sworn that to his ancestors across the river. Death would be their reward for sellin' out the mountains for pure greed. He would kill their families, too, if he ever crossed-up with 'em.

Chapter Sixteen

It is Good to Know Your Enemy

The word Dancing Bear was gettin' from the warriors of the Guard was troubling. He know'd what was comin', just wanted it not to. Knowin' his way of livin' might change made him concerned, sad, and angry. He and the elders at council had been havin' visions of white men lookin' for gold, killin' Indians, and stealin' homes and land. Of federal men trailin' through the mountains, cuttin' wounds into trees. The Indians could feel the evil of a body that would torture the trees. It scared 'em as a nation.

The talk around the smoke fires was of concern. It weren't gonna be good for the Cherokee what called the mountains of Choestoe home. The council know'd it. The broken treaties of past years had proved the white leaders untrustworthy. Dancing Bear had rather they stay away, but wisdom told him they would not. They was here, *in his home*. He feared blood would flow . . . know'd deep down it would flow. He'd seen the blue soldiers' work in his younger days. They could be ruthless, heartless, near soulless.

***

Dad know'd Red Hawk. Been on trail with him many times. So, when Momma told him about them meetin' on the trail to Cain's, it sparked Dad's need to know. *What would bring him down this low? Why was he near? Had he left any sign?* He would need to look around 'fore too long.

Dad figured he'd be talkin' with Red Hawk soon enough. He'd not showed himself to Cain. Time weren't right for talk yet. Dad would have no trouble findin' him if he was near. The warrior would show himself to Thompie Collins, if he went to search him out.

Dad weren't gonna put himself in no hurry - Red Hawk didn't seem to be. He thought to spend some time with Momma. He could feel the trail callin' down in his gut since Red Hawk was close. Know'd he'd be answerin' soon. The Guard bein' down low was uncommon. Somethin' was stirrin'.

***

Rose and Momma was havin' a big ol' time. They'd spent the better part of two days in the cook room; their nights talkin'. Rose had a shine to her skin. Momma noticed.

She was teachin' Rose how to use her indoor cook stove. For dinners and suppers, they was havin' boiled or baked vegetables, biscuits, fry meat and gravy. All the while, Rose was usin' Momma's old cook stove, learnin' proper. Rose had learned on open fire pit cookin' with clay bread ovens to the side. Cain had yet to get her outdoor cookin' pit or oven ready. Indoor cookin' was new to her, so she burnt most 'a what she cooked. Found it difficult settin' the fire proper for the food she was workin' with. Momma could see when she arrived Cain was sufferin' from what was probably feelin' like half-near starvation. He was a good eater when he sat for meals normal. He'd slimmed up a right smart now that him and Rose was hitched. Momma felt for him. Figured to stay, and in a polite way, teach her new daughter in the ways 'a home keepin'. Rose thanked her for the concern. She learned how to cook indoor from Momma. She'd teach my wife later on. I loved Rose.

Momma got her a new stove not long 'fore Cain and Rose ever married. Dad traded for it at the early season market in Gaines Town, then hauled it in a wagon all the way through the mountains to home. Black Oak went with him. Allowed it took two extra day's travel makin' it back. Dad said Jim had a time. It was special to Momma, knowin' Dad had done her proud. The stove had a bread bakin' side what draw'd enough heat to make the best cornbread, cathead biscuits or sweet cake you ever put your mouth to.

The old one Rose got cooked just fine. It was seasoned from several years' use in Momma's cook room. Food tasted so good when cooked on it proper. I reckon it was most likely an answer to one 'a Cain's regular prayers when Momma stayed to help his wife learn stove cookin'. Cain worked hard buildin' his place and providin', daylight to dark most days. He needed nourishment to go the long hours he stayed at it.

His place was sure nice'n up good, though. He had a fine touch about him. A lot like Dad when workin' with his hands. Dad had worked him a right smart over the years, watchin' him, teachin' him. Ever since the wedding, he'd been goin' over to help at Cain's when he had time. They got a lot done workin' together. It was a sight 'a help to Cain and Rose for Dad to do that.

Momma's teachin' Rose some cookin' skills helped a heap. With all 'a what they was buildin', Cain needed to eat good. Cain and Rose didn't have to ask my folks for help, neither. They saw a need the young couple had and took to makin' things better. It's what family did when I grow'd up.

Rose and Momma cleaned the house so well it was hard to know if folks even lived there. They sharpened the meat knives, re-worked the pantry puttin' the most used things easier to fetch, and just stayed busy doin' house chores. Rose learned a lot 'a home keepin ways from Momma, and Momma learned, too - mostly about her new daughter. They both enjoyed every minute of it.

At night, they'd sit by the fire for hours talkin', smokin', readin' the Bible, studyin' on things, and worryin' over concerns. They sipped hard cider warmed in a hangin' teapot over the fire while nibblin' on sweet cake. Rose braided Momma's hair. Momma brushed Rose's long beautiful mane. It made for a fine time 'a bein' together. They was growin' close just like a true mother and daughter.

Of course, if you studied on it, they was. Dancing Bear had adopted my family. We was all one.

They'd take walks durin' the warm part of the mornings all wrapped up in quilts, talkin', watchin' as they went, lookin', hopin' to see something wonderful — some deer, a wolf or bear, an eagle, or possibly a beaver workin'. An Indian? It wouldn't be a surprise if one showed, but, they weren't expectin' to see no Indian. Wouldn't be too worried if they did. So, they weren't surprised to be seein' the one beside the trail they was followin' not more than twenty paces away. They both froze, lookin' close, tryin' to figure it out.

Expectin' it or not, there he stood, handsome, strong lookin', seasoned. His winter skins holdin' marks for bravery and courage. His was a face of stone - eyes squinted, searchin' all his surroundings like a hawk. His head had been shaved on both sides with a strip down the middle that braided whole in the back reachin' near to the center of his shoulders. Full battle truck hung off various parts of his body. His bow, unstrung, was laced to his pouch straps across his back; a quiver of sharp-pointed arrows with it. His one long knife showed, but smaller ones were sure to be hid in other places. A hatchet was tied to his right side along with three separate pouches. Two pouches hung around his neck with one braided into his belt that carried his possibles: pipe, tobacco, flint and steel. A simple, braided leather cord threaded through a dozen big cat claws hung from his neck, a huge honor for him to wear. Very few Cherokee could claim a big cat kill, let alone one done by hand. Old Mother had mine.

He was draggin' a fresh kilt buck. Rose looked closer, then settled herself when she saw the friendly smirk at the edge of his mouth. Moon Shadow, her brother. From where they was standin', his appearance was amazing. His majesty stunning the way he blended with the woods, a part of the forest. Moon Shadow hadn't been seen or heard from in a long while. She had many questions for him, but they could wait. For the moment, she was just admiring the man he'd come to be. The strength he show'd was near frightening to her. He'd aged some.

He was bringin' fresh meat. A deer from the bunch he ran into feedin' on ivy earlier that morning. A sharp flint arrow to the heart from less than ten paces was all it took for him to make the harvest. He was the best hunter in the clan. But even for him, it was gettin' harder to find deer. He'd stopped killin' the mommas, if he could help it. The hide market south 'a the mountains was callin' for more. The Cherokee was obligen' 'em, tradin' hides for gold coin. Killed more than they needed collectin' them hides. Made for less food wanderin' through the woods come suppertime. Moon Shadow thought the overkill to be disrespectful to folks, deer, Mother Earth. Foolish thinkin'. A waste. The Guard hunted for folks who couldn't hunt for themselves. Them Indians what took deer for hides made some coin, which helped their families, but the deer was gettin' gone, and that hurt folks. Tradin' good for bad, really. Hogs and bears was still workin' the ridges. We liked that meat just fine, even though fresh deer meat was preferred.

Cain was real happy when he learned Moon Shadow had brought in a deer. Rose was in need of some fresh meat. What meat he'd worked up at Killin' Time was gettin' cold dried. Some fresh with real blood flowin' through it recent was gonna be good. Cain had made his mind to go for a hunt soon but could put it off for a while. Moon Shadow had taken care of that need for a spell. The Great Spirit had seen to it. Of Him providin', there was no doubt in Cain's mind. Deer was becomin' scarce. For Moon Shadow to bring one in was a near miracle at that time of the season. Critters would be layin' up most all day since the cold time was still goin' strong; savin' what energy they could to keep warm. Movin' to eat what little they needed, makin' sure to move no more'n what they had to.

There was a reason Moon Shadow had come to Cain's. Red Hawk had sent for him by runner a few suns back. Told him to meet at Cain's on the fifth sun risin'. He did not know the reason, only that he was to come. He would not question what Red Hawk ordered, just obey his duty. A warrior from the Guard was expected to do nothin' less. He was curious when he learned Dad was there.

It was the first Rose and Cain know'd of her brother's adoption into the Guard. It was hard to swallow, Moon Shadow becomin' a respected warrior of the Cherokee Guard, had been for many moons without folks knowin'. We understood. It made perfect sense to all who know'd him. He lived in the woods most all the time anyway. Moon Shadow was equal to most warriors at readin' sign, trackin' food critters, or folks. He was took on by the Guard shortly after his brother, Fox Running, had been murdered by the coward no one spoke of no more. The name of the evil warrior from south of the mountains had been forgotten by all Cherokee. Cain had seen to that.

The murder of Fox Running had changed Moon Shadow, same as it had Wolf. Made him mean in his thinkin'. Opened his eyes to the evil that could rise up unexpected like. His call now was to protect his people, to keep them safe when danger come to the valley and provide meat to those who could no longer hunt. He was good at it. His reputation among the Guard was favorable. Hadn't been too long what they'd give him his own part of the nation's boundary to watch over. He honored them by acceptin' his responsibility with courage, showin' no fear. He was the son of Dancing Bear. His fellow warriors expected him to be strong. He was bound by no less. He loved his life; know'd he'd been called to it by the Great Spirit. There weren't no doubtin' it, neither.

***

Dad thought Red Hawk looked older than the last time he'd seen him. Cain and Moon Shadow watched as the two warriors faced each other, their eyes answerin' questions, forearms molded as one, showin' they was friends. Nobody but them could know how close. I could see Dad was humbled. That was a rare sight for me.

"Thompie Collins, how has the Great Spirit watched over you since last we crossed ways?" Red Hawk asked, his eyes searchin' Dad's. "You are still a white man. I cannot help you with that. Maybe one day the Great Creator will send you a change spirit. Make you look handsome like me." They both smiled.

Dad replied, "I would be honored if the Holy One saw to it for that to happen my friend, but it is my prayer He sees fit to send the change spirit to your camp. You would still be handsome in a white skin. Do not worry."

They both smiled again as they broke forearms and sat. Red Hawk had a good size fire built that morning, the day after Moon Shadow come. It was a small camp he'd set at the edge of the woods south 'a Cain's. Those in the house would see the fire as they woke. Know he was ready to talk.

He'd watched as Moon Shadow come the day before with a fresh kill. Give him a taste for some roasted deer ham. Saw Thompie Collins; was glad he was there. Thanked the Great Spirit for sending him. Watched as Thompie helped Moon Shadow hang, then skin the deer. He longed for a taste.

He'd spied on the intruders' camp all he needed. It was time for talk to be made with his family, questions answered. He know'd Thompie would be lookin' for him to show himself. He was there at daylight. Made it easy to know he was there. The fire in Red Hawk's camp weren't to be missed. It was warm, too. They would smoke.

***

Back home, Anne and me reasoned our folks weren't comin' back straight away. Kinda obvious since they weren't back after three days, then four. It was a while after the marryin'. Momma was naturally concerned for her family, daughter and son. Worried they might need some teachin' from older folks what'd been through it all. If so, it would all be square 'fore Momma left. She'd see to it. That was a good thing for Rose and Cain. Life would be better from her visit.

Rose held no hard feelin's. No feelin' of disrespect toward her new mother. Momma's aim was to be helpful by showin' her things she should do concernin' house chores and cookin'. Rose know'd she meant the best. She loved my momma, respected her, and was smart enough to hold her emotions. To listen to Momma when she told how to do certain chores a woman was responsible for that were natural to a woman's way 'a thinkin'. Dad always said it was rare for two wives to live comfortable in the same house, even for a little while like a visit. But Momma and Rose did fine. Never had a cross word between 'em, ever. They respected each other from years 'a knowin' one another through families. That goes a long way when friendship is at stake.

***

Wind Is Strong was gettin' better day-by-day. She could walk some now. Could make her way to the porch easy enough when she needed to rock. We'd sit and rock with her, talk. Black Oak, too. He had to have his own special rocker. Dad built it for him. It was half-again bigger than a common rocker most folks used. Made from hickory 'cause he didn't want it to break into splinters from the weight of Black Oak's huge body as he'd sit down. It was fun to rock in when Black Oak weren't around. My feet would just hang, not near touchin' the board floor of our porch.

"You look stronger today, Wind Is Strong," Black Oak said as they sat rockin', lookin' out over the farm from the front porch. "I have prayed your strength would come back to you. I feel you are healing from your run to freedom. Anne says your wound is no longer angry. This is good. Praise be to the Great Creator."

She had her head laid back against the oak rocker. Her face turned to look at him as she spoke, "I feel a bit stronger, Black Oak. I'm hungry now most of the time. I can sense my body healing from the care my sweet, darling Anne has shown me." Black Oak dropped his head as if prayin'.

She moved her left arm up to where his right arm covered his rocker's armrest. Laid her hand over his forearm. He looked over at her, the green in her eyes nearly takin' the air from his lungs. He listened to the beauty in her voice as she spoke.

"I owe you my life, big friend. I owe Wolf, Jeb, Thompie, Old Mother, Anne, and the Good Lord only knows how much I can never repay to Celia. Will they ever know how deeply I hold the love they've shown to me? A stranger not of this land? Will you ever know?" Her eyes narrowed.

Quick as she'd got the words out clear, her eyes squinted shut hard. She jerked her head back straight as a sudden pang grabbed her side. It trailed up her back, then on through to her shoulders. Black Oak turned as he softly braced her shoulder off with his hand. Her eyes opened. He saw no death. Healing was bein' hard on her, though. She was fightin' with it constant.

"You owe me nothing, Wind Is Strong. You were hurt, needed help. That is what matters. I feel you would do the same for any of us. I know this in my heart. Your spirit speaks to me in dreams. I am comfortable with trusting what I see."

***

Red Hawk spoke words nobody wanted to hear. Unwelcomed visitors had made camp in the southern end of Choestoe. Nobody wanted 'em. They was not invited. Encroachin' on sacred land, killin' food the locals depended on, and if that weren't enough, they was takin' gold from the creeks. The Cherokee did not like that fact. Truth be told, the gold was why they was comin'. Everybody know'd that, even government men, too.

"Ten are fighting men," Red Hawk began. "Soldiers. They wear blue. Their lower legs covered by the long boots. A curved long knife strapped to their chosen side. Over all their clothing, they wear a heavy woven coat. Gray in color like the first light of the morning. The guns they carry are deadly. Their aim is true. Ten others share the camp. They are settlers. Gold searching settlers looks to be. Most likely given safe passage by the soldiers to find gold. The last three are Cherokee, their guides through the mountains. Lost souls who've sold out their people for the gold coin. Greedy ones who will never leave this valley. The camp is well stocked. Extra covers are up to keep their supplies dry. Provisions are many -- more than enough. I believe they aim to stay for a time. I expect more of the same to come. That is who we have as unwelcomed guests to our home."

Dad, Cain, and Moon Shadow listened close while Red Hawk was talkin'. Every word had meanin' when faced with the decisions that had to be made. They all fetched their pipes and tobacco pouches. Commenced to fillin' their bowls with their choosin' of smoke. This was a big problem to consider. These trespassers was uninvited by the locals and insisted on by the U.S. Government. That held weight. The Cherokee claimed the land. Wars with the Creek for huntin' grounds had ended, but wounds of the tribe was still healin'. The soldiers was backed by the U.S. Congress. Killin' one 'a them was like attackin' General George himself, even though he was long gone. We liked General Washington in Choestoe a right smart. We did not want to make war with his people. They'd whupped the British. Sent 'em packin' back across the Great Waters. That held merit with the folks what lived in the valley, Cherokee, too, as many who'd sided with the Red Coats got whupped right along with the rest of them British soldiers.

"The U.S. Government have come to our home," Dad said, after about an hour of nobody sayin' nothin', just thinkin'. "We may not like it, but they are here. We must be very careful. Make sure we give them no reason to stay in this valley. If they finish what it is they are doin' here, they will leave. If they find no gold, they will not come back. I would like to watch them for a while more, to see their true intentions, to know their purpose 'fore we face 'em for talk. When that time does come, I will take Cain. We will make the talk. Soldiers will not be as nervous around two common folks as two battle-ready Cherokee. How does this fit with the thinkin' of my brothers?"

"I, too, would like to watch this bunch for a while longer," replied Moon Shadow. "Killing soldiers is like killing the yellow bee. Its death brings more yellow bees. That will be worse than these few who are here now. I agree, if they find nothing, I believe they will leave. We should watch them for a time more."

"It is wise to give this more thought. It is good to know your enemy. The words you speak are wise, Thompie. We will watch," answered Red Hawk, speaking for the Guard.

***

It was her first walk out since she'd been healed-up enough to walk. Black Oak led her to the barn, then followed the south trail out from there to a small rise a little ways from the edge of the mule pasture where there was seats. Big pieces of firewood turned on end, with a fire pit in the center, and dry wood under a lean-to me and Dad had built. It was a great place to sit, think, pray, or have a smoke. The walk in winded her some, even though it was only a quarter mile 'a flat ground. She sat in a big, tall, old oak stump. Granddad had carved out 'a wood seat, comfortable back, and a place to put your feet. Black Oak started a warmin' fire. It was good for her to get out, move around some, get her lungs workin', breathin' in good, cool mountain air. She liked bein' out. It'd been a while since she made her run from The Lost.

"You rest while I build up a warming fire," said Black Oak as he squatted down on one knee. Grabbin' hold to the edge of the seat with his right arm to steady himself, he looked her in the eye. She slid up to the front of the seat to get close to him. "We will sit. Talk in this quiet place. Are you comfortable? Do you need water?"

"I have my water skin you filled for me. That is plenty. It is sweet how you care for me so," she said, leanin' in against his front, so close he could smell her. Taste her scent. Her emerald green eyes locked into his. "You, your family, you've all been so good to me. How can I ever return the favor of life I have received? I am very thankful it was Jeb and Wolf who found me. And you, my friend, I thank the Great Spirit for you. You make me feel welcome. I will never forget what has been done for me here."

Black Oak's world exploded as she slid her hands behind his head pullin' his face to hers. He felt her chest press against his as their lips locked in a passionate long awaited comin' together. The fire he felt in his soul was unlike anything he'd ever known as he wrapped her up in his arms, holdin' her tight as could be without causin' hurt. A feelin' so strong it's call was painful, but, it was a good pain he did not want to be away from.

Her mind was numb. The firmness of his embrace nearly made her quit breathing. His scent was overbearing. His strength a comfort. Being close to him was a pleasure she'd not known since just before her husband had been murdered in the raid that made her a slave. It was nice with such a man as Black Oak near. She'd begun havin' strong feelings for him. She did not mind that.

His heart was full as the kiss lingered for a while, then faded. The pleasure holdin' as well. He wanted to be away from this being that had entered his life, to come to an understandin' of the thoughts in his mind, the feelings in his soul. *What is this? How is it a woman could weaken a man so? Does she feel the same? How could one tell? Do you ask such things? It seems you do not. Oh, what world is it I have entered with this stranger from another land?* He wondered what his future was gonna look like now if he could not escape the pull of what must be... almost had to be... the thing a warrior fears most... the thing that gets good men killed... it was a dreaded word for a man... but one he was learning to cherish... love.

Chapter Seventeen

Leave 'em Be

The Indians was nervous about this new breed 'a gold hunter payin' visit to the valley. All visitors was watched for a time when they first crossed the nation's boundary. Once they was found to be of no threat, they was left be. Most was not a threat. Caused little damage other than what small bit 'a gold or what not they'd take. But these new lookers was different, heavily armed. Soldiers and settlers alike was both carryin' brand new flintlock rifles. Most settlers wearin' homespun over skins, these folks was considered threatenin'. A worthy enemy. The gold hunters what come before had been more of a nuisance, like parasites pickin' up pieces of this and that, scroungin', workin' for crumbs so to speak. This new bunch weren't like that. They was skilled, more capable, and much better equipped. They was bein' watched constant with great concern, their camp noted in full detail.

It was obvious these new folks know'd where they was comin' to. They'd made provision for their stay and was prepared for the cold world they'd be livin' in for a couple 'a months prior to makin' camp on Wolf Creek. Many fire pits layed around their camp. Firewood stacked in cords. Warm clothing for all. Settler traitors, too. Heavy wool top coats with lots 'a pockets for all who was there. Solid winter boots made from water turnin' leather with fur on the inside. Stacks 'a hand-quilted blankets, thick bedrolls with pillows, and hand-sewn sheets. Good stores of food. Fresh meat, cheese, milk, coffee, tea, sugar, and gun powder — plenty 'a gun powder. Couple 'a barrels full stored real careful-like inside a dry canvas tent. Wood standards drove into the ground with grooves cut in the top for the bottom edge of the barrel to sit on. That helped keep the moisture out by lettin' air flow underneath. The doors was folded proper on each end directin' air to move through. A guard posted at that tent constant, all day and all night. Never a time when their fightin' supplies weren't watched over. It was gonna be a challenge.

All their provisions would keep 'em alive, but it was their weapons that give 'em strength. Kept 'em safe. Each soldier had two U.S. .54 caliber flintlock pistols, a U.S. Harpers Ferry .54 caliber flintlock rifled long gun, and the very deadly curved long knife hangin' off their fancy belts. That thing could do damage to a body real quick like. I meant to have me one 'a them, sheath and all.

***

Dad told us everything about the camp he'd learned from Red Hawk first thing when he got home that afternoon. The folks in the camp, the soldiers, all the provisions they had stored, and the two mule teams. Everybody was bein' made aware of it. Indian and settler alike. Wolf and me know'd the very spot where they'd laid the camp. Been there many times. It was simple to get to. Easy place to slip in on. They was perched on a little rise east of West Wolf Creek. Sidin' to the north end of the upper Wolf Creek flats. Only problem was, we weren't allowed to go near it. None of us. An order was sent out by runner. A direct order to stay away from the camp given by Dancing Bear himself. He was leavin' it to the Guard for watchin' 'em. All others was required to stand clear of that holler 'til they'd got done and left out.

"Leave 'em be" was the exact words my dad used after he returned home from Cain's. He'd left Momma but was goin' back later that evening. He was there to collect his fightin' truck, gather some provisions, and have a talk with Black Oak about what all was goin' on. Ask him to stay at our place a while to protect things, watch over us, tend to the stock on the farm, and help Anne with Wind Is Strong, since Owl had gone back to Slaughter Mountain. He told me and Wolf to keep clear 'a the camp's doin's as he was leavin', said it as he was goin' through the door headin' to Cain's later that evenin'. Left us with no time to plead our case. He never would 'a given us permission no how. Dancing Bear had made the order. We weren't to go near that camp or any of the folks stayin' in it. That rule was spoke clear. We know'd exactly what was expected of us. Our fathers should 'a been sharper than to try and keep us from trailin' up to where the camp laid... or maybe they was.

It was interestin' hearin' what Dad had to say about our unwelcomed guests. Terrible we weren't bein' allowed to go see 'em. Wolf and me was dumbfounded, speechless, deep in thought. I know'd what Wolf's thoughts was sayin', same as mine. We had to go. We'd need to figure some way to not disobey our fathers, but still get a chance to have at that camp.

What we was bein' asked to do was not possible. What? Keep clear? Leave 'em be? Right. A treasure layin' for capture was just too much temptation for the likes 'a Wolf and me. If Dancing Bear and Dad weren't so serious in their instruction, it'd be near funny thinkin' we'd not go see it.

What was they thinkin'? The biggest thing to come to the valley in our lives — the enemy — and they thought tellin' us to stay away would do any good. Surely, they could reason Wolf would have to see it. It'd be like keepin' bees from their honey gettin' him not to go look in on that camp, like holdin' water in a homespun sock.

Knowin' Wolf, they should 'a figured he'd already made a list in his mind of the things he would take before that bunch pulled out 'a Choestoe. The first thing on that list? One 'a them shiny, new, U.S. issued long rifles. Just out 'a the box. Never fired. I could guarantee you, without question, I know'd my friend, he'd have one 'a them guns in his possession 'fore the soldiers got gone from the valley.

I made my mind to fetch what I wanted, too. They was takin' Choestoe gold and food meat, layin' trail for future folk to bring their trouble, changin' mine and Wolf's life forever, and takin' away our peace. Seemed fair to us for a couple mountain boys to trade 'em for some much-needed truck to protect ourselves with -- our families. They had more than they needed. Probably reasoned some would most likely get gone one way or another anyhow. Way we saw it, we'd oblige their suspicions. Take some 'a what extra they had stored in them tents. 'Sides, they was enemy to us. Better if they didn't have it.

We didn't care about any fear we had of the ones camped. No, what worried on us was how the Great Spirit was gonna take us doin' what our fathers told us not to. How Dancing Bear would react to the disrespect of bein' disobeyed if we got caught. God clearly said they'd be no stealin' in His book. We know'd that. But this weren't stealin' to us. Takin' from an enemy that's plannin' trouble for folks weren't stealin'. We considered it weakenin' the foe. And, the gold they took was just as important to us as possessions was to them. This was tradin' by stealin' from the enemy durin' a war kinda way. Our folks ought 'a be proud of the effort we was figurin' to make. However, I would never tell my dad I took nothin' from the government. He'd not want me to have it. He'd figure anything they had as evil.

The Cherokee saw it same as us. They cared little what happened to these varmints as long as death stayed away. I got to wantin' me one 'a them new guns to company the long, curved knife I planned on gettin'. Wolf and me would have to smoke over the self-inflicted danger comin' our way. Pray for protection. Pray our fathers never found out. We needed to plan very carefully. Dancing Bear had ordered us to stay away. My dad had told us as well. We would be goin' against both of 'em. A terrible thing for a son to do, but forgivable, as long as all went well. How foolish was I to think things would work out the way we first planned? It never did.

I believed somethin' was bein' done about the intruders, and I figured Dad to be a part of it. His mind was a mile away when he left that evening. I figured Cain would be in on it, too. Gatherin' fightin' truck will make a body take thought. Cause you to be quiet with all the expectin' your mind trails to. It's only human to be concerned when a fight is comin'. Yet, there was somethin' else. It seemed he had more on his mind than the trouble brewin' on Wolf Creek. I prayed for the family.

***

Wolf motioned me to the back door with a lift of his eyebrow the same evening as Dad went back to Cain's. He was ready to talk about all that was happenin'. He'd been full-on quiet since Dad spoke to us about the visitors earlier in the afternoon. We'd just finished all the supper clean up leavin' the cook room ready for breakfast the next mornin'. Black Oak and Wind Is Strong left for the great room to build up the fire. Rock together a while. They liked doin' that. Anne headed upstairs to finish makin' notes about Wind Is Strong's healin' trail. Things like what medicines she used, how the wound responded to different herbs or treatment, and what she expected to happen durin' the continued healin' process. The notes would be references for similar wounds. They would guide Anne on how to treat folks who got the same kinda hurt as Wind was inflicted with.

I followed Wolf out the back door. He didn't stop 'til he got to the bench beside the gate to the mule corral. We sat, it was a clear night. When you looked up, it almost seemed you could reach out and grab yourself a star. Stuff it in your possibles pouch. The new moon didn't have a lot 'a light yet so the surroundin's was dark. Couldn't see far.

Barely could make out Wolf's face. I didn't need to see it full on to know the look it was holdin'. I know'd his mind.

"Jebediah, my brother," Wolf said as he leaned back on the bench in distant thought. "I do not like the kind of people who have come to our home. These will leave at some point. Most likely be gone for good, or maybe they will return. I cannot say. But I know in my heart, as do you, more like this bunch will come. Our home will change now because of them wanting to come here. I want to know my enemy. See how he lives. How he fights. What he fights with. We need his weapons to match his power. More knowledge about the how of what they do will help us in dealing with them in the future. I must disobey my father's wisdom. I am asking you to do the same. Let us go to this camp. Watch these invaders. Lay eyes on the evil ones ourselves. It will be very important our fathers don't suspect we are going there. If they find out, it will be bad for us. Also, what we are going to do will be dangerous. If the soldiers find us, it will be bad for us as well. We will need to be like the spirit cat moving through the woods. Watch all around. Make sure no one ever knows what we are doing. What say you my friend?"

"It's a bad day when we do what our fathers have told us not to do. I agree we need to make sure nobody finds out what we're doin'. Yet, I feel we need to make ourselves a part of what is happenin'. I do not like this kind 'a folk bein' here, neither. There will be danger in the effort we are goin' to make, but I feel we must learn how our enemy thinks. We will spy on these heathens. Take from them as we can. I will not let this opportunity pass without understandin' their doin's. I want to know what will happen when more folks like them decide the mountains are where they want to live. I believe as you my friend, brother, our home is movin' toward change. We need to know who it is that is gonna be changin' it. Let's smoke this over. Come up with a plan. I will go with you. I will disobey my father."

I remember thinkin' it worked out good comin' to my reckoning in the chestnut tree holler several days before since we was havin' to act more grow'd-up and all. God is wise.

***

Dad and Red Hawk topped the last ridge north of the upper Wolf Creek level lands. Not to be confused with the Levelland Mountain to the east. This is a big flat holler that covers many acres of land in the upper Wolf Creek area. The camp was a ways off the creek at the north end of the flat. Upwind from where Red Hawk was aimin' to sit for a spell, watch the trespassers camped in his valley. He wanted them to leave, but the way the camp was set up made it look like their plans was to stay a while. He wanted to kill them all for not leavin', but that would just bring more of the same. There was really no way to win a war killin' the folks in the camp would start. For now, the Cherokee could only watch. Stay on guard for their families. Pray to the Great Spirit the lookers didn't find anything that would make them want to come back. Let the thieves take what gold they might find, then leave. It could not be soon enough for Red Hawk.

"They are dirty, Thompie," said Red Hawk as he and Dad squatted in the edge of a thick ivy thicket not fifty paces from their camp. "I can smell their stink in the air. They smell of grease, old rotten leather, hog meat, and tobacco. I wonder if their tobacco is any good."

"They are foolish," Dad said in reply. "I've not seen one soul leave camp for sentry duty and it almost dark. They've missed the best time to see an enemy slippin' in. That would 'a been the first thing General George would 'a done. He'd have a couple folks out watchin'. Idiots like these would learn a thing or two studyin' on how Mr. Washington made war. He run the greatest army the world ever know'd back to its homeland across the big water. Tail tucked between its legs. He was a great warrior. Most likely the best our new country has ever had."

"General George Wash-Ting-Sun. I have heard of him. The Father of this great nation you belong to. The one who gave my father, Water Runs Deep, the land Dancing Bear now lives on. It is a good place, too. Very generous of him. I would like to meet this General Wash-Ting-Sun. Smoke with him. Talk of battles. Listen to his thoughts on the future of my people here. Our people. He sounds like a wise man who might be friends with the Cherokee. What does his name mean? Where can I meet this great man? I want to go to where he is. Speak with him. Take him a gift. Maybe trade knives with him. You should bring him here if I cannot go to where he lives."

"Oh, my friend, Red Hawk, if only you could, if only I could. He is across the Great River with Jesus. We will only see him when our time to cross has come. I long for him to lead our country again. He was a God-fearin' man and a great leader. He gave his all for this country of 'mine'. I will die to defend what he gave us with his courage. Honor his sacrifice. The Great Spirit covered him. Many horses was shot out from under him durin' battle, but never did he know death. He was our greatest warrior. He is missed."

"Warriors like Mr. Wash-Ting-Sun are rare on Mother Earth. I've known many. All have died good deaths. I hope to be with them in the end, if I am worthy. I long for the peace they now know with no more bloodshed. We fight many battles in this life, Thompie. Some we win, others we must take the best way out. Then some, like we face here, we cannot win. We simply fight. Need only to survive. I believe your General knew this when he offered himself for his people. He was answering the call of duty. A duty no true warrior can ignore. That is the sign of a worthy leader."

Their talk was interrupted by a twig snappin' not twenty paces away from where they sat. Finally, one 'a the settlers was takin' his place as night guard. His choice of seats was not good enough to keep him safe, though.

"I would like to talk to this settler, Thompie. I want his long gun, too," said Red Hawk in a whisper. "Let us go to where he sits. Take him down the creek for a talk. What say ye, friend?"

"I'm thinkin' the same as you, Red Hawk. We could learn many things from him that we need to know, then leave him tied to a tree for them to find at daylight. It should not be a problem if we don't hurt him much, just a little. Enough to show them we have no fear. I think it is good for us to speak with him."

The man chosen for sentry duty was young. A kid really lackin' in experience. It was obvious by where he chose to watch from, all the noise he made gettin' to his perch and how he handled his gun. Never know'd what hit him as Red Hawk slipped up behind the rock he was sittin' on, stood for a minute to prove his bravery, then laid his war club upside the kid's head knockin' him out cold. Dad simply picked him up and carried him down the creek away from the camp. Blood runnin' down the right side of his head from a gash above the ear. Them war clubs was solid.

Red Hawk had him a new .54 caliber "smoke pole." That's what the Indians called 'em. Thompie would collect the pistols. He didn't feel right about it, really - kinda like stealin' - but he know'd if he had those two short guns, they'd never kill no innocent Cherokee or family.

They built a small fire several paces back from the creek. They wanted to see their prisoner's face when they spoke to him. For sure wanted him to see Red Hawk. His mouth bein' stuffed full 'a homespun kept him from makin' any noise to alert his campmates. The leather holdin' him around the tree would keep him secure while they asked him questions. He'd find the strap to be painful the longer it was tied around his wrist.

Weren't long 'til he was shook awake by the cold creek water throw'd in his face. His eyes got big as Red Hawk come into focus. Dad stayed hid. Poor kid probably never met a true, battle-hardened Cherokee warrior close-up in the wild before. He had now. The pee stink from him wettin' his pants was proof to it. That encounter with Red

Hawk had to be really scary for him. No tellin' the stories he'd been told about how savage the Indians was. Some of 'em true, no doubt. Good fortune shone on him that day as Red Hawk had no plans of killin' him. Too bad the kid didn't know that. Luck would be on his side, at least for a time.

"Young one. I am Red Hawk. Tribal elder of the Cherokee nation. A nation you have invaded," Red Hawk explained as he grabbed the kid's head by the hair shovin' it back hard against the tree he was tied to. Red Hawk wanted to look him eye-to-eye.

"You mean very little to me watcher. A settler turned traitor to your people. You are not a soldier. You are not marked as a warrior. I can kill you if I wish. You are unworthy. No one will care. As of now, I only want to talk. Ask you questions. If I find you of little help, then I will kill you. Agreed, young one?"

Agreed? Sean wondered. He'd never agree to dyin'. Who was this man abusin' him. Never had he seen such a magnificent figure. This aged Cherokee warrior stood tall. He was graceful in his movements. Clear in his speech. Deadly in his fully armed appearance. Battle ready. Looked as though he could kill in a thought. No hesitation. Sean was not raised a fool; careless maybe, but no fool. He would talk. He hoped to understand this amazing lookin' person he was facin'.

"I understand what you say. I am Sean. I will answer as you ask if you promise not to kill me in return… Uncle."

What? Uncle? Only family or clansmen was allowed to call an elder uncle! Red Hawk draw'd his knife meanin' to plunge it deep into Sean's chest when Dad come from the dark stoppin' him. It was a terrible show of disrespect to the ancestors unless Sean could prove what he meant.

Sean know'd he'd put his life on the line callin' Red Hawk uncle. He'd been around Indians enough to know the expectation of proper respect. He now had to prove his claim.

"It is true, Uncle. I am of the Cherokee. My father was full Cherokee. My mother Irish. My father is Boar Runs Wild. He has spoken of you often. Of your brother, Dancing Bear. He respects Dancing Bear as a council member. You as his brother. He believes you to be an honored member of the Guard. I will help you with all you need, Uncle. I praise the Great Spirit for bringin' us together this night… however painful," he finished, softly droppin' his head down 'til his chin laid on his chest. It was poundin' somethin' awful. The blow from Red Hawk's war club hurt. He know'd it was his own fault, though. He'd been careless in his doin's. He'd not let that happen again.

If he was speakin' truth about who he was, then he was Cherokee. Red Hawk know'd the Cherokee man he'd spoke of in name only. Didn't care for what he'd heard about him, but know'd of him. Never had they met. That meant his boy weren't due full respect. He'd turned traitor anyhow, helpin' the enemy the way he was. Still, the claim of bein' Cherokee held some call. Red Hawk would not kill him just in case he did speak true. Make sure the ancestors stayed pleased with him. Side's, the information he held is what mattered. He couldn't talk if he was dead.

"What you claim could be true," replied Red Hawk calmly. "I have heard of Boar Runs Wild. I am sorry. The things I've heard are bad. Folks say he is lazy. Provides poorly. Beats his woman, your mother. I would cut his throat while he slept for beating my mother. You should leave from him if those words hold truth. Your mother should find her another man. I feel for you having him as a father, but I don't care. You are helping my enemy. You are a traitor. You are enemy. I should kill you. But, I will spare your life so as not to anger the ancestors toward me. But, this man, Thompie Collins from Choestoe. He just saved your life. He is my friend. He is not blood Cherokee. He can kill you. No ancestor will be angry with him for sending you across the Great River, so you best speak what you know. Now, here is my first question. How long do the soldiers intend to stay here in this valley? And my second. What do they want?"

The first question, of what Sean figured to be many, was a two-part question: one part easy to answer, the second difficult. He would have to be very careful how he worded his answers. He could tell Red Hawk was anxious. It was clear the strange ones camped on Wolf Creek bothered him.

"One part of your question is easy for me to answer, Uncle. The soldiers are a scoutin' party for the U.S. War Department. They are lookin' for resources. Tryin' to find out if there is enough profit in this part of the mountains to make it worthwhile to purchase or for takin'. The settlers are bein' paid as guides and to do the labor. I do the labor. I do what I am told. We look for gold, count timber and take samples of the earth. We are also mapping the whole valley. That's why the first part of your question is difficult for me to answer. We do not know how long that drawing will take, so the soldiers will be here until the chore is finished."

Dad's heart sank. *Mapping the whole valley!*

Red Hawk merely grunted. He did not understand what that statement meant. He would 'a had somethin' hard to say if he did.

Mapping the whole valley meant the U.S. Government had taken interest in their home, noticed it, and was interested in what profits could be made off the resources located there. The new country had debt -- war debt. Millions of dollars in gold worth 'a debt. The folks what paid the bills for the government was lookin' for about anyway they could find to raise revenues. They needed money to survive, to pay its workers — soldiers, leaders, traitors and mapping folk. Me and Wolf found out later it was the amount of quality deers skins leavin' the mountains what gained the governments attention. Don't know for sure if that was gospel, but it made sense. Somethin' out in the world made them focus on the Choestoe Valley. That slave findin' gold across the ridge later on didn't help matters. His owner should 'a kept his mouth shut.

Living Where the Rabbits Dance

Chapter Eighteen

Our First Ambush

It was time we got our minds set concernin' what to do exactly about spyin' on the soldier camp. Wolf and me moved to the main fire pit after comin' to an agreement to purposefully disobey our fathers. We needed to smoke things over. Figure the best attack to our new-found problem. It took some time gettin' the fire makin's ready, so we thought on things while we worked. Didn't say nothin', just tryin' to cipher out what trouble we might be headed toward. How to go about avoidin' it if possible. It come to both of us simple. Sometimes the best plans are the easiest to figure out.

We needed some hot coals from inside the main house. Nobody'd fired the outside pit in so long the coal bed was out. You hardly ever saw that. I went to the great room fireplace where Black Oak and Wind Is Strong sat rockin', talkin', what-not; said my apologies for interuptin' while layin' some hot coals into a small, cast iron soup pot. We kept a small fireplace shovel on the hearth for handlin' hot coals. I told the rockin' folks we'd be out by the fire pit if they wanted to join the talk, pray with us. Didn't want Black Oak to get suspicious of our goin' on's.

I turned from them, headed straight for Momma's cook room. I wanted to fetch me a quick bite of her delicious sweet cake. I loved that cake. Sweet, moist, and perfect for when you needed that little bite 'a somethin' sweet. Sometimes she'd fry it for breakfast. I'd give up a sin mark for a piece of her fried sweet cake today.

I was greeted with the smell of Momma's past cookin' as I eased through the heavy quilt hangin' over the pass-way between the cook room and the great room. Weren't no real door what opened and closed year 'round, just a quilt Momma hung coverin' the openin' durin' the cold time. It held the heat in the great room. That's where we did most of our indoor livin' when it turned cold for the year. The cook room always smelled of skillet cookin', wood smoke, hot coffee, and that homemade bread. Oh, it was nice, comforting. Made me miss Momma. I hadn't seen her since I come for Anne to do healin' on Wind Is Strong. She'd been up to Cain's since I got back from the Panther Cave.

I fetched the hot coals back out to the fire pit — Wolf had it ready — poured 'em out in the center where he'd scratched the ash out 'a the way. We both commenced to layin' on dried kindlin', then sat and packed a full bowl 'a weaver tobacco as the flames steadily built to a nice size. Dad's wood was kept in the dry. Wet kindlin' was like a dull knife, not much use to a body.

"It is nice that we sit and smoke, Jebediah. We have not made time for our prayers like we should. You are a bad rub on my spiritual walk. White settlers do not pray as much as the Cherokee. I have noticed this. Is it that you don't know the Great Spirit the way we do? I will teach you to do better. Now we will smoke – pray -- ask the Great Spirit to give us His thoughts. Let our words be carried to Holy Spirit on the smoke of our pipes."

We both fetched a wood splinter off the edge of a piece 'a firewood, reached in to the flames with the small end of the splinter, and pulled a smaller flame from the main fire to light our pipes. Oh, the taste was rich, calmin'. The smoke filled your body with warmth, then carried your prayers upward where God would be waitin' to hear 'em.

It made me wonder what kinda pipe the Great Spirit smoked. Did He use dried burley or weaver. I reasoned His tobacco would be the best of all, whatever it turned out to be.

I couldn't reason about words travelin' on smoke the way Wolf believed. I know'd God heard my prayers. The Bible makes it clear as spring water in a drought, what Jesus done allows me to talk direct to God through Holy Spirit. I never read where the Word declared talk traveled on smoke. I've always wondered if they got it from that time Moses saw the light up on the mountain, talked to the Great Creator through a burning bush? They could read it as the smoke was carryin' his words up instead of the bush speakin' for God Himself. To them, it was reasonable. The Cherokee believed all things was alive, had purpose. But if He told the Cherokee He'd wait for their words to be carried up on smoke, then that was their choice to believe that. I'd not be held accountable. They know'd the Word same as me. It's the way their faith lived. Seemed to me it was easier to just speak straight to Him since those who accept the blood of the Peace Child are allowed the privilege. They had every right to speak straight to God through Holy Spirit same as me the way I saw it. No, that weren't the way for Wolf. Disrespect to the Holy One meant no peace in their lives. He accepted Jesus overcomin' death but did things the way his ancestors did out 'a respect, wisdom, and trust. It was the way. I understood that. I've said it many times in my life, the Cherokee do things their way. Weren't no explainin' some of it. A body just lived with it. I never minded them prayin' that way. To me, it just made time for a good smoke. I know'd my prayers was in God's ear 'fore I ever lit my pipe. I believe the Great Creator knows your thoughts 'fore they ever leave your heart. He just wants you to speak with Him about 'em, conversation-like. He's nice, and He'll listen to anything you got to say. He walked with the First Creation in the First Garden in the evenings. Can you believe that? The Great Spirit went to Adam for talk. Them beliefs was a difference between my blood brother and myself, but it was never a problem. I know'd his soul was safe 'cause of his faith in the love of the Holy One.

Weren't but a few minutes after we'd finished our smoke that the talkin' got goin'. We was alone. It was very quiet. The mules was all sleepin' 'cause 'a the cold. No critter noise was stirrin'. Not a breeze that you could feel. The only sound was the fire poppin' and cracklin', hissin'. I was glad there weren't no wind. The weather had gotten plumb cold. I worried for Momma. I thought of someone else, too, for some reason. I wondered what she was doin'? Was she warm?

Wolf started our little pow-wow. Seems like he was always the first to speak. That was fine with me. He usually had the best ideas. "Sometimes it is wise to just keep things very simple, Jeb. I cannot come up with any way to solve our betrayal. If we go to this camp, see things for ourselves, we are doing exactly what both our fathers have told us not to do. We would be disobeying their order. An important order. We could stay way back in the woods, watch anyone that might pass, and not go near the camp, but we would still be close to one of them. Possibly get caught. That's also disobeying. Even so, I do not feel like having to stay at home. Waiting for news of what is happening like a sister. The Guard will never let out all that is known of our invaders. I want to be a part of whatever this is that may change our lives forever. I want to know what there is to know. We should go to this camp, watch quietly, unnoticed, learn, then decide from our seeing what it is we will do next. Yes, I am going to disobey my father. I may tell him when the trail ends, whether he catches us or not. That is to be seen. I will accept my punishment. Ask him to forgive me. Live my life from there. This is the best my heart has given my mind on this matter. What does the voice in your heart say to you my brother?"

"I feel as you do, Wolf. But for us and our fathers, I believe this is a time when we are bein' forced to go against their thinkin'. I will accept my punishment because I know what I am goin' to do is a disrespect. I cannot help myself. The need to learn who these folks are is too great inside me.

There is no doubt in my mind I hear the voice of the Holy One. I know it in my heart. I understand the Word. He frowns on bein' disobedient, so I pray we have forgiveness from Him 'fore we ever get busy with the watchin'. I feel terrible inside. I know this will hurt my father's soul if he learns of it, that is for sure. Like you, there is a chance I will tell him when we finish our learnin' chore. I just don't want to get caught; made to stop 'fore we know what we need to know. But I think he will be proud of me, if our adventure turns out to be good for our families. I believe the Great Spirit will watch our backs, even though we betrayed our fathers. What we do will be important to our future families. Through that, I will be comfortable with our decisions."

"I want some of what they have as well," said Wolf, "A soldier's new gun so I can have his strength. Powder and ball, the long knife with its sheath, and other things I know they will have but don't know I need yet. We will go, watch. I am with you my brother. Let us leave here in the morning at Old Man Sun's first light. Slip in on them after the woods are showing good so we can see to not make any noise as we move. We must be as careful as we've ever been, Jeb. If they catch us, we will be punished. Let us be ready to fight."

All was settled. We both agreed we'd need to disobey our dads. That weren't good. We'd get it for doin' that, be it one way or another. We figured to deal with that if and when it come. Right then, we was gonna prepare for a trail I did not know if we was ready for. We was both mature for our age. Made grow'd-up decisions we'd had to live with. How could one know if you're ready? We'd never spied on any U.S. soldiers before. Never disobeyed our fathers like we was fixin' to. I guess you don't know 'til you find out. We was gonna find out, then we'd know. We sure needed to watch close. We did not want to get caught. That was gonna take some doin' on our part 'cause the Guard was on the prowl, too. They'd take us to Dancing Bear if they caught us. Not sure, but I believe I'd rather be caught by the soldiers.

***

Black Oak honored my father. Agreed to do what was asked of him. Stay the farm to look after things, us. It was possible he'd never see the soldiers. Did it matter to him right then if he fought another battle? There had been so many in his life. Some time with a special person seemed about right for a nice change. His last kill bothered him very little. Most killin's, war or not, he was shook to his soul. He would learn from this person growin' to mean so much to him. Her life mattered in his world. She'd fought hard to save it. He respected her strength, her beauty, her warmth when the air turned cold. Walks through the woods with her felt right. Bein' near her spirit felt right. She felt right. Her kiss was like the heat of a hundred campfires. Her emerald green eyes were doors to her soul. He sensed her thoughts. Know'd what she needed 'fore she ever had to ask. This woman was becoming a part of his life. It was fine with him to stay the farm 'til Thompie come back. Maybe he'd stay gone a while.

It was nice, her havin' Black Oak near while the healin' kept on. The warrior in him made her feel safe, protected. He was a comfort to her. Had helped her off the mountain and with her healin'. A joy to be with. He was strong, very strong, and handsome in a rugged, mountain-sized man sort 'a way. She really liked that about him. No enemy would dare approach her with a warrior like Black Oak guardin' her life. She felt like he might be growin' some feelin's for her. He held her hand when she was near. They had shared some intimate times durin' their talks and other times while on walks. They'd spent a good deal of time in the tub soakin' in hot water for her healin'. His body was beauty to her. She prayed to the Great Spirit to guide her in their walk. She was lonely, havin' no one to call family or friend. Courtin' could be in her future, which was fine with her. The pangs of love felt good squeezin' at her middle, much more bearable than the pangs of death or hunger. Life was good. Black Oak was good. She was happy. She wanted to feel more happy.

The time she was spendin' with Black Oak would've been perfect if her son had been there to meet him as well. She could feel he was still alive. She wanted him back. Her family together. It would be nice if George Black Oak was part of it as well. He had become something very special in her life. She had to wonder if he felt the same. She would know soon.

***

"I cannot believe what I am seeing," Wolf whispered as we lay behind a big, white pine top watchin'. Looked like the tree had been blow'd over in a heavy wind breakin' the top out. It run horizontal across the west side of a small top east of the camp. We'd searched all over for a couple hours that morning lookin' for the perfect place to watch from. The tree would be our main gatherin' point. It lay right on the edge of a good-sized ivy thicket just off the top. Easy to get to when comin' in from the north. A deer trail ran in close behind where we was layin', makin' it easy to come and go without bein' heard or seen. Couldn't help but notice at how the pine fell square sideways across the hill. As if it was a gift from the Great Spirit. Near perfect for what we needed. A good sign, 'cause most trees didn't fall straight across the slope. This one laid square across. Never saw many what fell the way that'n did. We settled in. Got ready to do our spyin'. It all felt right.

"O, Great Spirit, watch over us. Never have I seen this many soldiers in one spot," Wolf said in a kinda stunned whisper not long after we'd got comfortable behind our white pine log. The tree's bark was gray, smooth to the touch, and sticky where it'd been scratched in the fall. It smelled of rich pine tar.

"Look at how many tents there are," Wolf continued to whisper. "No wonder they're using the flats for their camp. They need the space. Your dad said Red Hawk counted ten. I believe he was correct. He watched for a time. The number is different now. Grown considerable. I count eighteen soldiers total. The new must have just arrived recent. The supply wagon is still being unloaded. What do you see, Jeb?"

"The same. You are not wrong. There are more. Eight more than when Red Hawk scouted the camp. I believe he will know of the change in number by now. The Guard is out watchin', too. They will be keepin' a sharp eye out for movement. The two unloadin' the supply wagon are dressed different than the regular soldiers. They most likely will leave with the wagon when it's empty. Maybe we could talk to them. Try to understand what it is the soldiers are doin' here. Make 'em tell us what's goin' on. One 'a them lead-head arrows 'a yours would take one of 'em out. The other I could slip up behind, catch him while he is distracted by his mate fallin' out, and bust him upside the head knockin' him out cold. Then when they wake, they'll be hogtied. We'll put rags over their eyes, so they don't see our faces when we question 'em. That way they won't be able to know us later on. Do you like my way 'a thinkin', Wolf?"

"It is good. Clearly thought out. You are growing wise my brother. Let me say more. They follow the Keowee Path. We know it runs behind where we watch not so far away. We also know where the path leads. We will go ahead of them. The Guard will not see us because their eyes will be for the moving of the wagon. We set up an ambush site far down the trail, far enough away that the Guard will have passed the wagon up. We will let the Blue Coats believe they are clear of all danger, then catch them by surprise a couple miles from here. That is the way I see it." He pointed the first two fingers of his right hand at his eyes. This meant he was done talkin'. It was time for thinkin'.

A couple miles. A couple miles away. Follow the Path for a couple miles, he said. I felt kinda lost, small. Wolf always saw things clear. Who'd 'a thought on the distance it should take to be safe from folks findin' out what we was aimin' to do. It'd take a couple miles to clear the eyes of the Guard. It was simple thinkin' to him. He was plumb savvy when it come to woods cipherin'. Dancing Bear had raised him well. Taught him the value of how to adapt to your surroundings. Work things out to keep safe.

The new moon was more lit than earlier in the week, but still weren't real bright. The Keowee Path could be seen well enough to know what was comin'. We'd walked the path for over an hour 'til we come to a good spot. Our first real ambush, I hoped I was ready. Didn't wanna let Wolf down. It's not every day you plan such things. It felt strange, not real. This bein' our first, we was kinda new at it. I don't think I ever know'd what an ambush was supposed to feel like, really. We'd figure it out as we went. We always did.

It could almost be considered another gift. Such a good place for us to post an attack from. An oak limb, about the size of a small barrel, reachin' level plumb across the Path. Be easy to walk out on the limb and wait for the wagon while holdin' a good-sized rock. Drop it down on one of 'em's head as the wagon passed underneath, knockin' him out. I'd leave Wolf to worry over the other one. Shootin' right behind the ear from the ground as the wagon passed by with one 'a them lead-head, coon-gettin' arrows. Our combined efforts should do what we needed.

It was a solid plan. It would work if everything went well. We'd found the near perfect spot. All should be fine. We commenced to gettin' ready. Our first ever ambush was about to be one for the story fires.

The first thing hit us was they weren't no limbs down low, so I couldn't climb up. We didn't have no rope. The tree bark was smooth as a sheet of ice froze across the river Notla. What to do? A body couldn't climb it without limbs. It was too big around to climb with your arms. Wolf studied it all for about a minute, then slid out his long knife and chopped out two toe holds on each side 'a the tree. Shimmied up it quick as a squirrel then out the limb over the path. He come back down the same way he'd went up. I was supposed to do the same as he done to get myself out on the limb. Weren't gonna be no trouble that I could see.

The next problem we had was findin' a rock. We had to get one big enough to do the job, but not so big it would bust the soldiers head open. That would kill him dead. We for sure didn't want to be killin' no soldiers. Lookin' took a little while 'cause we didn' have no light. Got me to wonderin' just how much time we we'd have 'fore the wagon come. Weren't long 'til we found one, 'bout the size of a half-grow'd hog's head, maybe a little bigger. I'd not wanna get hit in the head with it from off 'a that limb, I'll tell you that for sure. That feller was gonna have a bad headache when he woke. At least judgin' from the weight of the rock he'd be alive, hopefully.

I climbed the tree with no problem by myself, but there was no way I was gonna climb the tree while carryin' the rock. Weren't gonna happen. It was too heavy. If I'd been older, I might could 'a done it. But at my age, I'd not be doin' it. Wolf was kinda stumped, too. Our pouches weren't strong enough to carry it up. We looked around for some small grape vines. Didn't find any in what light there was. It was just too dark to be lookin' for stuff in the woods without a light. Finally, I thought of our pouches in a different way. We could tie 'em together across the rock, then lift the straps up to where I was on the limb. As long as the pouch straps was strong enough, it would work. I was feelin' like we needed to hurry.

I throw'd my possibles pouch down to the ground for him to use. It weren't no time 'til I was layin' belly down on top of the limb, reachin' to Wolf for our pouch straps holdin' the rock. My thinkin' worked. I would be proud 'a that when we smoked everything over later by the fire. It was a load to pull the rock up then get stood back up straight, but I finally got where I needed to be. Things was comin' together. I felt confident. Taller.

We was set up. Ready to get busy. I was standin' on the limb favorin' the outside edge of the Path, holdin' the rock. The rider ought to pass right under where I stood. He was the one I had to take out. All I'd have to do is drop the rock straight down on top of his head as the wagon passed underneath. Wolf was off in the dark some to their left of the Path, settled on one knee next to a young poplar tree. His bow notched with the widest of all his dubbed-off, lead head arrow points. He had it set so it looked to be pointin' the way to where the wagon would be rollin'. He'd started totin' a stronger bow than what I was used to seein' him carry. It was actually one 'a Moon Shadow's, his older brother. I hoped Wolf only draw'd it hard enough to just knock the guy out, it could kill him 'cause that bow was so strong if he draw'd it back too far. Maybe not, Wolf know'd what he was doin'.

 We waited. Thought about what we was fixin' to do while in the quiet of the wait. I had no worries about what I aimed to do, Wolf, neither. This was our home. We would be fathers one day. If these was the folks what was movin' to the mountains, then we needed to know who they was. The slight noise I heard off in the dark said our introduction might be commencin'.

 It weren't long after we got set up 'fore we heard 'em comin' down the path for sure. The rock was gettin' heavy, too. I was studyin' on settin' it down when I heard their wagon squeak. It was way 'fore Wolf did 'cause 'a me bein' up in the tree. I called to him with a soft owl hoot to let him know they was comin'. He signaled back the same.

 We had to wait a bit more 'til they actually come in sight. They seemed to not be in no hurry. The wagon and team bigger than I'd had in mind. Nervous run down the middle of my back when I first saw their mules — big, beautiful, movin' in time. They looked a lot like ours. Near made me drop the rock way too soon studyin' on 'em. It was very important I drop it at just the right time or I'd miss the target. If the rock didn't drop straight down on top of the soldier's head, it might not knock him out, or if in the wrong place, kill him Our surprise to the enemy would be wasted if that happened. The first guy had to be out cold from the rock or we'd be in a fight. We did not want that.

Them fellers weren't lookin' for no ambush. They was tired. Seemed as though they barely could keep their eyes open. Pro'bly been haulin' all day. Dark was on 'em now. Couldn't see much. They weren't haulin' nothin', so they probably figured why worry 'bout any trouble. Their main watch was while they was still loaded on the way in, but they had eight soldiers as guards for that trip to camp. The one steerin' had his head down kinda like he was asleep lettin' the mules follow the Path. The rider was slumped back some with his neck against the wagon seat back. Both was propped up on their new rifles bein' held in a side slot on the wagon itself. It was the head I needed to hit. Didn't want to kill him. Just knock him out so we could talk to him, but his head was laid back on the wagon seat. Not straight up and down like we figured it would be. I had to hit him on top of his head. This could be a problem for me. Made me uncomfortable.

The time come to drop the rock. I saw the rider good as the mules passed on under me. He was asleep. No question. His felt soldier hat laid flat in his lap. He had his arms forked behind his head, holdin' it from fallin' backwards. His face was kinda turned toward the sky. That was bad for me. He had his legs crossed out in front over the edge of the wagon. I was gonna have to hit him in the forehead. If I missed and hit him square in the face, it would kill him. I remember thinkin' he was probably a nice guy. He looked like folks I know'd. Mine was younger by about ten years or so from the driver.

I squared up good with my feet to the center of the limb. That way I could aim my drop better. More precise. The wagon come on. I dropped the rock, but I did it wrong. It slipped through my hand faster than I figured it would 'cause my arms was tired from holdin' it. I'd been holdin' it for a while. *Oh, God help me!* shot through my mind. The rock had left too early, fallin' on a line that would most likely take the soldiers face plumb off. Kill him dead for sure. The one thing I'd hoped would not happen. I was fixin' to be a murderer. I know'd for sure they'd be hangin' me 'fore long. I didn't want that. Just to hit him in the head was all we needed. Put him out for a spell. *Oh God, please!* I was missin' my mark.

The air sucked up complete from both my lungs. My mind was screamin' silently. I was lookin' straight down at the wagon. Could see the rock headed right for the man's face. That would kill him dead. *Please God! Keep it from happenin'.* I was helpless. All I could do was watch the rock fall. The man, die. Everything started movin' real slow like. I felt I was a watcher in a dream. I wondered what it would feel like to be hung 'til death. I got scared.

Mules don't usually stop quick. They're slow minded. Takes 'em a while to do about anything. But for some unknown reason, these did. I promise you. Before that rock could tear that man's face from his body, in the split second it took for the rock to make its journey, them mules stopped. Did it quick, too. God bless 'em. Kept the soldier from bein' kilt. Never found out why they stopped. It had to be the work of Holy Spirit.

A most important consideration in our first ever ambush was the need to take both soldiers out at as near to the same time as we could, and it happened much like that. Wolf hit square on behind the left ear of the driver with his lead-head arrow takin' him out complete. My rock did not hit the rider on top of the head, but it did its chore. I felt for him 'cause it didn't happen just as we'd planned. It worked out good, though, praise be. I believe Holy Spirit guided my rock and Wolf's arrow. The experience made a good smoke-fire story for many years.

Them mules stoppin' like they did would be all the luck the rider would gain from his first encounter with us. The rock weren't far off from where I was aimin'. I didn't miss. No, I didn't miss. That rock slipped right passed the man's face landin' dead square on his "acorn" pouch. The scream he made when that rock hit his privates was like a mountain cat what got its paw caught in a trap. Nearly made me jump scared from the limb I was standin' on to my death. Our rock must 'a weighed ten pounds or more. Took both of us takin' turns to carry it out to the path from the place we found it in the woods. It crashed into his lap with a sickening thud right below his belt buckle with him laid out flat kinda near sleepin' on the wagon. Immediately, both legs and arms shot plumb sideways. His whole body folded like one 'a them new jackknives I saw at market last trip. Dad bought him one. The expression on his face was complete surprise as his upper body folded up at me from the force of the rock landin'. I remember his face looked like he'd been dropped whole into ice-cold water. His eyes as big as chicken eggs. Fear, agony, and shock show'd on him. I weren't figurin he'd be able to walk too good when we turned him loose later 'cause of the swellin' between his legs that was sure to come.

The rock done its chore. It missed the head, but he was still out cold. Laid back in the wagon seat like a wet rag of homespun. Not movin' 'cept his slow breathin'. Somehow hittin' him in the manhood with a heavy rock dropped from a few feet above made him go right out. Weren't the way we planned it, but all worked out good for us in the end. I would have to remember how I did that. Might have to do it again sometime.

I prayed a prayer of thanks that God heard my need about the rock fallin'. It missed the rider's face by just a few inches. I know'd it was by His grace alone that happened. Wolf never missed. His arrow point hit solid, just behind the left ear. Drove the driver forward amongst the harness in front of the wheels. Them mules never frightened none, didn't offer to run off. They was good mules. I wanted to take 'em. Wolf thought better. Talked me out of it. Made me see reason. So, we didn't take 'em. I regretted leavin' those mules later on in my life. Them was good mules what belonged to the people. The whole put together got me to feelin' like Wolf a right smart, invaded.

Chapter Nineteen

Government Folk Camped on Wolf Creek

Them fellers was out cold. Weren't long 'til we had 'em laid out in back 'a the wagon on their sides facin' each other. Tied solid at the wrist with leather straps from Wolf's possibles pouch. Feet crossed, tied at the ankles with the same kinda leather straps. Wolf learned how to secure folks by watchin' the warriors in his clan. Weren't no need to put nothin' over their eyes, me and Wolf could stay out 'a sight while we talked to 'em. We tied 'em like we did so they could work loose without much effort after we'd got gone good. Planned on helpin' with their gettin' free by leavin' one 'a their knives stuck on the edge of the wagon. Stick it so it's easy to get to.

Wolf drove the wagon out into the woods a ways so no passin' folk would see us. Not that they would be any at that time of night, but we had to be careful. We built a small warmin' fire while we waited for any noise from back 'a the wagon . . . both of us wrapped warm in the wool long coats of the soldiers. We thought to splash water in their faces but decided not to. Figured 'em to wake soon enough all natural-like since they weren't hurt that bad.

Didn't have to wait but a short time. Just after we got our fire goin' good, we heard movement. The soldiers was comin' awake. This thing we was doin' had just taken on real life. I felt cold. I prayed we'd get some good information for our trouble.

We both eased over to the front of the wagon. Me on one side, Wolf around the mules to the other side opposite me. The mules stood tied in their harnesses. We was at their rumps facin' the back of the wagon listenin' for more movement. It come as voices.

"James?" one of 'em said real slow. "You alive? Tell me… You alive, James? James? I wished you'd talk. I can hear ya breathin'. Say somethin', Brother."

"What manner 'a hell you got us into this time, Brother? Where did that rock come from? Out 'a that tree? I believe that thing has near cut me in two. My privates hurt somethin' awful. I can tell they're swol' up. It's hurtin' havin' to lay with my legs tied so. Why'd they have to hog tie us like this in the back of our own wagon, Sammy?"

"Ain't got a clue, James. Reckon it's Indians? Got 'a be, don't it? Who else would leave us out like this? I ain't sure what hit me in back 'a my head, but it made lightnin' go off behind my eyes. One minute, I'm drivin' the mules. Next second, the world goes bright then dark. I remember fallin' forward, that's it. Woke up here like this with my head screamin' in pain. Can you reach your boot knife, James? Maybe we can cut these straps."

He weren't gonna reach his boot knife. It weren't there. We'd relieved 'em of all their weapons: knives, pistols, and rifles. Weren't gonna steal 'em. 'Fore we left, all their stuff would be layin' out nearby. We weren't common thieves. As much as both of us wanted one 'a them new guns, we'd not leave proper folk unprotected as they traveled. These soldiers still had a ways to go. Might meet trouble along the way and need their rifles. They could keep those.

Nothin' on their person much, 'cept for their pistols and a couple 'a dull short knives. There was little in the wagon besides their possibles. The two wool coats, some dried meat, a half sack 'a dried fruit, a couple small sacks 'a dried beans ready for boilin', coffee, some cookin' truck, two curved long knives, two poorly woven quilts, a canvas for sleepin' under, and a spare batch 'a clothes. Them was neatly folded, clean, and ready to crawl into. I don't know how they moved the way they dressed, everything so tight — the coats, the under layers, their pants, and the long black boots. The only thing that fit loose was the huge wool overcoats. Wolf and me owned them now. They'd come in handy while spyin' on the camp the next few days. We was keepin' the pistols, too. They could have their rifles, truck, and all their knives 'cept one. The long-curved knife. That was comin' with me. I picked the newest of the two. Looked to be just out 'a the shippin' barrel. It was a beautiful piece 'a craft work. U.S. Government sealed. The soldier wouldn't go without for long. He'd get a replacement after a while.

"You think you have been left here alone, soldiers?" Wolf asked. "That is not the case. I am here. My friend is here. You are our prisoners. We mean you no harm from this moment on, if you will help us. Is this agreeable?"

"Agreeable? What is it you want us to do?" replied James. "What in the world could we help you with tied up like we are. Let us go. We'll help with all you need."

"I do not trust your word soldier," Wolf kept on. "We will give you freedom, in time. Right now, we need information. Give us answers or I will cut pieces off your body to burn in our fire. Help us or suffer until you do tell us. It is your choice. Make your decision. I know you've heard of how savage us Creek can be."

We both near laughed out loud. Wolf was makin' fun with 'em. It had to feel strange wakin' up with your body hurtin', bound-up like an outlaw, then have some crazy Indian threatenin' to cut pieces off your person to feed his fire. On top 'a that, not ever really knowin' what put you in your situation of bein' near carved on, of havin' parts of your person burnt in a fire. I'm glad I stood on the questionin' side 'a that fence.

"What is it you wanna know, you heathen," Sammy spoke through gritted teeth. "Why you wanna cut pieces off me to burn in your fire? I don't know nothin' I wouldn't tell you about this stinkin' soldier life. Ask away. Don't be surprised at the answers."

"Answer then," Wolf demanded as he pulled the long, curved knife from its sheath in a way they couldn't help to hear it. "Why are you here in this valley? Why not somewhere else? The mountains reach for many miles in all directions. What brings you to Choestoe? My home? Answer soldier!"

"What are you doin' with that sabre, Creek? Leave it be. Leave us be," James near shouted back. "Ask your questions, then get gone from us. We just want to get back home. We have families."

"As do I," shouted Wolf mad like, shuttin' the man up. "That is why we are all here. I want to protect my family from the likes of you. I fear for the life of all Indians since you are here. Your kind will change my life without my say. I should kill you now; kill all who come here like you, but that would solve nothing. I'd rather know you, to understand who you are, then I can learn to live with you."

"I will answer," said Sammy, calm-like, not hard in any way. "We are here because we was told to come here. These mountains have resources, gold. Our government wants to know what and how much. We are here to look around so as to make a statement to the folks in Washington about what we found. What kinda folks live here? What crops grow good here? Is the soil fertile? Is there gold? These are the questions our leaders have sent us here to find out. Some with us are drawin' maps. We are doin' nothin' more than I've told you just now. They will leave when the information they need is gathered. I expect it to be some time in the early fall. The camp will stay where it is 'til the chore is complete."

"We don't want you here," I said in my deepest voice but still soundin' like a boy. "Go away from us. Return to your towns. Tell your leaders there is nothin' here worth the effort. The settler folk who live here have made this our home. We live in peace with the Indians what welcomed our ancestors when they first come to these mountains. This is our home. You have come here uninvited. Invading us like an enemy. You take food from our huntin' woods, but never share. You torture the trees with your axe marks. Steal our gold from the creeks. You've put fear in the hearts of many. All want this camp to go away. Not come back. I am sad to hear it will be here for a while longer. We will pray the Great Spirit keeps all hidden from the eyes of your lookers. Hopefully, you will go away and never come back, Good Lord willin'."

It was quiet for a spell after I spoke. Wolf got the talkin' goin' again after a bit. I didn't have a notion to say them words to those soldiers. My soul spoke for me. Them folks just bein' camped there meant our lives was 'bout to change for the worse. Kinda troubled a body if you thought on it. I guess I meant to let some mad out I'd been holdin' in for a while.

"You have heard my friend. We do not want you here," Wolf repeated just to drive it home. "You being here is bad for my clan. Bad for the ones who call the Choestoe Valley home. The future of this country is dancing with change. That is not always good. I have one more question. Answer true. I will know your words. How many more will come?"

It was a question that stopped time for me. One that may not should 'a been asked. But it was asked. In thinkin' back, I wished Wolf would 'a never asked it.

"There will be many more comin' here, boy," James said near happy soundin'. "This camp will leave 'fore long, but many others will follow as time goes. You are right, young ones. This country will change. It will be slow gettin' folks word to come here, but it will happen. The world you live in now will be gone. The Indians will be gone. Towns will be built along the rivers. Settlements will thrive. The way you live now will be no more. The U.S. Government will see to it. Write my words down. Believe what I say. It will happen in time."

Me and Wolf both felt like we'd been slapped upside the head. I think I know'd there would be change comin', but it kinda slipped up the way things had already turned. Comin' from their answers to Wolf's questions, change was there, really. It was time to accept it.

"I know your words are true, soldier," Wolf said after a minute of nobody sayin' nothin'. "Our elders have been having visions of you dirty people coming here. Answer me this, soldier. You think me a savage. I think of you as a heathen. My friend and I want to understand something. Why do you white skins not pray to the Great Creator as often as the Indian? Why do you not bathe? You smell. We Indians keep ourselves clean. Our scent down. I can smell you downwind from a long way. You would be surprised at how far. You stink like the old boar hogs we find back in the mountains. Greasy smelling, nasty. Your kind should wash themselves more.

"It is time for us to go," Wolf continued. "We will keep our word for answering our questions. We will leave one of your long knives stuck in the side of the wagon. The rest of your possibles are under the tree along with your food. It will take a while, but you can work yourselves out to where the knife is. Cut the leather straps holdin' you tied, then go on home. We apologize for any pain we have caused.

"Listen now, my ancestors speak to me. They want you dead. You are considered enemy, invaders to our home, worthy of death, but it will not be by our hand. It is dangerous to travel this path. We will leave your new long guns. Your pistols are ours. One say-ber is coming with us. The other we leave. Also, it may be cold for you on the rest of this trail. We are keeping your heavy coats. They are very warm, comfortable. I will think of our coming together here every time I wear it. Do not worry, I know your leaders will give you another of each thing we take. Understand this, folks here consider this trade for what you steal from us. What will you trade when you steal our way of life?"

We turned and left.

Our trail back home was a sad trail. We'd learned what we needed to hear, but not what we wanted to hear. It brought to light that we should enjoy every minute we had left to live the life we was livin' . . . 'fore it all went away.

Visitors to the mountains weren't uncommon. Most would come for a spell then leave. The cold time drivin' 'em away. It could get uncommon cold in the mountains. Colder than folks figured for. Now the Cherokee was dealin' with a creature that wanted things different than they'd ever been. I could sense it possible, if those in control of the new nation got greedy. Used the power they held over folks to gain profit. Power we give 'em. I was afraid it'd be the Cherokee that would suffer most if that fire got goin'. The words of Spirit Bear burned fresh in my mind. This was the beginnin' of the change he'd spoken of, I could feel it. My soul was troubled in a great way, 'cause I know'd my friends would be hurt. It was their way of life, a life I'd been adopted to, that would end if what the soldiers said was true. Many Cherokee would figure their mountain life a life worth fightin' for. Many would die. Killed to defend our way of life. I felt no different. God bless 'em and pass the gunpowder. I would stand beside my friend.

We left without sayin' another word, only a dull thud as Wolf stabbed the front side of the wagon with a long knife from their possibles. We hid what we'd took in a cave behind our home on Ben's Knob as Old Man Sun was just beginnin' to wake next morning. I was tired. It'd been a long night walkin' in the dark. Didn't want folks to know we'd been anywhere near that camp come first light. Let alone attackin' the two wagon soldiers. I wondered if they'd gotten free yet. They would if they hadn't.

***

Wolf decided he'd stay a few days at our place. Help me work the farm. He liked doin' that. We weren't gonna mind the soldier camp 'til later. Let any chance of havin' to face them two we attacked cool down. Anne, Wind Is

Strong, and Black Oak was all there, too. Our folks was still stayin' over to Cain and Rose's place when the runner from Dancing Bear arrived.

Nobody ever figured for sure what the news would be. We simply know'd bad news would come sooner or later. Them folks camped on Wolf Creek was bad news. Turns out, it was a girl got took. An assault near the England place. Stands to reason that'd be the area they'd trail to. Closest farm to where the soldier camp lay. Easiest to get to for 'em on foot. Young girl taken, but no name given. Trail led south toward the low gap. South toward slavery. My heart quit beatin'. I prayed for Elizabeth, my Elizabeth.

***

The trail had grown cold. The Indians makin' it had moved with swiftness and cunning. Moon Shadow could not tell where they'd gone for sure. It did not matter. The trail had told him plenty. It was the traitor Cherokee what led the white soldiers through the mountains. He recognized it bein' the same foot print as when he'd seen 'em leave camp before. Where was they goin'? The England place lay in that direction, the Weavers', Smith's and Southers', too. There was no soldier boot tracks mixed in with theirs. Moon Shadow decided to go look in on the farms what lay in the direction the trail was headin' to make sure folks was okay.

Red Hawk stayed the trail like a deer dog. It weren't hard to find where it left the Smith farm headin' south. As with Moon Shadow, the sign told him enough to know who'd left it. The traitor Cherokee camped with the soldiers. He know'd their foot skin tracks. No doubtin' who took the poor girl. He'd meant to kill those three 'fore anything happened. He and Moon Shadow had watched 'em constant for several days waitin' for a chance. Sadly for the girl, that chance never come.

The Cherokee traitors didn't spend all their time with the Blue Coats. Many days they would leave out on their own, just the three of 'em. Appeared to be scoutin' most 'a them days, nobody know'd for sure on many others. The Guard had trouble keepin' up with 'em once they was in the woods. It was common for 'em to split up after leavin' the camp, then come back together after makin' sure they weren't bein' watched. Made it near impossible to track 'em. Indians what don't wanna be found are hard to follow. Most woods savvy Indians could leave a trail that weren't nothin' but confusin'. These Cherokee was skilled warriors, traitors to the tribe, but skilled all the same. Know'd how to hide, stay hid, and move without sign. Would be easy for the three of 'em to watch different farms for an unsuspectin' child. Move in late one night to wait by the outhouse. Haul off with their catch after the young 'un finished their call. That kinda evil worked great for slavers. They caught folks unaware. Settlers couldn't understand the manner of demon what would take a child comin' from the privy.

They'd took Ruby Smith. A maiden of near fifteen years of age. I believed they might trail to regret not makin' a better choice 'bout who they stole. Ruby could have a meanness about her that was worse than a trapped hog. If she was conscious, they would be hearin' from her. That might get her killed, 'cause them Indians would hear her words as disrespect. They'd not tolerate that. She come from good stock. Hard-workin', respectful, God-fearin' folk that was tough. I never liked fightin' their boys. They bled a right smart 'cause it took a lot 'a hittin' to whoop one. I was friends with most my age. I liked their family. Cain got on with 'em, too, for the most part. They was one Smith family he didn't take to. A mean bunch who lived in a small log home up Stink Creek a ways. Folk's didn't pay 'em much mind they was so rotten. No tellin' how much grindin' they'd stole from old man Jep Souther's mill what lay in below their farm. Even the common Smith clan had nothin' to do with 'em. Cain'd whupp'd their boys many times growin' up. Once at Killin' Time, another at Big Camp, and a couple different times at Camp Meetin' for talkin' bad about the Lord. Didn't matter where Cain was if his temper sparked. He'd be in a fight if it come to it.

The Smith clan was a religious bunch. Some folks said they had family what made a big name for themselves preachin' their religion. They'd come to Camp Meetin'; thought different about the Word than us. Even had a Bible what looked different. Didn't sit good with folks how they thought. Worshipped. Bein' Christian held a lot 'a weight with the folks in Choestoe.

Them Smiths was good folks. Most all the clan I ever met was as nice as could be. But like all families, they had some bad ones, too. The ones what lived on Stink Creek was theirs. Them bad Smith boys hated Cain. A very tight family what never cared for folks beatin' up their loved ones. They got it in mind to teach Cain a lesson they thought he needed to know for whoopin' a couple 'a theirs one morning at Killin' Time. They should 'a let it be. Granddad always said, "Bein' stupid is hard to fix." Three of 'em jumped Cain one evenin' on his way back from the Souther mill. Them fellers at Killin' Time had it comin' for bein' mean to folks. Cain give it to him for teachin' purposes so to speak. Their brothers didn't care for that.

He was leadin' Big Jim home from the mill with three sacks 'a flour tied middle of the mule's back. Old Man Moon shinin' like a new gold piece a way up there in the heavens. Cain said it straight the night he told me at the smoke fire.

"Weren't fair what they did, Jebediah. I give 'em the what-fer, too, 'cause of it. They jumped me on the trail home from Jep Souther's mill one evenin'. Hurt me bad. I didn't let 'em get the best of me, though. Left all three of 'em layin' face down in the trail. Walked on with Jim aimin' to get home with the meal, but never made it. Dad found me in the edge 'a the creek 'bout a half mile from home next morning. My head bleedin' in a few spots, ribs busted, bruises on my arms, nose broke, and my gut hurt inside like hell's fire was burnin' me up from the inside out. Never had I been hurt that bad. Worried me some for a while.

"I'd turned most 'a the long curve just shy 'a Wolf Creek on the trail home when I run into 'em, standin' middle of the trail not movin' for nothin'. Me and Jim had to whoa. I didn't like that, neither did Jim. I asked 'em what they was wantin' blockin' the way like they was. They let out a growl then come on me. The first one from straight in front. I met him hard about the time somethin' solid hit me in back of my head. All went black. When I come to, all three was beatin' on me as I lay on the edge of the trail. One had a Cherokee war club. I know'd then what it was they'd hit me with. I believe it near killed me, really. Well, I got so mad seein' 'em with that club, blood shot from my nose I blow'd so hard gettin' up from amongst 'em. They all got mean then knowin' my aim meant to kill 'em.

"The first one to meet my resurrection was the oldest of the bunch. I hit him in the bottom jaw so hard with my right fist that I felt what must 'a been near all his teeth shatter in his head. He never got up from that lick. I learned later it killed him. That was the first death I ever caused that I know'd of. They buried him on the sly. I was glad about that. The second what got my attention was standin' holdin' the war club smilin' at me with rotten teeth. I figured then that was why the older brother's teeth exploded in his mouth. I turned to my left side, liftin' my right leg in the effort. Reached my right foot out to his mid-section with enough force to knock him down, droppin' the club. I picked it up 'fore the third Smith boy could get on me. I leveled him with a square hit to the side of his head with the club's front edge. He was out. Blood flowin' from his nose as he slammed to the ground. The one I figured to 'a used the club on me started to run. I threw the club by its handle on about his third big step. The club's end caught him hard in the back of his big ol' ugly head. He slapped forward hittin' the ground face first. Out cold. I know'd they'd hurt me, but I was alive.

Momma healed me up with Anne helpin'. She was still young back then."

As he told it for gospel, he ended up whuppin' all three 'a them Smith boys. Left 'em layin' while he walked away. He never made it home, but Jim did. That's how Dad know'd somethin' was wrong. He backtracked the home trail, findin' Cain passed out in the edge 'a Wolf Creek. Jim carried him home from there. They hurt him a right smart. Several days went by 'fore he could walk good or speak enough for a body to understand. Never taught him no lesson, though. I'd say he did the teachin' that day. Them Smith boys never bothered him no more. For sure not the oldest of the bunch.

***

It was a perfect night for a hot tub visit — cold, clear, no breeze whatsoever. Wind Is Strong found herself sittin' on the rock seats above our hemlock tub wrapped in one 'a Momma's quilts. Her winter skins layin' folded on the seat next to where she sat waitin' for Black Oak to fill the tub with hot water. That left her with nothin' on under the quilt. She sat starin' at a most beautiful full moon while Black Oak heated the water. The night was like day. You could see in all directions. Her body tingled at the thought of how the hot water would feel. Black Oak was bare from the waist up even though it was cold. The fire he'd built under the kettle keepin' him warm. That would be her chore soon. Keepin' him warm. Her inner thoughts made her normal tingle even more tingly. She longed for the tub. The comfort of a good soak. The sensation as she would sit in his lap surrounded by hot water and cool air. His strong arms wrapped around her whole person. Her head laid back on the front of his huge shoulder. Their faces touchin'. Her long legs laid across the top of his. She felt her passion rise with only the expectation of his closeness. She warmed quickly at the thought of it all.

"Your bath is ready, Wind. I have filled it for you. Come, let us enter while the water is hot. It will be good for you," he said as he stripped off his leggin's.

He commenced down the steps into the tub, turned once he got in good, and offered his hand back to help her. Old Man Moon shined on her like fire light. Black Oak's heart stopped as she stood loosenin' the quilt. Her womaness on full show for him.

"Thank you, my friend. You are so good to me. I have healed proper because of your help these last few moons. It has been truly a pleasure. I look forward too many more days of your care… if that is what you want," she said, the quilt slidin' off her shoulders fallin' back onto the rock seat with the slightest of movements. She slowly walked toward Black Oak stopping just shy of the tub steps for a few seconds to soak in Old Man Moon's light. Black Oak could not speak for what he was seein'. He simply nodded in awe of her beauty. Her black hair, which had grow'd out a good bit, was shimmerin'. Her lean body complete in the full light of Old Man Moon's glory. She entered the tub serpent-like, slitherin' to make a seat in his lap. His world could not be better. The Great Spirit had been kind to them both.

Chapter Twenty

Fresh Blood on the Breeze

The girl would not be quiet. Ever since she'd woke, her mouth had moved non-stop. Laughing Beaver could not stand the sound of her voice. He warned her many times. Slapped her hard more than once. Finally, he had to tie her mouth off with a metal cuttin' bit not much different than a bridle bit for a horse. It laid through the corners of her mouth with leather straps that tied behind her head. That shut her up. No way could she move her mouth to speak as tight as Laughing Beaver tied it. The bind so tight it'd cut her if she tried to move her jaws to talk. A typical slave-tradin' tool. He'd used it plenty in all the years he'd been takin' folks for slaves. He was ruthless in the white man's world. Tradin' come natural to him. He bought and sold folks, too. Fact was, most of his doin's was buyin' slaves cheap then sellin' 'em for profit. Didn't really matter who or what or if they was stole or not. If he could make a profit from the sale, he'd trade. Folks included, legal or not. Gold on the barrelhead ruled in his world.

His two outlaw mates said very little, even to him. Cherokee warriors who'd turned on their own people. Know'd they was givin' away mountain secrets only the Indian had knowledge of, but didn't really care as long as they had what they wanted. They'd betrayed the spirits of the ancestors for gold coin. Made life about takin' from Mother Earth all she would give. A lot she didn't want to give.

Payin' nothin' back. Death would be a relief for them. That made them dangerous, deadly.

This bunch was not your typical slaver crew. They'd been workin' the illegal side 'a the trade by takin' folks for many years. Good at what they did with gold at the root of their souls. The Great Spirit made it known to them their life would not be long upon His rock. It was accepted. The three of 'em lived the way they chose, no regrets. Folks suffered 'cause of it.

Red Hawk know'd by the direction the trail was holdin' that it would lead straight to Blood Mountain. There was a place close to the top on the west side facin' due west, where traders and slave folk made trade. He left the trail takin' to the higher ridges. If he hurried, he may make it there before the evil ones with their bounty.

Somethin' movin' on the ridge top caught Moon Shadow's eye. A second glimpse said, 'man comin'.' If the stranger stayed the ridge top, he'd pass by close. Moon Shadow sat, waited as the figure kept comin'. It was strange the way he moved. Not tryin' to hide. Not really watchin' the woods headin' west on the trail what run up the side of Blood Mountain. That trail would take him right to the west-facin' side. A slight turn in the trail brought the man much closer. *Red Hawk. Uncle is on the trail.* It all became clear. Red Hawk was on the move.

A simple ground squirrel chirp from Moon Shadow stopped the seasoned warrior in his tracks. Eyes sharp for movement. The raising of a right fist showed Red Hawk his nephew. It would be good to have him along. They must hurry. It was important to reach the tradin' place on the 'Blood' 'fore the thieves got there with Ruby.

***

The moon had moved on down the trail, but the cold hung on like skunk stink. The nights was dark while Old Man Moon went for more light. All his was used up from the new moon week before.

We had no trouble makin' it to our watch log east 'a the 'Judas' camp. That's what me and Wolf had got to callin' the soldier camp. Them Indians what stayed there was traitors. The name fit in a hateful kinda way. Didn't matter, us thinkin' mean. We didn't care for the folks what stayed in that camp.

The spirit of them new long rifles was callin' to us. We'd seen 'em; know'd from our first watch they had wooden boxes full 'a extras what didn't belong to a soul. They was stored in their supply tents for when needed. A stretched canvas tent with heavy ends folded identical left to right. We both felt the pull. The wagon soldiers each had one. Me and Wolf looked 'em over durin' our ambush. Fine works of art to us. Fit your shoulder good when aimed. The balance of the hold when aimin' one felt comfortable. You could hold the bead on a target for a long time before havin' to let the gun down. It was all we could do not to take theirs when we had the chance. That would 'a been wrong. Couldn't leave 'em without protection. They had a ways to go. Families dependin' on 'em. Weren't right for them to be without their long guns with considerable trail left.

Our plan was to watch all day, then go to our place on Ben's Knob at dark to smoke on what we'd seen. Try to figure out the best way to go about gettin' a chance at one 'a them brand-new shiny rifles each. We know'd it wouldn't be easy. The supply tent was manned night and day with a fully-armed soldier at guard. They meant to protect their supplies from the likes of us, the enemy.

After we got settled amongst the limbs of our white pine top blind, the camp started comin' alive. The smell 'a wood smoke got strong as the soldiers and settlers alike laid dried wood on the overnight coals in their fire pits all over camp. Coffee pots got placed just right on the coals to yield that perfect first cup 'a morning flavor. The smell of bacon fryin' with onions, potatoes, sausage, ham, and steak made me hungry as breakfast cookin' commenced. They come well provided for. The skillet fryin' smell got my mouth to waterin'. I wanted to slip down close. Take some 'a their fry meat. Wolf had other things on his mind.

"Jeb, look to the north side of camp. They've built a privy. No surprise it's in the wrong place. Should've been on the west side. Let the morning and evening breeze carry away the bad scent. These government folks are foolish. They make me laugh not knowing simple things like where to put a fire pit, how to keep fresh water, or where to put the outhouse. Cherokee would never be so foolish as these."

"I see it, Wolf, many have gone there this morning. Also, as you see, there's two supply tents now, both guarded. It is good they put it on the south side closer to us. Hopefully, they'll open 'em for air in a little while. Kindly show us what's inside."

The second supply tent was some behind the original to the north closer to us. With any good fortune, it would have guns stored in it as well. From where we laid, we could see right in the end of it not fifty a' Dad's paces away. The first of the two tents was at least eighty 'a Dad's paces away. It had less cover, too. Be our luck the new one held less important stuff such as clothes or food or what not. We were kinda partial to the heavy long coats. Brought 'em with us to wear while we lay watchin' the Judas camp. Bein' on the ground made a body colder than the air around their person. Them coats helped about makin' it more comfortable. They was a blessin' to have. I found myself wonderin' at the two soldiers on the wagon. *They got cold goin' home.* I smiled when I thought on it. *I hope they did. Maybe they'd stay gone. Not get no more rocks fell on 'em.*

Once breakfast finished, the whole bunch of 'em headed out. Left two guards in the camp to look after the place. One stayed with the supply tents constant while the other roamed around, then they'd trade places ever so often. Seemed fair. The camp weren't huge so they seen each other constant. Never saw the Cherokee traitors. They probably slipped out 'fore daylight. Run some on their own without the soldier men knowin'. I know'd I'd wanna be away from 'em all I could.

We laid on top of our heavy wool coats, watchin'. Several hours passed. We took turns sleepin', watchin', and takin' walks to stretch our legs. We ate in the blind, all the while takin' in the camp layout. Folks in and out all day. Located a couple small, hidden areas we believed was spots we could slip up to without bein' seen if the need come to us.

Near mid-afternoon our watchin' paid off. The two guards opened the ends of the supply tents to let air flow through. We got a look. Fate was not smilin' on us. The new tent had nothin' but what a body needs for livin'. Dried beans, jars 'a peaches, heavy sacks 'a cornmill and flour, a couple dozen salt-cured hams hangin' from the peak of the tent, three stacks 'a quilts done in dark blue material same as their short coats, extra long wool overcoats like the ones we had, boots, more short coats, and bags 'a what must 'a been under garments. Some 'a that stuff caught our mind for a minute, but we forgot about it quick. It was the long guns we wanted. We meant to have us a couple.

We left the blind headed for Ben's Knob 'bout an hour 'fore full-on dark. Got there just before Old Man Sun got to breakin' the ridge tops next morning. Sleep kept us from talkin' 'til we both woke way into the night.

The smoke fire was still hot when we sat the rock seats around the fire pit. Somebody had been sittin' there recent. It was a couple hours past normal bedtime. I figured 'em for bein' in the house sleepin'.

"Black Oak and Wind Is Strong have been here," Wolf said as we packed our pipes for a smoke. "I can still smell her scent. His, too. Her smell is much better. I've seen they are spending much time together recent. I feel for him. A woman can change a man if he does not stay wise. My father says a woman will play tricks on your thinking. That she has a spiritual power man does not understand. Makes him do things he would not normally do. I have seen it. A sickness what leaves a body helpless. I do not care to have one. I do not need one. That is how I see it."

His eyes had not been opened enough to know that was foolish talk. He would know the frustration of bein' concerned over a girl soon enough. The little chestnut-haired girl, Elizabeth, from over at the England place, she got on my mind a right smart of late. Would stay there constant if I didn't fight it. I'd never told Wolf.

I hadn't seen her since Cain's wedding; hadn't thought much about her. Then her folks come to Killin' Time last. Camped on the same part 'a Wolf Creek as we did. Proved to me the Great Spirit has a sense of humor. He put her right where I could see her at first fire every morning. Natural comin' together 'a nature one would allow? No! Most unnatural thing I ever crossed up with. Changed my life. Made me do things I'd never seen myself doin'. Spendin' time talkin' with her felt about as good as anything I'd felt in my life. I liked it. I sat talkin' with her durin' the last Killin' Time when I would 'a been runnin' with Wolf I liked it so much. He didn't care for that. My thoughts turned to her as we enjoyed our pipes in the silent by the fire. I did not feel the need to speak. Wolf must 'a not, neither. It was nice thinkin' on things she and I had talked over. She'd had a tough row in life. I felt for her.

They throw'd their camp right directly next to ours on a little bend in the creek just downstream from us. Made it to where all I had do was look off to the north some, there she'd be. Her wavy chestnut colored hair hangin' over her shoulders. I never thought about her much 'fore then. Well, maybe some, at times. I'd really only met her at the wedding. Oh, but that was a nice meetin'. I'd forgotten how good it felt to dance with her. My heart would beat so hard when our hands come together dancin' it hurt in my chest. Bein' close to her caused my knees to shake with weakness. I barely could draw air proper while breathin' when she was near.

I caught myself thinkin' on all that instead 'a helpin' Dad make camp. I guess he'd near put the sleepin' canvas up by himself 'fore I come to reason at one point. He said not one word to me as it was clear my mind was focused on somethin' other than our camp. I couldn't help it. Her memory jumped to the front 'a my thinkin' after seein' her family settle next to us the morning we arrived.

Quick as Dad said we was done, later that first afternoon, I fetched Momma's comb, some soap, and a washrag and went up the creek a ways where nobody could see me to wash. Cleaned myself up some. Soakin' my head with clear, cool water from Wolf Creek. Combed my hair straight. Washed my face and ears, then slipped back into camp. I put the comb back in its usual place among Momma's possibles. Left the soap and washrag on a stump by the creek, natural-like, then eased on over to the camp next to us to visit Elizabeth. Dad weren't really done workin' me that afternoon makin' camp but set me free regardless. Know'd I was eager to go 'cause I hadn't seen my friend recent. Probably better off havin' me out 'a the way if truth be told.

I stopped at the front 'a their camp to make sure they all saw me. Elizabeth was sittin' in a chair by the fire with several other kids sittin' on benches spread around. A man with a coonskin cap was sittin in a rocker smokin'. They all had a mug 'a somethin' hot. I could see the heat comin' out the top. Her mother, Martha, spoke first as I neared their fire. Elizabeth looked eager to see me, too. That brought comfort to my insides.

"Jebediah Collins," Martha said as she stood from her chair beside Elizabeth to come hug me. "It is good to see you again. Come, take my seat by our fire."

I would learn she was very sly.

"I hope your family is well. Tell Thompie and Celia I look forward to catchin' up. This is my husband, Mr. Benson. The rest is all our kids. I'll let Elizabeth name them. Tell you which ones belong to who. I know you two are acquainted. Y'all met when you and Thompie come to our place two nights after my last husband got killed. I remember you from then. Elizabeth does, too. I also saw you at Cain and Rose's wedding. You danced with Elizabeth, I believe."

Well, I'll be! I was half right when I said I figured her to marry Indian. The man she married was near-Indian. A settler what wore skins. He looked like somebody I'd trail with. We wore a lot 'a the same type clothes. Homespun over winter skins. Long foot-skin boots. Warm fur hat — mine was rabbit — soft leather possibles pouches, pipe and tobacco, and sheathed knives. A keen eye set him off as a woodsman. I liked woodsmen. That's what I was 'til Dancing Bear adopted us, now we was considered Cherokee to the tribe. We weren't real blood Cherokee. We lived like 'em, though. Why not? We lived in the woods.

"Yes, ma'am," was 'bout all I could answer as I turned my head to look at Elizabeth, her blue eyes shinin', "I remember. I believe I did dance with her."

"Yes, you did, Jebediah Collins. Have you forgotten so quickly?" Elizabeth said with a grin as we looked each other eye-to-eye. "I would hope I wouldn't be so easy to forget. I remembered you."

"I didn't forget. No, Elizabeth, I did not forget. I remembered as well. It was very enjoyable for me. I'd do it again, too. You know any folks bein' married soon? We can meet there. We will dance again."

"No, silly. I don't know anyone being married soon. We don't need a wedding if you want to dance. We can find music. We will have music here. Maybe we could dance then?"

"It would be my pleasure for sure. I look forward to it," I replied as I leaned closer to her ear tryin' to whisper. "Would you like to go for a walk, Miss Elizabeth? Do you think your mom would allow it? We could talk."

"No, she'd not allow it," she answered, whisperin' back as I turned my ear to her. "Mr. Benson, neither. I'm too young to go out alone with boys, but we can sit here when they all go to bed. Talk all night if you want to. It don't matter what time we stop. How would you like that?"

"Fine, just fine," I answered again, whisperin'. "Can we start tonight?"

She looked in thought for a minute. "I don't see why not," she said, droppin' her head a little from embarrassment. "I'll be thinking about you anyway. Might as well be here in person."

Weren't no need to go back to tell Dad I'd be over at her camp talkin'. I could see him sittin' by our fire smokin'. He could see me. Waved at me many times lettin' me know he seen me sittin' over by their fire. He had a smirk on his face. Yeah, he know'd where I was. No need to trouble him or Momma 'bout my whereabouts. Give them some time alone, too. I was learnin' that could be fun.

Old Man Moon smiled on us as we sat there that night, so bright I could see the sky blue in her eyes. The weather had turned cold recent, which made it good for Killin' Time, but was downright cold for folks sittin' outside talkin'. She went inside when her family left for the tent to tell 'em all goodnight. Probably got a talkin' to from Mr. Benson or her momma 'bout how proper girls act around young men. She come back to her chair wrapped in a quilt to keep the cold off. Her face showin' clear in the moonlight. Beautiful. I only had one layer 'a skins on. Could feel the cold cuttin' through for sure. She noticed. Weren't difficult to see I was cold shakin' like I was. I'd built the fire up some while she was in the tent. Didn't help much with our chairs back so far from it. I thought to move mine a little closer to the heat 'til she spoke. My heart kinda skipped whenever she'd speak. I liked hearin' her voice. Figured she could most likely sing pretty. It'd be nice to hear her sing.

"You look cold, Mr. Jeb Collins," she said with a kinda invitation in her voice. "I don't mind sharin' my quilt with you if you'd care to. I will tell you a story while you warm. How'd that be? Hmm?"

"Oh, Ms. Elizabeth, I would like that very much. *I am* cold. Your quilt looks very warm. Thank you for bein' so considerate," I answered as I moved my chair close to hers.

These was straight backed chairs, just a seat and a back, no chair arms for restin' on, which allowed us to get our bodies close together for warmth. That was real nice.

She opened her quilt so we could share as I moved closer. The scent from her warmth hittin' me square in the face makin' me dizzy. Her smell reminded me of sweet bread cookin' in Momma's stove. I gladly slid under my side while leanin' in toward her. My right arm layin' over her left as our bodies come together side-to-side under the heavy quilt. It got warm for me in a hurry.

"This is much warmer. Thank you, again," I said as we got settled. She snuggled up tight, drawin' the quilt up close as space allowed. I liked that a lot. Her body was warm against the cold night air. "I hope my cold self don't freeze you. You looked plumb cozy wrapped up like you was all by yourself."

We sat for a spell without speakin' starin' into the fire while sneakin' peaks at one another. Smilin' back and forth. Snugglin' under the quilt. I laid my hand over on top 'a hers. It felt like the palm of my hand would melt her skin was so hot. She looked at me steady for a minute, then back into the fire. Serious takin' her face.

"I remember," she said, never takin' her eyes from the fire. "I remember seeing you for the first time. We were young when your father brought you to our place for the bear meat a couple mornings after Mr. England was killed. He was a precious man. I loved him so much. Mrs. England stayed strong through all that, more so than I fear I would have, had it been my husband. I saw you leave the following morning. I snuck out before you left. Climbed a tree in back of our house to watch as you and Thompie left through the front gate very early. I never forgot you.

"Then, I saw you wrestling at the wedding. It made me happy to see you there. I thought you very tough as I watched you. I admire your friend, Wolf. I would like to go to his home. Visit his mother, A-Ga-Li-Ha. I met her at the wedding, too. She invited me over to visit anytime I wanted to come. I accepted her invitation. I plan to go there, to spend time with her, and talk to Dancing Bear. He is an extraordinary man. Unique in his world. I want you to take me."

She turned her eyes from the fire square on to mine as she said them final words. It weren't no question. It was a statement from her heart. She trusted me enough to lead her on a trail to Slaughter Mountain. That meant somethin' in my world. I would gladly lead her to visit Wolf's folks. She'd get no respite from me. I started lookin' forward to the time we'd leave.

"I'd be proud to take you to visit my mother, Sunshine. A-Ga-Li-Ha as you know her. She will be glad to see you. I know this in my heart. She is a good woman. I love her very much. I am her son, as the Cherokee believe. I too, believe this. Dancing Bear has adopted us as family. I love him like a father. He treats me as a son. Cain, too."

"I understand the rules of one who is adopted. I, too, am adopted. My true parents suffered from an encounter with trail bandits. My family was all there. Daddy, Momma, and me. A young family traveling the Keowee Path in our covered wagon. Daddy driving the team. Momma in the back tending to me. Two settlers, brothers who drank more than they worked, stopped us on the Path. Momma hid me behind a cedar chest when she recognized them as outlaws. The leader of the two shot my daddy for his pocket money, then shot my momma after she come from the back of the wagon firing Daddy's long gun. Her only shot killed one brother. She stared death right in the eye looking out for me. Gave her life for mine. They hanged his murdering carcass, but I was too young to remember anything that happened. Mrs. England had just told me days before the bear took her husband. It was still worrying on me when you came. Somehow, thinking about you kept me from thinking about them. I hated to see you go. I wanted us to be friends."

"What happened after they killed your folks? Why are you alive? Somebody must 'a found you. How is it the lone brother didn't find you. Sell you as a slave? I have to ask. Your story is very interesting. It's made me curious."

"The answer is simple, really. A warrior from the Guard was nearby. Heard the two shots. When he came to check, he saw my parent's bodies lying dead. Found the killer in the wagon goin' through the cedar chest I was stuffed behind. The warrior won their fight findin' me when it was over. That is how justice got the surviving brother. The warrior took me to Mrs. England's home to stay 'til somebody wanted me . . . nobody did. She ended up keeping me. I thank God she did. I love her just as I would my natural birth mother. Her husband became my new Father. I loved him so. Sadness held us all for many days after the bears visited our place. I do not like bears to this day, Jeb."

"Who was this warrior who found you that day? Fought for you. Captured the killer of your folks? He is blessed by the Great Spirit whoever he is."

"Red Hawk. His name is Red Hawk. He visits me often."

***

It was a lot for me to take in then. A lot to think on now as me and Wolf finished our pipes. Started talkin' on how to get us a couple 'a them fine military rifles. Wolf had an idea he allowed would work. He most always saw more to things than I did. His plans was usually more precise than mine, which turned out to be true of our newest effort as well. But first, I had somethin' I needed to talk to him about.

"My brother," I began, "I am troubled over what we are plannin'. I cannot come to peace with it. I feel like I'm takin' somethin' that's not mine. It seems we are stealin' from these soldiers. Tell me, why is it okay to break the rules of God? We are told to not steal. Explain how it is that we can justify what we take. My spirit is disturbed. My mind is not thinkin' straight. Help me to understand what we do so I may think clearly about our comin' trail."

"Jeb, my brother, these guns are for killing. They belong to the U.S. Government. The U.S. Government is the enemy of the Cherokee. They are much stronger than us. We are weak against their weapons. They betrayed us after the war with the red coats. Broke the land treaties our chiefs had agreed to with them, lied to those who trusted their words, stole our lands, and killed many of our tribe. Taking their weapons weakens them as our enemy, strengthens us as theirs. Taking their weapons helps the very folks these guns might kill. Our elders' visions are clear. These soldiers coming here is the beginning of the end to our way of life. When enough have come, they will run us from our land. Take our mountain home to make a way for more settlers to come. This is the home of our fathers. The Cherokee have been here many generations. My people will be made to leave by these very soldiers camped among us now. We will need these guns to defend ourselves. I will fight for my home. Do not think of this as stealing, my friend. Think of it as Cherokee that will live because the soldiers meant for the guns we take will not have them. We will be saving our people from the black death of the enemy's smoke pole, saving many Cherokee lives. For us, it is preparing for war. That is how I see it."

It brought the whole thing to home when Wolf informed me he considered us at war. I did not blame the Cherokee for seein' the U.S. Government as an enemy. The leaders of the new nation had broken many agreements with the Indians. Taken much land with lies. Cost many Indians, young and old, their very lives. To me, it was despicable. I had chosen my side.

Savin' Cherokee lives. I could fight for that. My spirit was settled, knowin' I was fightin' for a cause. His thoughts opened my eyes. I looked at our doin's different from then on. Bein' Wolf's brother meant my life would change if his did. It hadn't set good with me takin' the things we did from the wagon masters. Now, after Wolf explained it all to me, I was comfortable with what we'd done. What we was gonna do. A kinda war had come to the mountains for the Indians through the treachery of the U.S.

Government. A war unannounced, but a war just the same. It would not turn out good for the native folk. I still hadn't told Wolf about the secret room in Panther Cave. It might be time for me to do that.

***

Fortunately for the folk stealin' Indians, Ruby was still unable to speak or the whole of the woods would know they was there. Laughing Beaver could see the tradin' spot as he stayed the trail from the north. Saw as they got closer it seemed nobody was waitin' there like they should be.

Never had the traders from the south not been there waitin' for him when a time for meetin' had been set. Laughing Beaver stopped a ways back from the tradin' spot when he saw for sure that the traders weren't there. Scented the air. Studied things all around. Nothin' looked wrong, but he studied it some more. Somethin' weren't right. He squatted down. The air along the ground was wrong. He raised his head, leanin' it back as he stood. His blood was cold. Danger was near. He lifted his head even higher, near standin' on his toes he was streatchin' so tall, searchin' for the slightest smell. He caught it. Layin' on what little breeze they was comin' from up on the mountain. Fresh blood stink floatin'. It was thick. A quick look at the two warriors with him said they smelled it, too. Their faces holdin' a look of pure hate.

The blood scent meant the traders was gone, either dead or run off. No gold would be given for the maiden that day. Laughing Beaver know'd without a doubt this would be the work of the Guard. He turned mad as he figured on what was happenin' to his slave tradin' plans. Slippin' his right hand in behind himself, he slowly pulled a long knife from its sheath at the small of his back. Reachin' out with his left hand, he turned Ruby square on face to face in the middle of the trail. Lowerin' his right arm, he sliced the leather lead at her wrist. Their eyes met in that split second it took to set her hands free. Hers held fear—hope. His held hate. She could see in his eyes the evil what held his soul. As the truth come to light, unfortunately, she also saw her death in those cold eyes of Laughing Beaver. Her prayer was a quick one. God forgive him.

Rememberin' the anger he'd felt at how she'd not obeyed him when he'd told her to stay quiet, how she'd not minded him, disrespected him in front of his men, he turned the sharp edge up bringin' the knife blade back through her middle slicin' her deep, plumb through the thick homespun dress like it was a warm biscuit, stoppin' shy of the breast bone. Swithchin' the knife to his left hand, he plunged his right deep inside her chest grabbin' hold of the heart. A strong jerk tore the organ from its restin' place between her lungs. Her blood runnin' down his arm as he held it up for Ruby to watch its last beat, then held it up even higher for whoever it was near to see. Her body slumped to the ground in death. Ruby Smith had gone to be with Jesus.

The three rogues took off runnin' hard for Wolf Creek, soon as Laughing Beaver finished his murderin'. He hated killin' the girl, aggravatin' as she'd been. She was worth gold on the slave tradin' market. But, he had to let his enemies know he weren't scared 'a killin'. The gold could be made back. He'd seen many girls what lived in the mountains, settler and Indian, easy to take. Fetched much coin when sold. He was glad he'd decided to come with the soldiers to this valley. This place where the rabbits dance.

Chapter Twenty-One

Wolf Fights with Fire

Wolf had the attack plan laid out in his mind not long after we'd finished our pipes. It involved fire. Nothin' simple that might go unnoticed but by a few, no. He wanted to use fire to light up the woods. Draw their attention, then move while they looked the other way. He wanted to grab a whole box 'a them new long rifles, too. Have extra for when we might need 'em; of course he did. Why would I expect anything different? If it weren't dangerous enough goin' for a couple rifles, goin' for a whole box would be. But, gettin' a whole box meant we could spare one each to Cain and Rose as a wedding gift. Cain had a good rifle Dad give him, but a body could always use another dependable gun, even if you was as bad a shot as Cain. You'd not want him shootin' at your person with his bow, though. He could hit turkey gobblers as they spooked to wing he was so good. It would be okay to let 'em have a couple. They'd not tell a soul. I couldn't wait to get one 'a them new guns in my hands. I know'd the first place I was goin' huntin' with it.

We'd seen the soldiers shoot targets from one side 'a the camp to the other, hittin' dead on where they was aimin'. Like the center of a dried oak leaf some fifty paces away stuck solid to the side of a tree. That was uncommon accurate. The soldiers used a stick as a rest, reachin' from the ground to near shoulder height. It held the front end of the gun's stock in a fork while the shooter held the stick with his off hand to steady the bead; left hand or right hand dependin' on which shoulder the gun butt was braced against. Most shot from the right shoulder usin' the left arm to hold the aimin' pole, some from the left.

"I know how to get a chance at those guns, Jeb. It is simple when you stop to think, listen close. We wait for late in the afternoon, then work our way to the east until we can turn south into the holler just up the creek from their camp. There, we will set the woods on fire. The weather has been cold and dry of late. The old leaves will burn strong once lit. Let the settling evening breeze work the flames down the holler. When the smoke fills the whole of camp, we use the cover to make our way to the supply tent for the new guns. Hopefully, all the soldiers will go to the fire, leavin' the tents unguarded. We slip up to the east end of the first supply tent, slide a box of guns out, get one of us on each end while running all out toward the woods. If they all go to fight the fire, we should be able to make it out without getting shot. What say you, Jeb?"

"A whole box, Wolf? Shot? I don't wanna get shot, Wolf. How much do one 'a them boxes weigh anyhow? If they're too heavy, we won't be able to run fast enough to get away," I said real concerned like. "If we find ourselves needin' to run faster, will it slow us down enough for them to draw a clean bead on us? You know how straight they can shoot usin' them little sticks 'a theirs. I don't wanna get shot at, Wolf. If one of us gets shot, our dads will have our hides. Hear? We don't need to even come close to gettin' shot. That would be a really *bad thing*. Why don't we just watch. Snatch one 'a their personal guns each when we catch somebody not payin' mind? Wouldn't that work, too, Wolf?"

"No. Why get a couple when we can fetch a whole box for the same effort? Where is the wisdom in that? We need these guns to protect ourselves, provide for our families. The boxes can't be *that* heavy. We've seen two soldiers carry a box, one on each handle at the ends. We can carry a box if they can. It just has to be when there are no eyes on the supply tent. The woods are not far from the first tent where they keep the guns. We can get in there without being seen. Get out quick. Be gone before they see us. If the fire does what it should, we will have our guns. If not, we will do the best we can. That is how I see it." He pointed the first two fingers of his right hand at his eyes again. We was done talkin'.

He'd say no more on it; would listen to no more about it. Weren't no gettin' away from it now, we was gonna set the woods on fire. He'd do it without me if I decided not to go, so I figured I might as well oblige him. Watch out he didn't do somethin' careless like get holes shot in his person. We know'd them soldiers could hit what they aimed at. Just had to make sure they didn't aim at us.

At that time, I couldn't even imagine what "settin' the woods on fire" meant. The woods was big. Covered all the mountains. I would come to an understandin' soon enough 'cause he wanted to go the next afternoon. I didn't like it, but I saw his reason. It had been dry, probably stay that way for a while.

I started wonderin' if one 'a them new guns was worth all the risk we'd be takin'. One of us, or both of us, could get kilt. I prayed that would not happen. Put it all in the hands of the Great Creator. That settled it. I could take their guns, so they couldn't use 'em on me or mine. They would provide me protection. But I did not want to die.

We took our time workin' east. A long steep ridge ran dead north to south not far from where we watched in our white pine top that early afternoon. The late evening settle bringin' the air down from the ridges would not start for a few hours yet. We had time for travel. Time for makin' fire across the holler above their camp. I weren't in no hurry no how. My soul was at ease for the most part. Felt like a time between life and death.

***

Red Hawk and Moon Shadow watched from just south of the tradin' spot as Laughing Beaver cut the leather leash holdin' Ruby. They was hopeful since he looked to be turnin' her loose, but watched in regret as he slit her up the front quick as a spider strikin', then felt great anger as he tore the heart from her body, makin' her watch it beat its last. He took her heart with him as they run off. Most likely for his supper. Bad spirits believed in such as that.

Red Hawk and Moon Shadow went to Ruby quick as they could. It was steep where they'd been watchin' from, not far from the tradin' spot. Movin' fast down to where Ruby lay weren't really an opiton. Didn't matter, she was dead. The killers had run off, but Red Hawk and Moon Shadow know'd they'd find 'em soon. Make 'em pay. Red Hawk felt even more guilty after seein' Ruby up close. He'd meant to have them traitors dead by then. Regretted not gettin' the chore completed. The girl would still be alive if he'd 'a killed 'em earlier. They would not get away, he promised her. His aim was to see 'em die hard for murderin' such a child. A daughter of Choestoe.

"We must see to this, Moon Shadow," Red Hawk said as the two sat next to Ruby. Near-weepin' at the lost innocence layin' dead beside 'em. "This girl did not deserve what the evil ones have done to her. A life lost before it could be lived. We will see this settled. Those three will be going to visit their ancestors across the Great River very soon."

"I agree, Uncle. We will need to follow their trail. Set their spirits free. Demons told them we were close by watching. I think the scent from the blood of the traders we killed warned them of us being up there, caused them to quit their trading trail. It is a bad day when such as this young one must lose her life to the evil what has taken it. I want to bathe my knife blade in their blood. Hang their hair in my lodge. Let us wash in the sacred smoke. Cleanse ourselves for the fight ahead. I am eager to make this right."

They built a small warmin' fire a few feet upwind of where Ruby lay. They would not touch her. They would not take her back to her family. Nor would they ever speak of it.

Folks never saw members of the Guard and know'd it. They stayed secret. No, she'd lay right there 'til somebody else found her, which might be a time 'cause few folks ever traveled the trail those outlaws used. It was a hard trail to find first off, then it was a difficult one to walk. Ivy thickets, rocks, steep ground all made it perfect for an illegal tradin' spot to lay hid in. If the night time critters found her, Ruby Smith's disappearance might never be answered.

Their time would now be spent runnin' down the rogue Indians what done the killin'. It was their duty. Murder weren't tolerated in Choestoe. The settlers didn't allow it. Cherokee, neither. Law had to be maintained. Folks made to answer for their actions. These outlaws would answer soon. Their trial was over. The sentence was death, to be carried out soon as could be. Justice had now took to their trail.

It weren't difficult to read where the warriors went while they still ran. Red Hawk was havin' trouble keepin' trail once they'd slowed their pace to a walk. He come to a place by a small branch where the three had stopped, got a drink, sat, talked, most likely figurin' on what to do. These was trained Cherokee warriors who know'd how to move when bein' followed. He come to understand while he searched for their sign, like any other warrior, they'd not feel comfortable bein' looked for. Would want to know if they was bein' chased for sure. By who? How many? It come to Red Hawk how to find 'em once he seen they left three different trails when startin' on again after their talk. They'd split up. He stopped his trail readin'. He needed to talk to Moon Shadow.

"We must be very careful moving forward," Red Hawk said as he took a seat by the runnin' water of the small branch. Moon Shadow sat, too. "They are no longer on the run. They have gone on the hunt. Looking for us. If we keep on after them this way, it will be easy for them to hide from us, then wait 'til we come in range and attack. We would lose with these three, Moon Shadow. Death would find us. These are skilled warriors. No. We must be smarter than they. Use our cunning to hunt them. Let us move up high on the ridges. Travel east as Old Man Sun begins to go for sleep. Come down in the valley from on high at dark. That would put us ahead of their travel. Have them looking back while we are in front. I believe we should hunt them instead of following their trail. This is what I reason we should do."

"You are wise, Uncle. I know you are right. They will want to find us. Kill us for messing up their trade. I will follow you, Red Hawk. Your plan to move ahead is very wise. I, like you, want to see blood paid for with blood. That young one was a beautiful daughter, sister, future wife to some worthy young man, maybe one of our brothers. We must right this for her family's concern. I would like nothing better than to follow on, fight them now for the killing they have done. But I know your words are true, it will be as you say."

The rest of their day was spent gettin' in front of the Cherokee what done the killin' to Ruby. It was a little while 'fore dark when Red Hawk finally led he and Moon Shadow down from off the ridges. 'Bout the same time me and Wolf was gettin' busy. They'd reached the place where Red Hawk figured to start the back-trailin' hunt for the killers layin' at the north end of the valley just above the base of the big ridges. Ground laid easy for travel there. Woods was open. If the rogue Indians made it that far, and he believed they would, it made for a better chance at findin' 'em without bein' seen. The only thing Red Hawk couldn't figure as he and Moon Shadow looked for a place to set up watch, was why he smelled a faint hint of woods smoke. That weren't exactly right.

***

It only took us a short time to start a good fire across the south end 'a the holler where their camp lay. We had to wait 'til later in the afternoon to get it goin' than we'd figured on 'cause the air weren't movin' good. Made us have to hurry gettin' back north to our watch place. We wanted to get settled where we could watch good 'fore the smoke got to rollin' down the holler. Didn't have to wait long 'til the first little hints 'a woods-burnin' scent come to us just before dark. Weren't but a little while after we first smelled it that the camp got busy. The word "fire" bein' yelled from one side to the other. Lanterns was bein' lit all over camp so folks could see. Soldiers grabbed buckets and headed for the creek to fill 'em, then back to the supply tents to leave 'em on the ground at each end to have if needed. Others got all the mules to the west side 'a the creek. Tied 'em off there thinkin' the fire would stay on the east side. One would think a woods fire would struggle to jump water as wide as Wolf Creek, but it could.

"The smoke is getting heavier, Jeb, but where is the fire?" Wolf asked as he turned to me. "The fire will make all the soldiers leave camp. That will be our chance to move in for the guns. I don't understand. The smoke is thick enough that the fire should be here by now. We must keep watch. I hope the Great Spirit is with us."

I had the same questions in my mind 'cause my eyes was startin' to burn from the smoke. The inside of my lungs felt hot when I breathed in, too. The smoke was thick enough for the actual flames to be close, but they weren't. It could only mean on thing: that fire was burnin' hard. Wolf's plan may work out if the fire is big enough to get the soldiers out from camp. I felt a little hope.

"I don't know, Wolf. It seems as if the first flames should be here by now. The smoke is such that you'd think it was on us," I said as I looked back south. "We should just... keep... watchin'... 'til... see... light.

Wolf followed my gaze. It was fire, alright, but not down on the ground where you'd expect to see fire. No, this was up under the tops of the big trees. Over the tops of the smaller trees like the dogwood or half-grow'd white pines. Giant licks of flame jumpin' loose. Flyin' through the tree tops like huge bird flames leavin' out through the canopy of limbs overhead. Like mule-sized firebirds fightin' each other for space across the tops of the shorter trees.

The size of fire makin' that big 'a licks had to be huge, and when it come into sight, it was. You could hear it roarin' as it busted through the trees into the camp. What had we done? The woods was burnin' out 'a control. Flames reachin' higher than our barn was tall. It would be all the soldiers could do to get their possibles gathered and clear out without bein' burnt alive. Nobody was stoppin' that fire. This could get very bad for the ones who started it 'cause the Cherokee will know when they backtrack the fire's path that somebody did start it. That could get very bad for those what did it... if folks found out who did it.

Their privy got it first. We watched as flames caught the front right corner, then eased up the side catchin' size as it went. That side of camp was still kinda normal, 'cept for concern over the smoke, 'til their outhouse caught up. They know'd then somethin' bad was happenin'. I counted at least three what had to vacate the private house half-covered as the flames began to rip from the inside of the door. The tent layin' to the west caught it next. Didn't take but a short time 'til they weren't none left. That really got their attention. Wolf had done attacked the whole camp with his fire plan. He had many of 'em steppin' and fetchin' just hopin' to get out alive. There would be stories told about Wolf's fire for ages to come.

"We must move," said Wolf as the flames come full-on into camp, burnin' all in its path. You could feel the heat. "Our time will get short now that the fire is near. We must get closer to the supply tent. Wait for a chance to grab a gun crate, then clear out. Let the fire burn what it will. I hope it burns the whole camp to ash. Maybe then they will leave and never come back. They are cowards anyway. I do not respect them or their government. Forgive me Great Spirit, but I have a true hate for these white devils who have come to my home in hidin'. Sneakin' around, stealin' folks, and gold. Let it burn, I say. But, we do need the rifles. The protection they will provide for our families. The food it will allow us to harvest. Follow me, Jeb. Let's get on with it."

We moved to a place closer to the south side 'a camp, not far from the supply tent we meant to get in. Squatted there not twenty paces from the south end. It weren't exactly what we was expectin'. We watched as everybody who'd seen the comin' flames made their way to their sleepin' tents to gather their personals. They didn't want what they owned to burn up. *Was that what Wolf was talkin' about when he meant it would involve all the folks in camp when the fire come?*

The buckets of water sat exactly how the soldiers had left 'em earlier. Both ends of the supply tent was standin' wide open. Not a soul in sight on the outside. Seemed everybody had gone to take care 'a their own stuff first, then I guess they'd worry over the government truck. Made the situation perfect for us. Wolf know'd it, too. He hardly waited a second once he seen they weren't no guards payin' mind to the supplies. Sprang from his squattin' place like a rabbit jumpin'. His feet movin' quick to the end of the tent, makin' sure he stayed hid behind the canvas fold of the openin'. He motioned for me to do the same. I followed just as he'd done. We was now standin' only two paces from our intended, not a soul to be accounted for watchin'.

Wolf stood straight up next to the edge of the openin', while bendin' his neck for a look inside. The light from the fire makin' it where he could see good. There was four boxes of guns, two crates layin' open of small leather bags full 'a .54 caliber lead balls, another crate layin' open closer to the openin' filled with powder horns, and barrels of various goods. Whiskey and other stuff he didn't take the time to identify.

I couldn't believe it when he dropped his hand behind his back, motionin' me to follow as he disappeared into the tent. I trusted his decision, so I did just as he did. We ended up standin' on the inside next to the four boxes of guns. One of which we was aimin' to take. Wolf was standin' at the other end 'a the tent lookin' out, makin' sure nobody was comin'. We found ourselves inside the soldier's supply tent with not a guard nowhere. It was hard to believe.

"My friend," whispered Wolf as he turned back inside the tent to commence fillin' his possibles pouch with the small leather bags of shot, "Let's not stand here like girls. Fill your pouch with powder horns like I am filling mine with these bags of shot — quickly before they come — then grab your end of the top box. Let's get from this place to the woods. Hurry, before we are found out."

I did what I was told without thinkin' or feelin'. I stuffed as many 'a them brass horns in my pouch as I could fit, then reached to grab the rope handle at the end 'a the box just as Wolf reached for his. The weight was heavy as we headed out the tent toward the nearest woods as fast as we could walk. I never felt no pullin' back, so I figured Wolf had his end like I did. The box didn't feel too heavy for me to move good at the time. The trail to take was clear. I just kept movin'. Figurin' at any second to hear the explosion of the shot that would send a lead ball tearin' through my person while we struggled up a small hill we had to climb carryin' the guns. We walked as fast as we could 'til we was a good fifty or more paces clear 'a that small top and back in the woods a good piece. That's where the real weight 'a the box hit us. I could go no more. Wolf couldn't either. We eased up in the edge of an ivy thicket. Set the box down for a breather, strainin' hard to listen to our back trail. The dark woods all around us. Waited 'til our breathin' got quiet and listened close again. Nothin'. Neither of us heard anyone followin'. It was over. The guns was ours. The next chore was gettin' 'em home without nobody findin' us. I hoped Wolf had a plan for that.

We'd made it out alive. I thanked the Great Spirit as we rested, sittin' cross legged in the deer trail we was followin'. I looked down at the treasure we'd took, even the box was fine made usin' air-dried pine. The top was hinged. A metal lock plate opposite those hinges bent over the edge of the lid. One at each end. A stamped "U.S." was branded in the flat of the top. Only got to enjoy lookin' at it for a minute 'cause the fire was comin' on. We each grabbed our ends 'a the box to work deeper into the woods. It gettin' heavier by the minute. The rope handle got to cuttin' into the skin on the inside of my fingers. Weren't but after a few 'a them minutes, we had to stop again. I began to wonder how I carried such a load so easy leavin' the supply tent durin' the fire. Wolf would call it spiritual when we talked it all over days later. It was clear I did it with strength what left me once we made the woods good. *How many guns was in our box anyway? Felt like several.* I looked forward to opening it. Our pouches was heavy with ball and powder, too.

  We made it to a flat place where the deer trail we was followin' crossed the main trail what would take us to our hidin' cave 'fore we had to set the box down again. The same cave the rest of our stuff was put away in. It weren't near as big as some caves. Only camp three or four folks comfortable, but it was a good cave for hidin' in. Dry, as caves went. Dancing Bear named it Turtle Cave 'cause the entrance was like a turtle's head when pulled in its shell. Covered in front. Hard to see. A small branch run just out from the front of it for water. You could build a camp fire in it just like you could Panther Cave. The smoke would draw out the back somehow. Wolf and Dancing Bear found it on a walk many moons before while searchin' for gold. Wolf'd show'd it to me. Made me swear never to tell a livin' soul about it, not even Cain or Dad. Dancing Bear wanted it to be a secret place only he and Wolf know'd about, for safety if the government soldiers come. It was close to my home on Ben's Knob makin' it handy about keepin' an eye on our truck hid there. Me and Wolf would spend a fair amount 'a time in that cave as time went on. We liked it there.

  "Praise be to the Great Creator, Jeb," Wolf said as our backsides landed in the trail, the box between us. "I believe we have done this thing without being seen. I heard no shots. Felt no heat from any lead balls hitting me. No one shot you. I hear no following sounds from our rear trail. We have the crate of guns, some shot, powder horns, and our hides. God is good. He has given us truck that will feed our families. Protect us from our enemies. I thank Him for His gift."

"I, too, thank Him for his mercy. His protection from gettin' kilt. His gift to us for our future. I'm eager to lay eyes on what's inside, Wolf. I want to open the box. Put hands on what we risked our lives for. It is heavy. There must be several new rifles packed in there. My heart is beatin' like a grouse hammerin' after a rain. What say you, Brother?"

"Sounds good to me," he replied as he loosed the catch on his end of the box.

I did the same on my end. We stopped, looked up to stare eye-to-eye. Wolf nodded slightly then motioned his head to my right. We flipped open the lid. What met our gaze made the hair stand up on the back of my neck. Sent cold chills down my back and caused Wolf to suck in air like he was chokin'. His eyes near-poppin' from his head. I could but just barely breathe. Seven brand new Harpers Ferry .54 caliber flintlock rifles. There had been eight original. One was gone, like somebody'd needed a replacement. Seven whole long guns. We couldn't believe it. No wonder the box was heavy! Seven shiny new rifles of our very own. It was more'n we ever figured for. What was we gonna do with this many guns? I'm sure we'd figure it out.

After a short rest, we grabbed up the box with Wolf in front, me bringin' up the rear. He was facin' forward holdin' the box handle behind his back, makin' both hands bounce off his backside as he walked. The trail to the cave was easy travelin'. We'd make it in a couple hours. Store the guns there for now, make plans for what to do with 'em later. Wolf and me would take one each, maybe two. That would leave three. I'd wanted Cain and Rose to have one each. I think Wolf would figure the same. He loved his sister.

We was headed toward Turtle Cave. Stoppin' ever so often to rest. Our hands sufferin' from the braided crate straps. Them guns was killin' us toten' 'em. I wished Peter had been there. It was foolish not thinkin' to have a mule hid out in the woods to do our totin'. We would learn from that.

***

The flames was huge as they rolled down the holler toward where Red Hawk and Moon Shadow had found to wait. A small top sittin' between two big tops covered in ivy on the west side 'a Wolf Creek. If Red Hawk had figured it proper, the trio they sought was somewhere in the small valley runnin' south. Straight away from where they sat watchin'. Northeast of the soldier's camp, which was over a half mile away. From where they stood on the short top, it was easy to see the flames as the fire crawled down the valley takin' everything it touched. The smoke fillin' the woods thick. You could taste it while it burned your nose and eyes. Even the trees was burnin'.

They heard the explosion toward where the camp lay; felt Mother Earth tremble under their feet. Figured it for powder explodin'. They both hoped no folks died in that.

The winds from the evening settle died after a spell. The fire burned down to nothin'. Red Hawk and Moon Shadow laid down to sleep just off to the west of the top they was camped on. The smoke from the fire movin' over their heads. They both wondered how such a fire could 'a got started. Weren't common for a fire like that to get out lest they was lightning from an angry sky.

***

Morning brought a whole new world into focus for all who survived the fire. Everything was burnt. Trees charred up way higher than even Black Oak could reach with his bow. Stumps smokin'. Logs and trees still burnin'. Hot spots smokin' all over from puffy little humps on the woods floor. The smoke thick. Hard to see over fifteen to twenty paces in any direction. You had to breathe through homespun to keep from choking. Moon Shadow wondered at it all.

"Uncle, I have never seen such as this. All has been burned. What kind of demon fire passed through here? Have you been through this before? The woods are gone. How could a fire like that happen? Where are the animals?"

"Do not worry over where the fire has burned. We will come back here in the late spring. You will see the work of our Father's hand. Everything touched by this fire will grow new. Fire takes away the old. Lets new growth take its place. I have seen this many times. The whole of the woods will be better. Now, let us not forget why we are here. We must find those murdering traitors. We will move back higher up. Get out from this smoke. That is where we will find them, watching for the two of us. Look close as we travel. It is necessary to find them before they see us. Come, let us string our bows. Make ready for an arrow. Our search begins."

Red Hawk led the way as they moved higher up the mountain, while fadin' south to work up the edge of where the fire had burned. It was tough goin' havin' to slip along on the steep slow-like watchin', breathin' in smoke as you went. It was hard to see anything. Moon Shadow saw the heathens many times in the stumps or logs faintly through the haze. It didn't seem they could climb high enough to escape the torment of the woods smoke. Moon Shadow was determined. He watched closely with every step he took, as did Red Hawk. They meant to find the evildoers before death could draw near. Time would tell.

With Red Hawk leadin', he'd got several paces ahead of Moon Shadow as the two eased through the woods searchin' everywhere a body could hide. Nothin'. Midday come and went, but no warriors had been found. No signs. Moon Shadow began to wonder if Red Hawk had guessed correctly about where the killers might be, then he rememberd who his uncle was. If anybody could find 'em, he could.

He stopped for just a minute to catch his breath. Breathe in a few times through his homespun shirt collar. It was all he had. But he watched Red Hawk's back close as the elder took several steps on ahead. The movement he saw a few paces above and behind Red Hawk didn't really seem like nothin'. *Smoke driftin'?* He'd already been fooled many times into thinkin' they was folks where they weren't none. Not until the Indian crouched with bow in had did Moon Shadow realize trees couldn't move like that, smoke or not. He quickly slipped a sharp-pointed flint arrow from his quiver layin' it across his bow, then noched it. Looked up quick to find his target. Gone. No warrior there. His eyes shifted left then right, head still, bow at the ready, knowin' death was close for his uncle if he could not stop it. He must kill the evil one before his arrow sent Red Hawk across the Great River.

Moon Shadow saw that Red Hawk was none the wiser as he followed near motionless, easin' along the side of the ridge, searchin'. More movement. This time no more than twenty paces behind Red Hawk. A bow on its way to full draw. Only seconds 'til he released his hold sendin' death through the air. Moon Shadow could not let that happen. Just like shootin' a spooked deer, he drawed and fired without hardly even takin' aim. His instinct for the kill guidin' his movements. The arrow left Moon Shadow's bow with a true purpose. It did its job, findin' the warrior's center just as he released his fingers from the bow string. The evil arrow slit Red Hawk's leggin's just above the knee. Red Hawk hit the ground flat. Removin' himself as a target.

Moon Shadow did not. The second arrow, loosed by a hidden warrior Moon Shadow never saw, did not miss its mark, either. Hittin' Moon Shadow just below the shoulder through his left side. The pain he felt caused his world to go dark. He wanted to scream out but could not. Goin' to his knees he thanked the Great Creator for all He'd ever done for him. Asked Him in silent to watch over his loved ones as he fell face first to the ground. Red Hawk got to him just as the hidden warrior revealed himself.

Standin' over Moon Shadow, Red Hawk and the warrior locked eyes for just a moment 'fore chargin' each other for the kill. Their comin' together sounded like a bear gruntin' in death. A deep release of two sets of lungs. One from the slammin' of bodies, the other from a knife sunk through a lung into a heart. Red Hawk rose from the ground jerkin' the knife from the slaver's chest leavin' him to bleed out. Bendin' over he wiped the evil spirit blood off on the dyin' man's shirt. He left 'em both where they lay. The worms could have the meat. God was dealin' with their souls.

Moon Shadow!

Red Hawk jumped back down the mountain to where Moon Shadow lay moanin'. He was alive. A surprise to Red Hawk seein' where the arrow stuck out from under his arm. It was in a place that should have caused near instant death. The enemy warrior had made the shot he needed but did not notice Moon Shadow's arrow quiver had slid down beneath his arm with him havin' to shoot so quick. The flint point had struck one of the hickory shafts of a huntin' arrow inside the quiver, then glanced off one 'a Moon Shadow's ribs breakin' it plumb into, 'fore stoppin' just shy of his lungs. Red Hawk was able to remove it with a simple pullin' twist. Moon Shadow come to complete from the pain of the arrow bein' backed out. Red Hawk was proud 'a that.

"You there. Warrior," come a voice from up the ridge a short piece. Red Hawk rose to see Laughing Beaver standin' above him just a few paces away. "Thank you for riddin' me of those two parasites, brave one. I have been too many moons looking out for them. It is good they are dead. I, however, will not be so easy to kill. What is your name, warrior?"

"I am Red Hawk, of the Choestoe clan. And you, murderer, what be your name? I want to remember when I add you to those I've sent across the river. You should not have killed the young one last sun. The Great Spirit will see her done for square. Your death is coming. Your hair will hang from our lodge. You are evil. Never should you have come here."

"Red Hawk. I will remember this name. You, too, have a death coming. We all will face that battle, but you will not kill me, my new friend. There is a chance that I, Laughing Beaver, will take your life when the day of our coming together is on us. Fortunately for you, it will not be today. I must go from here. Make more trade with the white settlers. Take others from their stock of young ones. Make slaves for the market. But, hear me warrior, Red Hawk. One day I will return to this valley. We will bring the story of one of our lives to an end. I look forward to that day."

With all his talk done, he turned on his heels leavin' Red Hawk to simply shake his head. He, too, would also look forward to that day. Some comfort come in knowin' the two left rotting on the side of the ridge above Wolf Creek would never bother another soul. Would never make anymore slaves. He hated lettin' Laughing Beaver get away. That would not happen the next time they met. He needed to see to Moon Shadow.

***

Red Hawk smiled as the last of the wagons left the soldier camp two days after the fire, weeks before their figured time to leave. He silently offered up a prayer for the U.S Government to never return to Choestoe. He did not know how the fire come to be but praised the Great Spirit for the trail it chose. Right through the middle of the soldier camp. Burned everything. One supply tent with three boxes of guns blow'd all to pieces. They'd had the sense to move the barrels of black powder, but not the guns and powder horns. Nothin' was left 'a their outhouse, their tents, all the things they'd found, the words they no doubt wrote on paper about the valley, its resources — all gone. No time to do it all over again 'fore the spring thaw when folks all over would need regulatin'. Duty would call. The soldiers would be needed more some other place. Sadly, Red Hawk reasoned, in time, they would all return.

Chapter Twenty-Two

Life Changes Our Lives

Sean watched as the two boys left the burnin' soldier camp headin' for the woods carryin' their prize crate of guns best they could. Their haul looked to be almost too heavy for 'em the way they was strugglin'. He'd seen 'em grab the top box inside the tent not long before it blew up. His new gun had come from that box. A replacement for the one he'd lost to the Indian. One Cherokee boy, one settler. He could 'a stopped 'em when they went to the tent durin' the fire but didn't. Looked out for 'em, really. He weren't no soldier -- they was just boys. The supplies belonged to the U.S. Government, anyhow. Let 'em have what they can get was how he saw it. 'Sides, his head still rung some from bein' caught careless on sentry. Best he could do was gather what little truck he had 'fore it got burnt. His possibles for sure. New rifle, powder and ball, sleepin' quilts, spare clothes, long knives, jerky he'd stole from the supplies, and a wool overcoat, then he hit the woods away from the soldier camp. His job with them would end now 'cause 'a the fire. He was thankful for it. Watchin' the two make off with their take told him how that fire got started, too. He would follow these rebels. Make friends if he could.

***

We'd been headed down the main trail for the cave for several minutes when we felt the ground shake. Heard the "boom" of a hard load explodin'. Wolf and me stopped totin'. Squatted down to listen.

Wolf called it, "I believe the case of powder horns caught, Jebediah. It is good. The rest of the guns will be broken now if the soldiers did not move them. Praise be to Holy Spirit. I am glad we started the fire. Destroyed their things. Maybe they will leave now and never come back. Jeb, listen. I feel it might be wise for us to not mention our disobedience to the fathers for a while. Just get the guns hid, then circle around to the north trail. I will return to Slaughter. You will go to Ben's Knob. We will come together at Turtle Cave at the end of three moons. Put together what we know. Learn if we are being talked about when the fire stories are told. Let us hope we are not."

"You are right my brother. I believe we should wait 'fore lettin' our folks know we had anything to do with what has happened. That fire did a lot 'a damage. Caused a lot 'a loss. Whoever started it could get in a mess 'a trouble. I agree we should stay quiet for now. Our time with these guns will have to wait. At least until all is forgotten about what drove the first soldiers out from Choestoe."

We never know'd it 'til later, but Sean followed us all the way back to Turtle cave. Watched as we carried our load inside. It was a great place to have for hidin' things, not easy to find. He wouldn't 'a know'd it was there if he'd not followed us on trail. He waited 'til we left the cave, then got in behind trailin' us again. He had no pull to bother what was in the cave, it didn't belong to him. He weren't really interested. He wanted to see where Wolf lived. Son of Dancing Bear. He had a notion who I was, but his true desire was to meet Dancing Bear. He'd heard much about him from his family.

"I will see you in time, my friend," Wolf said as we made the north trail a couple miles from our place. "We have done a mighty thing, Jebediah. Now our keep includes weapons of war. If trouble comes to us, we can fight. Our lives have been protected by the Great Creator. I praise Him for that. I praise Him for you, too, my blood brother. Take care of your person, your family, the things important to you in life, and say many prayers. In three moons, we will meet at Turtle Cave. We will talk again there."

He turned from me as he finished his words. Left at a trot 'fore I could say anything back. My heart grow'd sad as I watched him leave in the early morning light. Never could a body find a better friend . . . or brother.

Our little adventure went off without any trouble for us. Plenty for them other folks. That was good. I had fear our trail would not turn out as safe as it had. One day I figured, and it might be 'fore we realized it, our plans would not work out so well. Old Man Trouble would find us in time, that was fact, 'cause 'a Wolf bein' who he was, me bein' who I was. There'd be no shortage of adventure for us. Odds just weren't in our favor for trouble not to find our path. I kinda looked forward to it. The things we did brought my spirit to life. Made me feel alive each morning I woke to see how blessed I was. To me, life could only get better one way . . . she lived on Wolf Creek.

***

It was time for Momma to leave from her visit to Rose and Cain's place. She wanted to stay longer, but her and Dad know'd they would be needed at home 'fore too much longer. The goodbye was hard for Momma as they all left the house headin' for the barn. A secret had not been told. One that needed tellin'. She know'd it, but not because Rose had told her, she'd seen it. Noticed it really, bein' a woman and all. She pulled Rose off away from Dad and Cain as they walked. They needed to talk 'fore her and Dad left.

"What is it, Mother Celia? Have I done something wrong?" Rose asked, kinda nervous like.

"Why yes, I believe you have, daughter," Momma said in a very calm, soft voice, near-whisperin' so's not to be heard by the men folk. "I am curious why you won't tell me your secret?"

"Mother, you must be mistaken," Rose replied with a soft smile stretchin' the corners of her mouth while her eyes dropped from lookin' into Momma's. Her fingers pickin' at the threads in her homespun shirt. "I have kept nothing from you that I can tell. I love you."

"Has Cain told his father yet? Hmm?" Momma asked while givin' her new daughter a look only mothers can.

"No... I mean... what would he tell him, Mother Celia?" Rose asked caustiously.

"Okay, I wonder then. Why is there a certain glow about you? Why is your skin so rosy in color? So beautiful to look at? Why do you have a constant smile on your face? What is it you are staring at when you have such a long-lost look in your eye at different times of the day? Have you grown a fondness for the privy? You go there several times more than you should every day. And trust me, when you start to show, you won't have to rub your middle fifty times daily to see if there's a hump growing. You will feel when your baby gets bigger than your tummy. The little hump you keep checking on will let you know. Now, how far along are you my sweet child?" Momma couldn't help but to latch on to Rose for a big ol' hug. They both cried softly.

"Oh, Mother Celia. I have wanted to tell you so badly for many days. I've wanted us to come visit, so we could tell you and Thompie in person. It has been the most difficult thing to not get word to my mother. Cain just doesn't want to talk about it yet. He thinks I am not far enough along to start letting folks know. He wants to wait until I am swelling in front. 'Proof to the truth,' as he says. I think he is being foolish, but he is my husband, and I will honor his words."

"Yes, of course. You are wise. But sometimes we women must straighten out our 'wonderful' husbands to the correct way of thinking. You come with me. I will teach you about husbands." Done with her say, Momma walked Rose right back to where the men stood talkin'. Got right up in

Cain's face. He know'd then he'd done fouled up. He just didn't know which foul-up he was gonna be charged with.

"How dare you not let me and your Father know what is truly going on over here Mr. Cain Collins. Son, I am hurt to the depth of my soul." She looked over at Dad with a little look 'a hers only he know'd so well, then back at Cain.

"What in the whole put-together are you thinking when you won't let Rose tell us she is carrying our grandbaby. I will never forgive you, beautiful son of mine. Now come here and give me your best hug. You silly thinking boy," Momma said as the tears started flowin' freely all around.

Dad was took more than all of 'em. He near fainted at the news. Momma know'd he would. They ended up stayin' on another day. Such news had to be savored, seasoned with a little time. We was gonna have a new Collins 'fore long. I wondered if it would be a boy or girl. Didn't really matter to me. I was gonna love on it either way.

***

Wind Is Strong was movin' around good after a few moons at our place. The tea she'd been drinkin' had built her up some. Anne had told us previous makin' blood was a slow chore. She weren't near full-healed. That trail still had plenty 'a climb left to it, but her healin' had come a long way. Breathin' was a lot easier than it had been. The lung sickness had moved on. Anne was proud 'a that.

Her and Black Oak went on walks every day. She could feel her strength comin' back, which give her hope. Her desire to see her son grow'd, too. It felt like a slice of her soul was missin' bein' apart from him. Not knowin' anything about his whereabouts, nor who had him. Hurt worse than all the pain she'd felt on her escape run. In her dreams, she could feel his soul callin' out. She know'd he was alive -- she had to find him. Her prayer asked God to speak with Black Oak. She had come to know him very well.

Could feel it in her heart he could be the one to get her son back if that was his choice.

"Wind Is Strong," said Black Oak as she helped him in the barn salt curin' the fresh hams we'd brought in from our recent hunt. The hunt that led us to her, "I feel there is something I've done to hurt your feelings. I don't know what it is. Your spirit is silent to me. My soul does not hear you. If I have worried you, I apologize. If there is something you need to say, I will listen. If your heart is heavy, let me help you carry your load. I am here for you. Do not be afraid to speak with me on any concern or worry you may have. I want to understand."

"Thank you, sweet friend," she said. Puttin' her hand over on his arm, she turned her face up to look into his eyes; her big doe eyes showin' him her sorrow. "I do have something to say Black Oak. My soul is angry. That is why my spirit is quiet. My insides want to kill the evil ones who took my son. If they walk Mother Earth, they likely still have their families. I do not. That is not fair. I want my son back, Black Oak. I want to go find him. I will know him when I see him. I will know him when I hear his voice. I will know him when he comes close by his scent. My soul will be troubled until I find him. My heart tells me the search begins when my healing is complete. This trail will be very dangerous for me alone. Strangers seem to be roaming the woods more and more. I will probably need someone to escort me for safety on this trail, maybe a couple of folks. Is there someone you might know that would be willing to see me safe on this path I will walk, Black Oak? Can you think of anyone?"

"Of course, I know this person" said Black Oak as he moved closer to where she was standin'. "You must be very careful of him. He is a dangerous man. A warrior of the Cherokee nation with a terrible reputation. A big man who moves like the wind. A strong man who can wrestle bears. A man of courage. Scared of nothing. One willing to take the trail with a vengeful woman. Does this sound like a protector you would want to travel with? Or does he scare you?"

"Oh, I tell you true, he scares me deeply, but he is exactly the kind of protector I am looking for. I know, together, we can find my son. My heart tells me, together, we can do many things. I hope yours speaks the same." They come together. Their kiss lasted for a while. His did speak the same.

***

Red Hawk helped Moon Shadow make it to Slaughter Mountain the night he was hit. Owl was there to tend to him. He sat with Dancing Bear at the fire the night they arrived. Talked over the things that had happened. It was good they got the chance to sit for a while.

"Moon Shadow fought bravely, Brother. Saved my life." Red Hawk began. "You have taught him well. We respect him as a warrior of the Guard. He makes us stronger in a time of need. Never have we seen so many strangers moving through our home. Another was killed only recent. It is a sign our life here in the mountains is changing. In my spirit, I feel war is coming. Many speak of moving west to get away from the change. I do not feel that way. I will fight for my home. Live free as I choose or die keeping my way. Let them come."

"I will not leave," Dancing Bear responded in anger. "This is the home of our ancestors. It is my duty to stay with them. I believe many may go away, but me and mine will stay. The U.S. Government is not trustworthy. You cannot put faith in their words. If all we ever get is what we fight for, then so be it. I will fight. I would rather die here in my home than be made to live under the law of greedy men. I will put my life in the hands of the One who created me. I can go no further than that."

"Good. Good, Brother. It is good to hear we are of the same mind. We may need to fight together one day. I will be ready if that happens," Red Hawk said as he stood to leave. "I must go now. My fate lies with one named Laughing Beaver. His trail grows cold while I sit here speaking on things that might happen. It is good to see you again, Brother. I will remember you in my prayers."

"As I you. Take care as you go, Brother. It has been good to see you. Thank you for bringing Moon Shadow to Slaughter Mountain. I would like for you to stay longer, if duty would let you. I know your mind is on the outlaw trail. Be careful when you find this murderer. I know of him. He may be evil, but he is a worthy foe. At one time, he was one of our greatest warriors, before his spirit was invaded by demons. Now he walks with the evil one. Watch yourself for his tricks if you fight him. Be surprised by nothing he will do. Remember my words, Red Hawk. They may save your life."

With their talk made, Red Hawk left to find the murderer, Laughing Beaver. See to it he paid for killin' Ruby Smith. It was a matter of honor. A terrible thing needed to be made square. Red Hawk aimed to make sure that happened.

***

The weather was perfect for a walk as Old Man Sun climbed that morning. I was tired. My arms, shoulders, back and legs hurt from carryin' the box 'a rifles over a mile to where we stored 'em in Turtle Cave. My legs more from no sleep than the walk. That box was heavier than Wolf allowed it was gonna be. I know'd 'fore we left it prob'ly was. He most likely did, too.

The walk home from where Wolf and me split up on the north trail would take a couple hours good walkin' if all was normal. I weren't walkin' normal. I hoped to make it by supper. That was fine with me. It'd give my mind some time to think, to study on all that'd happened in the last little while. We'd been busy.

Our hog hunt turned into a struggle for survival from a woman who'd now become part of our family. I was sure proud 'a that. I got introduced to a new people what lived across the big ridges to the west 'cause 'a her plight. Indians I never cared to see again. Then me and Wolf freed a slave woman from her torment while educatin' the evil old one who held her. That was pure fun. I never will forget that old man kissin' his nasty ol' mule right on the mouth; it flingin' him square in the creek. Wolf done him up good with Old Mother's dream powder.

If you thought on it, a body could say me and Wolf had our first-ever battle. We didn't get beat on. No blood was shed, but we did burn down most of upper Wolf Creek holler in hopes 'a smokin'-up the Judas Camp. God was with us in that fire. It did much more than smoke-up their camp, which will be talked about for generations. We did all that on the heels of attackin' the soldiers what mastered the camp's supply wagon. Folks we know'd was spiteful for us. The enemy of the Cherokee. I never wanted to see a soldier in the mountains again. Sadly, I would, plenty of 'em.

We spied on the soldier camp, even though our fathers told us to stay clear of it. Took fightin' stock from 'em to grow our store of weapons in Turtle Cave. It was wise keepin' all our fightin' truck there. Ready to use when the need for those kinda things might come on us. I hoped it would be in far away times. It was clear to us folks was gonna come to our mountain home after talkin' with our captives on the wagon. They weren't no stoppin' it. The Cherokee would be the ones to suffer. The U.S. Government was gonna see to it. It makes for a sad time when the evil ones in society become the leaders, then are allowed to make the rules. Folks suffer when that happens.

As I kept walkin', thinkin' on things, I enjoyed the freedom of the morning sun shinin' through the treetops, while soakin' in the woods all around me. The wet scent from the forest floor thawin', near burnin' my nose with its richness. Freedom was precious. I realized many lives had changed from the goin' on's of these last few moons — Cherokee and settler. Everyone who lived in Choestoe was touched, whether they know'd it or not, by the soldier camp. The information they'd be takin' back to Washington on what could be had in this new-found valley would catch a heap 'a interest. Honest evidence of the future trouble to come. Times was makin' these changes. Cherokee hearts broke all over the Southern Appalachian, watchin' the change begin.

Our families' lives would change, most of all from Rose and Cain — a new baby. It was hard to imagine Cain as a daddy. God help that poor child was all I could figure. Rose, too. My folks was gonna be grandparents. Dad was never happier, 'cept for marryin' Momma.

Anne was comin' into her own as a medicine woman. Folks from all over the valley come to her for healin'. Sometimes she'd be gone days. Dad give her a mule to save havin' to walk all the time. She'd use it to help tote her medicine truck. He also give her both the pistols we took for our trip to Panther Cave for protection. It was funny to see her boilin' kettle strapped across the back 'a that mule when she'd leave out, goin' to doctor some poor soul. Looked like her mule had two rumps with one tail. She carried it that way, though, had to have it when it was needed. Wind Is Strong was a livin' fact about all 'a that.

George Black Oak had changed. Wind Is Strong made his changin' happen. I prayed to the Great Spirit. Asked Him to guide them. I know she longed to find her true son. I believed she would, now that Black Oak was in her life. Nobody said no to him. His connection to Dancing Bear held weight in the Cherokee world, and he was as big and strong as a chestnut tree. If God would show them the boy, Black Oak would get him. I had no question over that. I hoped Wind Is Strong had that feelin' as well. It would give her comfort.

My next bunch 'a thoughts made me stop my trail. Find a place to sit, build a small fire and have a smoke. Weren't long 'til my fire was goin' good, and I fired my pipe with some good Weaver tobacco Wolf give me. That helped me settle with the knowin' I'd just come to while walkin' . . . I had changed. *A lot.*

The reckonin' I come to in the chestnut holler could not 'a happened at a better time. It was a gift from God. I had no doubt over that. He laid His Spirit on me knowin' what was comin' my way over the next several moons. I believe that. My whole way 'a thinkin' had become more like grow'd folks. I was losin' my childlikeness while workin' toward becomin' a man. Catchin' up to Wolf in my acceptin' of responsibility. I'd become his Blood Brother, a bond as strong or stonger than bein' birth family by blood. Also, I'd started down the warrior's trail. My heart was with the Cherokee. I would fight to the death to protect them. Their time was fadin'. I would fade with it.

Elizabeth had come into my life. I held concern for her constant. I loved Wolf. He was my best friend. We would take many trails in our time, survive much danger, live a life lots 'a folks only dream about, go places, see things, and fight with honor in battles we'd not avoid. That was all a part of my life from the time I met Wolf 'til I'd meet back up with him across the Great River. But I wanted Elizabeth to be a part of my life, too. I would make a trail for her soon. Bein' with her had become very important to me.

The one person who had not changed in everything that'd happened to us on the recent was Wolf. I don't believe anything we'd been through over the last several moons had changed him. He might 'a been a little more angry than at the start of our hunt weeks back, but that was it. He was just Wolf. Always the same curious person from day-to-day that he was born bein'. Full 'a spirit and questions. His whole life was an adventure in true, honest livin'. I never saw him act no different -- ever. He had the same ways about him the day he died as the first day I met him at our home on Ben's Knob. The day he and Dancing Bear visited us while out on a walk. He was just Wolf. A name never fit a person no better that I ever met. He was my friend.

Choestoe moved on. Our lives went back to normal once the soldier camp went away. Wolf and me come together three moons later. Neither of us ever heard our names spoke of concernin' anything that happened with the fire. We kept the guns hid for many moons. Never touched 'em 'cept to keep 'em clean and oiled. After a time, we started usin' 'em on occasion. Carried us one to hunt with when there was a hard need for meat at home, or for anybody else we know'd what needed it. Them guns shot so true. Never took it home, though. Always returned it to Turtle Cave. The pistols and sabre stayed hid with some other weapons we collected 'til a few years later. Them things was made for killin'. We had little use for such 'til the greedy folk started movin' in on the Cherokee. The fightin' truck we'd gathered over time come in real handy then.

Me and Wolf had learned a lot about what was gonna happen that would affect our families' futures in Choestoe. I reckon the mountains is just too special to share with a handful or two of common folk. Livin' there durin' my growin' up years was near to Heaven. More and more would want to come find that peace what lives free on the ridge tops or down in the valley along the river Notla. I could not blame them for wantin' to come. I just wish folks would 'a left the Indians alone.

THE END

Meet Our Author

J. R. Collins

J. R. Collins was raised in the valley he so passionately writes about. A descendant of the first pilgrims to the area, he proudly claims heritage and roots through the people of the Appalachian Mountains that settled in the Choestoe Valley sometime in the latter part of the 1700's early 1800's. Born and raised in North Georgia, he grew up like Jeb, hunting and running the ridges of Choestoe.

Collins is a graduate of Young Harris College in the North Georgia Mountains. His first novel of young Jeb, *The Boy Who Danced with Rabbits* introduces a folksy method of storytelling much in the style of another famous American author, Louis L'Amour.

Made in the USA
Columbia, SC
26 October 2018